A Gesture Life

RIVERHEAD BOOKS

a member of Penguin Putnam Inc.

New York

1999

A
Gesture
Life

.

Chang-rae Lee

This is a work of fiction. The events and characters
portrayed are imaginary. Their resemblance, if any, to real-life
counterparts is entirely coincidental.

RIVERHEAD BOOKS
a member of
Penguin Putnam Inc.
375 Hudson Street
New York, NY 10014

Published simultaneously in Canada

Library of Congress Cataloging-in-Publication Data

Lee, Chang-rae.
A gesture life / Chang-rae Lee.
p.   cm.
ISBN 1-57322-146-5
1. Japanese Americans—New York (State) Fiction.   2. World
War II, 1939–1945—Women—Korea Fiction.   I. Title.
PS3562.E3347G4   1999
813' .54—dc21   99-28382 CIP

Printed in the United States of America

5   7   9   10   8   6   4

This book is printed on acid-free paper. ∞

Book design by Marysarah Quinn

For Garrett Hongo,
great friend and poet

A Gesture Life

1

PEOPLE KNOW ME HERE. It wasn't always so. But living thirty-odd years in the same place begins to show on a man. In the course of such time, without even realizing it, one takes on the characteristics of the locality, the color and stamp of the prevailing dress and gait and even speech—those gentle bells of the sidewalk passersby, their *How are yous* and *Good days* and *Hellos*. And in kind there is a gradual and accruing recognition of one's face, of being, as far as anyone can recall, from around here. There's no longer a lingering or vacant stare, and you can taste the small but unequaled pleasure that comes with being a familiar sight to the eyes. In my case, everyone here knows perfectly who I am. It's a simple determination. Whenever I step into a shop in the main part of the village, invariably someone will say, "Hey, it's good Doc Hata."

The sentiment, certainly, is very kind, and one I deeply appreciate. Here, fifty minutes north of the city, in a picturesque town that I will call Bedley Run, I somehow enjoy an almost Oriental veneration as an elder. I suppose the other older folks who live here receive their due share of generosity and respect, but it seems I alone rate the blustery greeting, the special salutation. When I buy my paper each morning, the newsstand owner will say, with a tone feigning gravity, "Doctor Hata, I presume." And the young, bushy-eyebrowed woman at the deli, whose homebound mother I helped quite often in her final years, always reaches over the refrigerated glass counter and waves her plump hands and says, "Gonna have the usual, Doc?" She winks at me and makes sure to prepare my turkey breast sandwich herself, folding an extra wedge of pickle into the butcher paper. I realize that it's not just that I'm a friendly and out-going silver-hair, and that I genuinely enjoy meeting people, but also because I've lived here as long as any, and my name, after all, is Japanese, a fact that seems both odd and delightful to people, as well as somehow town-affirming.

In my first years in Bedley Run, things were a bit different. Even the town had another name, Bedleyville (this my attribution), which was changed sometime in the early 1970s because the town board decided it wasn't affluent-sounding enough. The town in fact wasn't affluent at the time, being just a shabby tan brick train station and the few stores that served it, some older village homes, several new housing developments, and the surrounding dairy cow pastures and wooded meadows, nothing fancy at all, which was how I was able to afford to move here and open a business. There were perhaps a few thousand residents, mostly shopkeepers and service people, and the small bedroom community who were their patronage.

I'd read about the town in the paper, a brief slice-of-life article with a picture of a meadow that had been completely cleared for new suburban-style homes, just white stakes in the frozen ground to mark where the streets would be. It looked sterile and desolate, like fresh blast ground, not in the least hopeful, and yet I felt strangely drawn to the town, in part because of the peaceful pace of life that the article noted, the simple tranquillity of the older, village section that made me think of the small city where I lived my youth, on the southwestern coast of Japan. I had already driven through the more established suburbs nearer to the city and found them distinctly cold, as well as too expensive. I'd ask for directions at a garage, or buy some gum at a candy store, and an awkward quiet would arise, that certain clippedness, and though I never heard any comments, I could tell I wasn't being welcomed to remain too long.

When I first arrived in Bedleyville, few people seemed to notice me. Not that they were much different from those in the other towns, at least not intrinsically. Fundamentally, it seems to me, the people in a particular area are given to a common set of conditions and influences, like the growth in a part of a forest. There may be many types of flora, but only the resident soil and climate provide for them, either richly or poorly or with indifference. I suppose it was because Bedleyville was still Bedleyville then, and not yet Bedley Run (though desperately wanting to be), and pretty much anybody new to town was seen as a positive addition to the census and tax base. It was 1963, and from what I'd seen during my brief travels in this country, everyone for the most part lived together, except, I suppose, for certain groups, such as the blacks, or the Chinese in the cities, who for one reason or another seemed to live apart. Still, I had assumed that once I settled someplace, I would be treated as those people were treated, and in fact I was fully prepared for it. But wherever I went—and in particular, here in Bedley Run—it seemed people took an odd interest in telling me that I wasn't *unwelcome.*

Did this suit me? I can't be sure. I do know that once I decided to remain in this country, and to live here in Bedley Run, the question of my status mostly faded away, to the point it is today, which is almost nothing; and I know, too, that this must have been beneficial to me over the years, to have so troubling an issue removed from the daily turns of my life. I did have a few small difficulties from time to time, but it was always just the play of mischievous boys, who enjoyed making faces at me in the shop window, or chalking statements out front on the sidewalk, even going so far as to slather axle grease on the dumpster handles. I never reported the incidents, or confronted the perpetrators, and eventually these annoyances ceased. Later on, after the boys had grown up into men, some of the ones who settled in town would come into the store, to buy a bed tray, or a walker, or perhaps an ice bag for a feverish child, and they would speak to me as if they had never done the things I knew they had done, they would just make affable small talk and docilely ask my advice as they might from any doctor, their eyes wavering and expectant.

I should mention now that I am not a physician of any kind, and that I only ran a medical and surgical supply store in town, though for many patrons it came to be regarded as an informal drop-in clinic, the kind of place where people could freely ask questions of someone who was experienced and knowledgeable as well as open and friendly, a demeanor that quite a few doctors, unfortunately, no longer feature these days.

I say all this not to boast or self-congratulate, but to remind myself that though I was ever willing to help, it was the generous attitude of the customers that drew me out and gave me confidence, and that every decent and good thing that has come to me while I have lived here is due to some corollary of that welcoming, which I have never lost sight of. I know there are those who would say I've too keenly sought approval and consensus, and if over the years I've erred on the side of being grateful, well, so be it. I think one person can hardly understand why another has conducted his life in such a way, how he came to commit certain actions and not others, whether he looks upon the past with mostly pleasure or equanimity or regret. It seems difficult enough to consider one's own triumphs and failures with perfect verity, for it's no secret that the past proves a most unstable mirror, typically too severe and flattering all at once, and never as truth-reflecting as people would like to believe.

Indeed, I have long felt that I ought to place my energies toward the reckoning of what stands in the here and now, especially given my ever-dwindling years, and so this is what I shall do. My old store, Sunny Medical Supply, is now run by a youngish New York City couple who three years ago purchased it, with all the stock and inventory, and the two one-bedroom apartments above. They haven't changed anything, really. A few weeks ago I noticed that the gold-leaf lettering I ordered when the town required all the village shops to put up the same rustic style of sign is now quite chipped and dull, and needs refurbishing. In fact the whole storefront is looking weatherworn, unlike the other shops immediately beside it on Church Street, the stationers and the florists, whose windows change regularly and have colorful sale announcements and displays of merchandise.

I know as well as anyone that it's challenging for a medical supplier to create an attractive storefront, that bedpans and insulin kits don't make for a naturally scintillating display, but with a little effort and creativity it's not long before you can come up with a window that is almost pleasing to look at. And while I never expected customers to flock into the store because of such attentions, I don't know how many times someone poked his or her head in to compliment me, saying, "Pretty as a picture," or "Best on the street," or "You've got some kinda style, Doc."

Three years later, however, the store still has the very same display from the last Easter window I made up. Really, it's a sad sight for the eyes. Everything's been ruined by time and light. The petals of the nylon tulips are dingy with dust and crumbling, and the blue plastic eyes of the stuffed rabbits have faded to a glazed, watery gray, the fur unevenly tufted and bare and generally feeble-looking. The only thing different is that the window's merchandise has long been reclaimed: the gowns unpinned from the walls, the potty now gone, and finally, left matted in the plastic grass, the faintest impression of a pair of orthopedic shoes.

I finally decided the other day to call on the new owners, just to see how they were doing. I take a walk of some length daily, part of my retirement routine, and so it's no trouble to make my way down Church Street, which is the main thoroughfare of the town. For the first month or so after I sold the business to the Hickeys, I'd make sure to drop by regularly, perhaps two or three times a week, to check on them and see if they needed any help or advice.

Initially, I know, they were quite happy whenever the bell on the door tink-tinkled and they saw me step inside, especially Mrs. Hickey. The Hickeys were both new to the business, not just to selling medical supplies but to selling anything, and their one tenuous qualification for the work was that they were formerly EMS workers, partners in fact, driving an ambulance together down in the city.

I worried, of course, that the Hickeys were gravely inexperienced, and that they'd probably borrowed enough money that their monthly payments were dangerously high, and that with a young child in tow, they would find the demands of running a retail business more severe than they had ever anticipated. I didn't speak about these concerns, as I did feel it was finally time to sell the store. But I was concerned. So whenever I visited them, I would do whatever was needed, calling on any past-due accounts at the county hospital and area retirement homes, negotiating with suppliers, and even checking the store books, reconciling inflows and outflows. I must admit that after the new days of inactivity, I found it pleasurable doing the work again, talking (and invariably joking) with former business contacts, appraising new products and brochures, and then taking my deli sandwich and pickles at my old desk with a mug of green tea, a canister of which I always brought with me on those days I thought I might drop in.

Mrs. Hickey would always greet me warmly and immediately ask how they ought to do this thing or that, and I'd set to work right away, until before I knew it, more than half the day had passed. It was Mr. Hickey, in retrospect, who was sometimes reticent, as he would look up and nod wanly when I entered the store, and after a few weeks I'd first check to see if Mrs. Hickey was there before deciding to go inside. And so it happened quite unexpectedly one day, when Mr. Hickey asked if I might let them run the business themselves, that it was what they had paid me for and if I would finally honor that.

I was confused for a moment, mostly by his tone, because it seemed I was merely there at their own wishes, but I realized that he was telling me in his own way that they had received orientation enough. Mrs. Hickey looked mortified and excused herself to go look for something in the storeroom, and Mr. Hickey politely held open the door for me, not saying anything more, and I resolved then not to disturb them again until they found it necessary to contact me directly, when I should be happy to contribute in any way.

Which they hadn't asked me to do, I admit, a few days ago when I stopped by. But the sorry state of the window case, and the sobering talk I had recently heard from some Church Street merchants about the illness of their son made me feel that I ought to call on them at least once again.

When I entered the store I found, to my surprise, no one there. The shelves were stocked, though somewhat lightly, and the desk and counter were haphazardly covered with volumes of papers and carbons, the unmanned cash register appearing particularly exposed. The aisles had not been waxed in some time. About the whole place there was the sense of a dwindling, the feeling you get when you enter a house people are moving out of, an alarming spareness and disarray that almost seems to be the cause of the leaving, when of course it's just the result. I said hello a few times toward the back storeroom, but I got no answer. Then I heard voices, muffled, coming from what one might see as a closet door but was actually the back stair to the second-floor hall, where the two rental apartments were. The doorway was behind the counter, and naturally I went around, and then I cracked open the door, to hear who might be talking. For a moment, I had the alarming idea that the Hickeys were being robbed, and had been taken upstairs to be bound and gagged.

But of course what I heard was their voices, speaking softly to each other in a low, weary drone, as if they had been arguing at length and now suddenly weren't. They were talking, I could tell, about their son, Patrick. Mrs. Hickey was saying something about getting on Medicaid, now that there was no point in struggling anymore. Mr. Hickey didn't answer, and I understood she was talking about the store and business. I thought I should leave then, for I suddenly didn't like the feeling of eavesdropping on them, when the shop telephone rang out. The sound froze me for a moment, and before I could get on my way, I heard a heavy gallop descend the short stair, and Mr. Hickey opened the door just as I swung myself around the end of the counter.

When he saw me he glared, raising his finger to say something, but the telephone was ringing and he said to me instead, "You hold on," and he picked up the handset, his eyes unwavering in their fix on me. Mrs. Hickey came down, too, and when she saw me she broke into an easy smile. Her face was wet, her nose and cheeks hotly flushed and rosy, and in spite of this it was wonderful to see her again, to remember what an attractive and pleasant young woman she was, with such genuine warmth of spirit.

"Doc Hata," she said, wiping her nose with a tissue. "It's so nice to see you again. Gosh, I'm sorry I'm like this." She blew her nose. "That's that. Now, how have you been? You haven't been by in so long."

"Forgive me," I said, "but you know how busy people are, when they have nothing to do."

She laughed lightly at this and said, "For a while I wondered if maybe you had moved to Florida or someplace. But then I thought about it and I knew better. You're not someone who would leave his home so easily."

"You're absolutely right," I replied. "Besides, that kind of heat has never agreed with me."

"Do you still go on your two-hour walks?"

"Every day," I answered. Mr. Hickey was still quiet, holding the handset to his ear. I said to her, "Why don't we go together some-time? I head up through the state park these days, on the trails there, which are very pretty with the leaves full and shading. It's hilly, but not so hard. What do you think?"

But before she could answer, her husband brusquely put down the phone. "He's not having a good morning," he said to her, inter-rupting us as though he had been in our conversation all along. He was looking straight at his wife. "The new doctor is going to see him at one-thirty. I better get up there now." He regarded me for a long, awkward moment. Then he said, "What do you want here, old man?"

"James!"

"Hold on, Annie. I'd just like to know what he wants from us. It can't be an accident that he's come today. Your buddy Mr. Finch at the bank didn't ask you to drop by, did he?"

It was a strange notion, and I had no reply.

"Well, you can tell him anyway he'll have the whole place soon. Lock, stock and barrel. We wish we could sell it, but do you know what the place is worth? I bet you have an idea."

"I can't say, Mr. Hickey."

"Sure you can't. You only say nice things, I guess. Should I tell you? About two-thirds what you sold it to us for. I'd have to find an-other hundred grand to clear the mortgage, *after* selling it. So it looks like foreclosure instead."

"He's not in the least at fault, James," Mrs. Hickey scolded. "So just please shut up now."

"This isn't blame, dear. I'm not blaming anybody," Mr. Hickey replied. He was regarding me with much umbrage. "This is just in-formation. Mr. Hata appreciates knowing what's happening in his town. We don't need a mayor because we have Mr. Hata. I'm sorry—*Doc* Hata. I never understood why you're called that when it's obvious you're not a doctor."

"I don't refer to myself as one."

"That you don't. That's true. But you seem to like the title. And I think it fits you, too."

Mrs. Hickey said, "Sometimes I despise you, James."

"Sometimes *I* despise me," her husband replied, suddenly looking hurt. He stared down at his feet. Then he tried to embrace her, but she turned away. "Oh, hell with it," he said, snatching his windbreaker from the rack on the wall. "Hell all." He marched out, leaving the door wide open.

Mrs. Hickey gathered herself and shut the door behind him. She was quite angry, though it was clear she was also deeply embarrassed and sorry for me. I told her she shouldn't worry about my feelings being hurt, for it was obvious her husband was under a terrible strain. Mrs. Hickey thanked me for my kindness, and though I assented, I didn't truly feel that it was kindness, on my part. Not really at all. It was an understanding, if anything. For I should say that I know from experience that the bearing of those in extreme circumstances can sometimes be untoward and even shocking, and we must try our best to understand what is actual and essential to a person, and what is by any indication anomalous, a momentary lapse that is better forgotten than considered time and time again, to little avail.

Mrs. Hickey asked if I might stay and talk a little while, and I was glad to. She told me more about her son. It was true what I'd heard, that his heart was congenitally diseased, and he was now in urgent need of a transplant. He was on the national registry, of course, and because of his age and condition almost at the top of the list, but the dysfunction had accelerated, and the doctors now told them that he was in real danger, that it was coming down to a matter of months, if a suitable donor wasn't located. This besides the fact that after two and a half years, they were almost out of insurance.

I had also visited on the day they were to inform the bank what their decision was about refinancing their mortgage, which was six months in arrears. Business wasn't booming, given that the local economy was in recession (which seemed to befall the area, unfortunately for the Hickeys, a short time after they bought my store), and that Sunny Medical Supply now had to compete with a franchise of a large regional supplier, which had opened in the neighboring town of Highbridge.

And yet with all this negativeness, Mrs. Hickey was still cheerful, joking and kidding and trying to put the best face on things, telling me how she took strength from Patrick, who never once complained about sleeping at the hospital, or eating the food. I had never actually met the boy, though I thought I could see him easily in his mother, whose sanguinity and resolve I admired without bound. I pictured him with her fair coloring and giddy spray of freckles, and the same sea-blue eyes, and then, too, possessed of the odd calm that very young children can sometimes have, even when they understand that dark fates may be near.

Eventually some customers came in, and I urged Mrs. Hickey to attend to them, while I should be getting on home. But before I could leave the store she had come over to see me out.

"Would you like to come see him sometime?" she asked me. "We take shifts, so you wouldn't have to worry about James, if you came when I was there. I could call you from the room."

"I'd be very happy to meet him," I said. "Anytime you wish to call me."

Mrs. Hickey seemed pleased, and she stepped outside. It was a social custom, strangely enough, that she'd picked up from watching me years before, the polite duty of a host or proprietor in bidding a respectful goodbye. It brought a warm feeling to my chest to have her come out accompanying me. But the customers were still inside, and I asked her please to go back and attend to them. I very nearly bowed, as if that might convince her, but then she did go in, and I'd already turned down the street when she called out to me once more.

"I just remembered," she said, her face brightening as she approached me. She was holding a dusty box, the kind photographic paper comes in. "I was cleaning out the storeroom last week, and I found this in an old briefcase. I'm sorry, I couldn't help but look inside. There are all kinds of neat pictures in there."

I could hardly remember leaving anything personal behind in the store.

"I noticed there's a young woman in many of them," Mrs. Hickey said. "She's very pretty. She's in quite a few, with you. Is she a relative?"

"Yes," I heard myself reply, accepting the box from her. "You must be talking about Sunny."

"Sunny? Did you name the store after her?"

I said, "I suppose I did."

"Where is she now?"

"She came from Japan," I said, "many years ago, and stayed for some schooling. She went back."

"Well, she's certainly lovely. She must be a grown woman now."

"Yes," I said, taking my leave. "I haven't seen her in quite a long time. But thank you."

"Will you call about our walk?"

"Yes."

"And Patrick, too?"

"Yes."

Before she could say any more I quickly made my way down Church Street, following it to the traffic square where it meets River and then Mountview, which is the street I live on. As I climbed the gentle rise of the old road, I wished that I hadn't spoken inaccurately about Sunny to Mrs. Hickey, but the moment, like so many others, passed too swiftly, as I didn't feel I could explain things without further complication and embarrassment. I went the half-mile to the road's crest, where the house I bought nearly thirty years ago stands amid a copse of mature elm and oak and maple. Inside, the house was warm and lighted. As usual I'd left the lamps on in the hall and kitchen, and I turned them off before going upstairs. I often prepared myself an early dinner of soup noodles or a casserole of oden with rice, but I decided to go straight up to my bedroom and read. It wasn't until the middle of the evening that I stopped, when it occurred to me that I should at least have a snack, so that I wouldn't toss in my sleep or wake up famished. I put on my robe and went out to the stairs, but instead of descending, I wandered down the hallway, to the far door, to the room where Sunny once lived.

For some moments I stood before the door. When I finally opened it, I was surprised by the sudden chill; the heating ducts had long been shut, and an icy curl of air lapped past my bare feet. I remembered, then, how it had taken longer than I expected to clear the room completely: it was crammed full of her furnishings, every sort of bric-a-brac and notion and wall hanging. She had left the house in a hurry. In the following weeks I worked on the room in my spare time, in the evenings and on the weekends. I remember patching and repainting the ceiling and walls, making sure to fix all the mars in the plaster. There were larger pocks, into which I found it easy enough to spade the filler. But it was the smaller ones, particularly the tack holes, which seemed to number in the hundreds, that took the greatest part of my time. In the end, I found myself doing the work in half-foot squares, pressing in the paste with the tip of a finger, smoothing it out, and it wasn't until much later, as I'd drift into the room to inspect for missed holes, running my hand over the surfaces, that the whole project was quite satisfactorily done.

2

MY HOUSE ISN'T THE GRANDEST in our town, but it's generally known that of the homes on Mountview, one of the original
streets in Bedley Run, the two-story Tudor revival at number 57 is
one of the special properties in the area. It seems it's every other
week now that I receive a card or note from a realtor, asking if I
might consider putting it up for sale. The local ones, of course,
know my situation, and as I'm retired and live alone in this large
house, with its impressive flower and herb garden, and flagstone
swimming pool, and leaded glass and wrought-iron conservatory,
they are right to hope that I might do as Mrs. Hickey had thought
I'd done, and move to one of those new developments in a welcomingly warm place like Boca Raton or Scottsdale.

"Now come on, Doc," Liv Crawford of Town Realty said to me
on the phone very early this morning, "that immensely beautiful
house of yours is also very high-maintenance. You don't want to be
worrying about clogged gutters and foundation cracks anymore, do
you?"

"I don't mind so much, actually," I told her.

"But how are you going to feel twenty years from now?"

I reminded her that I would be in my nineties by then.

"All the more so," she answered brightly. I thanked her for her very optimistic wishes for my health, and said I would let her know when I was ready.

"You never know until you are, Doc. But sometimes it's too late."

"Goodness, Liv."

"Just saying, Doc. Listen, I'm about to meet some buyers, and I think they'd just love your house to death. They're young and high-powered, and they're very desperate to find a place on a Mountview-type street. They're already talking an overbid, for the right kind of place, which yours is in spades."

"But it's not for sale, there's no price—"

"I know that, Doc. I'm just doing a drive-by with them, the whole neighborhood, but when I slow down in front of your place, can I at least tell them you're considering?"

"I don't think this is the best time for me, Liv. . . ."

"Fine, Doc, thanks. Gotta go."

Then click, she's gone. But really, in fact I don't mind her opportunism, her wishful pluck, the way her voice positively rings with the joyous vibrancy of commerce (a note I sorely miss). In fact I've had several market appraisals done in recent years, with the consensus being that my house hasn't fallen in price (as everything else in the county has, especially commercial properties like my former store), but has even appreciated somewhat; it seems that older, "vintage" homes in as pristine condition as mine rarely become available, and when they do there's not even time enough to stick the sign on the front lawn before they're sold.

If I were to leave this place, where would I go? Mr. Stark, who seven years ago bought Murasan's Smoke and Pipe, recently asked why I didn't think about going back and living out the rest of my days in Japan. I stop in at his shop some afternoons, near the end of my day.

"Imagine," he said to me, almost musically, waving his Churchill-length cigar, "spending one's days by a serene lake somewhere near Kyoto, wearing silken white robes and sipping rare sake served by knowing maidens. I can see you there, Doc. Like a dream I can see you."

Mr. Harris, a retired insurer who seems to pass most of his waking hours in Murasan's, added, "I'm drawn to the old country myself, Doc, though mine, of course, is Wales. Every year I wonder whether I should sell out and pilgrim there, to claim my ancestral seat." He took a lengthy, pensive drag from his pipe. "But then, of course, I realize my Muriel already has it."

"And in a sling," Mr. Stark added. They both cackled like old women, blowing smoke every which way.

I appreciated their interest, and what I took as their friendly concern, and I bore the notion with me for some days. Sometimes I still think of Japan, though much less in recent times than in my first years in Bedley Run, when it seemed it was every day I wondered how long I could last, and which morning I'd rise and know I'd have to return, though of course to what I couldn't know.

The other question in any retirement is, what would I do? These are things Liv Crawford cannot address deeply. But even if she can find me, as she says, a "prime zero-care condo with a 180° view of the ocean," her job stops there, for while I might have a decent place to live, I'd have to figure out for myself *how* to live there, and why. And the retirement lifestyle doesn't immediately draw me. I don't fish, for example, and I don't play bridge. I'm not a collector of figurines, or exotic birds, or antique toys. I'm not a connoisseur of drink. I don't really dance, and the related idea of companionship for someone like me seems at once complicated and vague. There are lectures at the junior college, and reading in bed, but most of what I come across seems to suggest that older folks like me might be better off just falling asleep forever.

What's left, perhaps, is golf, but I've played the game no more than a dozen times in my life, and then it was always with the same group of medical-supply wholesalers, who for several years in a row invited me on a spring junket to Myrtle Beach. I do remember there being a certain relaxation to those trips. We'd wake up late and stay on the course until dusk, and then eat a heavy dinner at a raucous lounge or striptease club where the others would drink like madmen until the early hours, when I'd have to drive us back to the hotel. And as much as I understood that they probably liked me well enough and found my company (and convenient stewardship of them) pleasing, what I looked forward to each year with genuine fondness was being with fellow businessmen, and passing those easy, jocular hours of camaraderie by the pool or greenside or in a smoky bar, when we spoke of nothing profound or consequential but still seemed to make the time somehow worthwhile.

I sometimes miss those trips, and others I took regularly when I was younger and more actively involved in the more social aspects of the business, the three-day Bahama conference cruises and the large, frenetic conventions in unusual cities like New Orleans and Minneapolis. All those many boisterous, various folks. I didn't crave their company as much as the opportunity to watch them in their enjoyment and reverie. But I suppose I also took easy comfort then in joking and laughing with pretty much anybody, and people seemed to respond with a surprising warmth, and I was often in-vited to late-night suite parties and next-day city tours with this group or that.

Once, I even met a Japanese gentleman from the San Francisco Bay area, who owned a store that sounded much like mine, and had opened in the very same year. He was American-born, his grand-parents among those who had long ago settled in Hawaii and then California. I think we both brightened on sighting each other. And yet there was an unexpected awkwardness. You would think we would have plenty to discuss, being of like race and age and occu-pation, but our conversation was oddly halting and strained. There was a very difficult moment, on being introduced to each other, when it was unclear whether we would shake hands or bow. Nei-ther of us wished to offend the other, and being peers, it was es-pecially difficult for one man to assume a posture of natural authority, or acquiescence. Perhaps had we been alone, and not standing in front of the other conventioneers, we might have bowed or shaken hands or done both without a flinch, and gone on to be friends. But as it happened, we exchanged only the mildest pleas-antries, and I sensed that he was immediately unsettled by my ac-cent (which was much stronger twenty years ago than it is now), for he seemed to speak with increasing softness, as if to diminish his perfect American-sounding voice. I first wondered if he felt he wasn't Japanese enough for me, or whether I thought myself not American enough for him. But later on, after returning home, I thought perhaps it was that we felt different from everyone by virtue of being together (these two Japanese in a convention crowd), and that it was this fact that made us realize, for a moment, our sudden and unmistakable sense of not fitting in.

I remember all this now because it seems to me the truer feeling of the time was somehow that uncomfortable one, rather than the collegial atmosphere of the convention or of my golfing trips, and it makes me now consider my many good years here in Bedley Run in a slightly different light. For what I didn't let Liv Crawford know this morning is that I'm probably nearer to actually selling my house than I've ever been before. I know I told Mrs. Hickey otherwise in the store last week, but more and more the time feels right to me, not so much from a financial viewpoint but from a sense of one's time in a place, and that time being close to done. It's not that I feel I've used up this house, this town, this part of the world, that I've gotten all I'm going to get, but more that this feeling I've come to expect, this happy blend of familiarity and homeyness and what must be belonging, is strangely beginning to disturb me.

What used to concern me greatly about leaving was the awkward impression you can sometimes have, say when you find yourself on an everyday street, or in a store, or in what would otherwise be a shimmering, verdant park, and you think not about the surroundings but about yourself, and how people will stop and think (most times, unnoticeably) about who you may be, how you fit into the picture, what this may say, and so on and so forth. I've never really liked this kind of thinking, either theirs or mine, and have always wished to be in a situation like the one I have steadily fashioned for myself in this town, where, if I don't have many intimates or close friends, I'm at least a quantity known, somebody long ago counted. Most everyone in Bedley Run knows me, though at the same time I've actually come to develop an unexpected condition of transparence here, a walking case of others' certitude, that to spy me on my way down Church Street is merely noting the expression of a natural law. *Doc Hata,* they can say with surety, *he comes around.*

And yet there is a discomfiting aspect to all this rapport. I don't know how or when it happened, or if it is truly happening now, but I'm sure something is afoot, for I keep stepping outside my house, walking its grounds, peering at the highly angled shape of its roofs, the warm color and time-textured facade, looking at it as though I were doing so for the very first time, when I wondered if I would ever in my life call such a house my home.

So after speaking with Liv Crawford, I changed into my trunks and walked out the French doors of the kitchen and past the gardens to the pool. I swim each morning, doing twenty-five steady lengths, rain or shine. It is July but has been unseasonably cool and dry, and with all the shade from the towering trees, the water is bracing in its chill, which is in fact how I prefer it.

So now I begin my swim the way I always do, taking a shallow dive from the far side and gliding underwater for much of the first length. It's always a slight shock to the system, and there's the bare second when I'm sure my heart has stopped, skipped in its time, though I'll keep going and gently rise, to begin my crawl. But this morning, beneath the surface of the lightless water (the pool bottom and sides were painted a dark battleship gray, to match the stone surround), I suddenly have the thought that I'm not swimming in my own pool at all, but am someplace else, in a neighboring pool or even a pond, and my chest gives a buckle and I actually swallow some water. Gasping, I peel off my goggles, and they lazily drift somewhere to the bottom. When my eyes clear, of course, I am nowhere else but home.

I decide not to swim anymore, and I pull my robe tight around me and step quickly inside. I'm shivering, almost uncontrollably, and instead of taking a warming shower, I have the odd compulsion to start a log fire in the family room hearth. Sitting crouched before it, arranging the kindling, I can't help but remember a story I once read in an old book of Sunny's, one she must have used in a high-school class. I found it among others on the shelves in the family room, and it had all sorts of interesting markings and notes in the margins. The story, which she had dog-eared, is about a man who decides one day to swim in other people's pools, one after another in his neighborhood and town, which, as described, seems very much like Bedley Run. The man, the story goes, has resolved to "swim across the county," and after some travail of walking in on his neighbors and scaling property walls and crossing busy parkways, he finally makes it back to his own home, which, to his desperate confusion, he finds locked up and deserted.

I'm not sure if I've ever appreciated fully the moral or deeper meanings of the story, which it no doubt has, but nevertheless it makes me think of many notions, the first being that the man has begun, whether knowing it or not, a sort of quest or journey, and ultimately finds himself, if in spiritual disillusion. This, naturally, seems reasonable. Another thought is that he has simply gone mad, or perhaps suffers a perennial state of upper-middle-class drunkenness, and his project is one of escape, to free himself from the realities of his fallen station. Or that (and this I draw mostly from the side notes, scribbled in several hands) he is making fitful passage, in a metaphorical sense, through the epic "seasons" of life.

Sitting before the fire, I wonder, too, whether someone watching me swim each morning in the peerless quiet of the pool, steadily pulling my way back and forth, would think I was entering a significant period in life, a time in which all I would do was swim every day in my backyard, a lovely place of my own making. And while this may seem a romantic, even triumphant picture of near-end, what we might well hope to achieve at the start of our adult lives, it strikes me that it could be a scene of some sadness as well, of a beauty empty and cold. It is an unnerving thing, but when I was underneath the water, gliding in that black chill, my mind's eye suddenly seemed to carry to a perspective high above, from where I could see the exacting, telling shapes of all: the spartan surfaces of the pool deck, the tight-clipped manicures of the garden, the venerable house and trees, the fetching, narrow street. And what caught me, too, was that I knew there was also a man in that water, amidst it all, a secret swimmer who, if he could choose, might always go silent and unseen.

Of course, when you read something like a story, you can find yourself thinking too long about all sorts of ideas, which usually complicate rather than settle the questions at hand. And while we understand that art and literature mean to do this to us, is there not a serious, thinking person who sometimes wishes the questions would be answered directly by a reading, with clarity and resolve, so that he might move steadily onward, to be further enlightened, improved?

The fire sputters and needs quick fuel, and so I decide to take the opportunity to burn the decades-old files and papers and other expired and useless documents packed in the oak drawer units that line one wall of the family room. I've been secretly eager to get rid of such stuff as canceled checks and mortgage and bank statements, and I'm perversely pleased to find that I've kept it all so orderly, which makes the disposal somehow worry-free and simple. I haven't yet changed into regular clothes, and though my robe is damp in the seat from my swim trunks, I no longer feel chilled in the room. Soon enough the fire is burning fiercely with the sheaves of papers, as too much goes in at once, the flames nearly dying out from the smothering; but then in a combustive rush they begin leaping up and out, to lick the underside of the marble mantel. I'm oddly unconcerned. There is a purity in the startling heat, its crave and intent, and I don't stop feeding in papers until I come to the folders of the most current documents, which I luckily notice before mistakenly tossing them in. I set them down on the carpet and pull the protective screen before the fire, and I go into the kitchen, where my breakfast is waiting.

I also nearly throw some old photographs into the flames, though not accidentally. This is always a difficult thing to do, even with pictures of no great consequence, which these are. There are scores of them, in rubber-banded shoe boxes, tucked at the backs of the file drawers—insurance shots of the store and its stock and equipment, and then many others of the house and its furnishings, the projects of steady construction of the patio and pool, the hothouse, the reroofing of the garage, and then the various cars and major tools and equipment I've owned through the years. I suppose it is the catalog of my life, my being's fill of good fortune, though what an estate appraiser might accidentally find and think nothing of discarding.

I was never one to keep albums and framed personal pictures, and it was only during the time Sunny lived with me that I used my camera for those reasons. I believe that among the photographs I received from Mrs. Hickey, there's one of Sunny at the piano, from her first year with me, when she needed a telephone book atop the bench to sit in the right position. Strangely enough, there isn't, among the boxes I found, a picture of the piano itself, a Baldwin baby grand. The box that Mrs. Hickey gave me I stowed upstairs, not in my room but in the hall table drawer, just outside the empty bedroom. I haven't looked at the photographs yet, but I can conjure some of them from my memory, images of the two of us, here and there, posing amid the chaos of renovations.

Sunny, I'm afraid, always hated the house. In those days the place wasn't as composed as it is now, and it seemed every door and molding and cabinet needed replacing, the lights flickering and burning brown, the plumbing fitful and spastic, the old structure nothing more than that, just simply old, and sliding swiftly into a final, dishonorable state. I had bought it on the confidence of the agent (not Liv Crawford, but someone very much like her), who assured me it was a solid investment, and also because my store was just beginning to do a steady business, the nearby county hospital having finally opened, and the land cleared and foundation laid for the large retirement home on Quaker's Ridge. I paid $45,000 for it, perhaps too much then. Inside, the house was dark and spacious and poorly heated, just the type of creaky, murmuring structure they make up at amusement parks to amuse and frighten guests.

I remember first walking Sunny into the foyer, with all that dark wood paneling that was still up on the walls and ceiling, smelling from the inside of rot and dust, the lights fading now and then, and she actually began to titter and cry. I didn't know what to do for her, as she seemed not to want me to touch her, and for some moments I stood apart from her while she wept, this shivering little girl of seven. She had learned some English at the orphanage, so I asked her not to worry or be afraid, that I would do my best to make a pleasant home, and that she should be happy to be in the United States and have a father now and maybe a mother someday soon. She kept crying but she looked at me and I saw her for the first time, the helpless black of her eyes, and I could do little else but bend down and hold her until she stopped.

And so after her arrival, it seemed that my every spare moment away from the store was devoted to fixing the house, at first attempting the renovations myself, and then calling in tradesmen, and finally, after disappointments with slow, shoddy work and the high expense, again taking on the projects solo. And there were many projects, too numerous to remember, but one that stands out is the smallest of them, the time I had to change the mirror and vanity in her bathroom upstairs.

I was cleaning the house as always that Sunday morning, vacuuming and dusting and disinfecting the kitchen and bathrooms. Sunny was nearly ten years old, and though she was more than capable of helping, I didn't think it was right to have her do such things. The house was still a terrible mess, and because I felt there was so much improving to do, it was clear I shouldn't include my daughter in the mundane drudgeries. My wish, as I had always explained to her, was that she study hard and practice her piano and read as many books as she could bear, and of course, when there was free time, play with her friends from school. A child's days are too short, and my sense then was that I should let her focus on activities that would most directly benefit her.

And so, besides the major ongoing renovations, I took up general maintenance of the house with the usual care and thoroughness, but as it happened every week something seemed to stall my efforts. Everything would go smoothly until a cabinet door wouldn't catch, or a hinge began to squeak, or a drain was too slow, and then a vise-like tightness came over me. That time in Sunny's bathroom, trying to rub out a persistent cloudy stain in the vanity, I somehow cracked the mirror, and my fingers began bleeding from the edges of the spidery glass. I must have kept rubbing and blotting, for it was only some moments later that I realized Sunny was watching from the doorway, her splintered reflection looking up at me.

Her round face, pretty and dark in complexion, was serene and quiet.

"Have you already finished practicing your Chopin?" I asked her.

"Yes."

"I couldn't hear you. What were you playing?"

"Nocturnes," she said, staring at my hand. "The ones you like. From Opus Nine and Thirty-two."

"I must have been vacuuming," I said, wrapping a rag about my fingers. "Would you play some of them again?"

"Okay. But can I help you now?"

"No, dear," I said to her, trying to stay the throbbing in my hand, my arm. "Why don't you play some more? Your teacher wishes that you practice more than you do. You must push yourself. It may be difficult for you to see, but even great talent is easily wasted."

"Yes."

"Sunny?"

"Yes," she said, folding the lacy hem of her green dress for Sunday school, where I would take her in the afternoon.

"Please leave the living room doors open, so the music can travel. And, Sunny?"

"Yes."

"You should do what we talked about last week. About addressing me."

"Yes, *Poppa,*" she said, saying the word softly but clearly.

She went downstairs, and I stood before the broken mirror, waiting for the first notes to rise up the stairs. She began playing Opus 32, 1, a piece she was preparing for an upcoming recital, and one I especially liked. The composition calmed me. Aside from the lyrical, impassioned musings, there are unlikely pauses in the piece, near-silences that make it seem as if the performer has suddenly decided to cease, cannot go on, even has disappeared. These silences are really quite magical and haunting. And just at the moment it seems the pianist has stopped, the lovely notes resume.

As I listened, Sunny played beautifully, with a style and presentation much beyond her years. She was as technically advanced as other gifted children, but she also seemed to have a deep understanding of a given piece of music, her playing rich with an arresting, mature feeling. And yet in the end, she never attained the virtuosity the best young performers must have in order to be promoted to the next ranks. In competitions Sunny was mostly magnificent, but it seemed that there were always a few difficult and even strangely blundering moments in her performances, perplexing passages marring what was otherwise wholesale surety and brilliance. It was perfection—or even near-perfection—that somehow eluded her, and as she grew up, the notion of attempting it seemed to fall farther and farther from her desire. Early in high school she ceased practicing seriously, and eventually she dropped playing altogether.

We had many arguments and bad feelings over her quitting, and for a long time during that period the two of us hardly acknowledged each other in the house. She was old enough then to move about as she pleased, and her friends with cars would often pick her up in the mornings before school, and not drop her off until late in the evening, ten or eleven at night. I'd hear the car roll up the cobblestone drive, the sweep of its lights in my window, the slam of the passenger door, her restless keys, the lock, the quick shuffle that trailed straight to her room. And then the quiet again. This went on, I'm afraid, for many months. In the mornings she seemed to wait until I had begun my swim to come downstairs, when she would leave the house and walk down the block to await her rides.

Perhaps I grew too accustomed to our distance. Initially I had tried to leave indications that I was unhappy with our relationship, putting out a bowl and spoon and a box of cereal for her, a glass of juice, a soft-boiled egg, but each morning when I came in from my swim the setting was just as I had left it, unmoved, untouched. I knew she'd seen it. I had watched her once from the pool, my goggled eyes skimming along the surface of the water; she stood staring at the place at the table, as if it were some kind of museum display, not to be disturbed, and then she turned away. But I continued each morning, and eventually I began sitting down to eat the breakfast myself, with more a taste of sorrow than spite. It wasn't long before I mostly forgot about Sunny refusing my offerings, and it became simply habit, part of my waking ritual that I still do now, without fail.

But then everything eventually shifts, accommodates. We began communicating again at some point, for no obvious reasons. This would prove a short time before she left the house for good. There was little warmth, I know, but at least she was hearing me, meeting my eyes. And there was talking, when it suited us. One day I went out to skim leaves and twigs from the pool, where she was sunbathing, and she asked if I was going to sell the piano.

"The piano?" I repeated, surprised by the notion. "Is there a reason why I should? I don't understand. Besides, you might want to begin playing again someday."

She didn't answer, turning over onto her back. She had on wrap-around sunglasses, and was lying in the recliner in the full sun. She had just turned seventeen that June, and in the fall would start her final year at Bedley Run High School. I thought she was spending too much time going to the seniors' post-graduation parties, staying out most of the night and then sleeping late, only coming out of her room to lie in the sun. I had often asked her if she would take better care with her skin, having seen certain patients come into the store suffering from melanoma, but in those days it was desirable to be tanned as dark as one could get, and Sunny was one who never had trouble in that regard.

"It's stupid to have the piano, when no one's ever going to play it."

"I hope that's not true," I replied.

"It is true," she said tersely, slinging her forearm over her face. "I don't like having to see it every day. It sits there for no reason."

"It doesn't bother me. I like it."

She didn't reply immediately to this. I kept working, gathering the flotsam with the long net. After a moment, she spoke up again. "I think you like what it says."

"I don't quite understand," I said.

"Of course you don't," she answered. "I'm saying, you like having it around for what it says. About me. How I've failed."

"That's not in the least true."

"Sure it is," she answered, almost affably. But there was real defeat in her voice also, a child's broad welling of it.

I told her, "If anything, Sunny, I should see it as a symbol of my own failure, in inspiring the best in you."

"That's right. I've failed doubly. First myself, and then my good poppa, who's loved and respected by all."

"You can always twist my words," I told her. "But you shouldn't take everything I do so seriously. I'm not doing anything wrong by keeping the piano. I would like you to play again, yes, this is true, but not because of me. Not anymore. I think it would improve you, like reading a book would improve you. Or even something as simple as swimming, which I've taken to heart. I don't believe I've ever compelled you to do anything. I've made suggestions, advised about certain things, like taking up the piano, but I try to follow your interests. Though you don't seem to like many things any longer, which I think I can fairly say."

"You *only* fairly say."

"Please, Sunny, I don't always enjoy your word games."

"Sorry, Doc."

"I wish you wouldn't call me that."

"I won't, then," she said, with some finality. Then she rose from the chaise. She wrapped the towel around her waist and headed for the house, and I didn't see or hear her for the rest of the day. I thought perhaps that this would be the start of another strained period for us, but the next day she left a note saying she was going to Jones Beach with her friends, and would be staying in the city over the weekend, at someone's apartment. She signed her name and added a "Don't worry!" on the end. I was worried, of course, and was annoyed that she hadn't mentioned her plans for the weekend earlier, but part of me was also greatly appreciative of the fact of the note, pleased by the simple thing of it, which she would have never thought to leave me some months before.

THE FIRELOG CRACKS SHARPLY in the family room, and I want to check it but the phone rings, and it's Liv Crawford. I can hardly hear her. She sounds as if she's half a world away.

"Doc," she says, obviously shouting. "Hang up! Will you hang up? I'll have to call you back!"

In a few seconds she calls again, and it's better this time. "Sorry, Doc, but this car phone is just rotten. Or maybe it's the car. I have to open the whole door to hear anything. You can imagine what hell that is on the Saw Mill Parkway."

"Where are you now?"

"Actually, Doc, I'm right outside your place. In the street. I'm not alone. Can I put you on speaker?"

"I don't think it's the right time——"

"Don't worry about it, Doc, we'll stay right here in the car, I promise. We won't budge." She sounds as if she's talking down into a hole, or that I'm listening to her from one. "Meet Karen and Dexter Ellings. They're from the city."

"Hi, Doctor Hata!" they say, in ill harmony.

"Hello."

There's a pause.

"You have a beautiful house!" the woman says. Her husband then adds, "It's really stunning. A winner."

"Thank you," I say, hoping very much Liv Crawford will come back. She does, and suddenly she's cut the couple out, the sound coming sharper again, just the two of us.

"They're so happy I brought them by," Liv Crawford says, clearly speaking for all involved, "even though I told them you weren't ready to sell yet. But they'll be patient and wait for your decision, however long it takes."

"It may be some time," I warn her.

"He says you guys will be the first to know," she says away from the phone. Now back. "Listen, Doc, we're going to the village for brunch, at Sffuzi's. If you're free, you ought to join us. I know you probably have lots of plans for a bright Sunday morning."

"I was just swimming," I tell her, though now my suit is nearly dry. "And I'm eating right now."

"Gosh! You should have told me you were eating! I'll stop pestering you. We're leaving right now. I'll call you tomorrow. Or maybe we can have lunch. Let's do that. . . ."

But as she is talking I sense in the air a lean, tight scent, almost chemical, and then it turns softer, into the fat odor of smoke. I don't see any, but when I crane around to the doorway I see the section of carpet in front of the fire starting to smolder. The heavy logs in the fireplace are crackling, roaring. Liv Crawford is mentioning times we might meet, and I am still listening to her, actually thinking about what she is saying about a lunch, even though a burst of flames is imminent.

"Doc?"

And then it happens, the fire, miraculously appearing from the deep pile of the rug where it meets the marble flooring. The flames are not high, or fierce; they are not spreading, and the whole sight, somehow, is a disappointment. It all seems perfectly controlled, the way fires burn in the movies and at theme parks, with a shut-off quality, and very colorful. But what there is volumes of is smoke, which now bellows and rises up in great flumes against the ceiling. Upstairs, I hear the piercing ring of the smoke alarm.

"Oh Doc . . ." Liv Crawford says in a singsong voice. "That sounds like your smoke alarm."

"Yes," I say, trying to find the doors out to the patio. "The family room is on fire."

"What?"

"I better get off now," I tell her, suddenly dropping to my knees.

I hear Liv Crawford's voice, now tiny and bleating, the cordless phone somewhere behind me. The smell is awful, and I feel as though I am underwater again, my eyes closed, holding my breath, gliding in the abyss, and I try my best to move, in my own measured crawl, my only flying.

3

HOW GOOD IT IS to see old friends and colleagues again. Even here, in the gray-green corridors of the adult ward of the county hospital, one finds that fellowship has not been forgotten in the shifting rush to efficiency and profits. There is Connie Kalajian, the head nurse of the adult unit, who seems to do all she can to make sure her young staff is attentive to me, and Ryka Murnow, the hospital administrator, whose father had terrible disc problems and came to my store quite often before he died. There is Johnny Barnes, the head pharmacist of the hospital and also a rising-in-the-ranks semiprofessional bowler, who has played in tournaments upstate and in Ontario and in the Midwest. And of course, there is Renny Banerjee, the hospital purchasing manager, who comes by my room every few hours to see if I need anything. He chain-smokes, so he stops by after his many breaks. He appears now at breakfast time, bearing a foil-wrapped plate containing a bacon-and-cheese omelette and toasted bagel from the neighboring diner.

He looks severely at my hospital tray, which I have only begun to pick at.

"Don't ever touch that stuff again," he says without levity. "You have no idea what goes on in Food Services." He peels off the foil and hands me a plastic fork. He pulls up a chair next to the bed while I eat. I'm not hungry, but I feel I'm able to eat because he's brought it along, because he is with me. "I used to date someone who worked there, a Puerto Rican girl named Julia. She was very sweet, but she told me how they really operate. They call it 'Jai Alai,' because you can use any surface for preparing the food—the floor, the walls, whatever. For entertainment they form hamburger patties by flinging ground beef up against the ceiling, then catching it on the way down."

Renny Banerjee, though East Indian of blood, is what I often think of as a very American sort of man—barrel-chested, tall, with an easy, directive way of gesturing. There is the feeling when he speaks to you in his lilting accent that he's addressing others in the room, who must be listening intently. Except that Renny is also polite. "My secret word to you, Doc, is that you get out of this place as soon as you are able. Or even before. I'll have a word with the attending, if you like. Better to be in your own home, in every respect. I've heard the damage wasn't very severe."

"Not at all," I answer, my lungs itchy, heavy-feeling. "Some carpet was ruined, and curtains. The family room and the kitchen need repainting. There is general cleaning to be done. A realtor is taking care of things right now."

"You're selling the house?" Renny Banerjee asks, a note of concern in his voice.

"No," I say. "She's just looking after the repairs for me. She lets in the workers. She's been a great help, really."

"Liv Crawford," he says, as if there could be no one else.

"You know her?"

"We dated," he answers matter-of-factly. "Long time ago. And we'll probably date one day again. I have a terrible weakness for that woman. It's quite specific. Something in me wants to hand over all my money to her. I hate the feeling, but it's true."

"She has a strong presence," I say, in way of support.

"You ought to be careful yourself, Doc. I mean with your house, of course. Make sure you know what you want. I know Liv's the one who pulled you out. Her picture was all over the paper. But what if you didn't live in such a pretty house? You have to wonder. . . ."

We have a hearty laugh at this, and though I start coughing and hacking, it is a pleasant feeling, to be talking with someone like Renny Banerjee. The circumstances are not ideal, yet it seems to me that life's moments don't have to be so right or not right anymore, so fraught and weighted with "value," but just of themselves, what they are, which in this case is myself and Renny once again sharing light times and jokes and notions. Since I retired from the medical business, neither of us has called the other (having nothing specific to call about), but none of that seems awkward or straining now, and lying here in this largish room (courtesy of Ryka Murnow), I feel as fortunate as a man my age should rightly be able to feel, who's had smoke inhalation and a racing heart and a good part of his house badly damaged by smoke. Liv Crawford did, with danger to herself, pull me out, while her frightened clients called emergency services on her car phone, and yesterday she sent a large bouquet of white roses, which sit on the windowsill in the brassy autumn light. They are beautiful, and I'm very grateful for them, even though in the Japanese tradition white is the signal color of death. But I don't mind even this, and perhaps it's right that Liv Crawford should be the bearer of these tidings, the mercenary angel who has saved my life.

"Sometimes I actually find myself missing that damned woman's company," Renny Banerjee says, looking over at the flowers. "Can you believe that? And I was the one who broke things off, Doc. I practically had to throw her out of my apartment. I changed the locks, though it didn't do any good."

"Is that so?"

"Absolutely, Doc. The local locksmiths love her because she makes sure to send them business. She can get into any house in the county. Truly. But it doesn't matter now. She doesn't bother me anymore. I never find her in my bed when I get home."

I nod at this, for lack of a better answer. Then we sit quietly for a moment, as I finish the breakfast he has brought me. One of the qualities I have always admired is Renny's unflinching forthrightness, more intimate than emotional, which the long hiatus in our friendship doesn't seem to have dulled. Of course I never knew that he and Liv Crawford were in a relationship, but even just the idea appeals to me; I know they say opposites attract, but in this case I imagine that their similarities in character made for an exciting and volatile mix, ready fuel for the fire.

"Who was that woman you used to spend time with, Doc?" he says, walking around the bed, to the window. "I remember you strolling around the village with a fine looker on your arm. Am I right?"

"I'm not sure if you are."

"Come now, Doc, don't play cute with me. She was quite tall, if I remember correctly. Statuesque, in fact. What was her name? You introduced us once, years ago, at a village festival. I'm not mistaken about this."

"A woman?"

"Yes, yes," he says, mirthfully annoyed. "A woman."

"Perhaps then you are talking about Mary Burns."

"That's right! Exactly. The striking widow, Mary Burns. What ever came of her? I thought you two were very much the item."

"We were always friendly."

Renny laughs, almost a guffaw, as he plucks a rose from the vase. "Friendly, you say. Hmm. I recall seeing some cooing and nuzzling beneath the linden trees, when they turned on the string lights for the evening in the park."

"Cooing and nuzzling?"

"Yes," he says, "I'm sure that's what it was."

"Mr. Banerjee," I say. "I'm not sure how to respond to these terms."

"No responses needed. I have an excellent memory. I see it now, very clearly." He casts his gaze past my shoulder, off and faraway. His brown face has the lustrous sheen of melted chocolate. "I see Doc Hata and Mrs. Burns, in silhouette, by the swan pond. How they stroll majestically. So very venerable. And look, here they are again, in a window booth at Jolene's Diner, spooning cherry ice cream from a shared dish. Do I see them once more? Ah, at the July Fourth parade, standing outside Sunny Medical Supply, waving at the procession. Are they holding hands? I can't see."

"I'm sure they aren't," I say in mock defense, acknowledging the scenes he is calling up. Renny Banerjee is remembering correctly, of course; I was with Mary Burns in those places (if not exact times), and I was more than content to be with her, to spend the idle hours together, in the park or a restaurant or the local movie theater. And yet as much as I happily recall those moments, there is an unformed quality to them as well, as if they are someone else's memories and reflections, though somehow available only to me, to keep and to hold. Their warmth is fleeting, like a winter sun passing through clouds, and what I have left is the nervous heat of my retorts. But Renny Banerjee pushes on.

"Mary Burns is a lovely woman, a lovely woman. If I could marry a woman who would look like that when she got older! If there were a guarantee! Amazing. Oh, Doc, I recall a striking figure as well. Firm, athletic. I'm sorry to say this, but that's one well-built woman. You still see her from time to time?"

"I'm sorry to say I don't."

"What's this?" he says, his face all clamor and disappointment.

I tell him, "She passed away last year."

"How terrible," he says, obviously stunned. "I'm so sorry. So sorry. I never heard anything."

"Yes. It was liver cancer."

"I imagine it must have been quite sudden," he says, still with a funny look on his face. He sits down again in the bedside chair.

"Yes," I answer. I wish to explain, but I realize there is nothing else to say. Owing to our health-related careers, we have come to know that with liver cancer, it can sometimes be a matter of months, which it was in Mary Burns's case, from diagnosis to end.

"I'm sorry now I talked about her like that," Renny Banerjee says. "I didn't know her, but I mean for your sake. I'm a very stupid man sometimes. I hope you'll forgive me, Doc. Maybe I ought to leave now, and let you rest."

"Please, please," I tell him, "there's no need to go right now. I was very happy to hear your compliments. And I'm sure Mrs. Burns would have been as well. This is an unnecessary feeling. I must insist. You've done nothing but cheer me with your visit."

"I'm a fool," he grumbles, knocking on his own head. "A big fool."

"Nonsense, I'm not upset, or offended. I'm very pleased, in fact, and look, you've even brought me a hot breakfast as well. Which is delicious."

He nods weakly. "I see I neglected to bring you coffee."

"You probably remembered that I don't drink coffee."

Renny Banerjee smiles. "I didn't, but it's nice of you to say. I actually do have to get back upstairs if I'm going to do some work today, but I'll be content to stay longer, whatever you wish."

"You know I'm not one to get in the way of someone and his work," I say happily. "But perhaps I will see you tomorrow? Doctor Weil wants me to stay until Wednesday morning. My breathing feels good, but I guess he's concerned about infection."

"Weil's overcautious. And he's pretty much a horse's ass."

"He is new, isn't he?" I ask.

"A couple years," Renny answers. "Young hotshot from the city. Everybody around here loves him. I don't. He's officious and arrogant. It seems they have to train them like that now." He turns for the door. "I'll bring breakfast again tomorrow. No, no, I will. No arguments. What do you want, omelette, pancakes, quiche lorraine?"

"I'll leave it to you," I tell him.

"Fine then. Rest well, Doc."

"See you tomorrow."

"Will be done. And I'm so sorry, again."

"No matter."
"Goodbye, then."
"Goodbye."

THE FACT WAS, I didn't see Mary Burns at the end. It was from mutual acquaintances that I learned she was ill, and by chance, this only a few weeks before she died. But I didn't call on her at her house or here at the hospital, where she spent the final days of her life. At the time, it didn't seem that I should, and the last thing I wished to do was to upset her or cause her distress in any way. But of course, I sometimes think that I should have visited her, sat by her bed and held her hand and said whatever words could have lent her comfort.

When I saw the newspaper notice, I didn't quite believe that she had passed away. I read the small print many times over, reading her full name again and again, the address of her house on Mountview (the same street as mine), the name of her long-dead husband, and her survivors and where they were living. She had two children and five grandchildren, none of whom I'd ever met. I did learn several facts about her that I was surprised I hadn't found out before. For example, she was a summa cum laude graduate of Mount Holyoke College, and served as a WAVE during the Second World War. There was a picture with the notice, but one taken from her early middle-age, which I supposed was how her children best wished to remember her, in the high glow and prime of her life.

We first met on our street, right in front of my house. I had lived there a number of years, but as it mostly is in towns like Bedley Run, and particularly on streets like ours, being neighbors means sharing the most limited kinds of intimacies, such as sewer lines and property boundaries and annual property tax valuations. Anything that falls into a more personal realm is only tentatively welcomed. I know certain families have enjoyed relationships because of their children, had carpools and holiday barbecues, and perhaps a shared weekend at a country house upstate or on the Long Island shore, but on the whole an unwritten covenant of conduct governs us, a signet of cordiality and decorum, in whose ethic, if it can be called such a thing, the worst wrong is to be drawn forth and disturbed.

From the time I moved here, I was very fortunate to understand the nature of these relations. Even when I received welcome cards and sweets baskets from my immediate neighbors, I judged the exact scale of what an appropriate response should be, that to reply with anything but the quiet simplicity of a gracious note would be to ruin the delicate and fragile balance. And so this is exactly what I did, in the form of expensive, heavy-stock cards, each of which I took great care to write in my best hand. Each brief thank-you was different, though saying the same thing, and I know that this helped me gain quick acceptance from my Mountview neighbors, especially given my being a foreigner and a Japanese. And as I've already intimated, they all seemed particularly surprised and pleased that I hadn't run over to their houses with wrapped presents and invitations and hopeful, clinging embraces; in fact, I must have given them the reassuring thought of how safe they actually were, how shielded, that an interloper might immediately recognize and so heed the rules of their houses.

But Mary Burns, somehow, decided to breach that peace with me. I was planting pachysandra in fresh beds beside the driveway, when I heard someone say, "Do you always work so hard?"

I turned around and saw a woman in faded red slacks and a sleeveless white blouse, a white velvety band holding back her sliver-streaked flaxen hair. She stood where the drive met the street. She wore delicate suede loafers and no socks, and I recall noting the differences in skin tone between her arms and shoulders and neck, and the narrow white shock of her ankles.

"You've been working all weekend, I know," she said, her hands locked behind her in an almost girlish pose. "And last weekend, too. Never anybody to help."

I stood up and brushed the moist sod from my knees. For the last few weekends, I'd been digging up the grass along the driveway, turning it over, breaking it down, and was only now planting. I recognized her face, but of course I didn't know who she was, and when she introduced herself by saying we were neighbors, I was immediately ashamed. I fumbled with my work gloves to shake her hand.

"Will you allow me to learn your name?" she asked with mirth.

"I'm very sorry," I said, feeling completely disheveled. "I am Franklin Hata."

"You're the doctor," she said knowingly, releasing her firm handshake.

"No, I'm not," I told her. "People call me Doc, but I'm not a physician. I own the medical supply store in the village. Many years ago some customers and other merchants got to calling me that, and somehow it stuck. I wish sometimes it wasn't so, but nobody seems to want to call me Franklin. I don't mind, but I would never wish to mislead anyone."

"You're not a doctor?" she said, still somewhat confused. She had stepped onto the grass of the front lawn, right onto the property.

She was casually surveying the house, which at that point appeared, at least on view from the street, to have been totally refurbished. "You know, I would have thought you were a doctor anyway."

"Many doctors live in this neighborhood."

"Yes, they do," she answered ruefully. "Many, many doctors. I used to know most all of them. Since my children left home, I don't know them anymore, especially the younger ones. My husband was a doctor. He's dead now."

"I'm sorry," I replied. Then I said, "May I ask, was he at Deacon or County?"

"At Deacon. He was also consulting to County, just after it opened. That's when he died. Dr. Bradley Burns. He was a cardiologist. Actually, he was chief of the unit."

I told her, "I'm sorry I never met him. I don't really meet the doctors through my business. There's certainly no reason for them to concern themselves with people like me. He must have been very impressive, to be head of cardiology."

"He certainly was," she said plainly. And then: "You could say impressive was his middle name."

I didn't immediately reply, for I was somewhat surprised by her tone, which seemed without a hint of longing or pride.

"I was saying," she went on, "that I would have thought you were a doctor, nickname or not. You do live in a doctor's kind of house."

"Perhaps, yes."

"But I think it's more that you have the movements and gestures of one. I haven't been spying on you, but I have noticed that you work like someone assured, confident, even as you put in your ground cover. You have that doctor's way, beyond any further questioning."

"Lately I've had much practice in this field," I said to her, toeing at the dirt.

She liked this and laughed. "I never see people here working in their yards. It would be nice if they did. But I often see that you do, at least whenever I'm walking by."

"I enjoy it," I told her, which was mostly the truth. I did find the work pleasing, basic and honest, but I didn't have any extra money for gardeners and groundskeepers back then, and so there were compelling reasons to find myself in the yard, kneeling and digging and rooting.

"My late husband would never do anything," she said, her arms crossed in front of her now. "He hated both the fact and the idea of working outside. That was fine, of course. But he always tried to argue about people having a certain expertise. He was a heart doctor, and he was good at that. Others did bookkeeping well, or they made a good doughnut or French bread, or they knew how to dig a ditch. It was when you tried doing someone else's specialty, in his opinion, that you courted real trouble. But I must admit I always thought he was just being lazy."

She smiled deeply, if not fondly, and she touched my arm as if to make a last, silent point. The contact surprised me. And then I realized at that moment how unusual it was that we were standing there at the head of the driveway, talking and joking and going on. In this area of expansive two- and three-acre lots, there is no such thing as gabbing over a hedge. There is too much buffer of fine landscaping and natural vegetation, of whitewashed horse fence and antiqued stone walls, that it's rare to see anyone outside, much less two people on the perimeter of a property, talking or socializing. But you could have driven by and seen us, these two neighborhood folks on a late spring day, a man and a woman conversing with leisure and calm, and it didn't seem that Mary Burns held any cares of being sighted, pointing down the street to her house and

asking me for a tour of my front garden, doing nothing to camouflage herself or otherwise hide. Of course, why should she have? She
was a widow, I a bachelor (if a father), both of us well into our middle years, and to step together among the drooping peonies was as
innocent as any Sunday excursion in a botanical park. And yet I felt
the burden of justification, of having a necessary reason for being
with her, besides simply enjoying the newfound company.

Which I was. As she examined the foliage and flowers on either
side of the front entrance, I found myself regarding her. She was
quite easy to look at, her coloring pale and soft and falling in a certain range, her light hair and her light skin and the milky, faded
color of her eyes. While moving steadily through my plants, inspecting, commenting, she described her own garden and the troubles she was having with caterpillars and leaf-eating beetles, wishing
aloud that her plants were as vigorous, and I suddenly realized I was
trailing quite closely behind her, as if drawn in by the air of her
wake. It wasn't so much that I found her so pretty or attractive,
which I would often come to hear about her from acquaintances
like Renny Banerjee or the fellows at Murasan's, for at the time I
didn't fully know how to look at a Western woman and immediately appreciate what should be beautiful and prized. They all
seemed generally tall, and with narrow faces, sharp and high about
the nose, which seemed to lead them all about. I know that I had
my own conceptions of female comeliness, those naturally developed in the years of my young manhood. But ever since my decision to leave Japan for good, I hadn't wished to think at length
about women and intimate relations and companionship, for I knew
there would be myriad difficulties ahead of me, in setting up my
small bit of commerce, and other things in life. This may sound like
an excuse, and perhaps even a little sad, but it's hard for others to

know how consuming one's arrival in a new land can be, how it will take up every last resource of spirit, which too often can lead to the detriment of most everything else.

But with Mary Burns I seemed to forget the place where I was. In the shade of the eaves, amid the fresh blooms of the lilies, a cool, tropical lilt seemed to unfold in the air. It was an almost memorial sweetness, rising beneath me like a lifting wave, as if it were intent on transporting me, sending me to a place across oceans. And for that moment I would have gladly gone there, or anywhere, for there was nothing but an immaculate calm in my heart. I wish to say this now, that it truly was a sensation of calm, and not the other thing, some pulsing, breakneck thump, a coursing furious and wild. I think it was because she seemed so perfectly at ease with me, as if our meeting was the most ordinary thing. And I the most ordinary man. She didn't seem to speak more slowly or loudly than she might otherwise, she didn't gaze at me too attentively, but paid as much attention as she appropriately should, all of which, at least for me, was the most unlikely kind of flattery.

"Mr. Hata," she said warmly. "You must have a family for this big house."

"Yes, I do."

"I don't know if I've ever seen your wife outside."

"No, no, you wouldn't have," I told her, thinking immediately that I should say something about that. But the need had not arisen, at least in such a situation, and all I could do was speak with expedience. Later on, I did remark to her on once having a wife, this many years in the past, but I made clear by my tone that it wasn't a subject that was very pleasing to me.

I said, "I've been alone for some time. But you may have seen my daughter. Sometimes she comes out with me, to garden." My gaze naturally wandered to the far first-floor window of the study, where I thought I saw a movement behind the lace curtain.

Mary Burns went on nodding, smiling. "How I wish my daughters would visit me more on the weekends. What's her name?"

"Sunny."

"Tell me, Mr. Hata, is she a mother or is she working? My youngest just finished her last year of college, and she's talking about working for ten years and then having children. Don't you think that seems awfully late to start having children?"

"No, no," I answered. "My daughter will be entering middle school in the fall."

"Middle school?"

"Yes," I said. "She's eleven."

Mary Burns was clearly confused, for it was obvious how near in age we were, in our fifties, and I quickly realized what an awkward situation I had placed her in. So I explained, "My daughter came to me four years ago, through a Christian adoption agency. I was very lucky to get her, being without a wife, and also because I'm somewhat older than is preferred. But I was able to convince the agency of my qualifications, and now I'm a happy father."

"Oh, I see," she said softly, brushing back loose ends of her wispy hair, which was fetchingly unkempt. "How wonderful for her, and for you. Truly. I sometimes wish that my children were as young as that again. What a rumpus they could cause. But it was worth every minute, as I'm sure you know."

"Yes. It's been very rewarding."

I decided to invite her to inspect the more extensive garden behind the house, and she was plainly happy to follow me there, to walk among the perennials that I'd recently planted in what used to be a small croquet lawn, adjacent to the pool.

She bent to smell the lavender-colored flowers of the blooming rosemary bushes, and then moved on to the other ornamental and fragrant plants, and as she did I excused myself to go into the house. When I returned, I took the pair of snips I'd retrieved from the kitchen and quickly cut a small bundle of the rosemary and thyme for her to take home, wrapping it neatly with a stripped branch. She clasped the bunch gratefully and thanked me, and though it seemed I should invite her inside for a soft drink or tea (as she herself seemed to anticipate), I remembered it was near the hour for Sunny to begin her afternoon practicing, and I feared it might be a disturbance for her to have an unfamiliar woman in the house.

For it was around the same time that I began speaking to Sunny about the possibility of her having a mother; I suggested that with a woman living with us, perhaps she would be happier, or at least less inexplicably agitated and anxious-feeling than she was, which it seemed was becoming an increasingly everyday condition. I had aimed to learn of a suitable woman through old friends back in Japan, depending on a small network of comrades from the war for a reputable contact, but so few Japanese of good background and means wished to leave their country, especially in those boom days. My only real chance was to locate a childless widow who might consider an opportunity for motherhood reason enough to leave her homeland, and I hoped, too, that a congenial understanding and companionship would at some point arise between us, as it is never ideal for a child to sense ill-feeling between her parents. I had tried to convince Sunny of all this, for it seemed certainly wrong for a young girl to know only a single adult, especially so if it was a man, but always she was vehemently against the idea, crying and going on whenever I persisted. And though I didn't do anything that day with Mary Burns to go against her wishes, it would be wrong to recall something other than a renewed lightness suffusing my spirit, a part of me which seemed, I was certain, to have been long ago dissipated, and lost.

Mary Burns, I know, was also surprised by the pleasantness of our meeting. She would later say I was gentle-seeming, and charming, and "exceedingly handsome," if I remember her words correctly. I don't know much about this; I've never thought—or even thought to think—of myself in such terms. And when she was even more comfortable with me, she confided how odd a recognition it was for her, at least at first, to find herself deeply attracted to an Oriental man. She laughed at herself and said there was no reason she shouldn't have been, that there was no good reason at all, but the feeling was there and she ought to be truthful, and whether it was shameful or not probably didn't matter in the end.

I agreed with her. Of course I didn't say anything about my own particular attractions. My initial concern was about the exact nature of our relationship, what we might do, share—what might, in fact, eventually occur in the more private moments. Soon enough, my thoughts were focused on these notions, these heightened wonderings, and I fear I lost some perspective along the way for what my daughter Sunny may have needed, which was not necessarily a woman or a mother or anyone else.

Mary Burns, I want to say now, tried her best to connect with Sunny. She made great efforts toward building a friendship, when there was no expectation for her to do so. How many afternoons did she await Sunny at the bus stop, so that they might walk home together, climb the steady hill of Mountview Street? How many evenings did she come over to the house to visit with Sunny upstairs in her room, to chat and "hang out" with her, and then later help with her homework? How many Sunday afternoons did they spend together, at the children's hour at Mary Burns's country club, or at Jolene's in the village for a treat of ice cream?

I remember when they would return from these outings, the front door creaking open, and Mary Burns would call out to say they were home. Her voice was always sprightly, aloft, but when I'd meet them in the foyer Sunny would be quickly ascending the stairs. I'd ask her if she had had fun, and she would answer, "Yes, Poppa, I did," and then continue on her way up. I'd remind her to say thank you, but of course she had already, without fail, having made offerings to Mary Burns in the car and at the door, and she'd even curtly bow at the top of the stairs before disappearing down the hall to her room.

Afterward, Mary Burns and I would sit in the family room or the kitchen, sharing a snack or a pot of tea I'd prepared, and though she wouldn't say anything I could see the disappointment ever settling in the fine lines of her face, her jaw perfectly steady. There was a sheerness, the smoothest rigor to her cheek, as if it were the keen wall of a canyon. And it was in these moments, strangely enough, that I believe I found her most arresting and lovely, that she appeared to me exquisitely composed in character, her bearing deliberate and unrelenting.

Only once did she break. After what she thought had been a particularly enjoyable day for them, full of shared gossip and even laughter, though with Sunny excusing herself as usual, Mary Burns began to cry. We were sitting on the family-room sofa. She cried very quietly, not covering her face, and at the very moment I thought she would come closer and lean on me, she rose and said she would be leaving.

"You're not going to stay?" I asked.

"No, Franklin, I don't think so."

"Not even for dinner?"

"Not tonight."

I followed her to the foyer. "I'm sorry about Sunny," I said. "She can be rude sometimes. I'll speak to her."

"I don't want you to do that," she answered, her voice strained and rising. "Please, Franklin. She's not rude. Not in any way. Never have I known a girl of eleven to be as polite as she is. She's never said an unkind word, and she's never complained. I truly thought she was happy today, to be together with me. She seemed happy. But the second we got home, the day was over. All at once, it was over. Just like that."

"Did Sunny say something?"

She shook her head. "Nothing. She was perfectly fine. But it was as though she was serving her sentence with me for the afternoon hours, and when we got home, she was released. It's not her fault. You've raised her impeccably. She doesn't have to have a deep feeling for me. There's no law." She lifted her purse from the hall table, curling the strap over her shoulder. They had been at the club, and she was still wearing her white tennis clothes, a short pleated skirt and blouse and a light sweater.

"I feel so unbelievably tired all of a sudden," she said, exhaling deeply. She touched my forearm and squeezed it gently. "Let's say good night now, Franklin, okay?"

"I'm very sorry."

"It's no one's fault. Least of all yours."

"Yes," I replied, though not intending to agree. I tried to think of an explanation, a way to tell her that Sunny was in fact a good-hearted girl who would never mean to upset or offend. But already I sensed the lateness of my providing any reasons, at least for Mary Burns's sake. For Mary Burns, it seemed, I was often too late. And the other truth was that even after several years, Sunny felt no more at home in this town, or in this house of mine, or perhaps even with me, than when she very first arrived at Kennedy Airport, accompanied by a woman from the agency. I noticed something even then. She was clutching a rough canvas bag of her things, the zipper flapping loose at one end, torn from the plain, soiled fabric. When I tried to coax it from her she crossed her small arms tightly around it, carrying it all the way to the car herself, the whole small picture of her both endearing and pathetic. She followed behind me and the woman, who was talking excitedly about the various projects the agency was developing for the benefit of Asian orphans. Whenever I looked around to acknowledge my new daughter, to try to catch her eye, she neatly tucked in her chin and pushed on, as if she were headed into a long and driving rain.

Mary Burns, I'm afraid, did not soon give up with Sunny. I saw how it was affecting her and tried to suggest that she cease, that she simply make an accommodation and not attempt to be intimate with the girl, who seemed to be growing more and more untouchable, becoming more and more distanced from her and myself and everything else.

"You don't understand, Franklin," she finally told me one evening, at the end of yet another day. "She's just a girl, and a girl needs a woman. To be there, if nothing else. I don't care if she doesn't love me. One day she'll have a feeling for me, perhaps, but that doesn't matter. I'm going to spend time with her, and that's that."

She continued scheduling their weekend outings, and attended the after-school activities that I could never go to because of the store, the soccer matches and the Brownie meetings and, of course, the piano lessons and recitals. Indeed, she was there, and always there, and had they looked remotely like each other, had they anything physical in common, I'm sure they would have seemed like all the other mothers and daughters, but even more so, arriving and departing together hand in hand, with hardly a sign of rancor. In fact, some of the mothers who came by my store would make sure to mention how delightful the two of them were, how gracious with each other, how wonderful it was that a woman like Mary Burns and my daughter could be so "good" together. It was wonderful, yes, yes indeed, how all girls and ladies had things in common. Of course I always thanked them, was appropriately pleased and proud, not saying otherwise, but I also wished secretly that for once I'd hear about Sunny speaking insolently, that they had had a terrible row in front of everyone, that once and finally Mary Burns had been most cross and vehement and had scolded her with great wrath.

But I never did hear that. Or ever would. And I remember vividly one of the last times Mary Burns and I spent together, this in the weeks before we drifted apart, when our relationship finally came to an end. She was sitting poolside while I swam in the August heat, her long fingers wrapped around a tall glass of iced tea. It was toward dusk but the air was still downy and insufferable and she was waiting for Sunny to come out. The two of them were going to a teen dance at the tennis club, Mary Burns having been asked to be one of the chaperons. She was of course dutiful that way. She looked pretty that evening, in a shimmering linen dress without sleeves and matching silken shoes. Her legs and arms had a glowing tan from all the tennis she played, and I thought she was the warm picture of goodness and health. She had been quiet on arriving, however, and as she didn't seem particularly interested in talking, I suggested she come outside and keep me company while I did my laps, for in the warmer weather I swam extra lengths in the evenings as well. I had originally planned to attend the dance myself, as Mary Burns's escort, but that afternoon Sunny had come to the store and asked me if I would be kind enough to stay at home.

"It's obvious you're not going to dance anyway," she had said right off. As she grew older, Sunny had a way of speaking unusually crisply, and with gravity, as if she were somehow in charge. Her English was of course impeccable, and had for a long time been much better than mine. "I don't see why you'd want to go. It's silly. You'll just sit at a back table and sip punch and watch the whole night go by."

She was right, certainly, as that was just what I'd probably do. There were no good reasons for my presence, except to be there for Mary Burns, as all the other chaperons would certainly have the company of their partners. And yet it was not for Mary Burns's sake that I pushed Sunny to explain her wishes.

Still, I said, "But who will accompany Mrs. Burns?"

"Mrs. Burns? She doesn't need anyone. It's her country club. She knows everybody there. She'll be busy all night with her club friends. In fact, she'll have a better time without you."

"But she's asked me to come."

"I know," she said, quite serious. "But I'm asking you not to come."

Her tone wasn't petulant, or fretful, for she was possessed of a remarkable equanimity, more the way one thinks distinguished, older people to be than young teenage girls. The way Mary Burns would no doubt conduct herself were she living now. But then Sunny displayed a ferocity as well, a flinty, coal-like hardness that should have been beyond the ken of her years.

I then asked her: "Are you afraid you'll be embarrassed by me?"

"Of course not," she replied. She was idly binding her wrist with a roll of sterile gauze. Whenever she came to the store, she played with some item or another. "Why should I be embarrassed? You know very well how much everyone likes you. Even my friends. In fact, they like you better than they like me."

"I'm sure that's not true."

"It is true. And it's the same with everyone I meet. But I don't care about that. I would like to be there by myself, on my own. I know Mary has to be there at this point, and I wish she weren't going to be, but if you come, too, I'll be the only one with my whole family there. I think that's a little strange, don't you, to be with your family at a dance just for kids?"

I nodded, for what she was saying seemed reasonable enough. I could understand the potential awkwardness of having the two of us present. Mary Burns and I went out together in public quite regularly, but rarely was it the three of us, the "whole family," as Sunny had put it, a phrase which stuck out, unfortunately, because it seemed amazing that she should say such a thing. Certainly, I wanted us to be as much of a unit as any, a "whole family" in whatever sense was possible. But I knew Sunny had no feelings of the kind. I had done as Mary Burns had requested, never bringing up to Sunny her ill use and her selfishness and her cold spirit; and my silence, I will say now, was hurtful to me, for I did have a genuine feeling for Mary Burns, as genuine a feeling as I'd had for a long time, and to stand by and witness their relations caused me severe distress. I was simply angry at Sunny, and so, finally, I think, was

Mary Burns, deeply angry and hurt, and though she never said a word to the girl, it seemed to happen that she was addressing me at the end, looking to me for the reasons why my daughter, after nearly four years, could still be so profoundly unmoved.

That night of the dance, Mary Burns quietly watched me swim. She waited to speak until I was done and had pulled on my robe. I sat down with her at the outdoor table. The automatic lights on the stone paths had gone on, and there was a coppery glow rising against the early evening sky.

"I wish we could have talked before you decided on your own not to come tonight."

"I called this afternoon," I said to her. "But you were out."

"You know I was at the club, helping with the decorations." She looked upset, though her voice was steady and low. "Though I suppose it wouldn't have mattered, whether we talked or not."

"Sunny isn't feeling so comfortable at the moment. You must understand that I wish to support her."

"Of course you do," she said, exasperated. She brushed her hair with her hand. She had recently changed the color, from its silvery tones to a very pale golden color, and though it was handsome, I wasn't certain it best suited her. She appeared much younger, and then not, and sometimes I was unsure how to think of her. "Listen to me, Franklin. She's your daughter, and so you ought to do everything you can for her. If you have eyes, you've seen that I've tried to do my part."

"I know you have, and I thank you."

"That's not why I bring it up," she said sharply. She paused and took a breath. "I didn't spend time with Sunny so you'd be grateful to me. I didn't do it because of you, or even so much to help you. She seemed to need guidance, the kind of company a mother or aunt or grandmother can give, and I wanted to try to offer that. I guess I was terribly wrong. I was naive. But I'm also not sorry. I would do it again, without hesitation.

"The reason I'm angry tonight is that I think you treat her wrongly. Perhaps you don't know it, but you do. I've thought it from time to time, and I'm sorry I'm such a coward that I can only say this to you now."

I cleared my throat and said, surprising myself, "I understand that I've not dealt with Sunny's jealousy of you very effectively."

This seemed to irritate her. "That's not what I'm talking about. That's not it at all."

"I try my best to treat her with respect," I said.

"Yes," Mary Burns answered earnestly. "Yes, you do. You treat her like a grown woman, which I guess is understandable because she's very mature for her age."

"You know how much I want her to be independent."

"Yes, she is," she replied. "But it's as if she's a woman to whom you're beholden, which I can't understand. I don't see the reason. You're the one who wanted her. You adopted her. But you act almost guilty, as if she's someone you hurt once, or betrayed, and now you're obliged to do whatever she wishes, which is never good for anyone, much less a child."

"This is quite unusual, Mary, to hear, but I'll think about what you say."

"For goodness sake, Franklin, you don't always have to assent!" she said, her voice suddenly rising. I thought she would speak most sharply to me then. But she seemed to hear herself, and I could see the control she was exercising over her face. She took a sip of her iced tea. "I might be completely wrong, Franklin. I hope I am."

"I have always trusted your judgment, Mary."

"Yes. I know you have."

We sat in silence after that, the night fast approaching, the crickets just beginning to arise in song. Mary Burns glanced at the house, to Sunny's bedroom window, which was still lighted. Shadows moved along a wall. They were already late for the dance, but it didn't seem to matter. It was one of those moments that appear to take forever, though somehow everything was the better for it. I didn't wish to go further in the conversation, nor did she, and if there was one true thing that we shared during our relations, it was that neither of us, for better or worse, had much stomach for these engagements, for taking certain issues to the necessary lengths. We rather floated the deep waters, just barely treading, although now I see how my friend Mary Burns held onto things more gravely than I, certain notions staying with her longer, more tightly clasped, so that in the end we were much farther apart in our feelings than I had ever imagined.

Sunny finally came out the patio doors, dressed in a resplendent swath of white. She and Mary Burns had decided on the outfit together the weekend before, on a shopping junket down to the city. It was a very handsome choice. The dress came just up to her darkly suntanned shoulders, the delicate material clinging to her torso but not so tightly as to be indecent, the handsome drape conveying only the suggestion of the young woman beneath. But the young woman was certainly there, too, the near adultness of her, and the sight of that shape made me realize why she had asked me to remain at home. It wasn't at all what Sunny had said in the store, about people liking me too much, or (as I had imagined it) her jealousy of Mary Burns, or even what was ventured of how I treated her, which was probably true enough. It was her bodily presence, the sheer, be-coming whatness of her limbs and skin and face and eyes. She was beautiful, yes. Exceptionally so. But it was also the other character of her beauty, its dark and willful visage, and with it, the growing measure of independence she would exercise over her world and over me, that she had hoped to keep hidden a little longer.

4

THE CANDY STRIPER, Veronica, finds me unusually good-natured. Almost everything I say makes her grin, and her full, ruddy face beams and blushes whenever she comes into my room with her cart. Most of the candy stripe girls are outgoing and talkative and even a little waywardly brash, which is naturally why they do the work. But Veronica, shyish and sweet, healthfully ample, with a shockingly full head of tight chestnut-brown curls, is the sort of girl you would wish upon all good people who have mourned the demise of that cardinal generosity of youth.

Veronica, of course, has little care for such things. She is unfretting, unsevere. She understands how to hearten a patient with a wide smile. And now, after two days and nights, she finds me familiar and trustworthy, enough so not to bother to knock on the always open door. She wheels her cart inside the room and then up beside the bed railing, and greets me with cheer.

"Were you able to sleep at all last night, Franklin?" she says, automatically fanning out the selection of magazines and books atop the cart. We are clearly on a first-name basis. She carries the usual periodicals, creased magazines of home and health and lifestyle, but the books are mostly crime novels and stories of the strange and the occult, all of which soft-spoken Veronica, it seems, has chosen for her selections. "The nurse said you were out of bed a lot, walking the halls."

"I was sure Dolly didn't see me," I tell her. "It looked like she was the one who was getting all the sleep."

"That's her job," Veronica says, and then adds, in a dramatic, mischievous tone: "She's the nurse of the night."

"Very true," I reply, wishing, all of a sudden, that I could change out of my hospital gown and accompany Veronica on her rounds. I say, "It appears she is also the nurse of jelly doughnuts. And perhaps of pastry and pie."

"Yes," Veronica cries, almost gleeful with the gossip. "I thought I saw cherry filling on her shoes. I didn't say anything, but I was half afraid it was blood!"

"How do we know it wasn't?" I say, knowing what it takes to goad her. "That she'd simply forgotten to hide a crime?"

"Yes, yes," Veronica cries, half-covering her mouth. "She raids the blood closet in the middle of the night. She's a ghoul, a vampiress. She needs it to live, but only the blood of young boys and girls, which she can smell through the packets."

"I hope this means I'm safe."

"No one is safe," Veronica states, almost seriously enough to alarm me. "But you, Franklin, you are. Even though you're young at heart."

"You think I am? Young, I mean."

"Definitely," she tells me, her voice buoyant again, the verve of fourteen. "But in a good way. Not like the boys at school, who are all incredibly lame and stupid. You're young like things are always beginning. Which I think is great."

"I always thought people your age think being grown up is most fashionable."

"Not me, I guess," Veronica says, handing me a stack of magazines, a book of word games, and an old jigsaw-puzzle box of the *Mona Lisa,* whose famous mien, I am beginning to think, is the expression of a young woman concealing a pure feeling of joy. "I don't want to grow up yet. It's too much trouble. And I don't care if I'm not cool. I can wait."

And so this we do, together, in my private room. I'm lucky, for since cable television finally arrived at the hospital, the patients are reading far less, and as they don't require that the candy stripers come around to them as often with material, I have Veronica's company for pretty much as long as I (and she) wish. She lives in the town of Ebbington, just east of Bedley Run on the far side of a large county reservoir, beside which the two villages are situated. Though Ebbington is not at all the sort of place Bedley Run is; mostly it's a working-class suburb of drab, unadorned homes and small motel-style apartment complexes. When you drive through town you notice how the trees hang a bit too closely over the streets, how the bushes and grasses are keenly in need of pruning and edging and clipping, how the main thoroughfare is rife with chain businesses and towering signs that glow and rotate and blink. In the older, quieter part of town, there are what seems a disproportionately high number of auto repair garages and beauty salons and churches and bars, all half-failed and dilapidating in their own fashion, and one's perception is that whatever uniqueness and charms Ebbington once had are being inexorably absorbed by larger, external presences both unknown and invited.

Veronica's mother is a Bedley Run police officer, whom I've come to know casually in the course of being a village merchant; her father, who used to be an officer himself (and the police chief of Ebbington, in fact), lost his life in a somewhat notorious local incident in which he was caught in a crossfire between his own officers and a group of out-of-town gamblers and loan sharks with whom he was enjoying the evening. I remember in the newspaper articles the mention of his wife and infant daughter, who was Veronica, and the question of whether they would receive his pension benefit, given the unusual circumstances of his death. They did not, and I was one of the few who took an interest in their welfare and wrote and called in support of Veronica's mother when word got out that she had applied for the officer's position in Bedley Run (our town's Chief Hearns being a longtime acquaintance of mine). After she got the job, Officer Como would often double-park her cruiser right in front of Sunny Medical while she got her lunch down the street at the deli or around the corner for takeout chicken, as if she was letting everyone know that she would be extra vigilant over my store, which mostly meant warning off the petty vandals. We rarely exchanged more than a few words, always simply a wave and a greeting, and it wasn't until Veronica mentioned yesterday what her mother did for a living that I put together who they were.

It particularly heartens me, in light of this, to see how well Veronica has grown up. As we read quietly together here in this sterile, unpapered gray room, me with a gardening magazine and Veronica a pocket murder mystery with gruesome, drippy, raised lettering on its tattered cover, I have to wonder what might have come of her had just one thing turned differently then—say, had her father survived the shooting, or her mother not found a job.

So much of the public debate and discussion these days is about the alarming fragility of a person's early years, how critically the times and circumstances can affect one's character and outlook and even actions. So the abiding philosophy is to help a wayward child develop into a productive member of the community, or if ignored, risk allowing someone of essentially decent nature to become an adult whose social interactions are fraught and difficult, or even pathological, criminal. How did Veronica, from the start fatherless, her family stigmatized, grow into her own fine self? What did her mother, Officer Como, do to enlist the native grace and good in her daughter's heart? Or did it all happen by ordination, by the slight chance of Being, that Veronica and the rest of us have actually one strain of life, and one strain only, and that the seeming variations are but particular contours, the everyday adornments?

Such as, I'm considering now, my being here in the hospital, suffering complications in the aftermath of the smoke inhalation. The fire in the family room was two days ago, and Liv Crawford has called more than a few times to let me know that "her boys" are just about finished with the renovations of the damage, so that the property will be fully "restored" and "secure." No doubt pristine and purchaser-ready. But then there is my situation. Dr. Weil is sure that I'm recovered, but from what I know and feel, I'm almost certain that I'm pleuritic, as my lungs don't seem to be improving the way they should. My chest still feels leaden and straitjacketed and generally out of sorts. I'm breathing well enough, but even the light activity of talking with Veronica (as well as my stolen wanderings last night in the corridors) seems to be taking a deep toll on my energy. And then there is the other, unrelated complication that has arisen, one far worse in my mind (and spirit-sapping), which is that I suddenly have an onset of the shingles. There is an almost caustic discomfort in my lower chest and then down my right arm and right leg, what feels like lines of internal burns that sharply prickle and itch and ache. There is no expression as yet, no outward sign of rashes or blisters, which I wouldn't be concerned about either way, except that I wouldn't want Veronica to see them and think it was better to leave me alone, to let me rest.

For being alone is the last thing I would wish for now, which is probably strange, given how I've conducted most all the days of my life. Save the time that Sunny spent with me, I've known myself best as a solitary person, and although I've always been able to enjoy the company of others, I've seen myself most clearly when I'm off on my own, without others in the mix. This may seem an obvious mode for most, but I think a surprising number of people prefer to imagine themselves through a filter of associations and links, perhaps Mary Burns being an example of a person who predominantly identified herself in this manner, through the lives of her daughters and her late husband, her country club and her charities, and then, possibly, through her attempted relations with Sunny, and with me. There is nothing inherently wrong with this. Indeed, there was a time when I held my own associations quite close to who I was, in the years leading up to and during the Pacific war, when in the course of events one naturally accepted the wartime culture of shared sacrifice and military codes of conduct. But then I eventually relinquished those ties for the relative freedoms of everyday, civilian life, and then finally decided to leave Japan altogether, for the relative—though very different—liberties of America.

Though here, in my town and every town, especially when you reach my age, you sadly find that the most available freedom is to live alone. There is an alarming surplus of the right. And though everyone accepts this, it's unclear to me whether anyone truly prefers it so. Few seem satisfied with the familial character of their latter years. Even Mary Burns, who no doubt taught her daughters the value of family, found that they honored her training of them by keeping to themselves, as if her involvement would be an adulteration. They didn't visit as often as she wished, nor of course did they ever ask if she would like to come live with them after Dr. Burns died, and even after her friendship with me came to its abrupt, unpleasant end. They let her be. Her daughters' distance was an ever-deepening disappointment to her (even if she never really expected them to be perfectly embracing and filial), and though she rarely spoke of it, I know now it was one of the reasons why she was so willing to spend time with Sunny, and why any time was still better than none.

Veronica, who is now nibbling on her fingernails, one by one, as she flips the pages of her book, has already told me that she wants to live at home as long as possible, through college and beyond, at least until she gets married. She waits in my room for her mother, who will come to pick her up. Veronica's future husband, who Veronica is certain will be a sculptor or a policeman or both, will have to love Officer Como as much as she does. Veronica herself will be a travel agent and murder mystery writer and the proud mother of seven bright-eyed, immeasurably happy girls. She doesn't care if they're not beautiful, in fact hopes that they aren't, for she has seen already how some of the prettiest girls in her class have become distant and superior and wholly ungenerous, and particularly how the blond, slim, protuberantly endowed Brittany, the self-appointed head of the shrinking cadre of candy stripers, will hardly even look at her, as if doing so would be to invite certain personal doom.

My initial impulse is to tell Veronica how she's absolutely right, how in this world (or the one we've made) beauty is the scantest blessing, and how, despite the appearance of ever-bestowed glory and celebration, it is mostly malice and misery that are returned to the bearer. I know this now, not from my own appearance, but from dealing with Sunny when she reached a certain maturity. She was beautiful, and in all the complicated ways I've already mentioned; Sunny thus educated me. In regard to myself, I've often been told I have a youthful, genial appearance, and am even a bit handsome. I remember what Mary Burns once remarked, after the first whole night we spent together. We were in my bedroom, and her spirit was ebullient with the clear light of the morning. She rose on her elbow and stretched, her exposed back still lithe and impressively athletic, and then she lay down and gazed at me from close range, as if she were tracing with her eyes the shape of my lips and nose and brow. I cleared my throat and sat up.

"I'm sorry," she said, blushing. "I'm being terribly rude. I don't mean to be odd. You must be wondering."

So I said, "You're making sure I'm the man you met last night?"

"No," she said, smiling easily. "I'm not. It's just that your face is so unlike my late husband's, I can't tell you. Bradley had such severe features, a long, narrow nose and deep-set eyes and a jutting chin. He was aggressive, in appearance. You have a wonderful gentleness to your face. A softer line to everything." She smiled and lightly kissed my shoulder. "Goodness, listen to me. I'm sorry I'm talking like this. I'm going to scare you away."

I didn't, or couldn't, reply, which wasn't my intention, as I didn't mind in the least what she'd said, but I had the urge to get up and dress and begin that Sunday like any other, although I had already slept through my swim time. Sunny had been downstairs for some time, warming up her hands with minor scales, up and down, in the dizzying series. I pulled on a robe and told Mary that I was going down to put the water on for our tea. I suggested she take a hot, soaking bath. She nodded, and from her weakened expression I could tell she wanted me to stay just a moment longer, that we might complete the conversation. But Sunny had begun playing intently and the night was done, and it seemed clear I should go downstairs and be present for her.

There had been indications that Mary's ever-increasing presence was disturbing to Sunny, as she had seemed to be practicing more fervently in the preceding weeks, particularly when Mary was over at the house. She took her warm-up exercises at an incredibly fast measure, running through them as though she were attempting to twist up her fingers. The pieces themselves she performed quite rudely, as if she would trounce them. She didn't miss a note, but the feeling in the playing was utterly perverse to what it should have been, as though she were critiquing rather than exploring the compositions. Mary would comment again how talented and skilled Sunny was, how dexterous and precocious, and I never thought to correct her appraisals, even though the performances were in fact maudlin and probably insulting to her, as they certainly were to me. I found them quite shaming. And as much as I tried, I couldn't inculcate the same sense in Sunny, as she pretended not to know what I was talking about.

"I'm trying my very best, Poppa," she'd say innocently, with her dark brown eyes gazing steadfastly up into mine. "You see that I am, don't you?"

Japanese fathers are famously overgenerous to their children (quite the opposite of what most Westerners would presume and wish to think), extremely permissive and obliging with their little ones, and so it was quite normal that I should be as well; though with a girl like Sunny, I should probably have exercised more rigor and sternness. But as it often was, I let the issue go in favor of moving forward, to the next hour and day. My hope was that she would change as she grew into a young woman, and that the minor indications of willfulness would gradually fall from her like any child's clutch upon a security blanket.

I, too, had been a difficult child. For me, it was the heady time of adolescence that unmasked and clarified my sense of obligations, so much so that I now view that period as the true beginning of "my life." This was when I first appreciated the comforts of real personhood, and its attendant secrets, among which is the harmonious relation between a self and his society. There is a mutualism that at its ideal is both powerful and liberating. For me, it was readily leaving the narrow existence of my family and our ghetto of hide tanners and renderers. Most all of us were ethnic Koreans, though we spoke and lived as Japanese, if ones in twilight. Of course, I didn't leave on my own. No one of my family's circumstance could expect to change his station, at least without a lifetime of struggle. But I was fortunate to score exceptionally high on several achievement tests, and was one of a few boys of my kind to be identified and enrolled in a special school in the nearby large city.

I lived with a well-to-do childless couple, a gear factory owner and his wife, who treated me as well as a son, providing me with every material need and advantage. I remember being accompanied by them on the first day of school, in my new serge uniform with brass buttons that they had fitted just for me, and how the other boys had let us pass without even a murmur, this prominent family Kurohata (a name, as is self-evident, I've since shortened). I think of them most warmly, as I do my natural parents, but to neither would I ascribe the business of having reared me, for it seems clear that it was the purposeful society that did so, and really nothing and no one else. I was more than grateful. And I knew even then as a boy of twelve how I should always give myself over to its vigilance, entrusting to its care everything I could know or ever hope for.

My Sunny, I thought, would do much the same. Not be so thankful or beholden to me, necessarily, but at least she'd be somewhat appreciative of the providence of institutions that brought her from the squalor of the orphanage—the best of which can be only so happy—to an orderly, welcoming suburban home in America, with a hopeful father of like-enough race and sufficient means. But now, sitting with Veronica, I realize the obvious mistakes that were made in regard to Sunny. Firstly, I shouldn't have made my desire for a child so paramount as to cloud my good judgment, which is what happened when I was interviewed by the woman at the agency. She had warned me on the telephone that it was exceedingly rare for a single man to be granted an adoption, that in fact there was no precedent for it and so really no reason for a meeting. I insisted, and when we met face-to-face she was able to understand the earnestness of my desire for a child, though of course earnestness should never be solely enough. I brought along a large donation to the agency, this beyond the regular expenses, as well as a like sum for the woman, which I explained as a most proper gift in my former homeland, and which would be followed by another. This wasn't actually proper, however, but she stopped talking and discreetly slipped the rice paper–wrapped package into her desk drawer, and on my way out she said she would see what was possible for a man in my special situation.

My second error was insisting on a female infant or child, when I should have known that a girl would likely do best with a maternal presence. But I wanted a girl, a daughter—I was (as I think of it now) strangely unmovable on the issue—and in the end the agency woman called to say they had found one, without any further explanation. My desire for a girl was unknown to me right up to the moment the agency woman spoke of locating a boy for me, but I interrupted her immediately and explained how I'd always hoped for a daughter, the words suddenly streaming from my mouth as though I'd long practiced the speech. I found myself speaking of a completeness, the unitary bond of a daughter and father. Of harmony and balance. The woman seemed impressed, or pretended to be, and when she called several weeks later with news of a suitable orphan, a girl from the city of Pusan, in Korea, I was overcome with a feeling that I can only describe as relief. There were no Japanese children available, but it didn't matter to me anymore. I thought only of the moment of her arrival, which I had hoped would serve to mark the recommencement of my days.

IT IS HALF PAST SIX, and Veronica's shift is all but done. Too soon, I think, her mother will curl the blue-and-white police cruiser around the parking circle and let the siren whoop sharply just once, to let her know she's there. I'm to be discharged by Dr. Weil in the morning, and as Veronica's shift doesn't start until midafternoon, I won't see her again unless I make a special trip, which I will consider, for I know, too, that Mrs. Hickey's son, Patrick, is in the children's ICU. Mrs. Hickey called early this morning to the nurses' station to check on my condition, and though I was fine to talk I asked Nurse Dolly to tell her I was still sleeping. We'd made tentative plans to meet here at the hospital, and of course my unexpected stay would seem good timing (of a sort) for a visit, but a part of me doesn't want to talk to Mrs. Hickey just now, or even see her face.

Last night at three, while Nurse Dolly was napping, I unhooked myself from the monitors and rose from my bed. I crept past the nurses' station to the elevator bank, and though I wasn't intending it, when the doors opened I pressed the button for the sixth floor, to the unit where Patrick Hickey lay.

I remembered the room number from Mrs. Hickey, which was easy for me to note because it was also the name of an anti-bacterial treatment we often used during the war, a solution of Salvarsan that was known as "606," the number of its compound denotation. It's one of those queer numbers that can appear with inexplicable frequency in one's life. In any case, the door to the room was ajar, and I slipped in without a sound, not having to trip the latch. I was breathing with some labor, though, from the exertion of walking quickly and perhaps the oddness of what I was doing, which in retrospect was completely silly. With flowers or a stuffed animal in hand, I could have asked one of the nurses if I could enter and look at him, and they would have simply waved me in. Instead I stole inside the half-lighted room, padding breathlessly in my slippers toward his bed. He was taking oxygen, which wasn't what made him appear so beset and wan; it was that he was amazingly slight and small, as though he were four or five years old instead of eight. With his weakened heart, he'd never grown as he should have, his wrists too delicate, it seemed, even to lift the tiny hands. But it was the features of his face that I could not look away from, his brush of hair, his nose, his tender, scant mouth. The sheer lids of his eyes. He looked like his mother, if his mother were boyish and unformed.

He lay with a sheet pulled up to his neck, and I had a strong impulse to draw it back so that I might see his chest, where they would open him if they could find a suitable heart.

Once, during the war, I witnessed our outpost's doctor pull apart the ribs of a man in order to hand-massage his heart. It's a strange technique to see, the procedure at once God-like and lowly animal. The patient was a Burmese man, a cobbler who was found stealing from the supply tent and who was condemned to death by beheading. But the doctor, a Captain Ono, asked the commanding officer if he would commute the sentence and give the man over to him, for purposes of instruction. So the morning of his execution, the cobbler was brought to the medical tent instead of the killing yard, where Captain Ono gathered us medics and interested others, including the commander, and put him into a half-sleep with a rag soaked in ether. The doctor, gloveless, maskless, as were the rest of us, quickly cut down his chest with a scalpel and then used the bone saw and the spreader and pushed aside the man's lungs to reveal his slowly beating, slowly galloping heart. It was all most unreal. Captain Ono himself seemed nonplussed. He took a paddle connected to a modified field telephone with a crank, which he turned quickly several times, and then asked us to give room. He flipped on a switch and then touched the paddle to the heart. It leaped into a faster rhythm, and then it stopped. He stood there for what seemed too long a moment, and then with his hand roughly grabbed the cobbler's heart and began squeezing. He did this rhythmically and with great purpose until it began beating again. It was nearly magical. He wished to show us a possible emergency maneuver in the field, in instances of the most grievous trauma. Though to me it seemed more academic than anything else. He repeated the exercise three or four times, which surprised him enough that he commented upon the vitality of the particular organ, until the last time, when his hand massage didn't work. He touched the heart with the paddle but nothing happened, and he attempted another manipulation, making a final remark on the importance of consistent, vigorous action. Then the instruction was over. Captain Ono wiped his hands with the etherizing rag, and the cobbler, solemnly agape, was carted away.

I wondered if I could perform the same on Patrick, if something terrible were to happen and his monitors alarmed and no one else could come. If I held the knife in my hand, could I make the quick, deep cut on him, could I reach inside, handle the thing, sustain him for the necessary time? The medic aims to keep a wounded comrade within the realm of being saved by a learned professional, and in this respect I think I was mostly good enough. To cease a hemorrhaging, get a man to breathe again. Pump down on a stilled heart. It is the mode I've come to know, that I'm able to sort out and address the primary disaster, at least. But the ongoing trouble, the chronic, complicated difficulty of the kind Patrick Hickey's parents have faced the last few years of his life is the one that shakes me from all my confidences. To be truthful, I am sure I'm not a creature who was made to endure. I'm not a long-chase antelope. I'm designed to withstand the hard, swift charges, or else am readily overcome. And so to have talked to Mrs. Hickey in the room with her dying son, and amid all their money troubles with my old store, seemed too much; I would never want to depress or disappoint her, in that I wasn't helping to alleviate her burdens, and so what else should I do but avoid her for now, even as I desperately wished to lend her friendly support?

Veronica has mentioned the putty-faced boy upstairs with the lavender-tipped fingers, how reserved and quiet he is; he's like a little old man, she says sadly, who knows his time is near. She's visited him the last few days, but he was too weak to use the puzzles or coloring books, and all she could do for him one afternoon was read a children's story for a few minutes until he dozed off. I tell Veronica she ought to visit him every day if the nurses will allow it, that she should talk to him and play with him and let him listen to her strong reading voice. In a funny way, she sounds like Liv Crawford when she reads from her books, a bit strident, overdramatic, with tones of succor. It's easy to listen to her. Veronica now suggests that I go up there with her tomorrow afternoon, that the sick boy would probably like me, but I can't answer, not only for my poor reasons concerning Mrs. Hickey but because I don't want to tell Veronica that I'm to leave in the morning. I haven't thought out fully or exactly when I am going to tell her, even as her mother is to pick her up any second, for what I really want and wish is that time could suspend for a moment or two, halt right here in my room, but such that I might still enjoy the company of Veronica and the intermittent visitors and the prodding charm of the nurses. And I wish it would stop especially for Patrick Hickey, stop bounding on for his unfit heart, which keeps counting toward its last.

A woman in uniform appears in the doorway. It's Officer Como, Veronica's mother, in midnight police blue. She's a striking figure, tall and sturdy, with a prominent brow, and with her two-way radio and holster and heavy black shoes she appears almost bristling; she doesn't look like Veronica at all. But there's a softness to her around the cheeks and jaw, a fullness that she didn't have years ago, when she and I conversed regularly on the sidewalk in front of the store.

"Nice to see you again, Doc," Officer Como says, extending her hand. She sits down at the bedside chair, while Veronica moves around to the one on the other side. "I hope you're feeling okay."

"I am, very much so."

"When Veronica began describing you last night, I realized who it was she was so smitten with."

"Mother!"

"Well, it's true. Hmm, let's see, an older, distinguished Asian gentleman from Bedley Run. That's not many people. I thought I should come up and say hello and see how you were doing. You're much missed in the village, you know."

"And I miss it," I say, my ready answer. "I know Church Street isn't on your regular beat anymore."

"Not for a couple years, since after you retired. I'm actually working back in Ebbington now. Private security."

"There's more crime in our town," Veronica says almost proudly. "Especially around the mall. That's where Mom works. She's known as the Terminatrix. She's head of security."

"Now who's talking out of school?" Officer Como says. "Actually, I spend most of my time supervising and doing paperwork. But it's better hours, if not better money. I can spend more time with the kid here."

"You're right to value that," I say.

"I'm trying. But you know it's amazing, Doc, what kids will do these days. It's not like it was in the alley behind your old shop. They're not just drinking and smoking pot by the back door. They're breaking in now, stealing computers and stereos, VCRs. Not to sell, but to have for themselves. Now these are truly bad kids for you. Most of them are middle-class. They feel entitled, and they're lazy to boot. It's a lifestyle. They bum change outside the mall, for candy and cigarettes. Can you believe that, kids with weekly allowances begging money? I'm sorry Veronica isn't older, so she'd already be away at college. You're going away someday, aren't you, darling, to a good school? Tell your mother you will."

"Not far away, Mother," Veronica happily answers. "Not far away at all."

Officer Como winks at her, and I say, "You must be very proud, Officer."

"We'll see how proud I can be," she answers. "Anything can happen. She could fall for some handsome jerk and get pregnant."

"Jesus, Mom."

"I'm only being realistic, darling. I have to be because you're too wide-eyed. You'd think she'd be harder, with those gory novels she reads, and with her mother a cop, but it's exactly the other way. She doesn't believe the world is the way it is."

"I don't want to believe," Veronica tells her, now glancing at me. "And neither does my good friend, Franklin. We share the same outlook. Don't we?"

"We certainly do," I answer her, though in truth the sound of the words is deeper than the feeling. I'm not sure anymore what I see when I "look out," if it's real or of my own making or something in between, a widely-shared fantasy of what we wish life to be and, therefore, have contrived to create. Or perhaps more to the point, what ought we see, for best sustenance and contentment and sense of purpose to our days? Veronica already seems rich in these re-gards, and seems, as much as a girl of fourteen can, quite unshake-able. So let her believe. I, Franklin Hata, retired supplier of home medical goods, expatriate and war veteran and now suburban lap swimmer nonpareil, can operate only provisionally at present, even in the wane of my life. I would gladly look to Veronica for a lead, and for the past two days, I probably have.

"Well, we ought to be going," Officer Como says, motioning to Veronica. "I can't leave the car out front forever. I'm not a public servant anymore. We've got to get dinner together, Ronny. And I want to thank you, Doc, for my daughter."

"What do you mean?"

"You've been very good for her. Most of the time she comes home plain tired, and I think this job is mostly a waste of her time. She should go right to studying after school. But she's been working hard at home the last couple days, full of energy. You two must have something special going."

"She's the one who has been providing the energy," I say.

"Well, I'm happy you're being discharged tomorrow, but I'm sorry for Ronny."

"You're going home?" Veronica says softly, knowing well that all discharges happen in the morning.

"Yes," I reply, though I'm looking at her mother. "Dr. Weil thinks I'm recovered."

Officer Como answers, "I talked to him as he was leaving the hospital. He helped a partner of mine once. He says you're coming back like a thirty-year-old."

"Do thirty-year-olds always feel like this?"

Officer Como smiles, touching my arm as she rises from the chair. "Don't get up, Doc. Ronny, it's time to go."

Veronica comes around the bed and stands next to her mother. They're opposite in shape, a white radish and a pear, the daughter seemingly half her mother's height, though of course she isn't. For a moment I wonder if she is an adopted child, but the thought chills me somehow, as if the possible fact should mean a certain set of complications and unhappiness is imminent for them, no matter how loving they are now. But I'm forlorn because Veronica seems forlorn, and all because of my stupid cowardice.

"Well, goodbye, then," Veronica says. Her face looks pale. She doesn't seem to know what to do. Then she reaches out and squeezes my hand for a second, and before I can say anything she's already out in the hall.

Her mother stares after her and, not wanting to leave abruptly, calls and tells her to wait in the car.

"I'm sorry, Doc," she says to me, her expression soured, "I don't know what's wrong with her. It's not like her to run off like that."

"It's my doing," I say. "I didn't tell her I was leaving tomorrow morning."

"She could have looked at your chart, or asked one of the nurses."

"Yes," I say, "but I didn't give her any reason to."

Officer Como considers this, working it quickly, and I can tell she's thinking back to the time when she and I knew each other much better than we might today, when we had a number of conversations whose subject was always the same. I recall how strictly we used to speak, and even sometimes disagreeably, so much so that the simple sight of her blue-and-white car slowly pulling up in front of the store would be enough to halt me.

"You know, Doc, it's amazing how fast the years go by. When we first met, Veronica was a toddler, if that. And your Sunny was what, around the age Veronica is now?"

"I believe that's right."

"It's truly amazing. It's nice to see how things can turn out fine, when maybe you thought it was going to be only trouble ahead. I guess that's why, in a funny way, I still worry so much about Ronny, even though she's generally such a good kid. You never know what's going to happen, for better or for worse. I'm happy that all is going well for you, except maybe this little mishap at your house. And to be a grandfather, well, that's just great for you. When I saw Sunny again at the mall, you know I hardly recognized her? She's such a grown-up now! We even had a nice little talk. Can you imagine, the two of us talking like two ladies at the club? And she showed me a picture of her little boy. Talk about who should be proud."

"You saw her at the Ebbington Mall?"

"I see her every day now. As Ronny said, I'm the new head of security. Sunny's been managing the store almost a year, right? She looks fantastic, all dressed up in those nice new clothes. She was always so beautiful. She's even more so now that's she a little older. So beautiful. I guess she always will be."

"Yes, you're right."

"I should be going. It was good to see you, Doc. I'm glad you met my daughter, or that she met you. Should I say anything to Ronny for you? I know she'll appreciate it. You might not have seen it, but she really is a good girl."

"I know she is," I say, wishing all of a sudden for my lungs to fill and tear, for my skin to burn, for things to fall apart for the benefit of Dr. Weil. "I know she is, I know."

"Well, so long then. Maybe we'll catch you at the mall."

"Yes, yes. Perhaps I'll see Veronica there."

"Sure, I'll tell her that."

And then that is all. I step to the window and I see a car parked in the circle where the ambulances come and go. It's hard to make out, but I think Veronica is sitting in the front seat, holding a book in her hands. Then I see Officer Como walk out to the car and get inside. They sit and speak for a moment, but not for long. They drive off and I watch them go down the hill, and I lose them with the angle. But I see their brake lights again when they reach the main road, the two-lane that follows Middle Pete Creek to the west where it crosses over the parkway, on the other side of which begin the stately rises of trees and easy rolling meadows of Bedley Run. They'll drive swiftly and quietly and without stopping until they cross the buffer zone of old warehouses and railyards, and they'll see reflected in the reservoir the many-colored lights of working-class Ebbington, home of the fast-food strip and the multiplex, and as well to those who would never get to live in my respectable town, the policewomen and the candy stripers and then all the others in this world who would hardly be known.

5

SUNNY, if I recall, was particularly hard on Officer Como. At her worst, she would sit diffidently on the hood of the policewoman's cruiser as it sat parked on Church Street, smoking a cigarette as though she were idly passing the time on a bench in the park, her favorite mirrored sunglasses perched on her head. I remember one incident quite clearly. It was one of those days of transitional warm weather in the late fall, when I had the door of the shop opened to the street. Sunny was one store down, in front of the stationer's, and I watched her obliquely from inside. This was long after the time that I could say anything directive or even meaningful to her, for I would have if I had thought it would do either of us any good. She was clearly waiting for Officer Como to come back with her lunch. I felt I was witnessing a staged accident, awaiting the trial run of something that I knew would be terrible.

"Get off the car," Officer Como said, perching the brown lunch bag near the lights on the roof. She stepped back toward the middle of the sidewalk, facing my daughter. Officer Como was still very youthful-looking then, sprightly and angular, and fresh of face like Veronica is now, which of course was partly what compelled Sunny to want to test her.

"Get off the car now!"

Sunny slid her hands behind her and pushed off the hood. She stood there on the edge of the sidewalk, inches from the fender. She wasn't as tall as the officer but her presence was remarkably severe and stolid and it didn't seem as though she were yielding any room. She was nearly sixteen and her body had filled out; she was just at the point when she was conscious of how to hold herself, how to gain a certain strength of repose by the set of her stance, her hips, her lofted chin. She wasn't the kind of bad girl who cursed or talked back, there being little of that loudness and bluster to her (except on rare occasions with me, who somehow inspired her), but rather she was intimidatingly and defiantly quiet. She just looked at you, or more accurately, she made it that you looked at her. There wasn't a hint of vanity or pride. The way she was facing Officer Como, you could tell she knew how to use her splendid appearance. For Sunny had always understood the cooler properties of her beauty, the ungiving stone of it.

"Now come over here," Officer Como commanded, pointing down at a spot a half-foot in front of her. "Right here, right now."

Sunny sighed and dropped her cigarette, not bothering to stamp it out. She acted more bored than anything else. And although she was but a couple steps from the officer, it seemed to take her whole minutes to reach the spot, enough so that I wanted to close the shop and rush out there and shake her to sensibility. But then I've always wanted to do that, and yet never have.

"You're really wasting yourself, you know that?" Officer Como said to her, less angrily than anyone could have expected from her at that moment. "You don't even know. Others have nothing, not brains, not money, not good looks. They've got nothing and they know it and they're bad. But you have everything going for you. It's ridiculous."

"You can't tell me what I have going," Sunny answered, keeping her voice low. "So don't try."

"I'll tell you whatever I want," Officer Como said forcefully, now holding Sunny by the arm. "And you know why? I wouldn't say a word to you if I thought you deserved it. But you don't. You drink and you probably do drugs and stay out all night with all kinds of sleazy men. It should make you sick to think what your father must feel, how scared he must be for you every time you leave the house. But you don't care about that, either. You can't think about that. All you have time for is being a stuck-up little girl who looks for trouble anywhere she can find it. You're so damn tough and cool, aren't you? So you sit on cop cars in your hot pants. Wow, young lady. Big deal. You're a big deal."

Officer Como let go of her but Sunny didn't move. For a moment I was certain that one of them would suddenly reach out and strike the other. There were no customers in the store and so I drifted out to the doorway; a few people were lingering about them on the sidewalk. I was perplexed as to what I should do. It's a strange thing, to have your daughter being publicly accosted by an officer of the law and to know inside that it's completely right and warranted, and yet on top of that having the impulse to shield her from criticism and unhappiness, and feeling, too, the purest, unbending aggression toward the officer. All this, I realize, is probably fatherhood in a nutshell, but I'm sure it's true that for most these instances are what they are, momentary and situational and thankfully rare, and not, as in the case of Sunny and me, our lives' chronic bout. That day my emotions were running particularly high, I think, because of what was spoken next, by both Officer Como and Sunny, as well as myself.

"What did you say about me staying out at night?" Sunny asked, her voice sounding higher and milder than I'd heard for some years, more like when she was just-arrived, the tone cut-off and vulnerable and like that of anybody else.

Officer Como answered, "Just what the whole town knows."

Sunny's face hardened, and she pulled her sunglasses down over her eyes and bent to lift her bicycle from the sidewalk. She began walking away with it, an expensive French racer I had bought for her recent birthday.

"Hey!" Officer Como spoke briskly. "Don't be running off. I haven't said anything about our being done, have I? We haven't finished our conversation."

Sunny stepped in front of the seat and straddled her bike, not answering the policewoman. There was a peculiar hint of innocence to the stance, despite how grave her expression was, as if she were simply asking the local officer for directions. She was on her bike because I hadn't allowed her to get her driver's permit and license, for I was deathly afraid of where she might end up if she had a car. After many weeks of intense arguments she finally gave up and took to riding the bicycle all around town. So much so, in fact, that it was a customary sight for everyone to see Sunny Hata pedaling on her powder-blue twelve-speed, here and there and at all hours of the day and night.

"Why don't you ask me again what I know about you?" Officer Como said. "Because I'll let you know."

"Sure," Sunny replied severely, sounding like herself again. "Go ahead."

I was at the door to the shop and as there were no customers on that unusually warm afternoon I couldn't help but head toward them. Officer Como's back was turned, but Sunny could well see me. She didn't give any indication that I was within earshot. She just glared defiantly at the officer without the least expression.

"I hear you're over at Jimmy Gizzi's house a lot these days."

Sunny didn't answer.

"Jimmy Gizzi. Now *there's* a nice young man," Officer Como said thickly. "Someone worth befriending. Let's see. What, he's twenty-five, a high-school dropout, and he's never had a real job? He used to beat up his mother every once in a while, before God blessed her and she had a heart attack and died. We had to go to the house and break things up. I know he's been selling pot and speed out of the garage, but I guess these days he's also scoring coke for rich kids at Bedley High."

"I guess you know everything," Sunny said.

"I sure do," the policewoman answered quickly, stepping closer to her. "I know you've been spending some weekend nights there, at his house, for example."

Sunny glanced at me, as if she were actually uncomfortable with my hearing the disclosure. I hadn't known for certain where she was spending those weekend nights, though I was confident that it was always with one of her girlfriends in the city. She'd go for trips to Jones Beach or for shopping or just "hanging out" in the downtown Bohemian neighborhoods, and if she was getting into trouble there, too, I hoped it was in the spirit of joyful rebellion and independence and enjoyment with her own set of comrades, which I should be glad to tolerate and understand. But to hear that she was staying in town, with a dubious young man whom she didn't seem to care to defend, was alarming to me, and even hurtful.

"I know a lot of the people who hang out at Gizzi's," Officer Como went on. "I hope you know that some of them are serious felons. They're not like you. They're not just there to have fun. It's life to them."

"Who says I'm there for fun?" Sunny said sharply. "You think I want fun? You think I'm having fun right now?"

Officer Como seemed surprised by her response, as was I. But the policewoman quickly took back her ground. "Don't ever talk to me like that again. Don't ever raise your voice. Do you hear me? I'll make things miserable for you, I promise. I don't have to care about you. I can write you off like any other good-for-nothing slut who's pissing her life away. Your father deserves better. I hear the stories about the parties, from Jimmy himself, actually. He was run in yesterday, as you probably know. He's out but we'll get him soon. He's a little punk who's in over his head with those brothers from the city. But he had a lot of colorful things to say about you especially. How generous you are to all the guys. What a good sport you are. He said you never get tired."

"Fuck you."

Officer Como lunged at Sunny, grabbing the handlebars and pulling them down to the sidewalk. Sunny fell over the bicycle, landing hard on her knee and forearm. Officer Como shouted, "Fuck me? Is that what you said? Little bitch!"

"Stop it!" I cried, barely able to keep myself from assaulting the officer. She'd turned just in time and by training had automatically unsnapped her holster. The sight of her reaction enraged me. "You cannot speak to my daughter that way. How dare you make such horrible accusations? This is slanderous. A public servant should not exhibit such unbecoming conduct."

"Doc—"

"I must ask you to leave her alone! If she's not done something illegal, you should move on and pursue your duties elsewhere. There are many other young people who are in fact committing crimes in this district, vandalizing and loitering. Why don't you berate and intimidate them? My daughter does sometimes go to the city with her friends, and what a felon says to you has no weight at all. None at all. Now please let us end this, Officer. You and I have a good relationship and I don't wish to see it ruined."

The officer nodded to me and stepped back from Sunny. With anyone else, certainly, Officer Como would have set in her heels, leaned in and returned to me what I deserved, but in deference (and respectful gratitude for my past efforts on her behalf) she grabbed her lunch bag from the roof of the cruiser and went around to the driver's side.

"I'm truly sorry, Doc, that I upset you," she said, opening her door. "I am. I wish you hadn't seen me just now. But I think you know better, too, about the real truth of things. Your daughter is this close to getting into some serious trouble, the kind you can't ignore or forget once it happens. I don't mean to upset you, but you're a good man and so I'm telling you just as I see it. I'm sorry that I am, but there's nothing else I can do. I don't really like your daughter and maybe I don't even care about her, but I owe you too much and so I won't lie. I'm sorry, again. You can call the station and ask for me whenever you want."

She drove off and left the two of us there by the parking meter, Sunny picking herself up from the pavement. I made her follow me inside the shop, for onlookers had begun to gather. The skin on her elbow was raw but not broken. When I tried to examine the abrasion more closely she shook me off, her hands raised diffidently in that long-familiar gesture of hers, as if my closeness were an unbearable weight. But this time the feeling was also mine. For the first time, I felt cold to her, like an ice sheet had fallen between us, and a picture of her began entering my mind, her dark form moving through the corridors of a dingy, slovenly house, peals of surly laughter trailing after her.

"Why must you insist on always provoking the police?" I said. "Officer Como wouldn't have bothered you had you not been so insolent. But you gave her no choice."

Sunny wouldn't answer me, instead propping her bicycle against the counter and drifting down an aisle, her back to me. When she was a young girl, she would skip along the racks and shelves, ticking the merchandise with her little fingers as she went, murmuring a made-up song. Back then I used to toy with the thought of her taking over the business when I retired, running Sunny Medical Supply as her own, even expanding it to open satellite stores across northern Westchester. I imagined her as a kind of mini-mogul who was raised in the trade, that she'd be well known in the business circles and be asked to speak before the audience at the colloquiums and conferences. Of course none of these hopes had much to do with who Sunny truly was, her personality and character, though it was my belief that she was actually well suited to the commerce of every day, for although she wasn't overly talkative she was strangely comfortable dealing with people, whether for better or worse.

"I'm going to ask you to stay here on the weekends from now on. I don't want you to go down to the city anymore. You've gone there all summer, and with school in session you ought to be studying more on the weekends."

"I haven't been going to the city," she said, handling a pair of aluminum crutches. She started using them, pretending to favor the knee that was skinned. "So there's nothing to change."

"Are you saying that you've been at that man's house, as Officer Como mentioned?"

"There and other places," she said. She ambled awkwardly to the far end of the store. The crutches were for a taller person, and she had to hop up slightly over the arm pads with each step. "What did you think, that she was making it up?"

"I assumed she was making a point."

"She wasn't."

"What are you doing there, then? Tell me, I want to know."

"Do you really?"

"Yes! Now tell me!"

She had turned back and slowly lurched forward, landing on both feet. She collected the crutches and looped them on the display hook.

She said, "I have friends there. But Jimmy Gizzi isn't one of them."

"The house is his?"

"I guess so. He's hardly there."

"Is he a dealer of drugs?"

"I suppose so. But I don't do them. I've never done them."

I believed her, for Sunny had never hidden anything from me, or told me untruths. It was actually mostly a matter of my confronting the issues, simply posing the questions.

"So then what do you do there? Are there other girls with you?"

"Some. Not always."

"So you're there alone, sometimes."

"It happens."

I asked her: "Are you having intimate relations?"

Sunny chuckled a bit and said, "What exactly do you mean?"

"You know what I'm talking about."

"I guess I do," she answered. "Is that what you had with Mary Burns?"

"Please don't speak about her like that," I said. "You know very well we're not spending time together anymore. It's disrespectful."

"I guess you're not," Sunny said, her expression souring. "I've been wanting to ask you about that. It's like she never was, isn't it? You just decided it was finished."

"I did nothing of the kind. The decision was mutual. But this is none of your concern."

"You're right," Sunny said. "Why should I care? What does she mean to either of us anymore, right?"

"I've asked you a question, Sunny."

"Yes, then."

"Yes?"

"I'm having sex, yes," she answered, "if that's what you want to know."

I could hardly speak in the face of her bluntness. Then I said, "Are you in love with this person?"

"What?"

"The person you're involving yourself with. Are you in love with him?"

"Are you kidding?" Sunny said savagely. "What do you think I'm doing, having a love affair?"

"I don't know," I said, confused by her sudden anger. "I'm trying to understand what you're seeking. What you may want for yourself."

"I don't want anything," she said, as though saying the words harshly enough would make it so. "Nothing. I don't want love and I don't want your concern. I think it's fake anyway. Maybe you don't know it, but all you care about is your reputation in this snotty, shitty town, and how I might hurt it."

"This is nonsense. You're speaking nonsense."

"I guess I am," she said. "But all I've ever seen is how careful you are with everything. With our fancy big house and this store and all the customers. How you sweep the sidewalk and nice-talk to the other shopkeepers. You make a whole life out of gestures and politeness. You're always having to be the ideal partner and colleague."

"And why not? Firstly, I am a Japanese! And then what is so awful about being amenable and liked?"

"Well, no one in Bedley Run really gives a damn. You know what I overheard down at the card shop? How nice it is to have such a 'good Charlie' to organize the garbage and sidewalk-cleaning schedule. That's what they really think of you. It's become your job to be the number-one citizen."

"I am respected and valued in this town. I'm asked to comment at all the critical council meetings. You have little idea what my position is. People heed my words."

"That's because you've made it so everyone owes something to you. You give these gifts out, just like to that policewoman, Como. She can't stand to cross you because you're this nice sweet man who's given when he didn't have to or want to but did anyway. You burden with your generosity. So even when I'm being troublesome, they can't bear to upset you. It was even that way with Mary Burns, wasn't it? You made it so that she couldn't even be angry with you."

"There was nothing to be angry about," I replied, trying to remember what it was that Mary Burns had finally said to me, after I had asked for one more chance to convince her of my feelings. *You always try, Franklin, but too hard, like it's your sworn duty to love me.*

"I never gave her any cause."

Sunny shook her head and walked past me to leave but I caught her by the arm.

"Let me go!"

"I don't want you sleeping at that house!"

"I'll sleep where I want," she said bitterly.

"Then I won't have you living in my house anymore," I told her, my blood rising. "I won't allow it. It disgusts me to think of what you're doing there. You cannot degrade yourself and expect for me to provide you with things."

"Whatever you want," Sunny answered, shaking herself loose from my grip. "I'll go right now and get my stuff from the house."

"You'll also lose the allowance I give you."

"It doesn't matter," she said, trying to open the door and walk her bicycle out at the same time. "I can get by."

"Sunny . . ."

She turned around to face me, her eyes moist and fierce, a hundred-meter stare. "I don't need you," she said softly, and without remorse. "I never needed you. I don't know why, but you needed me. But it was never the other way."

6

IN THE DAYS THAT FOLLOWED, I didn't see Sunny. Not for nearly three weeks. One would think that in a small town, I'd catch sight of her, coming and going into a shop on the main street. But not even that. I did call the school and subtly inquire whether her attendance was satisfactory, and the school counselor told me it was. He seemed to know Sunny somewhat and spoke glowingly of her exploits last fall on the field hockey team, though he wasn't sure if she was playing again this year. I told him she'd decided to concentrate more on the piano, that she was afraid of injuring her fingers and hands, all those players knocking the hard ball about with sticks. I could say this with confidence because I knew Sunny had in fact quit all her activities at the start of the fall, including the piano, and that really the only thing she had continued to do, strangely enough, was study, particularly her history books and world literature, piles of which always littered the surfaces and furniture of her room. She never ceased being the most avid reader, and I knew she was truly gone from the house when I got home that night weeks earlier and found the stacks removed, the shelves emptied save those books from her childhood, the ones I'd read to her when she first arrived, nursery and bedtime stories in a language she didn't know.

As I suspected, she was living now in the Gizzi house, on Turner Street, an unpaved dead-end road on the far east side of town, near the village line of neighboring Ebbington. I knew where it was from Officer Como, who was the only one I'd told of Sunny's leaving the house. I didn't want her officially listed as a runaway, as I was afraid the designation would remain indefinitely on her personal records, and I knew I could count on Officer Como to keep a watch on the place and its frequent visitors—mostly men in their twenties and thirties, many, according to her, known troublemakers and felons—and be publicly discreet about Sunny's habitation. Of course it was fairly common knowledge that she often hung out there, but most of my fellow merchants and colleagues thought she was simply wayward and difficult and not completely gone from me. I wanted to hide the real depth of the trouble, put it away not (as Sunny always contended) for the sake of my reputation or standing but so I could try to forget she was my daughter, that she had ever come to live with me and had grown up before my eyes.

But late one Friday evening I drove the station wagon down to the main road and followed it until it crossed the river, taking a smaller, unlighted road east past the bare land of the power switching station and the scrap-metal yard, to a large older subdivision called The Orchids that had never been fully developed, where Turner Street is. The neighborhood is more like one in Ebbington than in Bedley Run, a mix of cheaper apartments and small one-story houses, and had been left the way it was to satisfy a county requirement for lower-income housing units in towns like ours.

Mostly decent people live there, the few entrenched working-class of Bedley Run and new younger couples who are always fixing up the charming old cottages and the tiny treed lots they sit on. But fifteen years ago there were a number of boarded-up places with weeds and saplings overtaking the porches, the ivy growing through the broken panes of the windows, and among these were the derelict places owned by the likes of Jimmy Gizzi.

It was already late in the evening, and I don't think I would have found the house on my own had not the lights been on and loud music playing, various older-model pony cars parked in a bunch at the end of the dead-end street and up where the curb should have been. I knew it was the Gizzi place from the way Officer Como had described it, a squat high-ranch house with a bulging bedroom addition over the garage, the sole access to which was an exposed stairwell attached to the side of the building.

I parked halfway down the block and walked up to the property. From the soft light of the house I could see piles of trash and bottles and things like old shoes and undershirts scattered across the filthy yard, wrecked parts of appliances and cars in a heap in front of the open door of the garage, which itself was filled with junk. There was the decrepit, mixed-up scent of engine oil and stale beer and animal spray, the waft of which always seems to overrun certain locales and neighborhoods. And yet with all the lights on and the music and the silhouetted figures behind the curtains moving around dancing, there was a strange festivity to the warm autumn air, as if the place were the site of a favorite seasonal fete, as in those old English novels of Sunny's that I would glance at from time to time. This, of course, was no manor, but I suppose a house rife with any human activity has something over one unsettlingly spacious and silent.

There were two young men sitting on an old sofa on the front lawn, passing a bottle of liquor and a strange-looking pipe between them. One would tip back the bottle while the other lit the short pipe, and from the smell I knew it was probably marijuana they were smoking. The heavy sweetness of the odor was reminiscent of the time I was stationed in Burma during the war, when some of my comrades would hang certain giant leaves to dry and then cut them up to smoke. Everyone preferred real cigarettes, of course, but there was never enough of them (and toward the end of the conflict, none at all), and the leaves provided a bit of mirth and laxity to our spirits, if also a seizing headache at evening's end.

The men noticed me through the hazy light and motioned excitedly for me to approach them. They had longish hair in the prevailing style and swarthy, unshaven faces, though I could tell from their voices that they were in their twenties, the youthful ring still there.

"Hey, man, c'mover here, yeah," the skinnier one said to me. "Hey, Sonny, look, man, it's like, 'The Master.' Hey, old-timer, c'mover here and have a toke with us."

I decided to speak to them, as I thought to ask them if they knew Sunny, and whether she was inside.

"Hey, man," the same one said, handing me the pipe. "Would you mind calling me 'Grasshopper'? Will you say it?"

"I'm looking for my daughter."

"Yeah, sure. Will you just say it?"

"Do you know her? Is she inside?"

"Just a sec, old-timer, first things first. C'mon, say it for us. Say, 'Well done, Grasshopper.' "

"The entire phrase?"

"Yeah, that's right."

So I said to him, "Well done, Grasshopper."

At this they instantly broke out in laughter, the skinny one slapping his knee as he bellowed. His thick-cheeked friend was slower in his movements, not laughing as soundly but almost silently, as if he'd tickled himself with a funny idea.

I asked them, "Do you know my daughter, Sunny? Is she inside the house?"

The skinny one kept laughing but thumbed toward the front door, waving me to go in. All the while he kept saying the phrase to his friend in a choppy, halting voice, not at all as I had spoken it. My accent has never been perfect, and was less so then, but I've always been somewhat proud of my flowing verbiage, and that I speak in the familiar, accepted rhythms.

"Is she inside?"

"Yeah, yeah," the skinny one said, hardly able to look at me without gasping, "everybody's in the house."

"Thank you."

I returned the pipe (untried) and ventured up the tumbled, cracked concrete steps to the door. I banged the fake brass knocker but even I could hardly hear it for the loudness of the music inside. The knob hung loose and was almost falling off and the door swung open with a slight push. The place was raucous and crowded. As there was no foyer I was immediately in the small living room, where people were crammed onto the sectional L-shaped sofa, as well as sitting on its back and low arms. People were dancing everywhere, couples and then sole men unsteadily swaying to themselves. What struck me immediately was that a number of the partygoers were black and Puerto Rican; colored people were a rare sight in Bedley Run, especially at social events, and never did one see such "mixed" gatherings. I, certainly, would sometimes find myself at Mary Burns's country club for social hours and dances, the only one of my kind, a minor but still uncomfortable feeling, like the digging edge of an overstarched collar. But here everyone seemed unconcerned, and I was strangely heartened by the fact, though my next thought was that Sunny wasn't simply involving herself intimately with all these men white and brown and black, but was living with them as well, with no other company but theirs.

I didn't see her anywhere in the room. There were glances and bemused stares but no one seemed to care much about my presence as I went from one group to the next. I was surprised by how few women there were, perhaps a handful out of the crowd of twenty-five or thirty. They looked much older than Sunny, at least twice her age, sallow and fleshy and long-traveled from their youth. I was reminded of the women who sat on stools outside certain alley shops of my native seaside town, their faces painted the colors of crimson and ash, languorous popular songs filtering out beneath the lanterned eaves of their tiny "houses."

The house kitchen was a rancid, overflowing mess of bottles and ashtrays and spaghetti sauce–stained dishes, the doorless cupboards mostly bare except for a few cans of chili and soup. Down the corridor to the bedrooms there were people sitting on the floor against the walls, drinking beer and smoking while they waited for the bathroom. I could see the doors of the two bedrooms down at the end, and suddenly I was deeply afraid of what I might do if I found her behind one of them. I couldn't bear to imagine what awful sight it might be, what horrible tangle and depravity. I had only really seen Sunny with boys at the country club, all of them in their tennis whites and sneakers, or at the cotillion-type gatherings in the evenings, their bodies orderly and arranged and the touching in steady orchestrations, the careful waltzes and reels. Even then I used to wonder how I should feel when I saw some severely slim, tall lad place his hand on the small of her back, let it slip down a notch, whether I ought to burn with indignation or shiver or stand back in prideful and surrendering melancholy. And if she were only mine, of my own blood, would the feelings run different? Would I tremble and shake with an even purer intensity?

The first door was half-opened, and when I peered inside a group of a half-dozen or so young people were sitting in a circle, passing around a large pipe. Someone jeered at me and as I didn't see Sunny among them, I quickly shut the door. I knocked on the other door and announced myself as loudly as I could, but there was no answer. I repeated the action but to no avail. I tried the knob and found it, like everything about the house, unsecured. A stereo was playing its own blaring music. The room was illuminated by a bizarre flowing-liquid bulb of a lamp, the light poor and in a dizzying mix of colors, and in the dim I saw a large bed with high corner posts, a gauzy sheet thrown over as a makeshift canopy. Two figures languidly wrestled within the lair; I called to them, but again could hardly hear my own voice. Then one of them, I thought the man, kneeled up on the bed and lay on the other. The two began then, moving in that clipped, rolling action I dreaded to see. I shuddered with the thought that she was under him. I couldn't hear them and they couldn't hear me, and I approached the veiled bed. They didn't see me, being in their own realm. Were I an assassin, they would have been doomed.

I touched the netting at the foot of the bed, and at that moment the music paused and a murmur rose up—she had noticed me. And yet she didn't rebel. It was hard to see and I called her name and she cooed, and what I could make out finally was that she was beckoning me, darkly, taunting me with the vile display of her carnality. I had with me a small dagger, which I sometimes carried for self-defense, but now I felt its menacing weight in my breast pocket, its leather scabbard hard against my chest. My heart flooded black, and at that moment I wished she were nothing to me, dead or gone or disappeared, so that I might strike out at the bodies with the full force of my rage, tear at them with whatever strength I could muster.

"Hey, man, it's not like a block party," a gruff voice said. "You gotta be invited."

"Sunny," I said, suddenly unable to speak but weakly. "Sunny . . ."

"Let him in, sugar," a softer voice lazily answered. "C'mon. C'mon, sugar, yeah, come inside."

The record repeated and the woman inside the bed reached out to me. She had turned on a bed lamp. Her fingers were long and thin, and I realized it wasn't Sunny at all. She had a narrow, drawn expression with sleepy eyes. She smiled faintly, her lips moving, saying something. Her partner had already ceased caring about my presence, and he went back to his business, his hips working their way between her heavy, stippled thighs. But she kept her attention on me, unctuously gesturing, and even as he leaned and bucked into her she held out her open hand to me, as if I should take it when I crept my way inside.

I left the room straightaway, nearly stumbling over the huddled drinkers and smokers in the narrow corridor. All of a sudden the house seemed unbearably small and stifling. Someone was flicking on and off the hall and living room lights, and the effect was maddening and disorienting. Most everyone in the house began to dance, the music having changed from rock songs to the incessant beat of disco music, which was immensely popular at the time. But to me everything seemed a jangle of limbs. I began to feel that this house, these people, the party, were spinning out of control. The living room was transformed into a rank swamp of bodies, and having no path of exit, I stepped outside the back kitchen door as quickly as I could.

It was a great relief. And there, as I stood on the ruined cobble of the patio under a wide starless sky, the reports of music and voices playing off the hidden trees, an image of another time suddenly appeared to me, when I began my first weeks of service in the great Pacific war. I was initially stationed in Singapore, awaiting my orders to whatever front I would be sent to.

One evening, my comrades and I were on our way to a welcoming club, a grand house which was once a prominent British family's residence but was now used as a semi-official officers' club, with the usual entertainments. There was no sanctioned establishment as yet, and we young officers were more than grateful for the outpost.

My mates, Lieutenants Enchi and Fujimori, and I had eaten our dinner at a cart stand and were strolling to the club, a yellow two-story colonial structure with a double veranda and white columns. Enchi was already quite drunk, as usual, and Fujimori didn't have far to go. Drinking was never very alluring to me, but that night I had decided to take a few glasses of rice spirits with dinner. We were to be shipped out to our respective fronts in a matter of days, each of us assigned as medical assistants to bases that would serve the forward units. It was an august time, those first years of the war, and everyone to the man was supremely hopeful of a swift and glorious end to the fighting.

Enchi was talking about the girls that were to be brought to the club that evening. He was excited and speaking quite loudly, his face flushed with drink.

"I heard there are to be local girls there tonight, young ones, perhaps even virgins."

Fujimori said to him, in his customary dry manner, "You wouldn't know it if they were, Hideo, you grand masturbator."

"I certainly would!" Enchi cried, coming up and slinging his arms about us, so that we were a trio. "Your sister isn't a virgin, let me tell you"

It was an old joke from him, and Fujimori was of course unperturbed. He unhinged himself from us and replied, "Well, let's see if you can manage your way inside one tonight. The last time, I practically had to aim you. But you don't remember. You never remember."

I wasn't with them on their last "outing," as I had little interest in pleasure-for-hire, but that evening I thought I would at least accompany them, if only to see if their exploits matched the accounts I'd listened to, which were always extremely colorful.

"My good friend Jiro," Enchi said to me, lurching us forward with his heavy steps, "why don't you join us tonight? What is it? Are you not so fond of women? You can tell me."

"I'm not fond of women who are prostitutes," I said, though in truth I'd made several of my own visits, in secret. "Besides, they're all old and probably diseased. Made of face powder and cheap perfume."

"That's why you ought to stay around tonight!" Enchi replied, poking me in the chest. I pushed him away and he nearly fell down on the road. Fujimori was up ahead of us, calling in a strange voice after some schoolgirls walking on the other side of the canal. Enchi went on, "These are fresh girls who are coming. You'll see. They're not the old Japanese aunties who are shipped in. I'm tired of them, too, you know. It's like screwing a bag of soybean curds, just all mush and mess."

"I wonder what they must say of you, Hideo."

"No matter, no matter," he said, shaking his large, squarish head. He had the habit of closing his eyes when beginning to speak. Within a month, I would receive a telegram from Fujimori that Enchi had been killed in Borneo, torn apart by a mortar round outside a medical station. "I'm not proud, Jiro. Not proud at all. I'm only looking for a bit of satisfaction. Just a little bit and I'll die happy."

As we approached the clubhouse, we saw a crowd of soldiers outside. Fujimori had already reached them. Usually such gatherings would be loud and boisterous, but there was a stillness about the air that seemed unnatural. They were standing in a group at one side of the house, near the front of the wide veranda. Fujimori was ordering them to make way for him, being an officer. When we ran up, there were other officers now coming out from the main entrance, shouting orders at the group on the ground.

"Move back! Don't touch anything!"

"I'm a medical officer," I heard Fujimori say. He sounded grave and sober. "But it doesn't matter. She's in no need."

"I say move back!" The man speaking was Major Irota, chief of staff to General Yamashita. He was the only one out of uniform—in fact, he was wearing a blue silk robe and was slipperless. "Who saw what happened? Speak up!" The men stood silent, except for Fujimori, who was kneeling by a girl. Enchi and I were standing beside him. The girl was naked, and the skin of her young body looked smooth and perfect, except that her head was crooked too far upward. It was obvious her neck was cleanly broken. She was quite dead.

"No one saw anything?" Major Irota shouted. "Very well. I expect it to remain so. Now I want all of you off these grounds immediately. Lieutenant, you'll bring the girl inside."

He was ordering Fujimori, and as nobody had any choice in the matter I helped him carry the body inside. Enchi stood aside, looking slightly sick. Fujimori lifted her by the armpits and I took her legs. She was astoundingly light; one of us could have easily done the job. We brought her inside while Enchi followed. The major motioned for us to go to the back of the house, the duty officer leading us to a cramped room behind the kitchens. We laid her out on a butcher's table, and he ordered us to wrap her in burlap. We would do so and then report to the duty officer that the body was ready.

The girl was the first dead person I had ever seen. She was neither homely nor pretty. She was just a girl, otherwise unremarkable, perhaps fifteen or so. I kept thinking she looked to be Korean, with her broad, square face. She barely had any pubic hair. Her palms were lighter-toned than her hands. The same with her feet. I lifted and turned her as Fujimori spread the cut-up sacks beneath her. Enchi was sitting in a chair in the corner, watching us as he nervously smoked.

"It's only one floor," he finally said, quizzically. "She must have landed just so to snap her neck like that."

Outside, when I first lifted the girl, I had noticed two girls' faces peering over the ledge of a second-floor window. They looked scared more than sad. Then they were quickly pulled back inside.

"Perhaps she made sure to land on her head," he said, but Fujimori didn't answer. He had placed the sacks over her chest and shoulders and around her legs and was now winding the cord tightly to bind her.

"It's like one of those English-style roasts, eh, Fujimori?"

"Shut up."

"I'm not trying to be humorous," Enchi said.

"Shut up, anyway," Fujimori said again, this time quite grimly. He pulled a bag over the girl's head and wound the cord about her neck, then weaved the loose end through the bindings on her torso. He neatly slip-knotted it, and soon enough he was done. We then stood there for a moment, looking at his unusual work.

"How skilled, us medics," Enchi said from his chair. "The major will be impressed."

The atmosphere in the house that evening was typically rowdy. No one seemed mindful of what had happened a few hours earlier, that a girl had leaped to her death from one of the very rooms now being employed for the officers' entertainment. Enchi was so drunk with rice wine that he had passed out in the parlor room, never making it upstairs, and Fujimori, who always grew quieter as he indulged, was sitting glumly among the regular working ladies, sipping at his porcelain drinking cup. We didn't say much to each other after preparing the girl. We had caught sight of the duty officer and a corporal carrying her body out the back of the house, to a light transport truck. They counted aloud and swung it up and in like a sack of radishes. One could clearly hear the full sound it made on the metal bed, deep-voiced and surprising.

I wandered upstairs, eventually. I wasn't particularly interested in the entertainments of the new girls. But I kept thinking about them looking over the edge of the sill, how they'd gazed transfixedly at the body. On the landing, several men were playing a card game, gambling while they awaited their turn in the bedrooms. One of them was complaining that the wait would be longer, as now there was one fewer than before.

"Say, what are you doing?" he barked at me. I was walking down the wide, ornately papered hallway. "There's an order here, if you haven't noticed. We're the next group."

"I'm not waiting."

"You're surely not," he said, rising from his kneeling position. He teetered slightly before gaining his feet. "I'll make certain of that."

"I told you I'm not on the queue."

"Then where are you going?"

"Can't you see I'm a medical officer?"

He peered at my lapel insignia and nodded. Then he realized that I had been one of the men to carry in the body. "Oh, I get it. You're here to save us from the clap. But don't you think you ought to have checked the girls before they got started? It's a bit late now, isn't it?"

"Fortunately, Lieutenant, not for you," I said. My crisp tone seemed to convince him, and he bowed hesitantly as I walked down the hall and to the wing where they had quartered the new girls.

There was a group of six standing in the short hallway, which was almost a vestibule for the larger run of the wing. I strode past without incident. Typically, officers would have the privilege of spending hours and sometimes whole evenings with a woman, but in this instance a special rationing had been instituted. It seemed the men were all too familiar with the offerings of the professional aunties, and the arrival of these girls had most everyone edgy and expectant. General Yamashita, one presumed, had been first to take his enjoyment when they came in. It was said the four girls were shipped all the way from Shimonoseki, via the Philippines, and that in fact two others had been "lost" during the lengthy sea passage. Now there were three, though it was known that other new, young women would be arriving imminently, and in numbers that would be satisfactory for all.

But I didn't really care for these kinds of activities. It was true that I had visited the welcoming house a few times since being stationed in Singapore, but I wasn't enamored of the milieu, the transactional circumstances and such. Like any man, I sometimes had that piercing, wrecking want, and in moments I allowed it to propel me to frequent one of the women, Madam Itsuda. As noted, I did this discreetly. She must have been forty at the time, nearly twice my age, and I can't say I held deep feelings for her (as that would have been ludicrous). I appreciated her gentle, laconic manner and understanding mien toward my youth and naivety. She was never belittling, nor did she pretend that I was special, and I can still remember her smoothing her somehow always tidy floorbed, the sheets invitingly turned down.

Why I was going to the new girls, then, I couldn't exactly say. I was naturally disturbed by the earlier events, but the fact that I would be concerned in particular about them, even think an iota about their circumstance, confused and irked me. I kept imagining the three of them, one to a room, the lights unchastely left on. At the head of the west wing, it was strangely quiet. English-style houses were, if monstrous, at least sturdily built. One of the doors suddenly opened and a girl ran out, crying. She was naked, and there was a faint smudge of blood staining the inside of her legs. She tried to run past me but I automatically caught her, not knowing what else to do.

"Please," she said, her eyes frantic. "Let me go, please, let me go!"

"There's no place to go," I said, unthinking. "You must stay in the house."

She looked surprised at my words, staring at me as if I were someone she knew.

"Please," she said, crying even harder now. "I beg you."

A stout officer with a towel around his waist came stumbling out of the room. He was the group captain who'd come on the same transport as I. "There she is! I'm grateful to you, Lieutenant. We wouldn't want another leaper, would we?"

"I beg you, *O-ppah,* let me go!"

"She's a pretty one, isn't she?" he said, taking her from me. He slapped her once in the face, quite hard. She fell quiet. "She goes on a little, though. Say, what was that you were saying to her?"

"Nothing, sir."

"I thought I heard you say something, in her tongue."

"No sir, I didn't."

He looked confused for a moment, but then shrugged. "Ah, what does it matter? We're all here for relaxation tonight, right? And don't look so concerned. We won't be much longer. There'll be plenty left, for you and your mates."

"Yes, Captain."

He led her back down the hall to the open door. She followed him, in limp half-steps. Before they reached the room, the girl looked back at me, the side of her face raised red from the blow. I thought she was going to say something again, maybe *O-ppah,* how a girl would address her older brother or other male, but she just gazed at me instead, ashen-faced, as if in wonder whether I had uttered the words to her at all.

I WAS THINKING of that girl as I walked around the side of the Gizzi house and its waist-high weeds and saplings; I wondered if she had survived the war and was still living now, in Singapore or Korea or perhaps even here in this country. Or whether like Lieutenant Enchi she had been killed soon thereafter, by whatever circumstance, and been cheated of (or spared) the endless complications and questionings of a life duly spent. And what would she or Enchi think of me, an old man loitering in the shadows of a party house in America, peering into private rooms?

As I turned onto the front yard, the two young men who had first greeted me were still on the sofa, the skinny one passed out over the edge of the wide arm. His largish companion was sitting up, however, simply looking out at the night and laughing softly to himself. I thought he had gone mad. But as I crossed his field of vision he said something, whispering to me in a little boy's voice.

"What?" I said to him. "Excuse me? I can't hear you."

"She's up there," he was saying, his face screwed up in what I took to be mock fear. He repeated, "Up there."

He tipped his head toward the dormer over the garage. There, in the window, a seam of light shone through a break in the heavy curtain.

"You know my daughter, Sunny?"

"Don't tell him I told you," he answered more fearfully, getting up to walk away. He was already heading down the street, holding the neck of the big bottle between two fingers. "Don't say anything, okay?"

I ascended the flight of wooden stairs attached to the side of the house. The steep treads were spongy and rotting, and with each step it seemed the whole thing might collapse beneath me. At the landing I had to stop to catch my breath. The door was a half-window with a lacy curtain on the other side of the dingy glass.

And there she was. She was standing in the middle of the squarish room, her figure in profile. She had on only a gray tank-top and her underwear. She was dancing, slowly, by herself. Her jeans and her sweater were splayed on the floor in front of her. I looked to the side and saw her audience, two men sitting on the floor at the foot of a bed. They were calling and toasting her with bottles of beer. One was a young black man wearing a worn baseball cap; the other, I thought, was Jimmy Gizzi, whom I'd seen once or twice around town. A hand-sized mirror lay between them on the carpet, sprays of bright white powder salting the glass.

She wasn't playing anything up for them, performing. She was simply there, moving without music, hardly looking at them as she swayed and twirled and pushed out her hips, her chest. I kept myself far enough from the window to remain hidden. I could hardly bear to watch the scene, much less allow it to go on. And yet each time Sunny turned my way I stepped back and quieted myself and hoped the darkness would camouflage me.

I had never seen her move in such a way. I knew what her body was like, of course, from when she was a young girl, and later, too, when she'd swim or sunbathe at the house in a bikini, which was hardly a covering at all. She was always lithe and strong and sturdy-limbed, never too skinny or too softly feminine. I saw her as I believe any good father would, with pride and wonder and the most innocent (if impossible) measure of longing, an aching hope that she stay forever pristine, unsoiled.

But to gaze upon her like this. She was running her hands over herself, pressing across the skimpy shirting and down her naked thighs and up again. The two men were laughing still, but there was a new attention in their faces; they were sitting up a bit more, as if riding higher on the worn carpeting. The man I assumed was Gizzi was watching her intently, enough so that he picked up the mirror without looking and, wiping it with his finger, rubbed the stuff all over his mouth and gums. I could see the foul light of his teeth. The other man was nursing his beer, his face mostly hidden beneath the brim of his hat. But I could tell he was stirred now, too, his fingers anxiously tapping at the bottle. Gizzi was calling her names like *baby* and *sugar* and *sweet thing,* though she didn't respond, she didn't look or smile or even acknowledge him. But there was no coldness from her, either, no front of unwelcoming or remonstrance. I didn't wish to think that it was she who had initiated this moment but there was nothing to indicate otherwise. They weren't forcing her, or even goading her, or doing anything to coerce. She was moving and dancing with every suggestion, and then finally she was touching herself in places no decent woman would wish men to think about, much less see.

The other man finished his beer and let it fall to the side. He pushed off his hat and pulled off his shirt and approached her on his knees, his fluffy Afro matted in a ring. He took Sunny by the hips and with a palpable and surprising gentleness kissed her on the belly. She ceased her moving. She stroked his hair and pulled him tightly against her by his neck. Jimmy Gizzi was watching them, too, and he was already unbuckling his belt as he stumbled up toward them. Jimmy Gizzi said something and they ignored him, and when he tried to touch her the man reached and held him roughly by the shoulder and neck and said, "You sit awhile, okay, Giz?"

"All right, man, all right . . ." Jimmy mumbled weakly, a pained wince on his haggard face.

The man half-threw him back toward the bed, though Jimmy didn't lose his feet. He didn't look in the least shocked or upset. Instead he crouched down on the floor and cleaned up the mirror with his hand, licking and mouthing his fingers and palm.

"She's all yours, Linc. Eat her up, man," Jimmy Gizzi said, grinning and nodding. "Eat her up."

They ignored him again, and the man called Linc resumed kissing Sunny on the belly and down her sides, to the points of her lips. He was kissing her steadily, completely, as if he were simply there to mark her, above all else. Her body seemed tense, expectant. And then she leaned into him, hard, pressing herself into his face and hair. He bent and lifted her from the thighs, Sunny holding a standing position. She rose up as if nothing. He buried his face in the dip of her legs. Jimmy Gizzi had undone his pants and begun lazily stroking himself, and Sunny began laughing at him, first in chortles and then maniacally, in a dusky tone that seemed as illiberal and vile as what he was compelling on himself. And it was then that I wished she were just another girl or woman to me, no longer my kin or my daughter or even my charge, and I made no sound as I grimly descended, my blood already trying to forget, growing cold.

7

IT IS THE MORNING of my leaving and who should arrive to pick me up, bouqueted with lilies, but my friend and realtor and the likely future executor of my estate, Ms. Olivia Crawford, C.R.S. She tells me someone from the hospital left a message on her machine last night, to alert her that I was to be discharged today. She is almost certain that Renny Banerjee was the caller, though of course working through a third party, some nurse or assistant with a crowingly high-pitched nasal voice.

I don't inform Liv that it was in fact I who asked that someone to call—that someone being Nurse Dolly, who is one of those people who can seem insulted by any query whatsoever, and is thus naturally excellent at keeping secrets—not because I'm bashful for having requested her help, but because Liv herself looks deliciously intrigued by the idea that Renny Banerjee might be coming around again, perhaps finally regretting his decision to change every last one of his door locks. I don't wish to dissuade her from this suspicion, as Renny himself, stopping in on his way home last night, all but admitted to me that he's been driving by Liv's office at odd hours, as well as her condominium, to check whether someone else's car might regularly be there.

Matchmaker I'm not, and yet it gives me a shimmering, pearly gleam of joy to think of the two of them together again. Renny with his flashing, wicked grin and disarming bouts of tenderness, and Liv, of course, just being herself, a one-woman corporation and salvage crew and instant remodeling service, all in one.

"Now, Doc," she says, setting the immense bouquet on the rolling tray at the foot of the bed. "I brought this up solely for the purpose of letting everyone know how completely recovered you are. I don't believe in flowers only when you enter the hospital. You need even more lovely arrangements on getting out."

"From the grand looks of that bouquet, it may seem that I am 'getting out' forever."

"Doc!" she gasps, as if the idea were some awful, blaspheming joke. "You're always making it seem that I want you gone. Really. You're so awful these days! And cruel."

"It's the hospital, I think."

"Well, it's great timing, then, that I've come for you." As she flutters about like a hotel maid, and not looking the least bit odd in her slimming Italian blazer and silk scarf with the stirrup pattern, I realize what it is about her that I have always revered. Liv Crawford is helplessly, perhaps even morbidly industrious. She has already tidied up the room and made the bed, placing my hospital gowns in the plastic hamper in the bathroom and wiping down the surfaces with the used towels. All this because it is there to do, the same way she entered the ruined family room of my house and saw what was needed and lighted up the touchpad of her cellular phone, to call forth restorative good order. She's come with pictures of the renovations, all disarmingly, exactingly right. In a few minutes she will escort me out and drive me back swiftly to Bedley Run and show me the door to my prime vintage home, every last tint and scent of offending smoke steam-cleaned from the carpets, from the drapes, from the antiqued upholstery of the chairs, the place in showcase, immaculate, pristine and classic condition, appearing just as though I have not lived there every day for the last thirty years of my life.

And I think how strange (as well as lucky) it is that Liv Crawford is also the *only* person I could have called for such a task, whether I wished to or not.

"Hey, Doc, are these take-home slippers?" she now asks me, lifting a flattened baby-blue terry pair from beneath the bed.

"Whatever you think."

"They're sweet, in a downmarket sort of way. You can use them outside, before and after your swims."

"Yes, I can. Dr. Weil, however, is afraid my shingles will worsen with the chemicals."

"That's his malpractice premium talking. He's not a dermatologist, so what does he know?"

"Physicians must all have broad, sound training."

"Maybe you do, Doc, but I'm not so sure about Larry Weil."

"He's told me he's a graduate of the Yale Medical School."

"So what!" Liv cries. "The man plays golf four times a week. Two handicap, or so Renny used to tell me. Now how good a doctor can he really be?"

"He's perfectly fine," I say, feeling as though I've been his only defender. The nurses have also been harsh critics, as was Renny Banerjee the other day. And yet I've witnessed nothing to suggest that he's anything but a competent, knowledgeable physician. He is a good doctor, I am sure, but not what they call gung-ho, or else inspirational, in the way some are. What is obvious, unfortunately for him, is his somewhat stereotypical physician's mien, the stiff brush of his manner, the prickly tongue, that put-out-ness that is rarely endearing in a man so young, all of which is no doubt due to his frustration (as he's often expressed) that he works in this sleepy up-country hospital instead of in a big-city research and teaching institution with his own lab assistants and grant writers and ambitions of scientific glory.

I remember how I was when I was his age, heady with the quiet arrogance of a newly minted officer, feeling wise and capable and in command of any contingencies. Though not a true physician, I had been fully trained in field and emergency medicine in order to aid and sustain my comrades, to save them whenever possible, fulfilling my duty for Nation and Emperor. And while I was grateful for being part of what we all considered the greater destiny and the mandate of our people, I had hoped, too, that my preparation and training would be tested and confirmed by live experiences, however difficult and horrible; and more specifically, that my truest mettle would show itself in the crucible of the battlefield, and so prove to anyone who might suspect otherwise the worthiness of raising me away from the lowly quarters of my kin and reveal the essential, inner spirit that is within us all. And yet still I have always wondered if training or rearing tells more than the simple earth and ash and blood from which we come, or whether these social inurements eventually fall away, like the moldering garments of the dead, to reveal the underlying bones.

Liv Crawford, I have a feeling, would contend that neither is the case; it is what one does, right now, in the very fact of the act, that she champions. I like to hope that this is not simply the realtor modality. And the *right now* for her, thank goodness, is the business of getting me home.

"Ready, Doc?"

"Yes, Liv, I think so. Liv?"

"What, Doc?"

"I want to thank you for your efforts on my behalf. I am truly grateful."

"Don't start like this, Doc, or you'll get me misty."

"But I must tell you. Dousing the fire, helping to pull me out, the house renovations. Your coming today. I could not have asked a blood relative to do any of these things."

"The office head put me up to it," she says lamely, trying not to look at me. "She wants the exclusive someday. She's already written on the board that it'll be the listing of the year."

"But you must know that the house would be no one's but yours to sell."

Liv smiles, almost shyly, obviously having difficulty with self-admissions of generosity and kindness. Of course she's known. But she too much likes—and depends on—the blustery cover of commerce.

"You know me, Doc. I never take anything for granted. Not until closing. And even then, I make sure to read everyone's signature and date. Make sure it's right on the line."

"Perhaps I ought to leave it in my will, that you're to sell my house."

"You're being morbid again, Doc. But you know, it's not a bad idea," she says, perking up to her old self. She's able to eye me now. "Of course I don't have to say that I wish you would live for-ever. But"—and she pauses—"I do think I've made it clear that I be-lieve I'm the agent to list your beautiful home someday, and I hope all the time that I'm that lucky woman. But there's not a bone in my body that wishes that day to come any sooner than never."

"I thought sharks don't have any bones," says a familiar voice, and I see it's Renny Banerjee coming through the doorway, a sly expression on his smooth chocolate face.

"Ha, ha," Liv can only answer, taken aback and also, subtly and obviously, tickled by his presence. This is an expected surprise.

Renny, surveying the room, says to me, "I asked at the desk whether you had left, Doc, and they said they didn't see how, with all the flowers still arriving."

"We're on our way out," Liv replies tersely, pointing to the giant lily bouquet. "That one's yours, Mr. Banerjee. If you so please."

"I please."

"Thank you."

We thus march out as three, Liv with my bag over her shoulder and two smaller arrangements, one in each of her hands; Renny hardly apparent behind the lilies; and I ambling under my own power, having already refused two offers of a wheelchair and nurse, the latter walking along with us anyway. I don't tell anyone—including Dr. Weil, when he came earlier for a pre-discharge exam—about the strange burning in my chest that I awoke to this morning, an ever-angry tingle that feels to be webbing my lungs each time I breathe in tiny, almost electrical bursts. As we first gain the hall, I think there's a chance I might actually fall down. But I steel myself, for though it would be perfectly pleasant to stay indefinitely (and idle with Veronica Como), I don't want the messiness of further diagnoses and tests and proposed courses of treatment—in a phrase, the complications of complications. Simplicity seems all, or at least my expectations of it, which are my house and morning swims in the pool and my strolls down to the village, to view all the good people and shops.

At the ground-floor elevator bank, we come out and there is Mrs. Hickey, waiting to go up to the children's ICU. She greets me with warmth. I ask the heavyset nurse if she'll excuse us for a moment, and she complies with a hard grunt. Renny and Liv don't know Anne Hickey, of course, and don't pause on their way to the automatic doors. They hardly said a word in the elevator, only the four of us in the car, though I caught them gazing at each other quite intently if not lovingly, at least as yet; and so I tell them to go on to the parking lot, where I'll catch up to them soon, and they exit, murmuring, a mini-procession of my flowers.

Mrs. Hickey is nicely dressed in dark pants and black shoes and a short, woolly red jacket. It could be a church day, from her appearance, though I can see it is probably her attempt to maintain an optimism and order in her days, for both Patrick and Mr. Hickey. She looks slightly haggard otherwise, circles about her eyes, with the pallor that comes from lack of sleep. But she smiles kindly and takes my hand and we sit on a bench in the waiting area.

"I'm so sorry I couldn't come visit before you left. I tried, but you were always resting or with the doctor, and I didn't want to drop in unexpectedly."

"Nothing for you to be sorry about," I say, feeling remorseful already. "I'm the one who's sorry that I didn't have a chance to visit with your son while I was here. I could go up with you now——"

"Please, Doc, your friends are waiting for you outside. And I see you're not moving so quickly. Not like usual, anyway. Maybe you can come back, but only when you're feeling yourself again."

"Perhaps you're right."

"Of course I am," she says, trying to reassure me. "Besides, Patrick has hardly been awake the last few days. He's had much better weeks. I know he'll feel better soon, and when he does I'll call you right away."

"Okay, that's a deal."

"You bet it is," she replies, still holding my hand, and quite tightly. She looks down into her lap, and suddenly I realize she's crying.

"Mrs. Hickey," I say, crouching closer to her. "You must hold on as best you can. It will be very difficult, but you have to, a little longer. Your son is counting on you."

She nods and whispers, "Yes, he is."

"The doctors will find a heart for him, and soon enough Patrick will be home, playing in the store."

"I hope James is around for that," she says, wiping her nose with the back of her sleeve. "He's been terribly angry of late. I haven't seen him for days, and I don't know if he's even been in to see Patrick this week."

"Is it the money problems with the store?"

"It's always money problems. But they're mostly over now. He's really decided to give up."

"What do you mean?"

"He's going to give everything back to the bank. The whole building, the apartments, the store, everything. We haven't paid the mortgage in some months, you know, because of Patrick's bills. Business has been slow anyway. It has been, truthfully, ever since we bought the store from you. We only have about a month of insurance left. A few days ago we had a fight, and it was terrible. He said he wished they'd find Patrick a heart or not, and I went crazy. I asked him what he meant by 'a heart or not,' and he said we couldn't go on like this anymore, waiting for something that might never come, and maybe not work anyway, with the hospital costing us fifteen hundred dollars a day. I asked him if he really thought that way and he didn't answer. Then I told him to get out."

"It was a natural response."

"I know, but now I wish I hadn't. Sometimes, Doc, for a second, I'll think that way, too, but I don't want to admit it. James has been so frustrated with the business these last few years. It's never really worked for us. Then Patrick got sick and everything fell apart. We're losing everything, and I don't blame James for saying those things. He's under so much pressure. He was wrong to say it. But even I can't blame him anymore. I don't. Am I an awful mother, Doc? Am I horrible?"

"You're nothing of the kind, Mrs. Hickey."

"I'm glad you think so," she says, letting go of me now. Wisps of her light hair fall down over her temples and brow, and from this angle she reminds me of the obituary photograph of a younger Mary Burns, the clear, high sheen of the skin, the tender brow. "You've always been kind to us, and I hope you know that I appreciate it. James will, too, someday, when all this is over. We've just had bad luck with the store and he blames you for it, though there's no reason why he should. You sold us a nice business and it seemed like the next day the whole economy went sour. Somehow James has this crazy idea in his head that you sold us a lemon, that you knew the business would only get worse but made out as if otherwise. But even if that were true, I say we should have realized it ourselves, caveat emptor. I don't know why I'm getting into this except that nothing seems good for us these days, and I guess it would be nice to hear that it's all a run of bad luck that has to end soon."

"That must be what it is," I tell her, not wanting her to think ill of the store. "Bad luck can come but it cannot last, either. I know this myself. You do what you can under extreme circumstances, perseverance your only goal. After the difficulties, you can begin again, but you must put behind you what has occurred. Like your husband's words, for example. They were spoken under great duress, which makes people most unlike who they really are. We talk of people rising heroically in times of adversity, but I think that's rarer than we'd like to believe. I'm sure Mr. Hickey is remorseful for his thoughts about Patrick, just as deeply as you are. The task now is to forgive and forget."

There is silence between us, not so much because I've said anything profound or true but that we've gone much further in the conversation than either of us had anticipated. We both nod, trying to say how we appreciate the moment, although it pains me to think that the Hickeys have discussed the possibility that I might have made misrepresentations when I sold them the store in a neat and ordinary sale-by-owner. The last thing Mrs. Hickey needs is to wonder if I have had a part in their lamentable slide into misfortune, rather than focusing on the care and well-being of her son, and supporting her deeply stressed husband. With Sunny Medical Supply, I can say that I had no reservations at all of their prospects, except of course their own inexperience in general and Mr. Hickey's stubbornness in particular. Mr. Hickey can always contend that keeping certain contracts with the area hospitals was in fact an impossibility, given the immense buying power of the national franchises which had recently opened, and that I purposely overstated the relationship and loyalty I've enjoyed with those hospitals. But I've gone over this ground too many ways, and each time I conclude just as Mrs. Hickey has, which is that not only should one always be wary when buying into a situation, but once committed, graciously accept all realities.

Which, presently, is that I should find Liv's metallic green Saab and so make my way home. Mrs. Hickey offers to walk me all the way to the parking lot and to the car itself, but I refuse, saying how I'm disturbed that I've already taken time away from her son. Again I shudder with the thought of having to see him with her there, her mother's presence somehow an added burden to me, as if she might spy something damning in my face. She escorts me instead to the automatic doors, and we make tentative plans again, contingent upon this and that, all of it contigent still upon Patrick and Patrick alone, and the sad and peculiar notion of waiting for a heart.

One realizes, of course, what it will mean when a heart does arrive, that another young boy or girl has come to an awful end, and it makes me think again how the conservational laws apply to human beings and their endeavors as well as to energy and matter, and that for us, those laws are often ironical and cruel. I recall Fujimori posting me from Borneo, where he and Enchi had been assigned, writing about our friend's death. I still have the letter and read it sometimes for no burning reason.

"We could not find much of his body, Jiro. It was simply not present anymore. A corporal found a thumb some sixty meters from the spot where Enchi was last standing, but there had been others who were badly hurt and we couldn't be sure if it was his. He was the only one killed, somehow. There was nothing left of him. Nothing else of shape, just tiny bits of flesh on the ground and most awfully, up in the branches of the trees. The shell must have landed right between his feet, and he disappeared. The night before, Enchi had been going on and on at the officers' club, drunkenly, of course, about living here forever in this tropical paradise. He was obviously talking against his fear of death but he was doing so with great feeling and humor, and to a man we wanted to believe him. Later that night, after a service for him and then drinking alone, I walked past the spot. It was perfectly normal, having been cleared earlier. But I heard a rustle and I looked up into the trees directly above, and in the light of the moon I could see the tree limbs filled with small birds, what seemed like hundreds and hundreds of them. They were happily picking at the leaves and branches, and rather than feeling horror for our good Enchi, I began to bellow like a cow, and I almost fell down."

Fujimori possessed a dark sensibility, which wasn't always easy for me to appreciate. If I met him today, I'm not sure what I would say to him except to offer the standard greetings and inquiries about his work and spouse and family. It's not that I would feel cold toward him, but his personality was such that he always made you consider the oddest aspects of events and happenings, and so you never felt fully comfortable saying the most innocent things, for worry how he might interpret or reobserve them. For example, I have to consider how he might cast his eye on me now, after having spoken to Mrs. Hickey and once again excused myself from spending time with her dying son. How might he describe me as I step limpidly across this wide parking lot, holding a fading bouquet of my own? What would he say if I told him I had never married, and that the girl I adopted had decided to run away rather than live with me in comfort? And would he devilishly ask why I had been so careless with the fireplace in my most precious home, as if I'd wanted to bring everything down in a self-made conflagration?

The sun has come out from a break in the clouds, and Liv has retracted the convertible top to her brilliantine emerald car. She and Renny are sitting in the front seats, backs against their doors, conversing civilly and politely, without their usual gesticulations. I slow down almost to a halt, the pace surprisingly comfortable for me, this inching septuagenarian shuffle. This is the first instance I've had of feeling my age, which does not seem so beleaguering a notion but rather a strangely comforting one, as if a voice inside me is trying to proclaim, *I accept. I accept.* It's the way one relents when walking the last half-mile of a hike in light rain, to taste the sweet of the water on your face, and not just feel its chill. Why senescence should not have its hidden charms. . . .

Renny Banerjee smiles wide now, and though I can't hear what they're saying, it's clear they're getting along, with Liv extending her hand across the center armrest, drawing invisible curlicues on the shoulder of his bucket seat. The back is a gaudy parade float of lilies and carnations and roses in varying states of bloom and wither. He sees me approaching and immediately gets out and skips around the car, taking my forearm to guide me to his seat. Liv thanks him and turns on the ignition, and Renny neatly hurdles the fender behind her, snuggling himself into the backseat nest of petals and stems.

"So, where am I taking *you,* Mr. Banerjee?" Liv says blithely.

He answers, "I thought we were going to lunch, after dropping off the Doctor."

"Who said anything about lunch?" she says, quickly turning around.

"You did, going on about the new decor at Sffuzzi's. I thought you were sending me a message that I should take us out."

"Isn't he arrogant, Doc?" Liv replies, telling me more than asking. She's ignoring Renny, her eyes set low. "He implicates himself in everything."

"I'm like you that way, Liv," Renny murmurs from behind me, a sudden warmth softening his voice.

"I guess you are, Mr. Banerjee." Liv sighs, backing the car out. She puts it in forward gear and we begin to pull away. "Too bad for you."

From the hospital to home, it's a straight shot to the northeast on the narrow, curbless two-lane that snakes in tight up-and-down turns beneath the overhanging trees. The dark green canopy is rafter-like over us, a shimmering, tattered vault of cover. Liv keeps asking if we should stop and put up the roof of the convertible, as there is a fresh edge to the air, the sky depthlessly clear, but it feels so good to me, the rushing air and the speed of the open car and the oaty tang of just-cut grass. I know again why I favor it so much here, how I esteem the hush of this suburban foliage in every season, the surprising naturalness of its studied, human plan, how the privying hills and vales and dead-end lanes make one feel this indeed is the good and decent living, a cloister for those of us who are modest and unspecial.

The road routes to an old divided parkway that is faster and tighter still, and then, in a three-mile stretch, becomes the main commercial route of 3A, the signposted six-lane strip of the town of Ebbington. Liv has been taking us forth at a brisk clip, confidently riding the yellow line, but now it's halting traffic and four-way intersections and the rattle and hum of engines; though she's irritated and Renny's nodding off, I don't mind the sudden heat and exhaust and crowd. I can't help but notice, too, that beyond the expansive parking lot to my right, there sits the bulbous, tri-domed structure of the Ebbington Center Mall, its stucco facade stained dark along the top in large, creeping patches, the spindly trees infrequent in the mulched-bark landscaping, the whole thing looking weathered and faintly marine, floating in its blacktop sea.

When it was built, there was much fanfare and optimism, and I remember reading an editorial in the local paper about how important the Ebbington Center Mall would be in bringing new vitality to the area, enticing the shoppers (especially the affluent ones in Bedley Run) to stay here with their money, rather than trek down to the city. I myself received numerous solicitations from the mall management, special inducements and incentives to relocate my store as a "founding tenant," but even as some of my fellow merchants left the old village, I took heed of the comments I'd casually hear around town from the country and tennis club set, the matrons and well-heeled young mothers, that they never went over to Ebbington and would certainly not start now. This instant, unwavering judging did bother me a little, as it naturally made me wonder what thousand other predeterminations had been made, and kept to. Still, I remained at my spot on Church Street, and proceeded to watch the mall go up and grandly open to balloons and flags and enjoy the initial flush of good business, and then, in good time, settle in to its Ebbington-land destiny of steady dwindle and decline.

This being the place, apparently, to which Sunny has returned.

And so I look there now, with the impulse of asking Liv to turn into the lot, simply to drive slowly past the columned entrance, to peer at the scant activity inside. Originally there were plans for sixty or more shops, as well as a few large department stores like Macy's or Bloomingdales or Sears to anchor the bi-level wings, but the major chains weren't interested in a lower-middle-class hamlet forty miles from the city with no major highways running near its borders. So after failed attempts by lesser retailers, there are now huge yellow banners on each end of the building, courtesy of the temporary (two-week) tenants, a clearance "wholesaler" of brandless electronics and a discount Christian bookseller, their wares hastily set out on long, folding-leg tables, with pricing by the bunch. The smaller retail spaces are only two-thirds filled, the square-foot rents now around half the price originally quoted to me. Just recently, the grand indoor waterpool leaked one night and left in its wake a dusty, fungal odor that all the pizza and enchilada and chicken stir-fry of the food court can't seem to mask. Obviously I haven't been there since speaking to former Officer Como the other day, and I'm having trouble conjuring my former daughter even setting foot in such a place (self-styled anti-capitalist as she was, or at least, anti–Sunny Medical Supply), much less being a manager of a women's better-clothing store. And if all of this is true, I wonder now about the little boy who was mentioned by Officer Como, where he is staying while his mother works, and with whom, whether it's the whole day that he's with someone else, and again I want to tell Liv to tap her turn signal, get over to the entrance lane for the mall.

But I do not. I just sit quietly in the glove-leather seat and watch as the traffic light turns from red to green, and she lets up on the clutch to sling us forward off the line, and we are running, following Route 3A again as the stores and filling stations and kiosks gradually thin out, the horizon coming visible, the golden, burnished woods rushing back, dense and stately in their towering solicitude as we reach the kempt, rolling country of Bedley Run.

Renny Banerjee, perhaps inspired, too, by the glittering canopy, is talking now about this town of ours. We're gliding on the narrow two-lane road toward the old part of the village, the edifices of the dark brick town fire station and the turreted stone post office (once a mill) nobly guarding the entrance. But he's going on somewhat bittersweetly, not at all in a way meant to perturb Liv, who everyone knows is the first champion of this place. It seems he's had a few displeasing experiences around town in the last few weeks, despite the fact that he's lived here for nearly ten years.

"I don't know what it is," he says, pulling himself forward between our seats in front, "but I've been getting the most annoying comments lately, around the village. I'm confused. It seems everyone has completely forgotten who I am."

"Everyone but me," Liv sighs.

Renny squeezes her shoulder appreciatively. "Really, though. Have you noticed anything odd, Doc?"

"Not myself. At least I don't think so."

"I guess not, for someone like you. You're beloved. But I have. Even at Murasan's. Not-quite-funny jokes."

"What do you expect at that awful smoke shop?" Liv cries out. "They're a bunch of mean old geezers. Sorry, Doc, but it's true."

"I suppose they can be a little acid," I answer. I myself had been cutting back on my visits to the shop in recent months, as I'd decided to curtail my pipe smoking to one bowl a week instead of my longtime three or four; but also, I've been finding that the conversation there, which is usually entertaining and vigorous, has been somewhat sodden of late, as the fellows have been preoccupied with perceived "changes" in the character of the town and area, changes that Renny has obviously been compelled to address.

"Last week I'm there to buy cigarettes, just an in-and-out, and old Harris, who's sitting in his usual spot in the corner, says something about the millions of new smokers in the Third World. I turned around and he just waited. I asked him if he was talking to me and he said he was interested to know what I thought about the situation. I told him I had no opinion and got my change and was about to leave when he said, 'People don't even care about their own anymore.' Then the next day I'm walking by the duck pond in the park when I approach these two mothers with their strollers. One tries to hide, whispering something, and they quickly turn away like I'm about to mug them or steal their babies. Suddenly I don't know what the hell's going on around here. I mean, hey, I want to know, since when did I become the randy interloper?"

"It's because you're darker during the summer," Liv says matter-of-factly, evidently bringing up an old topic of discussion. She turns to me, smiling. "It's a fact."

"This is different, Liv," Renny insists. "And for the record, Liv darling, I'm always this dark. You should know. But it never mattered much before. Now people like Harris and Givens are talking about the 'direction' of the town. How the shop owners aren't like they used to be, your average middle-class Italian and Irish folk. I guess except for you, Doc."

"I guess so, yes."

"Don't get me wrong. I haven't really heard a bigoted word from anybody. Just 'observations.' There's every sort of merchant in town, the Viet people who bought the cleaner's, the French-speaking black couple at the old candy store."

"So what?" Liv exclaims. "People aren't allowed to talk about who runs the businesses in their own town? What's next, Renny? Will I not be able to even say you're Indian anymore? Or that Doc Hata is a noble Japanese?"

"Of course not," Renny answers. "But why this should somehow be of the most interest, I don't know. Most people could say anything they want in this regard, and I wouldn't blink. You know that's always been my view. But it seems to me the mood has changed around here. I don't know if it's this recession and that people are feeling insecure and threatened. Bedley Run was never an over-friendly place, but at least it wasn't completely unwelcoming. Now I'm not sure. The worst part is that I'm beginning to think I should have realized this long ago, and that I've been living for years inside an ugly cloud."

"You can be so dramatic, Renny!" Liv says, guiding us into the old village proper, the shops and boutiques lined up in a comely bend of a row, one of those fine doors once mine. "Two little incidents in the same week and all of history has changed. So am I included in all this business, too, retroactively?"

"Of course not. I'm talking about something different. Try to tell her, Doc. I know you've always been happy here but at least you can partly understand what I'm describing, yes?"

"I believe I do," I say to them, though unsure of why, and now sensing, too, how physically close we three are, even in the open car. We finally pass Sunny Medical Supply on the other side of the street, its window hazy and unlighted, with nary a glint of activity. "It's true that at times I have felt somewhat uneasy in certain situations, though probably it was not anyone's fault but my own. You may not agree with this, Renny, but I've always believed that the predominant burden is mine, if it is a question of feeling at home in a place. Why should it be another's? How can it? So I do what is necessary in being complimentary, as a citizen and colleague and partner. This is almost never too onerous. If people say things, I try not to listen. In the end, I have learned I must make whatever peace and solace of my own."

"But is this a situation that's okay with you, Doc?"

Liv throws up her hands at this, the leather-wound steering wheel for a lengthy moment subtly playing on its own. "Sure it is! Come on, Renny, can we please move on now to other topics?"

"This one is interesting enough."

"Okay then. Fine. Let's look at the Doctor's *situation*. He's not in too rough a shape, having lived in this town. Bedley Run, after all, is not Selma. He's recently had some trouble, but that was just a little fire. Otherwise, he lives in a gorgeous house in the most prestigious neighborhood, and he's enjoying the high golden hour of a well-deserved retirement, for having been a business and civic elder and leader. This from *anybody's* view. I could argue that in fact, Doc Hata *is* Bedley Run. He is what this place is about. Not the doctors and investment bankers and corporate lawyers who have ample cash and want sudden privacy and the airs that go with it. Though they're my clients and I love them, I have to say they mostly have it wrong and Doc Hata has it right. You *come* to a place like this, Renny; you don't make it yours with money or change it by the virtuous coffee color of your skin or do anything but welcomingly submit and you're happy to do so. Because look. Take one look at this street. The tumbled sidewalk and shabby-chic shops. It's all simple and beautiful and proportional. It has just the right amount of history, which, for the record, is welcoming and not. It's the place you want to arrive at, forever and ever."

"I once thought forever," Renny says tightly. "That's what I thought, and it was probably because you said it just like that."

"Everything is still the same," she answers him, curling her hand back to cup his cheek. "It will always be the same, if I have anything to do with it."

We glide to the end of Church Street, going past the yarn shop and the bead and millinery store and the cleaner's Renny mentioned, whose Vietnamese owners I met only recently when I went around soliciting donations for the local boys' and girls' soccer league, which I have long and enthusiastically supported. The couple at the cleaner's didn't seem to understand, staring at me stonily and wondering why I would be requesting such a thing, to give me money for others' children to play. I did not attempt to explain how this could benefit them in the end, as I believed it had benefited me and my business, at least in feeling and reputation. The man and his wife, their faces shiny from working the clothes press and extractor, did not say no or ask me to leave; they did not reply much at all, and we three stood there in the heavy, almost tropical, starch-laden air of the shop, waiting for something to happen.

On Mountview Street the trees are just of that color and scale Liv is talking about, and though it has been but a few days, the pleasing bulk and hang of the limbs makes me homesick for what lies in wait over the first rise of the street, and I feel doubly sorry for my carelessness in overstoking the fire. Liv is perfectly right in describing to Renny what store of happy goods I possess, my house and property being the crown pieces. And though it does occur to me as somewhat unfortunate that this should be so strictly true, I cannot help but feel blessed that I have as much as I do, even if it is in the form of box hedge and brick and paving stone. There is, I think, a most simple majesty in this, that in regarding one's own house or car or boat one can discover the discretionary pleasures of ownership—not at all conspicuous or competitive—and thus have another way of seeing the shape of one's life, how it has transformed and, with any luck, multiplied and grown. And as we approach I can already see the red maple I planted in the front yard the first days I lived in the house, a mere sapling that has widened and vaulted up to be much larger than it should be, its surprising

increase mirroring, I suppose, everything else I've invested in the
last thirty years—the values of the property itself, the blue-chip
stocks I bought intermittently, the store and building I sold to the
Hickeys, whatever I put time or money into ballooning inexorably,
magically, to great reward. It seems I have always been fortunate to
be in a certain provident time and place, which must be my sole
skill, and worth, and luck.

Liv slips the Saab gently into the driveway, and Renny lifts himself from the backseat before I can open the passenger door. He'll
bring the bags and flowers, Liv announces, and the two of us will
go directly inside. She wants me to see the work they've done, she
can't wait to see what I think.

The keys (hers?) are in the door and she swings it open with ceremony. The lights are all on and there are flowers in the foyer and
kitchen and on the hall table. There is music playing, an étude of
Chopin from one of the many classical records Sunny left behind,
its sober phrases leading me to the family room, the site of the
trouble. I see there is a neat stack of split wood in the vacuumed
and polished hearth, and that the Berber carpet is new and the
same top brand as what was there before the accident, the curtains
also having been replaced, as has the singed wall board above the
mantel. The whole room has been repainted in the exact shade of
pastel moss green Mary Burns once chose for me from a special
home decorator's palette book, the window mullions, too, damp-
dusted and sparkling, and the tile floors sheened. Everything appears fresh and vibrant but unmistakably familiar, of certain and
actual living.

Which strangely haunts, because as Liv Crawford guides me
through the rooms pointing out the distinguishing features of the
renovations, I have the peculiar sensation that this inspection and

showing is somehow postmortem, that I am already dead and a memory and I am walking the hallways of another man's estate, leaning into rooms to sniff what lingering notes of his person may remain, the tang of after-shave or slivers of soap, the old wool of his coats and leather shoes, the dust and spice of the cupboards. And I notice, too, the spareness of the rooms aside from the major furnishings, the few photographs showing him among groups of five or six in business attire or settings, and none including anyone who looks like him, distantly or otherwise.

This is my very house, my Mountview house in Bedley Run, understated and grand and unsolicitous of anything but the most honorable regard, and despite how magnificently Liv Crawford has directed its exacting restoration, I cannot escape feeling a mere proximateness to all its exhibits and effects, this oddly unsatisfying museum that she has come to curate for this visitation and the many that will someday follow. I cannot blame her, for there is nothing to assign blame about. It is the case that I have not been a man who has cultivated the relations that would make such a homecoming full and sanguine and joyous, and if anything occurs to me it is deep-felt gratitude to Liv Crawford and to Renny Banerjee as well, not only for the work and the ride home and the help with my things, but for the simple fact that they are present, walking the floors, pulling knobs, speaking and moving and filling the house with the most pleasing, ordinary reports.

Anyone, too, can glimpse through the wide doorway how they are lingering over each other in the kitchen, leaning up against the island counter from either side, and though Liv keeps asking to heat up the casserole dish of chicken cacciatore that she's brought for me, I insist that I can do it myself, so they might feel free to leave and go out together and do whatever they may. Liv and Renny are in their early forties, neither having ever married, and though they're certainly attractive people, it could also be said that they are approaching a critical time of middle age, when they should make clear decisions about their living situations. Whether they continue to live alone or not isn't my interest, as I don't have purpose or reason to hold a general opinion, but I do believe that they should choose one path without reserve and stay to it until the end.

I think the source of my trouble with Mary Burns—or her trouble with me—is that although I had decided to be a lifelong bachelor, I kept finding myself straying in both thought and deed, even so much as wondering aloud to her one night if she should sell her house down the street and move her things into mine. We were sitting intimately in the family room, enjoying, in fact, a fire and our customary pot of tea. When I spoke the words she had to stop sipping and put down her mug. Her usually placid expression broke open first in shock and then pleased wonder, and I knew I had slipped most horribly. In the ensuing quiet I already sensed that cold pitch of gravity and dissolve, as though something was dying in a corner of the room, invisibly and wordlessly. I didn't actually retract my suggestion, then or in the following days, nor did I repeat it, simply hoping instead for a gradual expiration. Of course, the whole thing did expire, and without further discussion, and almost exactly in the manner one would have wished.

"Hey, Doc," Liv calls out, in an airy voice provisional and solicitous, "I finally remembered something I meant to ask you about."

I enter the kitchen again from the family room. Renny is making ready to leave, putting his wallet and keys back into his pockets, while Liv is lifting the white casserole dish into the wall oven. The cacciatore (from Di Nicola's Deli) will be my dinner, along with a demi-bottle of Valpolicella and chocolate-dipped hazelnut biscotti, wrapped in picnic cloth and tucked by Liv into a wicker basket. I don't normally drink red wine, but tonight I am feeling particularly curious and unfamiliar to myself, and all I can do is try to recall if I even have a corkscrew somewhere in this house, left over from long past evenings of mirth and company.

"I've always meant to ask you, Doc, about the piano in the family room. I had a man look at it to make sure it was all right. It's a beautiful piano. I see it every time I pop in but I'm always going on about something else. It's fairly old, isn't it? I mean almost antique."

"Yes. I bought it a few years after I bought the house. It was used, about thirty years then, so now it may qualify as an antique piece."

"I should have figured that you played."

"I don't."

"But I've heard you play, haven't I, Doc? The last time we were all at Renny's condo, before Christmas a couple years ago, you played a song on his upright."

"Perhaps fooling around, but not playing."

"You were playing! You played, and we sang. "Good King Wenceslaus," wasn't it? You're a natural entertainer. I remember you added all these wonderful notes. Everyone wanted you to go on, but you were too modest."

"I don't remember playing. I haven't played at all."

"You had a bit of the punch that night, friend," Renny says. "We all did."

"I don't remember."

"Someone may have had to drive you home."

"It's hard to believe."

Renny says to me, "I wasn't all there myself. Neither was Liv, if

I'm right about anything. She was calling herself Party Girl that night."

"And you were Party Boy," Liv fake-scolds him, as it seems certain things are coming back into remembrance. "But anyway, you were great, Doc. You just sat down without a word and started playing. That was the first night we ever met, and when you told me where you lived, I pictured the house right away, the beautiful Tudor with the slate pool. I knew we'd be friends. I knew we'd all be friends."

"Okay, Livvy, let the Doc settle in now," says Renny firmly, turning to pat me on the shoulder. He does it with great kindness, enough to make me feel a tinge paternal. "You must be happy to be home. I'm glad you are. If you need anything, you be sure to call. I left my number on the refrigerator. I'm sure you have Liv's. Really, call about anything."

"I had them put up new smoke detectors, upstairs and down," Liv breaks in. "They're hard-wired so you don't have to worry about batteries going dead. The flue was cleaned, too. It's all ready to go. It's a big, old-fashioned hearth and you can build a big fire in there."

"Too big, I suppose."

"Well, you'll be careful, I know," she says, naturally pecking me on the cheek, though it's the first time she's ever done so. She looks as concerned as I've ever seen her. "I'll stop by tomorrow, if you want. I've stocked the refrigerator with a few basics but we can pick up whatever else you'd like. You have all your prescriptions?"

"Yes, thank you."

"I know you've managed all these years by yourself, Doc, but it's nice to have a hand after spending time in a hospital. How are your shingles?"

"The shingles?"

"Your condition . . ."

"Oh, very mild now. I'm recovering quickly."

"Okay then, we're going," she says, gathering her bag and cellular phone and pager, and motioning to the foyer to Renny as though she were urging him, and she says again, "Goodbye, say goodbye, Renny." Then all the leave-takings are exchanged, the reminders reminded—of the fireplace and the oven and the new locks on the doors—and in a small caravan we all move to the foyer and open the door to the warm late afternoon light and in three breaths they are in her car and they are gone.

Upstairs, in my bedroom, I take off my clothes and change into a pair of swim trunks, the ones I was wearing at the time of the fire misplaced somewhere at the hospital. I fold myself in a heavy terry robe and descend the stairs barefoot, smelling the tomatoey, garlic-laden chicken warming in the oven. Following Liv's written instructions, I've set the timer for forty-five minutes at 325 degrees, and I open the wine (having found a brass corkscrew, a gift from Mary Burns) to let it "breathe," though this certainly makes no difference to me. The time is just past four in the afternoon, and the leaves are petaling down from the treetops to float across the surface of the pool water like a fleet of tiny, colored punts and rafts. I don't dive. The water is cool, bracing and fresh as with the first morning's swim, and I'm surprised by my strength, or the strength the water seems to lend me.

For years I would never enter water that was even slightly cool, being accustomed to the shore in Singapore and Rangoon, the tropical, bath-like waters of the Andaman Sea. In the days before the war began to go badly, my comrades and I would take trips to the beach on our leave days, to swim and play volleyball and eat fresh-caught sea porgies and spiny lobsters and eels. The natives had been instructed to prepare them with a tiny ration of shoyu and the local palm wine, an attempt intended to make us feel comfortable but which unfortunately served more to remind us of Japan than anything else, and our immense distance from it. There was (for the others) much drinking, of course, and then the usual exploits of the balmy, lanterned evenings, singing folk songs at the stars with girls who hardly knew how to speak our language.

I used to swim after sunset on those occasions, the water placid and unrippled as I pulled my way through it. I could hear the laughter and joking of my comrades, and sometimes the strained, rote blandishments of their companions, the awkward attempts at flattery and passion which seemed unbearable to me, sober as I was. But as I swam I sometimes listened for the other ones, those girls who didn't make much noise or speech, wondering at their quiescence as they lay beneath the palms of the shore, the snorting and grunting of men skipping out over the surface of the water in soft reports. Down the shoreline I would go, in my usual steady crawl, and each time I'd lift my face for air I glimpsed the limp strings of lights and the kerosene torches and the arm-in-arm straggles of youthful soldiers, joyously barefoot on their way back to the base, overfilled with wine and the mercies of fallen women.

Once, in admonishment, I mentioned to Sunny what could happen to young women who strayed from the security of their families, how they would inevitably descend to the lowest level of human society and be forced to sell every part of themselves, in mind and flesh and spirit.

"Is that so?" she answered.

"Yes, it is."

"And how do you know so much about it?" she muttered, continuing to fold her clothes from the dryer. She had returned from the Gizzi house, to stay only briefly before moving on, this time out of town completely. There had been an incident at the house, a stabbing, in fact, a week or so after I made my visit there. James Gizzi had been the victim and was in critical condition at the county hospital. His friend, the black man named Lincoln, was accused of the crime and had not been arrested, having fled Bedley Run.

I said, "I witnessed many things during the war."

She visibly paused at the notion, which was new to her, and had to refold a blouse before placing it on her neat stack of things.

"You must heed me on this, Sunny. I have seen what can become of young women. It is often unpleasant. Perhaps even more so these days than during wartime. The newspaper is filled with stories of awful happenings in the city, where girls are tricked and abused. You're going to live down there, you said."

"For now," she answered limply, going back to her laundry. "I'll probably move on."

"Where will you stay? How will you support yourself? You're only eighteen and you have no skills or experience. You'll need to work. I can't give you enough money to support you forever."

"Don't give me any then. I don't want it."

"But how will you manage? I've always provided everything for you. I'm not saying this to criticize. It is simply the truth. You haven't lived on your own. These past few weeks, for example, you've been under the care of others—"

"I haven't been under anybody's *care*," she said stiffly, her voice sharpening. She pulled the rest of her clothes from the dryer in a bundle. "You know where I've been."

I didn't answer her.

"You were by the house, I bet, weren't you?"

"I have no interest in watching you degrade yourself."

"But you came around, all the same."

"I was in the area and wanted to speak with you about coming back home. I should have known it would be a mistake."

Sunny carefully balled up a pair of red socks, her face quiet. "When did you come?"

"On just one night. There was a party. But I assume there are always parties."

"Where was I?" she asked, not looking at me directly. I sensed she was feeling vulnerable, even ashamed, the latter emotion something I had rarely seen in her, and this took strong and sudden hold of me. She said in a far-off voice, "I must have been there."

"I did not find you," I quickly told her. "I looked around the house. There were many people, and I saw things I would not wish to see again. But I did not find you."

Sunny didn't pursue this line, and I was glad, for although my aim was to warn her of the disastrous life that lay ahead if she departed so young and unsupervised, I couldn't bear to revisit the scene of that room at the Gizzi house, with the dull yellow lights and the two men and the piqued want of the faces. I had left before being subject to the sight of her being fully embraced, enjoyed by the kneeling man, and yet it was that moment's picture of her pleasure and enthrallment that lingered with me, the expression she bore for the man who knelt there, the careless, open mouth, the hips turned out, the cord of her neck like an exposed wire.

"You never talked about the war," she said, now finished with the folding. She didn't seem to want to leave the cramped laundry room. And there was a willingness and interest in her tone that softened me. This was in the period after the Vietnam War, when the young people weren't so quick anymore to denounce those who fought, but began to consider the grim and terrible price all involved must have paid.

"It's strange to think of you as a soldier," Sunny said softly. "I can't imagine you in a uniform, with a rifle."

"I only carried a pistol," I told her, seeing the chance to engage her. "It was an officer's revolver, which I never shot, save a few times for practice. I was no good, you know. I never hit anything."

She smiled at this, freely. "You still have it?"

"No, no. I think it was lost during a maneuver. And everyone had to surrender their weapons at the end of the war, so I wouldn't have it anyway."

"I thought you might have hidden it in your closet."

"What are you talking about?"

"In one of those lacquered boxes," she said innocently. "Up on the shelf. There are so many of them, I remember. I saw them when I was little."

"I never showed those to you," I said.

"That's true," she answered, somewhat sheepishly. "I snooped one day. One day, that's all. I opened one of them, and there was a piece of cloth folded inside."

"A what?"

"A piece of cloth. I think it was silk. It felt like it. It was shiny, and a little tattered, I think. I thought it was someone's, or used to be. Like a woman's scarf, though it was completely black."

"It wasn't," I snapped at her, annoyed by the picture of her going through my things. "I don't know where you learned to do things like that."

"I'm sorry, but I used to explore sometimes, when you were at the store all day. I thought you knew."

"I certainly did not. In any case, it wasn't a scarf. It was a flag. From the war."

"Fine," she said. "No need to get upset now."

"I'm upset," I told her, "because what if I had stored a pistol there, or something else dangerous, and you had found it? What if something terrible had happened?"

"I'm here, aren't I?"

"Yes, but it's like you, isn't it? You've always been smart enough to know better, Sunny, and yet you've always had to push right up to the limits of others."

"Here we go, huh?" she said, stuffing her folded clothes into the white plastic basket.

"Yes, here we go," I answered, following her out and into the kitchen. She sat down at the table, the basket at her feet, almost waiting for my lecturing. This was often her stance, not slamming her door on me or departing the house, but rather defiantly sitting there and half-submitting, too, as if taking medicine from a doctor whose diagnosis she didn't quite believe.

"I'm happy that you decided on your own to stop living at that house. But you should have come to that decision earlier, certainly, or never gone there in the first place. Your willfulness will get you hurt someday. I think you know this, and yet you persist."

"I persist," she said darkly.

"Please don't mock me. You are eighteen years old and you can show adult comportment and respect, the same I have always tried to show to you, even when you've been so troublesome."

"I've been more trouble to myself than to you, but I know you can't believe that."

"I do believe that!" I said, my errant loudness surprising both of us. "This is my point precisely. You persist in behavior, despite your own knowledge of what is good for you and what is not. You must have known what leaving here and staying at that house would result in."

"You don't know the half of it. . . ." she said sharply, the color falling from her face.

"I know enough!" I replied. "I know, for example, that you were often the only female in that entire place. I know what kind of men frequented there. Officer Como and her colleagues have records on a good number of them. When I heard of James Gizzi getting stabbed, I was almost sure that you had been hurt as well. Luckily, this wasn't so, but your fortune cannot last for long. This path is reckless, and doomed."

"Well, you don't have to worry anymore. I'm out of there, and tomorrow I'll be out of here. I'll be on my way."

"Is that man hiding down in the city? This Lincoln Evans? Are you going to meet him?"

She seemed surprised that I would know his name. She said, "It's none of your business. And I wouldn't tell you if I was going to see him. You'd just tell Officer Como, anyway."

"That man is a fugitive! He's an attempted murderer."

"It wasn't his fault!" Sunny shouted.

"How can stabbing someone in the belly not be his fault? How is this possible?"

She turned away in her chair and for a moment did not speak. Suddenly I felt afraid for her, and she said, "He was protecting me."

"From James Gizzi? Why?"

"Just forget it."

I said, "This is what happens when you offer yourself so freely."

"I never gave myself to that shit," she said, her voice breaking. "Never. And don't you say I did. It was his house, but I never wanted anything from him. I never let him touch me. He's disgusting."

"What was Gizzi doing to you? Please, you should tell me."

"It was in the morning," she said, not looking at me. "Lincoln was out getting breakfast. I woke up, and he was holding down my arms."

"What are you saying? You didn't say anything to the police. There was no mention of anything like this."

"Why would I bother?" she rasped. "Your cop friends all think I'm a whore, and they'd do anything to get their hands on Lincoln. They don't want to hear that he was helping me."

"Did Gizzi . . . did he hurt you?" I asked her. "I'll alert Officer Como, if this is true."

"I don't want to talk about it anymore," she said, picking up the laundry basket. "It's over. Nothing like that is ever going to happen to me again. I'll kill myself before it does, I swear."

She stood up and hefted the basket and went upstairs. I would have suggested something then, that she stay a little longer before moving on, that I'd be happy to close the store for the weekend if she wished to do some shopping for clothes or other things I might provide for her, but she spoke those last words with such a finality and resolve—like a grown woman, in fact, charged and right-eous—that there didn't seem the appropriate moment and space in which to offer anything myself. I was simply shocked and outraged by what she had implied, but even more, if I'm to reflect fully, I felt the drug of fear course through me, and with it the revisitation of a long-stored memory of another young woman who once spoke nearly the same words.

Sunny stayed that night at the house, though not in her bedroom. I hadn't touched or disturbed a thing in there, not her many hairbrushes, not her books or records or her posters, in fact I hadn't even cleaned or vacuumed, as I thought I should wait for her return. But instead of her own bed she chose to pull down from the closet some old quilts to make up a floorbed, spreading them three high in the family room in front of the fireplace. I sat in one of the wing chairs, somewhat to the side of her. She lighted a fire, which she always liked to do, and sat down before the small flame, blowing on it and feeding it with newspaper and kindling. When she was young, she would ask me nightly if we could light one, even when the weather wasn't cold enough to do so, and often I would oblige her. She could spend hours in front of it, letting her face and limbs grow hot to the touch, and I would have to ask that she move back, for fear of her getting burned. She never wanted to use the fireplace screen because it dulled the heat, and that night of her brief return to the house, she pushed it aside as well. I used to lecture her on the dangers of flying sparks, reminding her that even one fiery mote could set a house ablaze, but she never seemed to hear me, only propping the screen to one side, happy to shield but a small corner of the room.

It is ironic, of course, that I should have been the one who caused a near-conflagration, and put my beloved house in danger. But as with everything else, I have begun to appreciate—perhaps like my old friend Fujimori—the odd aspects of things, unsettling as they may be. Take this pool, for instance. I've always esteemed the dark stone inlay, not the painted blue surround that one sees so clearly from the sky when landing in most any American city, the azure rectangles and circles beside the dotted houses. The water in

mine appears nearly lightless, whether in bright sun or dusk, and
the feeling sometimes is that you are not swimming in water at all,
in something material and true, but rather pulling yourself blindly
through a mysterious resistance whose properties are slowly re-
vealing themselves beneath you, in flame-like roils and tendrils,
the black fires of the past.

8

WHEN I WAS A YOUNG MAN, I didn't seek out the pleasure of women. At least not like my comrades in arms, who in their every spare moment seemed ravenous for any part of a woman, in any form, whether in photographs or songs or recounted stories, and of course, whenever possible, in the flesh. Pictures were most favored, being easy. I remember a corporal who in his radio code book kept illicit slides of disrobed maidens, a sheaf of which he had salvaged from a bombed-out colonial mansion in Indonesia. Whenever I walked by the communications tent he would call out in a most proper voice, "Lieutenant Kurohata, sir, may I receive an opinion from you please."

The women in his pictures were Western, I think French or Dutch, and caught by the camera in compromising positions, like bending over to pick up a dropped book, or being attended in the bath by another nude woman, or reclined in bed and pulling up a furry scarf between the legs. The corporal had perhaps a score of these, each featuring a different scene, replete with detailed settings and whatever scant costume, and he slowly shuffled through them with an unswerving awe and reverence that made me believe he was a Christian. Of course I shouldn't have allowed him to address me so familiarly, but we were from the same province and hometown and he was exuberantly innocent and youthful and he never called to me if others were within earshot. I knew at the time that he had never been with a real woman, but he seemed to know their intimacies, as if in going through his photos he had become privy to the secrets of lovemaking, the positions and special methods and the favored styles of the moment.

I myself, up to that time, was hardly what one could call experienced, but unlike the corporal I found little of interest in the hand-sized tableaux. They held for me none of the theatrics and drama that he clearly savored in them. Instead, I was sure, they smacked of the excess and privilege of a sclerotic, purulent culture, the very forces that our nation's people and will were struggling against, from Papua New Guinea and Indonesia to where we were posted at the time, in the foothill country of old Burma, approximately 125 kilometers from the outskirts of Rangoon. The women in the photocards were full-figured, not quite young, though several of them were attractive in an exotic manner, such as circus performers who do bizarre tricks to force one's eye.

The one image I preferred was the one of the bath. It was a mostly unadorned scene. With no other props but the tub and a coat hook for the robe and towels, the staging was quite plain. A woman was receiving a bath as she stood exposed, the attendant to the side of her in the midst of sponging her long, pale back. Somehow, I always noticed the helper more than the featured bather. She was younger, and more delicately limbed, like a Japanese, though in truth it was her face that struck me. From her expression, one could think she was truly intent on washing the woman's body, as if she weren't concerned with the staging or the camera or the oddity of her own nakedness, but of her task alone.

Several times the corporal offered to give me that particular card, but I didn't want the bother and worry of keeping it among my few personal things, should I be killed and those items along with my remains be tendered to my family in Japan, as was customary. In most all cases the officer in charge of such transferrals checked the package to include only the most necessary (and honorable) effects, but one heard of embarrassing instances when grieving elders were forced to contend with awkward last notions of their dead. I feared it would be especially shaming to mine, for as adoptive parents they might shoulder the burden of my vices even more heavily than if I had been born to them, blood of their blood, as there would be no excuse but their raising of me. Troubling to me was the image of my mother, peering at the photo of the bathers, and so inescapably remembering me, and then having desperately to hide it in her cosmetics chest before my father arrived home from his factory. Still, being twenty-three years old and a man and having been only with that Madam Itsuda during my first posting in Singapore, I was periodically given to the enticements of such base things, and unable to help but step into the radio tent whenever the corporal addressed me.

"Have I shown you this new series, sir?" he said one sweltering afternoon, reaching into the back inner flap of his code book. His eyes seemed especially bright, almost feral. "I traded some of mine to a fellow at munitions. He had these. He said he was tired of them, sir."

There were several photographs, which he had pasted into a small journal book, the cardstock and image of much lower quality than the corporal's Dutch assortment. But these were pictures of women and men together, from a close-in perspective, patently engaging in sexual intercourse. I had never seen such pictures before, or even imagined they could exist. The depicted acts were crudely staged, but seemed actual enough, and the style of the photography, if this could be said, was documentary, almost clinical, as though the overexposed frames were meant for some textbook of human coitus. To my mind, there was nothing remotely titillating in them, save perhaps the shocking idea that people had willingly performed the acts while someone else had photographed them.

The corporal, unfortunately, took more than a customary delight in the pictures. He seemed to be drawn into the stark realism of them, as if he desired to inhabit them somehow. I would notice him every so often around the camp, lingering about on his own, the private journal always in his clutch. In the week or two after he had first shown them to me, I encountered him several times, each instance finding him further disheveled in appearance, wholly unwashed (and reeking most awfully, even more than the camp norm), as well as being slightly jumpy and skittish, with a scattered gaze. His face had erupted in a sudden rash of pimples. He was, as mentioned, callow and youthful, as yet, at nineteen, without much developed musculature or hair on his lip. He was the youngest boy of a fairly prominent family, whose holdings in our town included a trucking firm and an automobile dealership. He had been trained in coded field communications to take advantage of his obvious intelligence, and to avoid the likely consequences of his physical immaturity if he were an infantry regular, which would be certain injury and possible death at the punitive hands of superiors, long before an enemy confronted him.

I took pity on him because of this, though I was afraid that lurking beneath his quick mind was a mental instability, a defect of character that I was certain would lead him to a troubling circumstance. As one of the brigade medical personnel, I decided to write a memorandum to Captain Ono, the physician-in-charge, advising that Corporal Endo be evaluated and possibly even relieved of his duties and disarmed; but as with much else in wartime, it was lost, or ignored. I should have understood the corporal's strange behavior to be an alarm—for example, he had placed among the photographs of his elders in the small shrine next to his bed several of the newly traded pictures, and actually cut out certain lurid forms and applied them in a most dishonoring fashion beside the portraits of his stolid-faced grandparents. When I lingered over this personal shrine, the corporal assumed I was admiring his artistry and even offered to refurbish mine if I so desired.

This was in the early fall of 1944, when it seemed our forces were being routed across the entire region. Ever since Admiral Yamamoto's transport plane had been ambushed and destroyed by American fighter planes some eighteen months before, the general mood and morale, if still hopeful, had certainly not been as ebullient and brash as it was in the high, early times of the war, when the Burma Road fell, and Mandalay. And now with our being under threat of attack from British and American dive-bombers—though none seemed to come for us, as if we'd been forgotten—the behaviors of the brigade, and most notably of Corporal Endo, grew increasingly more extreme. Sometimes, if one stood outside the communications tent, one could hear him talking to himself in a singsong voice, pretending—as he readily admitted to me—to be a film star like Marlene Dietrich or Claudette Colbert in the midst of a romantic seduction. Of course the corporal didn't speak English, but he memorized well enough certain dramatic tones and utterances such that his gibberish seemed almost real. Others had heard him do this as well, and there was soon suspicion among some of the officers that the corporal was a homosexual, and one of the captains even asked me if in my opinion he was a threat to the other men, like a contagion that should be checked. I told him I did not think so, but that I would be watchful of his activities and make a full report.

I knew, of course, that the corporal was constituted like most men. And not because of his interest in pornography, which was all too typical and rampant around the base. His unusual conduct was, I believe, a simple by-product of the deepening atmosphere of malaise and fear. I myself had developed a minor skin condition on the lower calves, and I was treating many others for similar irritations such as boils and scalp rashes and an unusual variety of fungal infections. It seemed the whole encampment was afflicted. Corporal Endo had no such physical problems, save his acne, and so I began to consider the possibility that his expressions were of a besieged mind, one perhaps innately tenuous and fragile and now—under duress—grown sickly and ornate.

Late one evening he came to my tent behind the medical quarters and asked if he could come inside and speak to me. He had washed up somewhat, and he looked much like the corporal of old. After awaiting my permission, he sat down quietly on a folding stool. I had been reading a surgery text on fractures under the dim oil lamp, and though I was weary and about to retire, it was clear the corporal was disturbed, and so I thought it best to give him some attention. There was a trenchant, focused look to his eyes, as if a notion or thought had taken a profound hold over him and he was useless before it.

But he didn't speak right away, and so I asked him if I might help him with something.

He replied, "Please forgive me, Lieutenant. I'm rude to request a moment from you and then waste your time." He paused for a few seconds and then went on. "You've been most generous to me, and I feel I've only returned to you the most inappropriate conduct and manners. There is no excuse. I feel ashamed of myself, so much so that I sometimes wish I were no longer living."

"There's no need for such a sentiment, Corporal Endo," I said, concerned by his words. "If your shame comes from showing some of your pictures to me, you must obviously know that it was always my choice to look at them. You did not force them on me. Now, on the other hand, I would only be insulted if you suggested that I had no autonomy where your pictures were concerned, like any child. If this is so, Corporal, then you had better leave my tent immediately or ready yourself to suffer the consequences."

"Yes of course, Lieutenant," he answered, bowing his head in a most supplicant angle. "I'm sorry, sir, for the implication. But if you'll excuse me, it wasn't only the pictures I was talking about. Please forgive my insolence, but it is another thing that makes me feel somewhat desperate."

He paused again, crossing his belly with his arms as though he were ill or suddenly cold. Then he said, "You see, sir, it's about the new arrivals everyone has been talking about. It's known around camp that they're scheduled to be here soon, and I've received messages for the quartermaster that the supply transport and complement will likely arrive by tomorrow."

"What about it, Corporal?"

"Well, sir, it's not my task to do so, but I've looked around camp yesterday and today, and I haven't been able to see where they'll be housed once they're here. All of us enlisted men are in the perimeter bivouacs, and the more permanent buildings in the central yard are of course being used. I thought as one of the medical officers, you might know where their quarters would be."

"I don't see where this is any of your concern, Corporal. But if you must know, they'll probably be housed in tents, like everyone else. Where exactly will no doubt be quickly determined, but not by me. I'm not in charge of their status or medical care. That will be Captain Ono's area, as he's the chief medical officer. Anyway, none of this is a matter of great importance, particularly to someone like you."

The corporal bobbed repeatedly, his face still quite serious. "Yes, sir. Should I then speak to Captain Ono?"

"If you must," I said, feeling that I would soon grow most annoyed with him if our conversation went on any longer. But I felt somewhat protective of him, and I feared he might provoke Captain Ono, who was known in the camp for his sometimes volatile outbursts, a mien which should have seemed quite odd for a medical doctor but somehow didn't seem so at the time. In fact, Captain Ono was quite controlled, if a bit grimly so, wound up within himself like a dense, impassable thicket. A week earlier, however, he had beaten a private nearly to death for accidentally brushing him as he passed on a narrow footpath near the latrines. Ono ordered the man to kneel and in plain view of onlookers beat him viciously with the butt of his revolver, until the private was bloody and unconscious. He treated the same man soon thereafter in the infirmary, in fact saving his life with some quick surgical work in relieving the building pressure of blood on the brain. I know that the commanding officer, Colonel Ishii, had actually spoken to the captain afterward of the benefits of meting out more condign discipline, and the captain seemed to take heed of the suggestion. In fairness, it was an isolated violence. Still, I was concerned for Corporal Endo, and so I said to him: "Will you tell me what your interest in all this is? You won't find the captain very patient, if he agrees to speak to you at all. He's a very busy man."

The young corporal nodded gravely. "Yes, sir. I should not speak to him until asking you. I'm grateful for your advice. You see, sir, I was hoping that I could be among the first of those who might meet the volunteers when they arrive. If there is to be a greeting in the camp, for example, I would be honored to take part—"

"Corporal Endo," I said sternly. "There will be no public greeting or reception of any kind. You ought to strike any such notion from your thoughts. As to meeting the female volunteers, it is the officer corps that will first inspect their readiness. Enlisted men, as I've been informed, will be issued their tickets shortly thereafter, and it will be up to you to hold a place in the queue. I'm new to this myself, in fact, and so my advice is that you make do with the limits of your station and rank and fit yourself as such to best advantage. I see you are most anxious to meet the volunteers, as will be most of the men when they learn of their arrival, and so I suggest you remain as circumspect as possible. I am also ordering you not to corroborate or spread further news of their arrival. There will be time enough for foment in the camp."

"Yes, Lieutenant."

"The other piece of advice I have is that you put away all the picture cards you've collected. Don't look at them for a while. Resist them. I believe you've developed an unhealthy reliance upon them, as if they and not rice and tea were your main sustenance. Do you think this may be true, Corporal?"

"Yes, sir," he said regretfully.

"Then take my advice. Bundle them up and put them in the bottom of your footlocker. Or give them away to someone."

"Yes, sir. I'll try," he replied, his voice drawn low in his throat. "Would you be willing to take them from me, Lieutenant?"

"Certainly not," I said, anticipating him, and so, unangered. "You'll have to find somebody else. I'm already disappointed in myself for having taken an initial interest. As I've said, this is not your fault. But now that I consider it, you ought to throw them away or destroy them, rather than blighting another. There's an atmosphere of malaise in the camp, and I believe it's partly due to a host of anticipations, both good and bad."

"It's assumed the British and Americans will soon mount another major offensive, in the northern and eastern territories."

"No doubt they will. As the commander instructed the officers last week, we must all be prepared for a cataclysm. We must ready ourselves for suffering and death. When the female volunteers do arrive, perhaps it would be good if you make your own visitation. This is most regular. But keep in mind, Corporal Endo, the reasons we are here as stated by the commander. It is our way of life that we're struggling for, and so it behooves each one of us to carry himself with dignity, in whatever he does. Try to remember this. I won't always be around to give you counsel."

"Yes, sir. Thank you, sir."

"Is that all?"

"Yes, sir," he answered, rising to his feet. He bowed, but didn't lift his head immediately, and said, "Sir?"

"Corporal?"

"If I may ask, sir," he said weakly, almost as a boy would who was already fearing he knew the answer. "Will you be visiting the volunteers as well?"

"Naturally," I immediately replied, picking up the text I had been reading. "You may take your leave now, Corporal."

I didn't look up again, and he left my tent shortly thereafter. I was glad. In truth, I hadn't yet thought of the question he'd posed, and for the rest of the evening and part of the night I wondered what I would do. I had answered the way I had for obvious reasons, to assure the corporal of the commonness of all our procedures, and yet the imminent arrival of these "volunteers," as they were referred to, seemed quite removed from the ordinary. Certainly, I had heard of the longtime mobilization of such a corps, in Northern China and in the Philippines and on other islands, and like everyone else appreciated the logic of deploying young women to help maintain the morale of officers and foot soldiers in the field, though I never bothered to consider it until that night. And like everyone else, I suppose, I assumed it would be a most familiar modality, just one among the many thousand details and notices in a wartime camp. But when the day finally came I realized that I was mistaken.

THE CONVOY ARRIVED a few days after I spoke to Corporal Endo, just as he had heard reported. It had been delayed by an ambush of native insurgents and had suffered significant damage and loss of supplies. There were at least a dozen men with serious injuries, for three of whom there was nothing left to be done. Two trucks had had to be abandoned en route, and I remember the men immediately crowding around the lone one bearing the twenty-kilo sacks of rice and other foods like pickled radishes and dried fish. At the time we were still in good contact with the supply line, and there were modest but still decent rations available to us, though it was clear the supplies were growing steadily feebler with each transport. The ambush had left the truck riddled with bullet holes, and one of the sergeants ordered a few of his men to pick the truckbed clean of every last kernel of rice that had drizzled out of pocks in the burlap. They appeared as if they were searching for insects or grubs. It was a pathetic sight, particularly when the sergeant lined up the men after they finished and had them pour their scavengings into his cap, which he in turn presented to the presiding officer-in-charge.

In fact I believe the whole group of us had nearly forgotten about what else had been expected, when a lone transport drove slowly up the road. It stopped and turned before reaching us in the central yard, heading instead to the commander's house of palm wood and bamboo and thatch, a small hut-like building situated at the far east end of the expansive clearing. I could see that the doctor, Captain Ono, had just emerged from the commander's quarters and was standing at attention on the makeshift veranda. The driver stopped in front and jumped out and saluted the captain. Then he went around and folded down the back gate to the bed. He called into the dark hold and helped an older woman wearing a paper hat to the ground. She seemed to thank him and then turned to bark raspily inside. There was no answer and the woman shouted this time, using a most crude epithet. It was then that they climbed down from the back of the truck, one by one, shielding their eyes from the high Burmese light.

They were dressed like peasants, in baggy, crumpled white trousers and loose shirts. One might have thought they were young boys were it not for their braided hair. The older woman and the driver pulled each of the girls by the arm as she descended and stood them in a row before the steps of the veranda. Captain Ono didn't seem to be looking at them. Instead he stood at attention, clearly waiting for the commander to call out and have him bring the arrivals—five in all—inside for inspection. That there were only five of them seems remarkable to me now, given that there were nearly two hundred men in the encampment, but at the time I had no thoughts of what was awaiting them in the coming days and nights. Like the rest of the men who were watching, I was simply struck by their mere presence, by the white shock of their oversized pants, by their dirty, unshod feet, by the narrowness of their hands and their throats. And soon enough it was the notion of what lay beneath the crumpled cotton of their poor clothes that shook me as if I had heard an air-raid siren, and which probably did the same for every other man standing at attention in that dusty clay field.

The commander must have spoken, for Captain Ono ordered the older woman to gather the others and march them up the steps. The girls looked frightened, and all but one ascended quickly to the veranda landing. The last one hesitated, though just momentarily, and the captain stepped forward and struck her in the face with the back of his hand, sending her down to one knee. He did not seem particularly enraged. Without saying anything he struck her again, then once more, and she fell back limply. She had not cried out. The older woman waited until Captain Ono stepped away before helping the girl up. Then the captain knocked on the door. The house servant opened it and he went inside, followed by the four girls and the older woman bracing on her shoulder the one who had been beaten. The house servant then closed the door and stood outside on the veranda, his hands at his sides, stock-still as we.

That night there was an unusually festive air in the camp.

Groups of soldiers squatted outside their tents singing songs and trading stories in the temperate night air. There was no ration of sake in the supply shipment except a few large bottles for the officers, but the men didn't seem to mind. They weren't raucous or moody. Instead they beheld the drink of their anticipations. Strangely enough, Corporal Endo alone seemed in a dark mood, and he sought me out as I took my evening walk. Even then I enjoyed a regular period of daily exercise, like my morning swims later in life, to reflect on and review the day's happenings and thereby try to make sense of them, contain them so. That evening, as I wended my way along our camp's perimeter, subsumed in the rhythmic din of birds and insects calling out from the jungle, I couldn't help but think of the sorry line of the girls entering the commander's house, led by the physician, Captain Ono. They had spent the better part of the afternoon inside with Colonel Ishii, shielded from the intense heat of the day. The captain had come by the infirmary soon after their entering to inform me of my new, additional duties—that I, and not he, would be responsible for maintaining the readiness of the girls, beginning the next day. Very soon the fighting would resume (he said this with a chilling surety), and his time and skills would be better spent performing surgery and other life-saving procedures.

As I was the paramedical officer—field-trained but not formally educated—it would be more than appropriate for me to handle their care. They were quite valuable, after all, to the well-being and morale of the camp, and vigilance would be in order. He was as serious as if we had been discussing the commander's health, though for the first time he seemed to be addressing me personally, even patting me lightly on the shoulder. His general implication, of course, was that their present good condition was likely to change with the imminent visitations by the officers and noncommissioned ranks and then the wider corps of the men, and that their continuing welfare would soon present me with difficult challenges.

Corporal Endo found me just short of the far southeast checkpoint, beyond which our squads were regularly patrolling the watch. To the left of us, one could see the faintest glimmers of light filtering through the half-cleared vegetation of the perimeter; it was the commander's hut, some fifty meters away. There was no music or other sound, just weak electric light glowing through the slats of the hut's bamboo shutters. Every so often the throw of light would flicker as someone moved in front of the window. The corporal and I were both drawn to it, and as I glanced over at him I could see the tiny play of illumination in his eyes.

"Lieutenant, sir," he addressed me gloomily, "I've been thinking all afternoon about what's to come in the next days."

"You mean about the expected offensive from the enemy?"

"I suppose, yes, that too," he said. "There's been much radio traffic lately. Almost all concerning where they'll strike, and when."

"Near here, and soon," I replied, echoing what Captain Ono had pithily said to me.

"Yes, sir," Endo said, "that seems to be the conclusion. But what I was thinking of mostly again was the volunteers."

"You'll have your due turn," I said, annoyed that he was still preoccupied with the issue. "It will be a day or two or three, whatever becomes determined. In the meanwhile you should keep yourself busy. It's an unhealthful anticipation that you are developing, Corporal. You must command yourself."

"But if I can make myself clear, sir, it's not that way at all. I'm not thinking about when I'll see one of them. In fact, sir, I'm almost sure of *not* visiting. I won't seek their comforts at all."

This surprised me, but I said anyway, "Of course you're not required to. No one is."

"Yes, sir, I know," he said softly, following me as I made my way on the path that headed back toward the main encampment, directly past Colonel Ishii's hut. We walked for some time before he spoke again. "The fellows in the communications and munitions areas drew lots this morning, to make things orderly and have some excitement as well by predetermining the order of the queue, and by sheer chance I took first place among my rank. There was much gibing and joking about it, and some of the fellows offered me cigarettes and fruits if I would trade with them. I had to leave the tent then, and they probably thought I was being a bad winner."

We had reached the point on the path that was closest to the hut. The sentry noticed us and let us pass; he was a private I had recently treated for a mild case of dysentery. Again there was hardly a sound, save the sharp, high songs of the nighttime fauna. The hut, with its thatched roof and roughly hewn veranda, was the picture of modesty and quiescence.

I asked, "So why did you leave?"

"Because I didn't want to so freely trade my place in front of them," he said, his voice nearly angry. He gazed anxiously at the hut, as though the humble structure were some unpleasant memorial. "You see, sir, I've decided not to visit those girls. I don't know why, for sure, because it's true that every day I've been in this miserable situation I've been thinking about being with a woman, any woman. But yesterday after I saw them arrive in the camp I suddenly didn't think about it anymore. I don't know why. I know I must be sick, Lieutenant. I do in fact feel sick, but I didn't come to ask for any treatment or advice. I don't want my lot anymore but I realized I didn't want any of the others to have it, either. So I thought I could ask simply that you hold it for me, so none of the fellows can get to it. Some of them would try to steal it from my things, and I'm afraid I'd misplace it on my own."

He then showed me a torn-edged chit, a tiny, triangular bit of rice paper with a scribble on one side. It was nothing, or less than nothing, not even something to be thrown away. His fellows would certainly just push and jostle for their place when the time came, chits or not. But the corporal handed the scrap to me as if it were the last ash of an ancestor, and somehow I found myself cradling it. I thought for a moment he had deceived me about his virginity and was suffering from something like an untreated syphilitic infection, but I saw nothing but the straining earnestness of his narrow, boyish face. I knew he was unsteady, but now I was quite certain his mind had descended on a most infirm path. His only tempering note was how he had described the present time as a "miserable situation," an appraisal that seemed highly regular, if somewhat disloyal to our morale and cause, and which, no doubt, was undeniably true.

I unbuttoned the chest pocket of my shirt and deposited the bit of paper. I said nothing to the corporal, for I did not know what I could say or otherwise do except attend to his present circumstance as any decent and clear-thinking medical officer would. He was genuinely grateful and relieved, and he bowed almost wistfully before me, making me feel as though I had indeed come to his aid, that I had helped save him from whatever fate he supposed would befall him were he to visit the ones delivered for our final solace and pleasure. And I recall understanding this last notion. For although it was true the talk throughout the camp was still of the glorious brightness of our ultimate victory and its forever dawning reach, the surer truth as yet unspoken was that we were now squarely facing the dark visage of our demise.

Famous, of course, is the resolve of the Japanese soldier, the lore of his tenacity and courage and willingness to fight in the face of certain death. But I will say, too, that for every man who showed no fear or hesitance, there were three or four or five others whose mettle was as unashamedly wan and mortal as yours or mine. As the defenders of the most far-flung sector of the occupied territory, we understood there was little question of the terrible hours ahead of us, and it was a startlingly real possibility that every man in the camp, every soul one looked upon, would soon be dead. This, I know, was a constant thought of mine, enough that my dreams were wracked nightly by the burden of it. And perhaps even more than my own death, my nightmares spelled the chance of Captain Ono and the few other medical personnel all being killed, and that among the scores of the horribly wounded, I'd be the lone surviving medical officer, the last hope of the broken and dying.

Corporal Endo seemed all too beleaguered to me, and I began to guide him quickly past the commander's hut, his gaze almost rigidly locked upon the shuttered windows. We had gone past the hut by some thirty paces when all of a sudden he grabbed me roughly by the shoulder.

"Lieutenant . . ."

I looked up and saw that the door was open, and that the figure of a man stood out on the open porch, his hands perched on his hips. He seemed to be surveying the darkened compound, and the corporal and I both stopped in our tracks, trying not to make a sound. From the silhouette it was clearly Colonel Ishii, with his thick torso and bowleggedness and the distinctly squared-off shape

of his head. He was naked, and he was sonorously inhaling and exhaling, deeply up from the belly. From our angle we could glimpse
as well inside the two-room house, but the only sight was a clothes
trunk against a far wall and a few lighted candles set atop it. There
was no indication of anybody else being inside, no sight of the girls
or the house servant or Captain Ono, who besides being the head
physician was also something of a confidant to the commander, his
personal surgeon and counsel. Many evenings after supper Captain
Ono could be seen on his way to the commander's house, and when
directives from central headquarters in Rangoon had come concerning preparations for the inevitable enemy offensive, the doctor
was always included in the briefings.

The commander himself was someone whom these days people
might call a "health nut," as some of his ministrations were quite peculiar. For example, he would exercise vigorously in the early
mornings, an intense regimen of calisthenics and stretches that
would challenge a seasoned drill sergeant. Following this, sweating
like a plow ox, he would allow himself to be bitten by descending
swarms of mosquitoes, as a way of bleeding himself. Out behind the
hut, he would cover only his face and neck and let the ravenous insects feed freely on his belly and chest and back. One would assume
he'd have suffered terribly from malaria, as a large number of the
men did, but he seemed perfectly fit right up to the day we received
news of the Emperor's surrender, when he committed ritual sui-
cide. Captain Ono made it a point to describe the commander's
daily methods to me, I believe, in the hope that I would find them
intimidating and remarkable, and back then I probably did consider them so. I was deeply impressionable and unassuming and
full of dread, knowing little else but whatever was provided to me
by professional men like the doctor, who were authoritative and

born into an elite caste, and who seemed the very incarnation of our meticulously constructed way of life.

The colonel took a step down. He was a bit wobbly. I thought he had seen us, and I was ready to address him to avoid seeming as if we were trying to conceal ourselves in the darkness, but he bent down to peer beneath the floorboards of the hut, which was set up off the ground on short posts. After a moment's inspection he stood up and began speaking down toward the crawl space, his tone eerily gentle, as if he were speaking to a niece who was misbehaving.

"There is little reason to hide anymore. It's all done now. It's silly to think otherwise. You will come out and join your companions."

There was no answer.

"You must come out sometime," Colonel Ishii went on, taking another tack. His effort seemed almost ridiculous, given that any other commander would have simply had soldiers retrieve her, or just shot her dead with his pistol, and perhaps on another evening the colonel himself would have done exactly that. "I suppose it's more comfortable under there than out in the jungle. But you know there is food inside now. The cook has made some rice balls. The others are eating them as we speak."

"I want to be with my sister," a young voice replied miserably. She was speaking awkwardly in Japanese, with some Korean words mixed in. "I want to know where she is. I won't come out until I know."

"She's with the camp doctor," the colonel said. "To have her ear looked at. The doctor wanted to make sure she was all right."

The girl obviously didn't know the doctor was the same man who had struck down her sister. There was a pause, and the colonel simply stood there in his blunt nakedness, the strangest picture of tolerance.

The girl's voice said, "I promised my mother we would always stay together."

"You are good to try to keep such a promise", the colonel said to her. "But how can you do so from down there? Your sister will be back with you tomorrow. For now you must come out, right at this moment. Right at this moment. I won't wait any longer."

Something must have shifted in his voice, a different note only she could hear, for she came out almost immediately, slowly scuttling forward on her hands and knees. When she reached the open air she didn't get up, staying limply crumpled at his feet. She was naked, too. The clouds had scattered and the moon was now apparent, and in the dim violet light the captured sight of them, if you did not know the truth, was almost a thing of beauty, a scene a painter might conjure to speak to the subject of a difficult love. The colonel offered his hand and the girl took it and pulled herself up to her feet, her posture bent and tentative as though she were ill. She was crying softly. He guided her to the step of the porch, and it was there that her legs suddenly lost power and buckled under her. The colonel took hold of her wrist and barked at her to get up, the sharp report of his voice sundering the air. She didn't respond or move, but lay there feebly, her head lolling against the step. She was sobbing wearily for her sister, whose name, I thought she was saying, was "Kkutaeh," which meant bottom, or last.

The colonel made a low grunt and jerked her up by her wrist, and it looked as if he were dragging a skinned billy goat or calf, her body thudding dully against the step and then being pulled across the rough planking of the porch. He got her inside and a peal of cries went up from an unseen corner of the room. He shouted for quiet with a sudden, terrible edge in his voice. All at once he had become livid, and he shoved the girl with his foot as though he were going to push-kick her across the floor. Meanwhile the sentry had heard the outburst and ran around to the front, instinctively leveling his rifle on us as he came forward. I raised my hands and the sentry yelled, "Hey there!", and I realized that Corporal Endo, inexplicably, had begun to sprint back into the darkness of the jungle.

I barked, "Don't shoot!" but the sentry couldn't help himself and fired once in our direction. The shot flew past well above me, though I could feel it bore through the heavy air. There was little chance that it could have hit the corporal, or anyone else. The sentry seemed shocked at his own reaction and dropped his rifle. I was relieved, but the colonel had already come out of the house, this time a robe hastily tied around his middle, a shiny pistol in his hand. Over the sentry's shoulder I could see the colonel take aim from the veranda and fire twice. It was like watching the action through a very long lens, when everything is narrowed and made delicate. Then a questioning, half-bemused expression flitted across the sentry's face, and he fell to the ground like a dropped stone.

The colonel walked over and motioned to me with the gun to let down my hands. He had recognized me as the doctor's assistant. "Lieutenant Kurohata," he said unseverely, not even looking down at the sentry's body, which he practically stepped over as he approached me. I knew the man was dead, as one of the bullets had struck him in the neck and torn away a section of carotid artery. The ground was slowly soaking up his blood. The colonel said, "You are a medical man, are you not?" Up close the colonel was more inebriated than I had surmised, his sleepy eyes opaque. "You can help me then, I hope, with a small confusion I was having this evening."

He paused, as if trying to remember what he was saying, and in the background I could hear the chaotic shouts of orders and foot-falls coming from the main encampment. I replied, "However I am able, sir."

"What? Oh yes. You can aid me with something. I was being en-tertained this evening, as you may know, and it occurred to me that there was a chance of . . . a complication."

"Sir?"

"You know what I'm talking about, Lieutenant."

"Yes, sir," I said, though in fact I had no idea.

"They are young, after all, and likely fertile." He paused a mo-ment and said as if an aside, "And of course, being virginal, that can't protect them, can it?"

"No, sir."

"Of course not," he concurred, as if I had asked him the ques-tion. His ignorance surprised me. The colonel was in his mid-thirties, which is not old in the world, but late in the war he was practically ancient. He crossed his arms in an almost casual pose, though he kept a tight hold on the pistol, which poked out beneath one folded arm. "And yet one grows up with all kinds of apoc-rypha and lore, yes? I mean us men. A young woman naturally re-ceives guidance and training about such matters, estimable information. While it seems we are left to our own methods, each by each and one by one. To our own devices, yes?"

Immediately I thought of Corporal Endo and his interests, and then with alarm wondered where he was now, but I couldn't an-swer, as a squad of armed men came running up to us. The colonel waved them forward. The squad leader, a corporal, seemed shocked to find the lifeless body of the sentry lying in awkward repose by our feet.

"Remove him," the colonel said, prompting the corporal to

order two of his men to lift up the corpse, which they hefted by the armpits and calves. Someone gathered the dropped rifle and the bloody cap. Two other men were to remain as sentries. Soon enough they were bearing the body off, the assemblage disappearing beyond the pale ring of lamplight about the hut. I realized then that neither the colonel nor I had spoken a word of explanation to the men, nor had any of them even whispered a question.

"You'll look after this," the colonel said to me matter-of-factly, referring, I understood immediately, to the death report, which was filled out whenever time and circumstances allowed. He was not requesting that I cover for him or whitewash the situation in any way; rather, he was simply reminding me of one of my usual duties, as though not wanting me to be remiss. The next day I would note in the necessary form that the sentry, a Private Ozaki, was shot dead by a forward sniper who was sought out by our patrols but never found.

I bowed curtly and the colonel acknowledged me with a grunt. I waited while he ascended the low porch and went inside. As I started back for my own tent, I could hear him speaking again, in a calm, unagitated tone, the same way he had spoken to the one of them who had hidden beneath the house. "Look at my girls," I heard him saying, repeating himself slowly, like a father who has been away much too long. "Look here at my girls."

9

BY MID-MORNING the day was already muggy and bright. I hadn't gone in search of Corporal Endo the night before, nor did I have any interest in doing so amid the usual early bustle of the day. No one knew he had instigated the shooting, or that he had even been present, and when it was announced that patrols would be increased to prevent further sniping, I hoped he would keep quiet and let the event pass. Colonel Ishii, whom I saw during the morning exercise, seemed fresh and fit. I had not confided in anyone, for there was no one to confide in. But in truth I was more than just annoyed with the corporal. In fact I felt sure my association with him—and indeed, my continued tolerance—should come quickly to an end. I didn't care about him, or perhaps closer to the truth was that I didn't wish to care about him any longer. He had plumbed the limits of my patience, and I was sure I should be done with him.

I was also aware that a half-humorous notion about me had begun circulating about the camp. It was not so awful, but embarrassing all the same; namely, it was being joked that I was intending to become a professional mental therapist or psychologist after the war, and that I was employing Corporal Endo as a "practice patient." Of course I found the jest insulting, and to know my name was being snickered about the infantrymen's tents, but it was particularly shaming when Captain Ono casually mentioned during an inspection of the ward that I might take an interest in one of the soldiers who had just come in from the front, who had not a scratch on his body but could no longer see or hear or speak. Captain Ono had effected all manner of examination on the man, and finally ended up restraining his arms and legs and beating him on the feet with a switch. But even this had not worked, for the man just moaned torturedly from his throat, as though he were drowning in the pain.

"Why don't you sit with him awhile, Lieutenant," he had said thickly after that, his brow crinkled. "Perhaps it's only you who can reach him now."

At the time I was almost sure the captain was being serious with me, and in fact I spent a quiet hour that evening at the man's bedside, inspecting his stoic face for the least indication of sentience. It was soon thereafter I understood that the doctor had been teasing me, and I felt, for a moment, the sharp heat of anger and shame. I was a young man, yes, but one of some learning and modest position as a junior officer, and if it was true that I was trained in a military school, not having his kind of university pedigree, it still seemed somewhat unfair of the doctor to belittle me so before a ward of enlisted men. I tried not to give further quarter to the feeling. The doctor was highly skilled and noted throughout our theater of operations for his innovations in field surgery, and I hoped that I could learn from him techniques and procedures that my textbooks and manuals could only hint at, such as his preliminary forays into open-heart surgery. In this sense it could be said that I genuinely admired Captain Ono, even held him up as a model for my future career. I had known from the first moment I met him that he was a person of singular resolve and even hardness, particularly when it came to the disposition of what must always be for him the patent, terrible frailty of his patients and others under his care, but I assumed it was his necessary mode, his own way of focus and concentration.

So it was with the girls whose charge he had left to me. And they were left to me, just as the captain had instructed, immediately after the commander was finally done with them. In the afternoon, I was the one who ordered that they be housed temporarily in one of the barracks, displacing a handful of men for several nights. The final receiving house was nearly completed, being built by a crew of native tradesmen who were following specifications provided by Captain Ono. I was to oversee this as well, but there was little left to be done.

In fact, it was all but finished. The comfort house, which is how it was known, was a narrow structure with five not-quite-square doorways, each with a rod across the top for a sheet for privacy. The whole thing was perhaps as long as a large transport truck, ten or so meters. There were five compartments, of course, one for each of the girls; these were tiny, windowless rooms, no more than the space of one and a half tatami mats, not even wide enough for a tall man to lie across without bending his knees. In the middle of each space was a wide plank of wood, fashioned like a bench seat but meant for lying down on, with one's feet as anchors on either side. At the other end, where the shoulders would be, the plank was widest, and then it narrowed again for the head, so that its shape was like the lid of a coffin. This is how they would receive the men.

After their duties were over, they would sleep where they could in the compartment. They would take their meals with the older Japanese woman, who was already living in her own small tent behind the comfort house. She would prepare their food and keep hold of their visitors' tickets and make sure they had enough of the things a young woman might need to keep herself in a minimally respectable way.

I alone was responsible for their health. Captain Ono had briefed me fully. Well-being aside, I was to make certain they could perform their duties for the men in the camp. The greatest challenge, of course, would be venereal disease. It was well known what an intractable problem this was in the first years of fighting, particularly in Manchuria, when it might happen that two of every three men were stricken and rendered useless for battle. In those initial years there had been houses of comfort set up by former prostitutes shipped in from Japan by Army-sanctioned merchants, and the infection rate was naturally high. Now that the comfort stations were run under military ordinances and the women not professionals but rather those who had unwittingly enlisted or been conscripted into the wartime women's volunteer corps, to contribute and sacrifice as all did, the expectation was that the various diseases would be kept more or less in check. Certainly, it was now the men who were problematic, and there was stiff penalty and corporal punishment for anyone known to be infected and not seeking treatment. I had one of the sergeants announce final call for the camp in this regard, as I hoped to quarantine anyone who might infect a girl, who in turn would certainly transmit it back among the men many times over, but it was very close to the time of their visits and only two men came forward complaining of symptoms, both of whom were in the ward already.

I was also to examine the girls and state their fitness for their duties. I was surprised that Captain Ono had given me this responsibility, though of course he had already completed an exam for the personal sake of the commander. But as there were procedural considerations, it was up to me to ask the older woman, who was called Mrs. Matsui, to bring them to the examination and surgery room of the ward.

I had put on a doctor's coat and was sitting at the desk with several folders of paperwork that needed completing for the Captain. I usually did this work for him, though it wasn't part of my stated tasks, but that afternoon I found I had no real patience for it. The intense heat of the day seemed to bound and treble inside the room, and the stiff white coat was yet another layer atop my regular uniform. I hadn't eaten anything yet that day, because of the sticking temperature and the crabbed feeling of an incipient illness, which I knew was due partly to my shock at events of the previous night, as well as the anticipation of this present moment, which should be nothing at all for an experienced medic but was unnerving all the same.

The woman, Mrs. Matsui, poked her head through the open doorway and bowed several times quickly. She was pale and pock-faced and dressed in the tawdry, over-shiny garb of a woman who had obviously once been in the trade. She was clearly, too, a full Japanese, and the fact of this bothered me now, to see her cheapness against the line of modest girls that trailed her.

They were all fairly young, ranging from sixteen to twenty-one. At the head of them was a tallish girl with a dark mole on her cheek. She was pretty, in an easily recognizable sort of way, with arched eyebrows and a full, deep-hued mouth. The two beside her were more retiring in their appearance, their eyes averted from me and everything else; they seemed to be clinging to each other, though they weren't touching at all. The next girl, I realized, was the one who had hidden beneath the commander's hut. She had firm hold of the hand of the girl behind her, her eyes unfocused, as if she were blind.

Her sister, whom I had not seen up close until then, was the only one of them who gazed directly at me. She did not stare or hold my sight; rather she met my eyes as someone might on any public bus or trolley car, though her regard was instantly fixing and cold. She had a wide, oval-shaped face, and there was still some faint bruising along the side of her jaw and upper neck. She had been housed with the captain while the rest of them had gone on to entertain the commander; the doctor had reserved her, implying to the commander that she was not a virgin like the others, who would offer him the salubrious and then other ineffable effects of his taking their maidenhood, which to a soldier is like an amulet of life and rebirth.

But in the end, I believe, it was not that the doctor thought her to be simply beautiful. For it is a fact well evidenced that there were many attractive, even lovely girls that one could have as a soldier of an occupying army. It was a more particular interest than that, and one I think perhaps he himself could not (and would not) describe. Like a kind of love, which need not be romantic or sexual but is a craving all the same, the way a young boy can so desire something that he loves it with the fiercest intensity, some toy or special ball, until the object becomes him, and he, it. Early the first morning after the girls' arrival I chanced upon him going into this very room, and in passing the closed door I heard him asking questions of someone concerning parentage and birthplace and education. A female voice had answered him clearly and evenly, and I knew it must be the fifth girl, the one called "Kkutaeh."

I told Mrs. Matsui to ready them for examination and she ordered them to remove their clothing. They were slow to do so and she went up to the girl with the mole and tore at her hair. The girl complied and the rest of them began to disrobe. I did not watch them. I stood at the table with a writing board and the sheets of paper for recording their medical histories and periodic examinations. There was special paperwork for everything, and it was no different for the young women of the comfort house. The girl with the mole came to me first. I nodded to the table and she lifted herself up gingerly. She was naked and in the bright afternoon light coming from the slatted window her youthful skin was practically luminous, as though she were somehow lit from inside. For a moment I was transfixed by the strangeness of it all, the sheer exposed figure of the girl and then the four others who stood covering themselves with their hands, their half-real, half-phantom nearness, which I thought must be like the allure of pornography for Corporal Endo. But then Mrs. Matsui came around the front of the girl on the exam table and without prompting from me spread her knees apart.

"You'll probably see they're all a bit raw today," she said hoarsely, like a monger with her morning's call. "Nothing like the first time, right? But you'll believe me when I say they'll be used to it by tomorrow."

Her cloying tone and familiarity put me off, but the woman was right. The girl's privates were terribly swollen and bruised, and there were dried smears of crimson-tinged discharge on her thighs and underside. Mrs. Matsui had just delivered the four of them from the commander's hut, and the faint, sour odors of dried sweat and spilled rice wine and blood and sexual relations emanated from the girl. When I reached to examine her more closely she curled her hips away and began whimpering and crying. Mrs. Matsui held her steady but I didn't touch her then, nor did I do anything else but visually inspect the others. Their condition was more or less the same. I was just beginning to examine Kkutaeh, the only girl who had not been with the commander, when the door quickly swung open. It was the doctor, in his fatigues, entering the room.

"What do you think you are doing?" he said sharply, staring at the girl on the table.

I answered, "The required examinations, Captain. I've nearly completed them, and I'll have the records for you shortly—"

"I don't need *records* from you," he said, not in the least hiding his irritation. He pushed Mrs. Matsui aside, then took hold of the girl by the back of her neck. Her shoulders tightened with his touch. He was applying subtle pressure, enough so that she was wincing slightly, though not letting herself cry out.

"I need order from you, Lieutenant. Order and adherence to our code. And yet this is a challenge. Time and again, what appears to elude you is the application of principle. It is never how one acts or reacts. It is never simply efficiency. The true officer understands this. It is the keeping to certain standards which is the only guide. You examined them, yes. But in doing so you abandoned far more important principles. This examination room, for example, is a disgrace and besmirchment upon our practice." He nodded at the clothes in piles on the floor, the scattered sandals; in the course of the examinations I had completely neglected to tell the girls they could put their clothes on again.

"You perform your duties but your conduct is often still so middling. In truth, I remain unconvinced of you. Now I am to prepare for a procedure this afternoon. You'll get them out of here and ready for receiving the officer corps tonight. The comfort house is done?"

"Yes, sir."

"Then go to the rest of it, Lieutenant."

"Captain, sir," I said, glancing at the girl beside him. She was stony-faced and still grimly silent. "I have not yet completed the examinations."

The doctor was staring at the girl on the table, not acknowledging my statement. Already he seemed to consider us gone. He was a person most centrally focused, someone who—in his own mind—could almost will his thoughts and desires to bear upon the wider truth. Of course it is often in the military, where one has fixed standing, that this can be seen, but in the case of the doctor I was sure he was as unimpeachable in civilian life as he was here, in this, his surgeon's room. He had a wife and young child back in Japan, whose attractive portraits on his desk had been steady witness to scores of bloody procedures and assays and mortal extinguishments, and I thought surely that any other man would have long retired them to the confines of a drawer or private cabinet. But now here he had the girl, Kkutaeh, unclothed on the table, and was pushing her to lie down on her back, his drawn, humorless face hovering above her shallow belly.

Mrs. Matsui immediately gathered the rest of the girls and then with a swift slap quieted the one of them who was unwilling to leave her sister in the room. She was inconsolable. Mrs. Matsui and the other three girls had to work together to drag her out, her sister on the table remaining oddly unmoved, almost dead to her and everything else. Through the shouting and the clamor I removed the doctor's white coat and left it folded on the desk chair. When I shut the door I did not look back into the room.

I was relieved to be outside. I came upon the enlisted mess tent, and the steward there saw me and offered to prepare me a cup of tea, as he sometimes did in the afternoons. I sat on an upended crate and waited, welcoming the small kindness. In the corner of my vision Mrs. Matsui and the others were half-carrying the still hysterical girl in a tight formation toward the comfort house, which seemed, being newly built, a lone clean island in the growing fetor of the camp. With dusk, I knew, the officers would begin their visitations—myself as well, if I chose.

I also noticed what I thought to be the slight figure of Corporal Endo, crouched at the far end of the central yard where it gave way to dense jungle. He was sitting back on his haunches, his canvas radioman's cap pinched down over his brow to shade his eyes from the fierce late daylight. He must have seen me but he did not wave or nod or make any gesture; he appeared to be surveying the goings-on, particularly the troop of girls making their way to Mrs. Matsui's tent behind the comfort house. Perhaps he had been waiting for them to come out from the medical hut, or perhaps he had just then crouched to rest, the timing being mere coincidence. Whatever the case he would later not say to me or anyone else. And thus what he committed next is also a mystery.

He rose from his crouch and began a medium trot toward Mrs. Matsui and the girls. The initial distance between them was not too great, perhaps sixty or seventy meters, and I was able to see the whole of the event, from start to end. The corporal was not a natural runner, lacking any real physical gifts, and he could have appeared to be awkwardly exercising, oddly stretching his legs, though hardly a soul was exerting himself any more than was necessary those days, given the shrinking rations of food and fresh water and the sapping seasonal heat. Some small part of me probably fathomed what he intended, and yet I simply watched the scene like a disinterested spectator, whose instant glint of prescience is somehow self-fulfilling.

The corporal approached and ordered them to halt. I could only partly hear them—the supply transports were being fueled and sent back to the south—though I could gather that Mrs. Matsui was objecting to what Endo seemed to want, which was an immediate private audience with one of the girls. As if to counter his rank she motioned back to the medical hut, but he pushed her aside, the girls falling away except for the one girl they were holding. She fell weakly to her knees, and it was Endo who raised her up with a stiff pull. She was not fighting him; in fact, her gait seemed to lighten, as if he were an old acquaintance and she was pleased to see him. Some men by the trucks had noticed the commotion and began calling to him, asking what was he up to, but shouting it in a hearty, knowing way. He ignored them and dragged her along quickly, until they reached his original position at the edge of the bush. When the two of them disappeared into the dense foliage and did not come back out for several minutes, the corporals and privates working near the trucks began to jog over, and it was then that I knew something irregular had occurred. I slipped beneath the netting of the mess tent and slowly made my way across the dusty red clay of the yard, past the officers' quarters and privy, then past the narrow comfort house, its walls rough-hewn and unpainted and smelling of fresh-cut wood, to where the canopy rose up again and the shade cooled the air. My legs felt unbearably heavy, and infirm. They were gathered there, in the trodden entrance of a patrol trail, the half-dozen or so men and the couple in their midst, him sitting on the ground with her lying down beside him.

She was dead. Her throat was slashed, deeply, very near to the bone. She had probably died in less than a minute. There was much blood, naturally, but it was almost wholly pooled in a broad blot beneath her, the dry red earth turned a rich hue of brown. There was little blood on her person, hardly a spatter or speck anywhere save on her collar and on the tops of her shoulders, where the fabric had begun blotting it back up. It was as though she had gently lain down for him and calmly waited for the slashing cut. The oddity was that he was unsoiled as well, completely untouched. There was nothing even on his hands, with which he was rubbing his close-shaven head. Repeatedly I asked him what had happened but he did not seem to hear me. He merely sat there, his knees limply splayed out, his cap fallen off, an errant expression on his face, like a man who has seen his other self.

Finally someone asked me what they ought to do, and as I held rank, I told the men to take Corporal Endo under arms to the officer-in-charge. While I stood at the edge of the trail they led him off. I recall myself, now, as having remained there after Endo had been escorted away. I ordered some others to fetch a stretcher for the girl's body, and after a few moments, I was left alone with her. In the sudden quiet of the glade I felt I should kneel down. Her eyes were open, coal-dark but still bright and glassy. She did not look fearful or sad. She was no longer in mourning. And for the first time I appreciated what she truly looked like, the simple cast of her young girl's face.

Endo was kept that night under close watch, and after a brief interrogation by Captain Ono, he confessed to the deed. The following morning, just after dawn, under witness by the entire garrison, he was executed. Mrs. Matsui was present, and the girls, as was the dead girl's sister, Kkutaeh, who looked upon the proceedings without the least affect. She stood somewhat aside from the others. The officer-in-charge announced that Endo had been charged not with murder, but with treasonous action against the corps. He should be considered as guilty as any saboteur who had stolen or despoiled the camp's armament or rations. Endo looked terribly small and frail; he was so frightened he could hardly walk. They had to help him to the spot where he would kneel. By custom he was then offered a blade, but he dropped it before he could pierce his belly, retching instead. The swordsman did not hesitate and struck him cleanly, and his headless body pitched forward lightly, his delicate hands oddly outstretched, as if to break his fall.

10

ON ANY SATURDAY MORNING in the Village of Bedley Run, one can see everywhere the prosperity and spirit and subtle industry of its citizens. There are the running, double-parked cars in front of Sammy's Bagel Nook, where inside the store middle-aged fathers line up along the foggy glass case of salads and schmears with chubby half–Sunday papers wadded beneath their arms, impatiently waiting for the call of their number. There are the as-if-competing pairs of lady walkers, neon-headbanded and sweat-suited, marching in their bulbous, ice-white cross-training shoes up and down the main avenue, strutting brazenly in front of the suddenly tolerant, halting weekend traffic. There are the well-dressed young families, many with prams, peering hopefully into the picture window of the Egg & Pancake House for an open table, and if there isn't one, strolling farther down Church to the birchwood-paneled Bakery Europa, the fancy new pastry shop where they prepare the noisy coffees. And all over the village is the bracing air of insistence, this lifting breeze of accomplishment, and whether the people are happy or not in their lives, they have learned to keep steadily moving, moving all the time.

Though I shouldn't, given the doctor's strict orders of convalescence, I now drive through these Saturday streets for perhaps the thousandth time, slowing at the pedestrian crossing and then by my former store, which should be open for customers at this hour but is instead shadowy and shuttered. I notice that a royal-blue-and-white Town Realty sign—PRIME RETAIL & APTS FOR SALE/LEASE—has been placed in the window case, and the name of the agent on the bottom is of course Liv Crawford, whose multiple phone numbers in bold lettering, despite my resistance, I have somehow accepted into memory.

The second-story apartment windows are dark as well, but curtains are up and the Hickeys' car, a red Volvo station wagon with rusty wheelwells, is parked at the curb. In the past two weeks I've been home, I haven't heard a word about the store or the Hickeys, or news about their son, and I've been too afraid to call the children's ICU to find out what, if anything, might have occurred. I don't wish to hear the nurse's voice stiffen and lower. I don't wish to hear her ask if I am family. During the quiet, inactive hours I've been stuck inside the house, I've been thinking again, too, of what it would mean for Patrick Hickey to survive, of the awful accident or gradual demise of another young boy or girl with the exactly right heart, and I begin to imagine—or even hope—that the necessary and terrible thing will happen, just come to pass, for it seems that if there should be a price to pay for darkly willing an innocent person's fate, I may as well pay it, and not the beleaguered Hickeys, who must endure constant torment by such conflicting thoughts.

I didn't even hear about the store being available from Liv Craw-

ford, who probably thinks I would find it too disturbing in my recovering state to learn that Sunny Medical Supply has finally gone
out of business. Well, I do. It's not that I believed the shop would
be there forever, or become a village institution, but I did hold out
hope of the store's being passed along in the coming years, if going
by a different name, from the Hickeys to whomever and whomever
else, a humble legacy that a decent man had once begun and built
up and nurtured. In fact, it becomes even more troubling a notion
to consider how quickly the memory of the store will fade away,
once it reopens as something else, say a bookshop or a beauty salon,
and how swiftly, too, the appellation of "Doc Hata" will dwindle and
pass from the talk of the town, if it's not completely gone already.
I realize, probably too late, that I wish to leave something of myself,
a small service to Bedley Run, and not simply a respectable head-
stone, but after seeing the generic, forlorn closedness of the store,
I feel precipitously insubstantial behind the wheel, like an appari-
tion who has visited too long.

But I am bolstered by Liv Crawford, whom I haven't actually
seen in some time but whose daily contact with me is most regular, in the form of a different catered box dinner delivered each afternoon by her new assistant, Julie, a cheery, bouncy young woman
whose talk and dress are uncannily like Liv's. Yesterday it was mous-
saka from the Aegean Shack, with flatbread and a Greek side salad,
and though I've asked Julie to please tell Liv this catering must
cease, when the doorbell rings at six o'clock I find myself swiftly
ambling to the door, my senses keen for what Liv has decided on
that day, whatever delectation and surprise she's thought to order
for me. In fact, I think I have never enjoyed such a range of dishes,
or known they could be had in the immediate area, though even
more satisfying than the cuisine has been the simple idea of Liv

taking a few moments from her busy afternoon to think of me. For a long time, particularly after Sunny left, I was certain that I would never get to enjoy the pleasantness and warmth of this kind of filiation and modest indulgence, and had resigned myself to a bachelor dotage of one-pot meals and (if careful) one-log fires and the placid chill of a zone-heated house. And I wonder if the spartan clime and space I've carefully arranged for myself has nearly shut me off, made me believe I ought never need to know what a sweet acceptance it can be, what good true ache can come by the door-to-door delivery of a hearty casserole in foil and a half-bottle of fruity red wine.

In this regard, I suppose, I feel as if I have been warmly taken up, in some manner adopted by Liv and then also by Renny Banerjee, who called on me two evenings ago to see if I was "getting enough rest." He was his customary bright and lively. Of course his stated intentions could not mask the real reason he stopped in, which was to spy out whether I was possibly growing gloomy and depressed, as can often happen after a physical trauma or accident, and particularly to someone of my age. Renny did not call beforehand but rather showed up just after seven, I thought perhaps to see if I was really eating my Liv Crawford meal-on-wheels, or was in fact spooning most of it down the disposal, as might an old injured man with no more savor. I happily invited him in, and we sat at the kitchen table. Before eating I had changed into pajamas and a robe, and Renny seemed to consider my dress, patting me on the shoulder, as though he were wondering if I had never changed out of them, or had just risen from an unhealthfully long daytime nap. He had just come from work at the hospital, and I urged him to take off his suit jacket and tie and have the rest of the wine, only a third-glassful of which I was able to drink. I rose to get him a goblet but he jumped up first and went to the cupboard, lingering for an instant over the sink, where dirty dishes and utensils from dinner (and lunch, and the dinner before) lay half-submerged in a bath of filmy water.

"Your color seems real good, Doc," he said, patting about his own chin and cheek. "You look like you're coming along great. Just great."

"I feel pretty good. Though I'm not swimming or taking my walks yet."

"But you will soon, right? I guess we've got maybe a few weeks of good weather left, and then it'll all turn to crap. You'll have to join a club or something. I think Liv belongs to a posh one in Highbridge, and I'm sure she'll get you initiated, or whatever they do."

"You don't do that yourself, Renny?"

"Are you kidding me, Doc? Renny Banerjee? You know me, if there's anything I do after work it's straining my elbow at O'Donnell's on Church Street."

"Or paying visits to the area shut-ins," I added, feeling a bit humorous, and maybe even sharp.

"Now please, that's unfair," he cried, smiling widely at me, loosening the knot of his tie. He took a big, washing gulp of the Beaujolais. "I come of my own accord. Really. Not even Liv put me up to anything, at least not in regard to you. Toward the end of the day I just thought, 'I want to say hello to Doc Hata.' So here I am."

"I'm happy you came, Renny. Please don't let me suggest otherwise."

"Certainly not," he said brightly. "Well, what's it been, almost two weeks now? You sound fine, and you haven't coughed since I've been here."

"I do, but just a little in the mornings."

"That's expected. But no fever, or infections, no other complications, right?"

"I'm fine. You should be my doctor, Renny."

"I probably should! I don't think you're fragile. My medical philosophy is that after troubles, one resumes the normal routine, as long as it's not totally damaging. I tore up a knee some years ago, when I used to play squash, and for months afterward I religiously did my physical therapy, and then I even changed my diet, and soon after that I stopped smoking and drinking. I was so completely wrapped up in fixing myself, fixing my weak knee, that I began to discover all sorts of other infirmities, and potential ones. I was so health-conscious that I felt sure I was becoming utterly decrepit. This of course coincided with something of a life crisis, and also my first go-round with Liv, and I can tell you she was a monster then, not like now. Not a good combination, you'll know. So it's no surprise I became quite deeply depressed."

"You?" I said, having some difficulty imagining the ebullient Renny Banerjee sitting in a darkened room, dolefully rubbing his face.

"Absolutely. I never told anybody. I don't go to doctors, you know. But I got bad enough that I asked Johnny Barnes to put me on something."

"He's only a pharmacist," I said. "He could have gotten in big trouble."

"He's a good man, Doc. Anyhow, after a couple weeks I stopped taking them. You know what I did? I said hell with a perfect knee and I didn't bother anymore. The thing clicks a little but it's okay. I can run around. And the meds were giving me another problem, of a performance nature, and there's really nothing more depressing than that for a still youngish man. So I go back to eating animals and smoking and drinking, back to the way it was and always should be. Back in my own skin, you'll know. But you can see this."

"Yes I do," I told him, appreciative of his friendly disclosures. And I began to glance about the kitchen and family room, and in my mind's eye back to the hall and parlor, and I put myself in Renny's place, or Liv's assistant Julie's, to consider if on initial impression there were obvious indications that I was conducting myself differently since coming home. It was true that I had not been swimming or walking or doing much of anything outdoors, not even the early raking and planting or the minor restorations about the house and garden. But someone who knew me would probably wonder about the unswept walk or the dishes in the sink or the pile of held mail in a bin by the door that hasn't been gone through yet, despite sitting there for a week. If they went upstairs, they would see several hampers of laundry to be done, my bathroom basin and tub and toilet in dire need of a scrub, and all kinds of robes and towels hung over the doors. Perhaps most other seventy-odd-year-old men of decent means would have the usual help, especially in a house as large as mine. But I've never required it even when I was running the store full-time, as I've always been active and vigilant and perched right atop the ever-threatening domestic entropy and chaos. Though now, or in the recent now, I've begun to understand how easily one can stand by and watch a pile of dross steadily grow, allow the fetter of one's quotidian life to become an unwieldy accumulation, which seems somehow much more daunting to clear away once it has settled, gained a repose.

"You probably don't see, Doc," Renny said, pouring out the rest of the small bottle into his glass, "how critical and difficult it is for me to remain my own wretchedly constituted self. Particularly now that I'm back with Lightning Liv. Yes, it's true. We're at it again. Just a few weeks now. You could say I hold you solely responsible."

"It can be said I lighted the fire," I murmured, going to the pantry in the hope of finding another bottle for him, which I did, a crusty-looking Italian-style wine in a basket. He gave me a thumbs-up, and a sly Renny grin for my modest joke. I said to him, "I hope you know I'm very pleased for you both."

"I know you're happy about the development, Doc, but what about us? We're sort of thrilled about it all, sure, but also definitely miserable again, like we're sharing the same low-grade fever. At least I am. To tell the truth, I'm not sleeping so well at night, and I'm not talking about when we're together. I'm a nervous wreck, thinking about all the things Liv is talking about me doing."

"What kinds of things?"

"Oh, it's a mess, you'll know." He had pulled off his tie and was winding it around his hand, then letting it unravel. "For starters, she has me looking around for a better, bigger job. But really I don't want a bigger job. She thinks I've settled, gotten too comfortable at the hospital. I say what the hell is wrong with too comfortable? I've got a pretty much worry-free system for myself. Next thing she brings up is how I should sell my condo and buy a real house. And what a 'real house' really means scares me. Liv herself is one big stressor, with a host of others ready in her pockets. She's MIRVing, Doc, targeting me all over."

"She has much warm feeling to offer, I think."

"I know, I know. You're absolutely right. You know what she said last night at my place? You won't believe this. She's talking about the big one. 'Renny,' she says, 'I'm going to be forty-two in a few weeks. I'm past my time.' I didn't answer her, because you'll know,

Doc, I was sort of scared to awful death, and then she gets up from bed and goes to the bathroom and starts to cry. She comes back with a washed face and she turns out the light and just clings to me, real tight. I didn't get a wink of sleep."

"She would like to get married?"

"Oh, God, no. I can't believe that. But maybe everything just short of it. This morning she's got that farness in her eyes, staring at me over her coffee mug, the I'm-closing-this-one-if-it-kills-me look. Doc, I feel my life passing before me."

"If I may say something, Renny, it seems that perhaps you might want some of the same things as Liv. . . ."

Renny didn't answer right away, helping me instead with the screwpull, as the cork was old and crumbling. When he finally got it open he poured it out and I could see from his expression that the wine was no good anymore, if it ever had been. It was brownish and a bit cloudy. But I had nothing else in the house and Renny poured a full glass anyway, and I found him some pretzels to mask the taste.

"I've never been against having children or getting married, never. But in my imagination I assumed it would be with a woman not at all like Liv Crawford. Not at all. Maybe I'm more traditional than I know, but I thought it would be someone more like your late friend, Mary Burns. I didn't really know her, of course, but this is what I thought. A woman with a quiet grace and stature. But not in the least unproud. Someone who couldn't *help* but be a good mother. Now Liv is quite a woman, a real bolt of light, but I'm not so sure she's motherhood material. Not just from my point of view, but hers as well. She's right about running out of time, but I'm afraid she's just doing this because it's a final opportunity, like coming across a good house whose owner is in danger of foreclosure, just automatically plowing ahead because there's no other reasonable option. I may be too hard. But should I be the one to plow ahead with her, Doc? I think yes, certainly, I will, I will, and then, definitely, absolutely, not. You'll know how this is making me quite upset."

I could see that, but Renny Banerjee is a fellow who never appears too perturbed. He drank most of the bad bottle of wine and ate the entire bag of pretzel twists, and I would have improvised something more substantial for him to eat, but he had dinner plans with Liv.

On the way out he noticed the full bin of mail and picked it up for me and asked where I would like it. Usually I opened mail at the desk off the kitchen, and so he walked back in and put it down, and suddenly he had his jacket off and sleeves rolled up and he pulled up another chair. "Let's get this done," he said, taking a fat handful. He did the work quickly, first sorting out the fliers and bulk mail and solicitation letters, then separating the bills and credit card statements and other semi-important notices from the other first-class letters and cards, of which there were quite a number. He held one up and I nodded and so he opened it, calling out the name, and then he went through the rest like that, cards from the florists, and from the deli woman, and from practically every other merchant on Church and Main streets who had been there at least a few years, long enough to know who I was. There was a card from the Hickeys, or Mrs. Hickey, with a little "Patrick" scratch. There was one from Liv, and then a few sent by her competitors at Century 21 and Better Homes and Prudential, who also called me periodically and were likely keeping abreast of my general state of health. There was a card from Mr. Stark at Murasan's Smoke and Pipe, enclosed with a small packet of my favorite tobacco, which I gave to Renny, who has taken up pipe smoking to go along with his cigars and cigarettes. And finally there was a get-well card from no one, subdued in style with only slightly curled script lettering, without even a signature or "Dear . . ." handwritten around the poetry/sentiment, just a blurred red postmark on the envelope and no return address.

After throwing away the junk mail and stacking the bills in order of payment, Renny carried the bundle of cards to the family room, where he and I set each one up on the mantel, so that it looked almost like Christmastime, when I still receive many cards from around town, though the number grows steadily smaller each year. He seemed quite satisfied with our work. "I wouldn't bother trying to respond to all these," he said. "There are too many. Besides, no one expects it. Just say thanks to everyone you see again in town. That'll do, you'll know. Just step out and go around and say how you feel."

I WANT TO DO that very thing now, of course, slow at each door and awning and window case and flip down the passenger-side window of my old and lumbering gray Mercedes coupe and perhaps not so softly call out my general gratitude for the collegial thoughts and kindnesses, but it's the selling hour, after all, and what would I be doing but disturbing the bustling morning of the town's activity by showing myself in an odd one-man parade that evokes no one's great nostalgia or longing. Even with a mantel full of cards, I know that more often than not in the past few years of my retirement, I've found the collective memory here to be shorter than I wished to believe, and getting shorter still. I've gone from being good Doc Hata to the nice old fellow to whoever that ancient Oriental is, a sentence (I heard it whispered last summer while paying for my lunch at the new Church Street Diner) which carries no hard malice or prejudice but leaves me in wonder all the same. For while I'm certain this sort of sad diminishment befalls every aging gentleman and -woman, and even those who once held modest position in the town's day, I am beginning to suspect, too, that in my case it's not only the blur of time and modern life's general expectation of senescence, but rather the enduring and immutable fact of what I am, if not who; the simple constancy of my face. I must wonder then, too, whether a man like me should be happy enough with the accrued comforts of his life, accepting the minor losses, or else seek out those persons who no matter how sharp their opinion or emotion at least know him in all his particulars.

And so as I come upon our poor-cousin town of Ebbington, with its shut-in facades and littered sidewalks and grubby rash of convenience stores, I'm struck low with the thought of where I am actually going. Winding around the main traffic circle and then down the commercial strip to the Ebbington Center Mall, the place where my erstwhile daughter now makes her living, I think back to yesterday morning, when I called the store, a Lerner's, and asked for the manager. After a long pause a voice came on to say, "Yes?" with hardly anything but the most solicitous tone, rising and heedful, the pitch of the word so terribly willing, and thus for me unanswerable, that I gently put down the handset.

It was Sunny, of course. And from the silent lingering, I was sure, she had sensed it was me. For the rest of the day and evening I tried to set the house right again, following Renny's lead with my bin of mail, but somewhere in the course of the good, mundane work I had to rest for what first felt like a shortness of breath. Dr. Weil had warned that I might experience very brief episodes of asthma-like attacks, but the sensation was sharper than that, not like a constriction but a pointed, burning ache deep in the square of my chest, like a rifle shot passing cleanly through. And then, as swiftly as it struck, it was gone, leaving me half-gasping with my temple pressed against the divided panels of the French patio doors, to gaze outside at the late summer colors gloriously burnished by the majestic, clarified light that should, by most any account, be guide to my life's last sweet dawning.

But the light, alas, is not. Rather, as I now make my way down the half-empty commercial boulevard, the traffic signals all changing to green so that I can hardly slow down or delay, the brightness seems hard and scrutinizing, everything I look upon appears over-real and starkly patent. To my dismay, I've arrived in what seems half the usual time. It being just after ten, the immense mall parking lot is practically deserted, save the hulking, older-model and econobox cars of the store employees, which sparsely line the far periphery in a gesture to the large weekend crowds that have long gone elsewhere. I pull in across the wide stretch of blacktop and although I have my choice I park perhaps a dozen spaces from the open spots nearest the entrance, and I wish I could obscure myself somehow as I walk to the grandly hideous, domed building, the lone customer heading inside.

The mall, everyone knows, is failing. There are other shoppers, of course, perhaps ten or fifteen wherever you look, but only a few are holding store bags of purchases. Mostly it's single parents or teens who have bought an orange drink or cinnamon bun at the food court, strutting about for nothing better to do, or the people my age and beyond, who gather beneath the central glass dome of the mall, sitting on the benches set beneath the artificial palms, which replaced the real ones that looked wretched from Grand Opening day and finally died last year. The old folks await an early lunch, then will take a slow stroll or sit again to watch the passersby until the middle afternoon, when they'll drive home before the rush hour and shut their eyes for a nap. The sense here, unlike in Bedley Run, is not of brisk and free commerce but rather the near-sickly, leaden atmosphere of a terminal, where people wait and linger under the fluorescent lights and kill time in any way they can.

At least a third of the shops are vacant, the bath and linens store gone under and the oak furniture place, too, and across the sorry divider of plastic ferns the Waterbeds Plus is in the midst of a closing sale, drastic final markdowns and reductions. The few notes of life in this wing come from the bulb-lettered signs of the Dollar Store, which is always in disarray and crowded with children, and the floor-to-ceiling display of the T-shirt and baseball cap seller, and the windows of the fish and pet shop, where dirty puppies climb and tumble over one another to scratch at the thick glass. There is the forlorn plastic playground of the Kiddie Kare hastily set up inside yet another empty store, and where the clock shop used to be, several Middle Eastern–looking men are papering the entrance with cardboard cutouts of goblins and cats and maniacal pumpkins, and unfurling a banner announcing the grand opening of their (temporary) store of Halloween gifts and costumes and crafts. There's more than a month to go, but a few children already stand by reverently watching them slide their ladders from side to side as they trim the windows with black and orange crepe paper ribbons, hanging witches and skeletons.

The effect is festive, at least, a lively contrast to the dank grimness of this place, even if it is morbidity being celebrated. Perhaps it's the most the Ebbington Center Mall can hope for now, the commemoration of pretty much anything. As I make my way down to the far wing where the Lerner's is, the running skylights above dingy with neglect, the dark water stains creeping down the plaster, I am suddenly overwhelmed by a tide of pure and awful feeling. And so the questions beg: Is this the place where her child must play? Is that the seat where she takes her day's break or lunch? Is this all the world she would have, so as not to be with me?

When Officer Como casually mentioned at the hospital that she had seen Sunny, I instantly saw in my mind the picture of her at the age when she first came to me. A skinny, jointy young girl, with thick, wavy black hair and dark-hued skin. I was disappointed initially; the agency had promised a child from a hardworking, if squarely humble, Korean family who had gone down on their luck. I had wished to make my own family, and if by necessity the single-parent kind then at least one that would soon be well reputed and happily known, the Hatas of Bedley Run. But of course I was over-hopeful and naive, and should have known that he or she would likely be the product of a much less dignified circumstance, a night's wanton encounter between a GI and a local bar girl. I had assumed the child and I would have a ready, natural affinity, and that my colleagues and associates and neighbors, though knowing her to be adopted, would have little trouble quickly accepting our being of a single kind and blood. But when I saw her for the first time I realized there could be no such conceit for us, no easy persuasion. Her hair, her skin, were there to see, self-evident, and it was obvious how some other color (or colors) ran deep within her. And perhaps it was right from that moment, the very start, that the young girl sensed my hesitance, the blighted hope in my eyes.

The Lerner's, I'm relieved, has fared much better than most of the stores. It's clean and tidy, for one thing, the display window sparkling and warmly lighted, the wide marble-tiled entrance spotless and waxed. It's just how I would try to keep it, were it mine, and for a moment I allow myself the thought that I've bestowed at least this tiny scruple on Sunny, from years of example. I can't see back to the main island register because I'm sitting on a bench one store down, happy to watch the steady traffic of women (and their children and some men) go inside and come out. The clothes in the store look to me eminently respectable, of conservative styling and subdued color, not too fancy or too cheap, the blouses and pantsuits and skirts of office managers and junior executives and the young real estate agents who aren't Liv Crawford quite yet. Part of me still can't accept the idea of Sunny running this kind of squarely middle-class franchise, or for that matter running any kind of business at all, and then one so expansive and peopled and professionally staffed. From this bench, lodged behind the cover of broad leaves of faux tropical plants, I survey the saleswomen working the floor, guiding customers to changing rooms with armfuls of clothes, offering other sizes and colors, this active squad she's charged with certain missions for the day. And it's almost too much for me, too felicitous perhaps, to imagine the fantastic idea of what Sunny Medical Supply might be instead of half-emptied and shut, what kind of vital, resplendent establishment could have been built, not for pride or for riches but a place to leave each night and glance back upon and feel sure would contain us. For isn't this what I've attempted for most all of my life, from entering the regular school with my Japanese parents when I was a boy, to enlisting myself in what should have been a glorious war, and then settling in this country and in a most respectable town, isn't this my long folly, my continuous failure?

Sunny, I am partly relieved, is still nowhere in sight. There is no reason of course she should necessarily be working today. But now I'm moving again, this time, finally, to the store itself, drawn in past

the airy entrance to a fragrant, music-filled space. I'm greeted by
a redheaded saleswoman who smiles and quickly checks around to
see if there's someone who looks to be mine, a daughter or a wife.
At the main register there are only two other employees scanning
items for the shoppers. One of them has ASST MANAGER printed on her
name badge, and I take a place in the line she's serving. Although
my hands are empty and I'm the lone man, I have only one question for KARI, who looks too young to be assistant managing, with
her stooped, spindly shoulders and frosted razor-cut locks, which
I learned at the hospital from Veronica Como is the popular style
these days.

"May I help you?" Kari says breathily, trying her best to sound
energetic and eager.

"I wondered if the manager is in today."

"Oh, sir, I can help you," she immediately says, leaning forward
and glancing over my shoulder at the line of women behind me. On
her collar I see she has a small, rectangular button with a very
contemporary-looking portrait of Jesus, under which it reads *Luv
Conquers All.*

"What can I do for you?"

"I had hoped, actually, to speak in private with the manager."

"Oh," she says, suddenly looking closely at me, and her face
brightens. Her voice changes, sounding more girlish and casual.
"Sure. Are you related? You must be."

"Yes," I say, amazed to hear myself answering such a question.
"We are."

"You sort of look like it!" she announces, for some reason excited. "Neat. Because she's usually not here on Saturdays until three.
But she said she would be in early today, around eleven, and then
leave early, too, so I'll have to do double-shift and close up. She

should be here in ten or fifteen. It's been really busy, actually. You can sit on the couch and wait, if you want. Hey, are you Sunny's uncle or something? Are you visiting from out of town?"

But I don't answer, or can't, as I've already turned back around and gone straight out to the mall, walking with all the speed I can muster, almost skipping into a trot, and I feel my chest start to ache and then balk, and before I know it I'm staring at the tops of my knees and the dirt-colored tile floor and coughing as though it's for the sake of my very life. And then, too, it is a nearly wondrous sensation, between hacks, for just as I've expelled every last ounce of breath, nearly coughed out a whole lung, there's also a feeling of something like purity again, a razing and renewal, as if I might wholly banish all that I was just a moment ago. It reminds me of swimming the final length of a morning, when in those last yards one refuses to take air, as if becoming something else, almost half-dying in the crawl. But when I open my eyes what is there but the alarmed expressions of unfamiliar faces examining this sorry old Japanese, these others bracing him, patting him, holding him up from under his arms.

"Hey, pops, just breathe easy now," a bearded man in a cap says. He looks down at me earnestly, nodding his head. "Guess it's time to trade in the hookah, huh, chief?"

A very large woman with a kind, rosy-hued face shoots him a look and then takes my hand and leads us a few steps to a bench, asking if I want her to sit with me awhile. I can't yet seem to breathe. I just shake my head weakly, unable to thank her, though part of me would like nothing better than to pass some long minutes leaning up against her ampleness, to rest upon the soft pad of her shoulder and arm and try to forget where I am. Soon my air comes back and with it my voice, and I thank her profusely for being patient and kind. It occurs to me, too, that this is probably my last chance to go back and tell Kari not to bother giving the manager any message, that it was my mistaken (and utterly sentimental and foolhardy) impression that this was the right store, or the right mall in the right town, and that I'm doddering and failing and should be completely ignored. But the samaritan woman now wants to walk me to my car, or drive me home if I can't, her eyes saying I'm in no suitable condition. I assure her I'm all right, and I quickly get to my feet to indicate the extent of my semi-decent command. I'm faking, of course, and desperate to keep myself upright for the time it takes to thank her again and say I'm fine and wave goodbye as she resumes the path of her shopping day. And it is only when she is out of sight and I've regained myself and am retracing my steps to the store in a tentative gait in order, I must oddly hope, to persuade the assistant manager Kari of my senility and madness, that I realize how merciful and lucky it is to have avoided such a meeting with all those difficult, murky remembrances.

But how near, indeed, all this presently ends. For there, inside the scratched and hand-smudged Plexiglas windows of the Kiddie Kare, is Sunny Hata, once daughter of mine, whom I have not seen in almost thirteen years, bending down to kiss a young boy on the crown of his head. She looks almost exactly the same, except her figure is fuller and her hair pulled neatly back with a band. She's still quite beautiful, in her way, perhaps more so than ever as Officer Como had said, now that she is a woman. She must be thirty-two. I think the boy must be hers, bestowed as he is with her high, narrowing eyes and her black hair, though it's tightly curled, near-Afro, and her warm, nut-colored skin (though I wonder why he isn't darker). She cups his ear and his cheek and before leaving gives him a quick, tiny wave of goodbye with her finger, which he tries to dismiss with a diffident shrug. But he can't, and runs to her, not with open arms, but with his head lowered and his shoulder dipped, throwing a slight, willful block into her side. She roughly runs her hand through his hair, then scoots him off.

As she comes out of the Kiddie Kare she sees me, which happens almost by accident, for she drops her keys and turns on an oblique angle, back toward me, opposite her way to Lerner's, and finds me where I'm standing stock-still in the middle of the mall. She stares, and for a moment we are transported back in time, as if we are caught up again in the long dry stare of her youth, that severe, bloodless regard she'd offer up from across the kitchen table, or the dark water of the pool, or from the sidewalk in front of the store, where she'd lean against the parking meter and smoke her spice-scented cigarettes. But now I see that more than anything else she is simply acknowledging me, her eyes half-angry and half-sad, and I wonder if in my threadbare red cardigan and bulky corrective shoes and loose-hanging slacks I am something of a horrendous sight for her eyes.

"Don't let him see us," she says, slowly approaching and then passing me by. "We'll talk at the food."

I realize what she means and start walking past the Kiddie Kare without glancing in, though now I wish to look upon him, once again take in his shape. Instead I loop around the large planter and head back toward the food hall smelling thickly of tacos and burgers and Chinese food warming in steam trays. Sunny is sitting at one of the tables on the inner "veranda" of the court, a plastic cup of iced coffee in her hands, and when I sit down she rises and asks if I want some tea. The consideration surprises me, and as she heads to the Java Hut I think we must both be glad for the momentary reprieve.

Soon enough, though, she returns with a paper cup of steaming green tea.

As there's silence, I say, "I was grateful for the card."

She pauses, but it's too late to act as if she doesn't know what I'm talking about.

"Sally Como told me. I bought it that day. I guess you know she works here. I wasn't going to send it, but then one morning I put a stamp on the envelope and dropped it in the box. It was stupid to think you wouldn't know who it was from."

"It wasn't stupid at all," I tell her.

She doesn't answer this, jiggling her iced coffee instead. "Well, now that's done with, and you're here. You look okay to me. But you lost some weight. I mean, over the years."

"I feel quite fine."

Sunny nods, not exactly smiling. "Did you really almost burn down the house?"

"Not at all," I say, taken by her sudden feeling and interest. "There was some minor damage from the smoke. Really nothing serious. I've had it all fixed, and the curtains and carpet in the family room have been replaced. There's hardly an odor anymore. If you came by and saw it you might think nothing had ever happened—"

"I'm sure you're right," she breaks in, sounding busy all of a sudden. She checks her watch. "I have to be at work pretty soon."

"It is quite lively there," I tell her. "It's a very nice shop, you know, very efficient, very well run. It's clear that there are good systems in place. You must have been managing the store for some time now, I suppose."

"No, not a long time," she answers. She seems a bit nervous, even almost shy, but acting as an adult might in an awkward situation, forward and harried. "We moved here in the spring. I was doing the same job in Long Island, at a Lerner's in Great Neck, but it was too expensive there for us to live and when this came up nobody else seemed to want it. So here I am."

"With your son."

"Yes," she answers, taking a sip through the straw.

"May I ask his name?"

"It's Thomas."

"What a good solid name for a boy. How old is he?"

"Almost six."

"He looks sturdy, very strong."

"Well, I didn't want him to see us together," she says firmly, unapologetic. "He doesn't know about you. And I would like it to stay that way. I don't want him confused."

I have an impulse to ask about the boy's father, if he is with them or at least somewhere around, and if it is Lincoln, in fact, but from Sunny's tone I realize the question is one I should set aside. She's here now with me, and willing enough. And from where I am sitting, I see how Sunny has aged as well. She's still someone at whom you must stop what you are doing and take a moment to look, her rich color, her beautiful eyes. I was last this close to her nearly half her lifetime ago, in the bristling flush of her adolescence. But now, too, I see the first lines at the corners of her mouth, a strand (or two or three) of silvery hair, the barest perceptible sag to her cheek. If there's anything one can say it's that she's a young woman of a lovely cast who has been worn down in the course of the years in the ways a woman of privilege or leisure would never have been.

"I'll let you say hello to him, if you want," she says now, looking squarely at me, as if I have already asked her and she's long been considering it. "But you can't say anything like you're his grandfather, or related to him in any way. I don't want you to tell him there was a connection. I'm having trouble enough with all his questions about his father and me."

"I would be very pleased to meet him," I say. "If he asks who I am, well, I can tell him you once worked at my store, when you were young."

"Fine," she answers curtly. "But I don't want him to have expectations. Because those would be impossible. You understand me, right? I want you to understand."

"Yes of course," I reply, wishing certain expectations wouldn't be so potentially hurtful or damaging, when all I might do is make myself available to him, in any possible way. "I'll do exactly as you wish."

She acknowledges this and we sit in silence, sipping our drinks. And it's striking to me—almost unacceptably so—how *not* awful it is to have passed all these years, with a host of all manner of difficult feelings, and have between us now such mild and mature accord. As if there had once been a hint of something more than just duty and responsibility: something like love. It's what I hadn't allowed myself to hope for as I drove to the mall, the ambient progression of such a meeting. At the same time, however, it grieves me a little now to see how Sunny has tempered herself, or worse, been thus tempered by her life, how my standing by and letting her leave at such a young age has led her, somehow, right back to this wan town and wan mall, to sit here with this innocently crouched old man who once tried to conduct himself like her father and not despise him to his death.

But how this moment, too, surpasses me. And I say, "I'm not surprised to see how well you're doing. For yourself and your boy, Thomas. I've had some worries, of course. I assumed I would find you in a good way, but like this, I must admit, as the manager of so wonderful a store with such attentive employees. And then to hold an obvious position of leadership here in the mall, which has some lack in this regard, well, it's quite an accomplishment."

"Oh, it's nothing," she mutters, looking over at the teens and children milling around the frozen yogurt bar, the burger and fry place. "All I've done is be persistent."

"Yes, of course," I tell her, "that's ninety-five percent of any success. You must know the secret. Sometimes I want to go into a shop on Church Street that isn't doing so well and tell them just to hold on. People give up so easily these days. A few bad months and it's time to sell everything off. The economy isn't helping matters, but it doesn't mean certain failure. It means having to provide better service, better goods. For a long time, you know, when you were in middle school, I was almost sure the store wouldn't make it. I had to convince Mr. Finch at the bank to give me more time. I was behind several payments, and I had to beg him."

"Isn't that when you were seeing Mrs. Burns?" Sunny asks, the mention surprising me. "I thought she helped you, because she'd known him."

"Mr. Finch?"

"Yes. I remember her saying to you, at the house, that she'd have a word with him. Their families being close for a long time. I thought she sort of vouched for you."

"Well," I reply, "I suppose you can say she did. Mr. Finch didn't know me then as he does now. But it was nothing irregular."

"I'm not saying it was," Sunny says, sighing a bit. "I just remembered her all of a sudden. What she looked like."

"She was quite dignified, you know. And kind."

"Yes," Sunny answers, nodding a little, though perhaps more to herself than to me. And then, almost sadly, "She was the sort of person who was always kinder to people than they were to her."

I don't have an answer to this, and after a moment Sunny makes some business of adjusting the cuffs of her suit jacket. I know what she's going to say but she's cut off by the sudden presence of Kari, the assistant manager, who's holding an immense waffle cone of chocolate yogurt. A girlfriend, enjoying the same, is standing with her, grinning through her braced upper teeth.

"Hey, you guys!" Kari beams. "Don't worry, Sunny, I've got good old Sheila at the desk. I waited for you before taking my break, but then I figured you guys might be here, bonding and stuff."

"I'm coming right now," Sunny tells her, just getting up.

"Don't sweat it, boss. Sheila is handling it. You guys take your time. Hey, is Tommy here today?"

Sunny, now sitting, nods.

"Well, let's go see Tommy," Kari announces. She and her friend bid us goodbye and march off to the Kiddie Kare.

"I should go anyway," Sunny then tells me. "It's not really fair to Sheila."

"Yes, of course," I say, though no part of me wants her to go just yet. For sitting right here, I think, is the daughter—considerate, fair, attentive—most anyone could be happy for. And I say, "You must return to your proud establishment."

"It's not so proud for long."

"Why shouldn't it be?"

"Business is terrible."

"What do you mean? What about all those customers, all the fine merchandise?"

"It looks better than it is," she says somberly. "It's not at all good, really. The corporate office wants to close the store. I think they knew it when they hired me. It was a horrible summer. People in Ebbington don't have much extra money to spend. No one else knows this yet, but we'll be closing at the end of the month."

"This month? But that's less than three weeks from now. . . ."

"I know." She says softly, "On Monday I have to give everybody notice."

"But what about you?"

"What about me. When there's no store, there's no manager. I've been looking around, but this whole town is in the dumps. Lerner's doesn't have openings anywhere else. I'll have to be a salesclerk somewhere again. It doesn't matter. I'll get by. I always have."

"But there's Thomas. Who will look after him? I know that day care can be very costly. You must look harder. You must find another management position. I can help you. I still know a number of businesspeople in Bedley Run—"

"Please!" she says quite forcefully. "I've been *fine* all these years. Let's not start. I didn't send the card to you to start something like this. And you should know I won't take one step in that town, and neither will Thomas. There's no chance of that. So please don't try to change my mind."

"But I can help you with Thomas," I tell her. "I'll pay for a sitter, or for day camp. Whatever else he needs, I'll provide. Please let me do this, at least. Please, Sunny. It can't hurt, to let me do this."

And yet, invariably, we all know how it does. In a few moments Sunny leaves to go back to the store, and I decide to walk about the mall with the last of my tea. We've made a plan to speak once again, sometime next week, after which I'll go to their apartment in Ebbington to pick him up for a short visit; we'll take a fun shopping trip, for some new sneakers or toys. And now, though I half-promised Sunny I wouldn't, I go past the Kiddie Kare once more, slowing my pace by the window, to see what he's up to inside. I can find him too easily amid the plastic barrels and chutes; he's by far the oldest and biggest, towering a bit too much over the other boys and girls, and I think how it is that Sunny was able to send that card to me, unsigned as it was, a message and non-message for the sole sake of her boy. And the idea entreats me once more, to wonder if something like love is forever victorious, truly conquering all, or if there are those who, like me, remain somehow whole and sovereign, still live unvanquished.

11

HOW I AM STILL UP SO LATE and sleepless in this darkened, unwarm kitchen, after spending the entire afternoon with Sunny's energetic boy, is an amazement to me. I must be rejuvenated, or at least somehow, for now, made over. Surely it is in good part Tommy's presence happily lingering with me, the slightly dizzied, hyperactive romp of him, the constant, as if self-winding locomotion of his sturdy, pumping limbs. It seems to me I should be tucked away in my bed and dreaming of myself on younger legs, running after the boy with joyous, flowing ease, instead of sitting here at the table with shoots of a draft prickling my feet and a tepid cup of green tea cooling in my hands. I am certainly concerned that I might be rubbing Sunny the wrong way, encroaching too far and too fast into the wide territory she has set between us, which I have never thought ill of her for and have even looked upon with a certain measure of relief and gratitude; she has always been able to exercise her resolve, a trait that was difficult to handle when she was young but one I am beginning to appreciate more with each passing day. So I am starting to think that the real cause of my rest-lessness is something that I saw this afternoon, which was most or-dinary and trivial.

It was after I dropped Tommy off at the mall at the end of our appointed day together. He and I had thoroughly enjoyed a shop-ping spree along Route 3A, where we visited, in turn, the Toy Palace and the Sports Section and the old roller-skating rink, and then sat side by side on revolving stools at the ice cream counter of the Woolworth's. It was a wonderful day for me, really, beginning at the toy shop where the stout little boy—whom I told people was my grandson—shed his initial shyness and healthy suspicion of me and suddenly bounded down the aisles touching and handling as many of the brightly packaged toys as he could. I told him he could pick out two things, though looking upon his desperate expression of trying to choose I weakened and said three, and soon enough I lost all resolve and it was five items he could have, then somehow seven. In the end he'd filled up the cart to the exact number, and I could tell he was fundamentally a well-raised boy because he picked out the smaller, modest things rather than some pedal-driven car or grandly boxed building set.

Sunny was somewhat cross with me when we arrived at the store, me bearing the bulging bags of his things and Tommy, drool-ing and gregarious, methodically aiming his special noise-and-light-making pistol at the Lerner's customers. But I could see that she was taken, too, by the lightness of his feet, his giddy, errant leaps and twirls, and maybe, as well, with the way he kept circling the racks of clothes and then returning to me, to shoot me square in the belly, clicking away again and again. Sunny didn't say much except to tell Tommy that he should thank "Mr. Hata," and then nodded to me with a lukewarm smile and a wave of her hand. But she was not being unkind. She had given her employees the news of the store closing a few days earlier, and the mood on the floor and among the staff was decidedly somber, all the more distinguished from Tommy's brusque, overpleased activity.

And then, surprisingly, I was caught off guard by my own stirring, at least the sudden thrum-thrum in my chest as I shook his small hand goodbye, which was a sensation one might usually describe as both sweet and bitter but to me was also squarely, terribly rueful, as I realized how brief and few my times with him might be in future days. It seems curious, all these years alone and my rarely thinking twice of the larger questions, perhaps save certain reconsiderations in the last few weeks, but now the simple padding touch of his boy's fingers seemed to have the force of a thousand pulling hands. It was everything I could do to heed his mother's unspoken (though readily clear) wishes and keep a dignified face and uneventfully leave him until our next time together, which was as yet unarranged.

So I went out from the Lerner's feeling as though my spirit was being loosed into the expansive, dusky caverns of the mall, wafting upward against the bank of skylights whose grimy filter recast the bright autumn sunshine into a hazy, gauzy glow. I felt lacking, of course, bereft in the thought of my adopted daughter and her son simply staying behind in the store, as they must do at the end of every afternoon and with hardly a thought of missing anything or anyone. And I thought if I were the boy, what would I know tonight except that a silver-haired man with wiry fingers had taken me around and bought me things and seemed to know Momma well enough and had plenty of the money she did not? What would I remember by the next afternoon, except for his old man's voice like a soft bellows, the strangely slow shuffle of his feet, his high, weak cough? For who was I to him, really, or to his mother, for that matter, but a too-late-in-coming, too-late-in-life notion of a grandfather, a sorry, open-handed figure of a patriarch, come back hungry and hopeful to people he never knew?

As such, I wouldn't have blamed Sunny if she couldn't help but make a scene and denounce me in front of all. Perhaps I would have welcomed it had she thought twice about my reappearance in her life and flashed me those hard eyes from her youth; that way, at least, I might not have come back to this house of mine sensing that it had grown even vaster—and me that much smaller within it—in the wake of the easy, joyful hours I spent with her son. And then my having the companion feeling, too, that my life had all at once become provisional again, the way a young man's might be, open to possibility and choice and then vulnerability as well, a state of being I have always treated with veritable dread. For it is the vulnerability of people that has long haunted me: the mortality and fragility, of the like I witnessed performing my duties in the war, which never ceased to alarm, but also the surprisingly subject condition of even the most stolid of men's wills during wartime, the inhuman capacities to which they are helplessly given if they have but ears to hear and eyes to see.

In my car in the parking lot, I sat for a few minutes with the engine running before I drove away. A particular sight was arresting me—and not of Tommy or Sunny. Rather, it was an otherwise insignificant notice: that group of Middle Eastern men who had opened the temporary Halloween store just the week before were already dismantling their modest, homespun window displays before Halloween had even arrived, stripping the shop. I was on my way out but stopped to watch them for a moment. They did not appear too upset or disturbed, just went about their work the same steady way as they had begun it. I felt badly for them, of course, knowing that they must be losing a decent amount of money, and that they were presumably stemming their losses with this very quick closing. They were again out in front of the place with ladders, unsticking the paper banners and signs, and I noticed inside the store a teenaged boy and girl sitting at chairs and working beside each other, the girl folding up various-sized squares of black cloth, Halloween table linens and napkins, and placing them in boxes. The young man wasn't as serious as the girl (his twin sister?), in fact he was clearly enervated by the task and was effortfully closing up each small box, fitfully running a tape dispenser across the tops. He was talking to her, but it seemed in a haranguing sort of way, his jawbone working continuously. There was a short stack of the taped boxes beside him, which he kept kicking lightly with the side of his foot. The girl, a slender young woman with high, wide-set eyes, wouldn't be annoyed by his attitude. She steadily made her way through a heaping, messy bin of the dark fabric. She would take each piece and shake it free of its haphazard folds and smooth it down flat on her lap, then begin to fold it again from corner to corner. The boy finished sealing a box and, having no others, watched her diffidently. She was picking another square of cloth from the bin and beginning her procedure, when he reached over and meanly picked at it, causing it to fall to her feet. She paused, then retrieved it and started over. But again he messed up her work. This happened twice more until finally the girl took the cloth and shook it open and placed it over her own head. The boy was confused. She sat there with her face covered in black, and he yelled at her once and then rose abruptly and left her.

The girl remained there, under the veil, unmoving for some time. And as I sat parked in the mostly empty lot in the long shadow of the mall, I felt I understood what she was meaning by her peculiar act, how she could repel his insults and finally him by making herself in some measure disappear. As if to provide the means of her own detachment. It was because of this notion—as well as the simple cloth itself, similar enough to the swath Sunny once found in a lacquered box in my closet—that I remembered the girl again, Kkutaeh, the one I came to call simply K, and the events in our camp in those last months of the war.

AFTER THE KILLING, and the execution of Corporal Endo, it was unusually quiet in the camp. It was then that K was placed under my care. This under direct order by the doctor, Captain Ono. He determined that she was despondent and suicidal, and possibly dangerous to others, particularly to the other girls. I had no reason to doubt his appraisal as I hadn't observed her or spent any length of time with her, nor would I have disagreed with him had I believed otherwise. He found me one afternoon doing paperwork and called me out into the small clearing behind the infirmary, where our medical wastes and other garbage were discarded. He said gravely, "I have determined that the girl (he always called her this, never referring to any of the others) is a risk and should be quarantined periodically. What will happen is that I will let the intervals be known to you, and under my authority you will remove her from her service and examine her thoroughly."

"Yes, sir," I said. "But what shall I examine her for?"

"For infection and disease," he said sharply, staring at me as if I were a total fool. "You will prepare and treat her if necessary. I expect her to be free of illness when she comes to me. Keep her and isolate her beforehand."

"Here in the infirmary, sir?"

"Where else, Lieutenant! Come up with something, can't you? For all I care you can use the surplus supply closet. In fact, that will do. You'll lock her inside, of course. Do you understand, Lieutenant?"

"Yes, sir," I told him, though not being completely certain of what he was actually ordering me to do. I stood waiting at attention, but he was silent. I could normally "remove her from her service" for medical reasons, with his permission, of course, but to select her out regularly, and only her, before indications of an illness or malady was unusual indeed.

"Resume your duties," he muttered, turning to go back inside the infirmary. He paused at the door. "Another thing. About the sign."

"Sir?"

"So that you know when to get her ready. I don't want to have to speak to you every time. In fact from now on I want to minimize such contacts between us. I'm too busy to be supervising you."

"Yes, sir."

"Then what shall it be?" he said sternly.

I had no hint of an answer for him, and I shuffled my feet. He then looked somewhat pleased, while regarding me.

"Well, it should be that then."

"Captain?"

"Since this will now be a critical responsibility for you, Lieutenant, perhaps it ought to be fairly obvious, so that you won't have any confusion and waste my time."

"Yes, sir."

"In this spirit, then, you will look out each morning for a black flag."

"Pardon me, sir?"

"A black flag. What do you think, Lieutenant? I will affix it on the front of the infirmary. I suspect even you will be able to notice this."

"I believe I will see it clearly, sir, yes."

He waited for me to respond further, as if he hoped to provoke me with his choice of sign. But I remained at attention, not meeting his piercing eyes, trying as hard as I could to imagine myself far away from him and this place, perhaps swimming in the quiet sea that lapped the shore of Rangoon. I had been thinking lately of that posting, which was mostly a last, brief R&R for us as we awaited transport to a more forward base. I remembered having the thought then in the glowing dusk on the beach that the war, oddly enough, was not so awful; that a young man uncertain of himself could find meaning amidst the camaraderie of his fellows working in such shared purpose, and that in fact there was no truer proving time for which he could hope. And yet it seemed everything fell away whenever Captain Ono addressed me, all my carefully built-up perception of things, and in the sorry depletion I could feel the searing, rising surges of what must be pure enmity. I have never quite shown this expression, and I did not then with Captain Ono.

"Look for it, Lieutenant Kurohata," he finally said, and with a flit of his surgeon's hand he turned and left me.

What he had determined as the sign, the black flag, was of course meant for me. Hata is, literally, "flag," and a "black flag," or *kurohata,* is the banner a village would raise by its gate in olden times to warn of a contagion within. It is the signal of spreading death. My adoptive family, I learned right away, had an ancient lineage of apothecaries, who had ventured into stricken villages and had for unknown reasons determined to keep the name, however inauspicious it was. Captain Ono's choice, of course, was intentionally belittling, though I could see, too, how the sign would serve to keep others away from the infirmary who would naturally assume there had been an outbreak. As there was no recent fighting in our area, the infirmary, was in fact empty and had been so for some weeks, and he could have a privacy there that was not possible anywhere else in the camp, even for an officer.

A few mornings later I rose before dawn and the morning call. I dressed and began my usual ablutions: a quick wash with a dampened rag, a fitful, pulling shave with a knife's edge, and then a meager, rationed morning meal of barley porridge and tea from the officers' mess. It was much the same as any other morning, but as I finished I realized, gazing out at the lightly fogged-in camp, how actually pitiable the condition of things had become. There was of course the threat of an enemy offensive looming about like a pall, but even that, too, seemed to be dissipating, the notion grown more enervating, somehow, than frightful. Soon enough, we would understand that the fighting had indeed passed us over, but we did not believe that then. There were various scatters of litter about the encampment, and all about the air was the fouled, earthy smell of the far latrines, which had filled up again and needed to be cleared. This was the unheroic state of our far-flung outpost, in fact one forgotten by both home and foe, and under the increasingly retiring leadership of Colonel Ishii, who was hardly to be seen anymore outside his house.

As I took my early morning walk I decided not to go directly to the infirmary but rather to detour toward the latrines, where I passed by the longish, narrow comfort house, with its five modest, unadorned doors all set in a row. It was quiet, no doubt empty, but I made my way toward the nearest door and swung it in on its dow-

eled hinges in order to look inside. There was no one there, as I had
expected. Just the oddly shaped plank of wood, like a strange, otherworldly pew in the middle of the tiny space more like a stall than
a room, the wood stained dark at its bottom end. This is what the
enlisted men had been queuing for these past few afternoons. I
hadn't done so myself the week earlier, when it was the officers
who visited exclusively (and still did, in the late evenings now,
sometimes for the entire night), and though I was publicly saying
to my fellows that I still would, I could not yet remove from my
thoughts how Corporal Endo had offered to give me his ticket,
how desperately he had wanted to relinquish his turn. The night before I had felt uncomfortable when I saw the men waiting in lines
outside the doorways, smoking and taunting and singing to one
another as they waited, their exuberance amazingly whole, unat-
tenuated. I wished I could be just the same as they, I wished for the
simple sheerness of their anticipation, whether it was born from
desire or lonesomeness or fear or anger or dread.

But I did not have such a feeling, nor could I call it forth. I supposed I should be half-glad. Maybe it was because I knew enough
of what would happen in the tiny room, or what would occur in
turn over the long hours of the afternoon and evening. One could
say it was a medical knowledge. Or so I chose to encounter it. I
knew that twenty or even thirty or more would visit each one of
them, and that the resulting insult would be horribly painful and ig-
nominious. The older woman, Mrs. Matsui, had brought over one
of them after their first full evening with the enlisted men; the girl
could hardly walk and was bleeding freely from her genital area,
which was bruised and swollen nearly beyond recognition. She was
weakened from the blood loss, and I had the orderly wrap her in
blankets and instructed Mrs. Matsui to give her an extra ration of

porridge from her supplies and some dried fish broth as well, which she stridently protested but could do nothing about. The girl had no other injuries, per se, though she hardly responded when spoken to or even when examined. Her eyes were lightless and nearly fixed. I had intended to keep her in the infirmary for several days, for observation and treatment and rest, but after Mrs. Matsui complained to the doctor about having to give her extra without compensation, he ordered that the girl be sent back to the comfort house immediately in order to resume her duties. As for the other three girls, he instructed me in a carefully written note, I would remove them only if they were diseased or if a malady was imminently life-threatening, and in all other instances I was to employ the least wasteful treatment and have Mrs. Matsui take them away.

Which is what I did in this case, and each subsequent time one of them was brought in, despite their terrible condition. It was not against my field training, certainly, to treat a patient in such a way with the aim of returning him to his duties as soon as possible, for in wartime it was never a question of salubrity, really not for anyone. Rather, as the doctor had already pointed out to me, it was a matter of standards, in this case to apply the level of treatment that was most appropriate for the situation, and for whom. In this schema the commander had his level, the officers theirs, the enlisted men and others yet another, and so on and so forth, until it came to the girls, who had their own. All this was inviolable, like any set of natural laws.

So as I left the cramped room and went out into the drifting mist of the morning, what struck me, what gave me pause, was the note Captain Ono had written. I would treat the girl, K, quite differently, in a manner of his private choosing, perhaps before she was even sick or afflicted. I wasn't against the order itself, which seemed in fact a good idea, to examine the girls regularly, with an eye toward prevention (if we were truly attempting to avoid the trouble with venereal outbreaks that had debilitated whole units of the Imperial Army), but what his order rankled against, which was the very code of all our association, and community. And yet I did not think doubtfully of the doctor for long, as I convinced myself to hold a deeper faith in his judgments, which must, I knew, be informed by years of study and experience and the accrued knowledge of his line of noblemen and scholars. He had seen something in K, I wanted to believe, he had discovered a curiosity in her, a uniqueness scientific or medical or otherwise, that attracted beyond her physical beauty, which was by any standard transcendent, somehow divine.

I stepped around the side of the comfort house and peered behind it, where Mrs. Matsui's broad tent stood. It was quiet there, too, in its sag and tilt, and beyond it (though still close, as if they were all part of one unit) were the larger corps' tents, spread out in less than strategic groupings. Across from these, set on a rise of land, was one of the officers' houses, and then behind that and partly in my sight the infirmary, everything in this morning remaining unto itself, and as such appearing remarkable and unremarkable at once. Such an observation is a symptom of living but it is one especially true during wartime, when simple, real things like a tent or a house (or a body) can take on a superreality, in the acknowledgment that they can be blown literally into nothingness, instantly pass from this state to the next. This the fate of my good friend Enchi, killed in Borneo. I was given over to these thoughts, somewhat negatively so, perhaps due to the grim events that had occurred in recent days, which seemed to be accepted by the men but none too easily. No matter what Corporal Endo had done, or the blanket necessity of his punishment, it was never a simple matter to conduct an execution of one of our own.

The image of which, I must say, I did not wish to let trouble me that placid morning, for in the solitary spell of my walk, amid the fog lightly huddled with a strange near-beauty over even this, a military camp, I tried to imagine how time itself could somehow stop, how the slumberers in Mrs. Matsui's tent and in the tents beyond might remain just so, unto themselves, as it were, peaceable and unmolested. As if untouched by the practices of wartime. And if this hope was most egregiously naive and sentimental, which it no doubt was, I only wished for myself that I could bear whatever burdens might fall to me, that I might remain steadfast in my duty and uphold my responsibilities and not waver under any circumstance, and by whatever measure. For I feared, simply enough, to be marked by a failure like Corporal Endo's, which was not one of ego or self but of an obligation public and total—and one resulting in the burdening of the entire society of his peers.

I have feared this throughout my life, from the day I was adopted by the family Kurohata to my induction into the Imperial Army to even the grand opening of Sunny Medical Supply, through the initial hours of which I was nearly paralyzed with the dread of dishonoring my fellow merchants, none of whom had yet approached me, or would for several weeks. It must be the question of genuine sponsorship that has worried me most, and the associations following, whose bonds have always held value for me, if not so much human comfort or warmth.

I would have spent the rest of that predawn taking a steady, lone walk about the perimeter had I not in the half-light nearly run into

Captain Ono and the girl, K. They were coming from the direction of the yard, where the commander's hut was, approaching at an almost marching pace, the doctor tugging her along by the hand, his thin, tall frame bent resolutely. He looked quite agitated, stiff in the face, and nearly slung her to the ground when he saw me.

"Lieutenant Kurohata!" he said sharply, eyeing the women's tent behind me. "You should be in your quarters or at the infirmary. I've been searching all over for you."

"Forgive me, sir. I woke early and thought to take a walk."

"I don't want to hear your explanations. They mean nothing to me."

K was half-kneeling beside him, propped on the ground by her forearm. Her thick hair had come undone, and it fell in a shiny black cascade, totally covering her face. She hadn't yet moved. Her clothes were disheveled, her blouse crumpled and hastily knotted in front, her baggy pants torn at the side along the seam, exposing a pale sliver of skin.

"You must have a penchant for disturbing me," the doctor said lividly. He was speaking uncomfortably close to me, his breath sour with waking. "It so happened that the commander sent his sentry to my quarters to have this one escorted back to the infirmary. He was extremely upset. It seems she's bleeding."

"Bleeding, sir?"

"*Menstruating*," he said. "How is this possible, Lieutenant? I entrusted you to anticipate these kinds of complications."

"Forgive me, sir, but I'm not certain how I could have known."

"You could have asked her, Lieutenant," he said with some disgust. "Simply asked. You should know this wouldn't be tolerable for the commander. He has particular requirements."

"But what could I have done, sir? I cannot stop her menses."

"Don't be insolent as well as stupid!" he shouted. "You should have made certain that it was another of them who would stay the night with the commander. But as is your character, I'm afraid, you are satisfied with leaving things to tenuous chance and hope and faith in the arbitrary. If I had patience I would wonder once more about your training. And so now you see, because I couldn't find you to escort her, and with the commander requiring a medical officer only, I had to be roused. And so you've made me undertake the task of an errand boy. Now you take her, for I don't want to gaze upon her even once until you hear from me. Do you finally understand me, Lieutenant?" He marched off toward his quarters before I could reply.

The girl waited until he was completely gone before rising. She didn't brush away the red-brown dirt from her shirt elbows and her knees, nor did she pull up the hair that was messily covering her face. The light was just now up, and I could see her dark eyes veiled through the skeins of her hair, staring out blankly across the loosely organized squalor of the camp. She was certainly not aware of me in the way she was of the doctor, with her shoulders narrowed with steel and hate. Nothing like that at all. With him gone, she was suddenly present but not present, and would hardly be a person at all were it not for her seemingly insoluble beauty, which the time in our camp had not yet worn away. I spoke to her then, asking her to follow me to the infirmary, where I had already prepared a small space for her behind a curtain in what was originally intended as a second supply area but was no longer, as we were now sorely lacking in most everything and would be until the end of the war. But she did not acknowledge me or move. She barely seemed to breathe. I spoke again, a bit more forcefully, though to no avail, despite the fact that she understood Japanese well enough, as she'd shown on several occasions.

"Young lady," I said finally, in her own language, "why not come with me now? The captain could return, and he won't be pleased on finding us still here. It will make things easier for us both, which is preferable to another course."

Her expression turned instantly, not in mood so much as aspect, the way she gazed at me as though I had magically appeared from nothingness. She searched me with her eyes but did not speak, and as I walked to the infirmary she trailed me at a few meters, not from fear or deference but more as though trying to regard the whole of me. When we reached the building I directed her to the examination and surgery room and she went in without pause. As the doctor had generally instructed me, I was to "disinfect" her, treat her for anything she might have contracted en route to us, though of course without lab equipment and certain obvious symptoms it was impossible to tell anything with certitude.

With Captain Ono, in fact, it was more a point of "purity" than disease; he was particularly fastidious in his personal practices, as he was always groomed and shaved like any town physician, and most often took his meals alone in the officers' mess, unless he was to dine there with the commander. I was surprised that he didn't prepare his own meals, given his attitudes, for he was often disgusted with the general state of the camp and of the men, particularly now, when conditions were less than orderly. None of it could measure up to his private standards of cleanliness. The infirmary was of course a model of hygiene and efficiency, which I was most willing to maintain for him, despite his sometimes searing criticisms in this very room (and in front of others), which were aimed not at my specific conduct but at the legacies of my "training" and "background"——the ultimate question being of my *ethos,* as it were, a term (from his brief university schooling in England) that he seemed to employ often, for my edification.

In the surgery room, I had the girl sit up on the table. She watched me silently as I laid out the instruments, a swab and probe and speculum, with the uses of which, in all frankness, I had no experience whatsover. I had very briefly observed the doctor conducting such an examination, but my knowledge was relegated to the little I could remember of anatomy texts, with nothing of the practical. I hadn't expected ever to treat a female in the course of my war service.

So I was ever more uncertain and confused. I also felt suddenly quite different. I had particular "feelings," to be sure, though not necessarily or discreetly for her. At least not yet. Rather, these came in the manner in which one normally has a feeling, which I think is governed as much by context as by what is actually happening. And the context that early morning, before the camp had arisen and the day begun, before the resumption of everything having to do with wartime and soldiering, which is the grimmest business of living, was one I had not quite conceived, or experienced, before. There was no protocol I could pattern myself by. Of course one might point out that I had been with Madam Itsuda in Singapore, but there the situation was in fact wholly defined and contracted. K was a young woman, my same age——and in the almost civilian calm of the pre-reveille, with us set apart from all manner of order and rule, I realized I did not know how I should begin to comport myself with her, whether to be forceful or distant or kind. Finally I decided to put away the instruments and asked her if she had any sores or other outbreaks. She shook her head, and I decided not to give her a shot, which would make her terribly sick. I then handed her a vial of a simple cleansing solution, which I told her to mix with clean water and flush herself with several times in the next few days.

"You should go back now to get your things," I then told her. "But return here directly."

She nodded and stepped down from the table. I locked the cabinet of instruments and supplies, hearing the rustle of her rough-spun trousers as she was leaving the room. Normally I should have had to escort her, to prevent a possible escape, but there was nothing but hilly jungle and forest for many kilometers. One of the others had already attempted to leave after the first rounds with the officers but was eventually found some days later (and quite nearby), dehydrated and half-starved, and when she was recovered she was beaten very badly, as an example to the others.

But when I turned, K was still standing in the doorway. She had been watching me as I put away the supplies.

And then she said, quite plainly: "You are a Korean."

"No," I told her. "I am not."

"I think you are," she said, not looking away as she spoke. I didn't know what to say. She sounded much more confident and mature in her own tongue than when she mumbled and half-whispered in Japanese. And there was an uprightness about her posture. Certainly I had an impulse to order her to be silent, harshly command that she leave immediately. But I felt unsettled by her forward bearing, as I was at once amazed and strangely intimidated.

I replied: "I have lived in Japan since I was born."

She nodded and said slowly, as if testing my willingness, "But I think, sir, that most Japanese would never bother to learn to speak Korean as well as you do. And if they did know how, they wouldn't reveal it. There are many Japanese settlers where my family lives, merchants and administrators and police, and this is how I know. When you first spoke outside, I thought it was my younger brother talking to me again. Your voice is just like his."

I did not wish to go on conversing with her any longer, and yet I found myself listening to her closely, for it was some time since I had heard so much of the language, the steady, rolling tone of it like ours and not, theirs perhaps coming more from the belly than the throat. It was almost pleasing to hear the words, in a normal register. But her talk was also not vulgar or harshly provincial-sounding as was the other girls'; she was obviously educated, and quite well, and this compelled me even more, though it shouldn't have. She seemed to sense this, and remained where she was standing, waiting for me to say something. I cleared my throat, but nothing would come out.

She then said to me, "I thought there was something different about you. I think you are not like everyone else."

"I don't know what you're speaking of," I said. "I'm a medical officer of the Imperial Forces, and there's nothing else to be said. Yes, you are partly correct. I spoke some Korean as a boy. But then no more. Such things are not easily forgotten, and so I have the ability still. But this is none of your concern."

"My Korean name is Kkutaeh," she said, speaking over me. Her expression had brightened, her face wonderful to behold. "But I never really wanted the name. I'm the youngest of four daughters, so you can see how I got it. May I ask yours?"

"I don't have one," I told her immediately. But this was not exactly true. I'd had one at birth, naturally, but it was never used by anyone, including my real parents, who, it must be said, wished as much as I that I become wholly and thoroughly Japanese. They had of course agreed to give me up to the office of the children's authority, which in turn placed me with the family Kurohata, and the day the administrator came for me was the last time I heard their tanners' raspy voices, and their birth-name for me.

I said to her, "This is not necessary conversation."

"I simply want to talk with you."

"We have talked enough," I told her, sitting down at the desk, with my back turned to her. "You'll go now and get your things. When you return, you'll remain in the other room, where I left you the blankets for your bedding. Please don't disturb me further. I have much work to do today."

"For Captain Ono?" she said.

"I have many duties, in various areas."

"Will you tell me what he wants from me?" she said now, a little desperately. When I turned she was but an arm's length away. I could smell the lingering air of a musky perfume, which Mrs. Matsui required the girls to wear. But compared to the sharp, sour reek of the men, even the tawdry scent was transporting. She asked, "Why has he kept me from what the others must do?"

"What are you talking about? You haven't yet been at the comfort house?"

"I have not," she answered. For the first time she looked somewhat frightened. "Last night I was to visit the commander, and so he had to send me. But before that the captain has always ordered Matsui-san to keep me in our tent. Sometimes he has her bring me to his private quarters, when he examines me. He runs his hands over my body and examines me everywhere. But that is all. He has kept me from the comfort house."

"You are lying to me."

"I would not lie about such a thing. You can ask Matsui-san. I would rather be killed, like my sister, before going to the comfort house. But I am growing afraid of what the captain will do with me. It can only be horrible, I am certain. He is the only one who truly frightens me, and I think he must have a terrible plan. Forgive me for speaking like this, but you have a gentle character to your face. You seem kind and careful, and I feel I can say these things to you."

I could not believe Captain Ono had ordered what she described, even if he thought she was "dangerous," which I could not at all see. I wondered, too, if the commander knew of this arrangement, or whether he would find it (as I or anyone would) to be an egregious mark on the captain's *self-respect,* at least in the Japanese sense of the term, which has little to do with pride or one's rights but with the efforts a person should make to be viewed well by his comrades. Yet I was not about to question the captain in front of her, or show my own hesitance. It was all very disturbing, though in truth a large part of me had indeed begun to sense the irregularity of his requests and the broadening license he seemed to be taking in respect to the camp. The commander, as noted, was hardly evident anymore, and it was Captain Ono who was increasingly charging and addressing the corps of the men; it was his issuances that were being enacted and followed, with Colonel Ishii appearing these days only intermittently before the officers on the veranda of his hut, often pink-faced and slow of speech.

"The captain must have his reasons," I said to her, "which I am not privy to and would not speak about if I were. I am responsible for certain medical duties and that is all. I need know nothing about this matter. Furthermore, I think you should not dwell on the present circumstance. Please let me finish. If you are not serving at the comfort house, then there are undoubtedly other duties awaiting you. Whether they will be better or worse no one but Captain Ono can say. And just as with the rest of us here, a fate of life or death awaits you; in this regard, as the commander once said to us, it is best if we all take an accepting path. This way destiny can find its right station."

"Is that why the soldier was executed?" she asked. "Because he was resistant?"

"He was ill of mind," I said, trying not to remember Corporal Endo's adolescent, pockmarked face. "And obviously dangerous. You should be thankful for what was ordered for him."

"I am only thankful for what he did. I am happy for my sister now. I don't cry for her anymore. And I am hoping that someone like you will do the same for me. That is why I ask if you know what the captain wants. If I'm to have the same misery, then I would beg you, as a countryman, to take your gun from your holster and put me down right now."

"I am not your countryman," I said to her, pushing my chair back as I rose. "And I will certainly do nothing of the kind. Please stand back now."

"But what if I were attacking you?" she said, stepping forward. "What would you do then? If I took one of those surgeon's blades from the cabinet, and I rushed at you with it, you would have to, yes? You would have to shoot me."

"I will not be shooting anyone," I said to her, almost shouting, my hand hovering at my side, grazing the pistol handle. "I am a medical officer. I have never fired at another human being, much less a young woman. I hope I will never have to. You had better go now and get your things. I am ordering you to do so. I order you!"

But she stepped forward again and her hands, pale-white and small, lunged out for my throat, my eyes. I had to step aside and then strike her across the chin with the ball of my open palm, and she fell awkwardly and hit her head on the steel leg of the examination table. I was shocked with how hard I had struck her, and it was a half-minute before I could get her to regain consciousness. When she did and opened her eyes she began crying, from the smelling salts, certainly, but also, I thought, from her realization that I had not in fact shot her dead.

"I didn't intend to strike you so forcefully," I said to her. "I am sorry. But you gave me no other choice."

"Why won't you help me?" she said, raising herself out of my grasp. Her mouth was bleeding, as she had bitten her tongue on falling. "If you have any compassion you will help me. You should know I won't let him do anything to me. I won't. I will kill myself before that. Or I will kill him first somehow, and then myself."

I let her words pass as she got to her feet, and I decided that I ought to escort her to Mrs. Matsui's tent to get her things immediately and lodge her inside the makeshift quarters. I was to lock her in the surplus supply closet, which was a lightless space with a narrow door and an iron loop for an old-style brass lock, the kind typically used on a cabinet or chest but this one quite large and heavy. The idea of confining her like this seemed somewhat more reasonable to me now, for it seemed she ought not to be allowed to roam freely about the infirmary or the camp. But it was the first time I had actually spoken at length to any of them, and then in my childhood language, which stirred me in an unexpected way. As we walked to Mrs. Matsui's tent and back I felt a certain connection to her, not in blood or culture or kind, but in that manner, I suppose, that any young man might naturally feel for a young woman. This may sound ludicrous, and even execrable under the circumstances, but I was youthful and naive enough that I possessed much more of a kind of hard focusing than any circumspection, which one may argue has remained with me for my whole life.

But I could not lock her inside the supply closet. It had no slatted window or other means of decent ventilation, and with the rays of the afternoon sun directly hitting the outer wall, I feared she might die of heatstroke or else suffocate in the cramped, lightless space. So as often as I could during the day I allowed her to stay with me in the examination room. She was weary from not sleeping the night before and lay down on the floor while I attended to my usual administrative work for Captain Ono. I knew that he could stop by at any time, but somehow I was not thinking about that chance. I was thinking only of K. She did not speak very much, nor ask any more about me, and after some time I turned to see that she had finally fallen asleep, her knees drawn up toward her chest. I stared at her for quite a long moment, taking in her figure and loosely fisted hands and the serene, pale oval of her face, when she slowly opened her eyes. She did not otherwise move. She merely met my gaze and acknowledged it, and then fell asleep again, her breathing light and even. Or perhaps, I thought, she had never really awoken.

If someone had asked me then what I felt, I would have been unable to answer. But if I can speak for that young man now, if I can tell some part of the truth for him, I would say that he felt himself drawn to her, drawn to her very presence, which must finally leave even such a thing as beauty aside. He did not yet know it, but he hoped that if he could simply be near to her, near to her voice and to her body—if never even touching her—near, he thought, to her sleeping mind, he might somehow be found.

12

FOR THE BETTER PART of the next four days our company was
undisturbed, the whole of the infirmary standing empty. On those
mornings I awoke especially early, finishing my camp-wide duties
as soon as I was able, and by nine o'clock or so I could hurry back
to my tent and get myself in decent order. With a washcloth I
would swab my neck and underarms and feet and put on a clean
shirt and trousers. I rubbed tooth powder along my gums and
smoothed down my crewcut hair and set my cap on straight. I made
sure to empty my pistol of bullets before placing it in the holster,
which I would then attach to my belt. Then I would go to the officers' mess and ask for a half-ration of cooked rice from the mess
sergeant, who would nod and not say a word. When I reached the
infirmary I'd wash my hands and then mix it with two rice balls I'd
saved from my own meal the evening before and make them larger,
dusting them with shrimp powder.

K seemed to like the pink-colored powder. Not the taste so
much, I suppose, which was more salty than fishy, but the fact that

I had taken the time to prepare the rice balls for her, form them into rounded wedges and brightly color one corner. When she looked at them set on the paper in my hands she said, with an acknowledging tone, "All they need now is sesame seeds." So on the next day I took a pinchful from Sergeant Takagawa and carefully sprinkled it over the rice balls. When she saw what I had done she didn't take them from me right away (as hungry as she was) but took my cupped hands and held them for what seemed many seconds. I wished then that I could have found some strips of dried fish for her, or a partridge egg, or anything more substantial, for she appeared quite thin to me, the bones of her shoulders seeming pronounced all of a sudden and her eyes darkly sunken in her face. In fact there was a full ration of food for her at Mrs. Matsui's, but she had refused to eat in the days before she was sent to the commander's hut, and it was only in the time with me that she finally began relenting before her hunger.

I watched her eat on those mornings. We didn't talk much, but rather sat in the threshold of the closet door, like people waiting for something to happen. In the afternoons, I had to leave her and lock her inside the closet again for a couple of hours, in order to complete the rest of my non-medical responsibilities, and by the end of them I began to feel anxious, as though the dwindling of the day was not coming fast enough. I couldn't help but picture her in the closet, barely two meters square, lightless save for the sunlight pushing through cracks in the wall, the heat blooming and redoubling in the tight space. But it was not her so much that made me uneasy. I felt as if my lungs and heart were detaching, moving outward to the skin, and that this was all too obvious to everyone I dealt with. As I was checking the state and condition of the mess hall and the latrines and supply dump, ordering men to clean and organize and raze (the secondary rounds of busywork in that long, odd probation from any fighting), I was almost certain that the soldiers were sensing my impatience and discomfort. They could not know, of course, the first thing about what Captain Ono had instituted, or my own increasing involvement, and yet I thought they kept meeting my gaze, not insubordinately but with a wonder and a host of questions. Who is the one we haven't yet seen? What is he doing with her, there in the empty sick house? Has the poor medic actually fallen for her?

And what if he had? Would he have truly known it then anyway? It was nearly unimaginable, of course, to think such a relationship was possible, and yet in a strange way the doctor's untoward interest in her, and his highly irregular orders, let me believe that my befriending her and showing her kindness and constantly thinking of her when she wasn't present was almost ordinary. In fact, K admitted to me that she had not been menstruating some days before, that she had intentionally pricked her thumb with a wood splinter and smudged the blood around her private area and thighs, in the hope that the commander would reject her. Normally I could not have abided such information; and yet what was happening to me was so quick and sure, like one of the late autumn deluges that were sweeping in on us more and more often, the red-brown water suddenly ankle-deep, seeping in everywhere, and in the last minutes before I would go to her again I was practically trembling.

But it was really only toward dusk and evening that first day, when she was willing to talk with me, that I lost myself. I brought her some more rice, and after finishing she didn't simply turn away and dwell in a corner until it was time for me to go. The daylight grew weak and dim and was almost gone, the exam room we were in becoming nearly dark. She asked again after my childhood and my families, the Ohs and the Kurohatas. To my surprise, she didn't want to know only about my first parents; in fact, the Kurohatas seemed to intrigue her more. She was curious as to how they had treated me and raised me and if they loved me the way she was sure my birth parents must have loved me, even though they'd given me up.

I told her I believed the Kurohatas felt a strong bond with me, that they had provided me with every advantage and opportunity they could muster, a respectable house and schooling and outside lessons, and had always treated me like a son.

"But I was wondering if they love you like a son."

"I think so. But I am not sure if there is a difference," I said, "if they have always treated me like one."

"I suppose not," she said, her face hardly apparent to me in the darkness. I offered to light an oil lamp, but she wanted to keep the room dark. Then she said: "Have you always treated them like parents?"

"I can only hope I have," I replied, instantly picturing them as they stood by their German sedan and waved to me as I boarded the troop ship at Shimonoseki. But I had not felt moved enough to cry, as did some of the other young men leaving home for the first time, even at the sight of my mother weeping fitfully into a kerchief. This is not so awful a farewell, was my thought, even if I am to die. I will miss them and feel sorry for them, and if I return I will be happy.

"You sound uncertain," she said.

"I am only uncertain of my honoring of them, which I am always failing in. But that is a child's lifelong burden."

"Yes," she replied, her voice a bit softer. "You're probably right, Lieutenant. Even for those of us who would not wish it, like me, one of four unwanted daughters. Yet I know that if my father were to come to me tonight and ask me to wash his feet with the last drops of water I had I would not hesitate for a second."

"You would be good to do so," I said.

She didn't answer immediately. All I could make out was the vaguest shape of her face.

"But he would never ask me such a thing," she said. "He would hardly ever speak to me, you know, or to any of us girls. To him we were unaddressable, even before all the trouble that happened to our family. He might say, toward my mother or one of our servants, that I should fetch his slippers for him, or that I should be quieter, or go play outside. I didn't sense hatred or bitterness from him. But what he had for me was mostly nothing at all, as if I were of the most distant blood. He touched me only once I can remember. A light hand touching my head, when my brother was born. I thought it would be the touch of a god."

"Was it?"

"No," she said. "It wasn't. Not at all."

"But he must have been pleased at the birth of your brother."

"Of course he was. But they became so protective of him, he and my mother both. So in turn we were to be as well, the four of us girls."

"And you were not?"

She didn't answer for some moments. I heard the rustle of her trousers as she shifted in her chair. "I loved him when he was born. I love him now. But I wasn't like my sisters or my mother, that way. Perhaps it was because we were closest in age. I was never quite filial, and my father and everyone knew it. Yet my brother never minded. He's a kindhearted boy."

"Is he still at home?"

"I must hope so," she answered, her voice low and quiet. "Or my sister has suffered and died for nothing."

I told her then, "I am sorry for what happened."

"Are you really?"

"Yes," I said, thinking too of Corporal Endo, and how I might have helped him more. "I know you are thinking that it is better that your sister is dead, than serving in the comfort house. But it's also possible that she could have eventually gone out of this place and had a long and decent life. She could have persevered, as I believe you will."

K laughed then, though gently and without any tone of derision. I asked her again if I might light the oil lamp, and this time she said I should. The light came up quickly, and in the warm cast she was perfectly radiant, her round face golden and smooth. She seemed to be gazing on me somewhat somberly, as if I had just been born into the difficult world, her eyes bearing a sadness and awe.

She said softly, "You are an unlikely fellow, Lieutenant Kurohata. You should know I am grateful for at least your hopefulness. I do hear that, and I am appreciative. But please let's rather continue what we were speaking of before, than talk of my sister, or this place. I don't wish to think of her right now. You understand, I know."

"Certainly, I do."

"Thank you, Lieutenant," she said, bowing her head, just as she might in everyday, civilian life, and I felt suddenly illicit in her presence, as though we'd slipped out of sight of our chaperons and found ourselves in a darkened, private park somewhere.

"Will you tell me more about your growing up? About your schooling? I always like to hear of what others have done."

"It was nothing too unusual," I told her. "I finished the upper school and was admitted to the university, but when the war broke out I was reassigned to the military institute instead, for field medical training. Eventually I'll go to medical school, but I am more than willing to serve in this way now. I'm looking forward to my final training, though, and becoming a surgeon."

"What kind?"

"I'm not certain yet," I said to her, though I already knew I'd like to specialize in something like cardiopulmonary surgery. I was afraid to speak aloud my wish, lest it never come to pass. In fact I have always been fascinated by the workings of the heart and lungs, the immortal constancy and vitality of their operation. Before I witnessed the doctor massaging the cobbler's heart, I had in my childhood seen a butcher quickly kill a small pig, slitting its throat and then immediately cutting it open as it hung from its hind legs. The first swift cut at the sternum was for an instant strangely unbloody, and I could see the quivering heart and the pliant sacs of the lungs, still alive as the pig was for a few moments longer. Since then, I have had the thought from time to time that indeed these were the vessels of the animal's spirit, and that perhaps our souls, too, reside not in our minds but in the very flesh of us, the frank, gray tissue which seems most remarkably possessed of the will to go on, to persist. Sometimes when one is a physician or a medic or a nurse, the physical body can take on an almost mystical presence, and whether living or not becomes a certain marker of the world, a sign of the wider circumstance. And though she was before me I thought of her again reclining in her sleep before I unlocked the door, this person in a tiny closet-room, this solitary girl in a box.

I said to her, "I'm curious. Why don't you tell me of how you grew up? Of the schools you must have attended."

"I don't have much of any schooling," she said, surprising me.

"Not of the formal kind. I went to grammar school for several years but it was decided by my father that as with my sisters I shouldn't continue."

"But you seem quite well educated."

"I have tried to educate myself," she answered, with the barest edge of pride. "So after that, all this time, I've studied at home, first with my older sisters, and then with my brother. He and I would climb the hill behind our house and I'd secretly read the lessons along with him, and also help him whenever I could. I don't mean to brag, but I know more Chinese characters than anyone in my family, except, of course, for my father, who was renowned in our province when he was a younger man for his learning and his public recitations of classical poetry. My mother would tell me and my sisters of his speaking, how impressive and brilliant he was, and we grew up idolizing him. We made sure to be absolutely quiet in the mornings, when he read and smoked his pipe in the study."

"I like to read, too," I spoke up, "whenever I can. Mostly medical texts, of course, but literature as well. I have enjoyed some modern novels, too, especially several French and German, which I have found to be passionate and distinctly dark, in turn."

She nodded with a half-smile, and I realized how enthusiastic I probably sounded, as though we were on an initial date, like any two university students. And yet I could hardly contain myself, able to broach such subjects after those many months of drudgery and routine and anxious inaction.

"You're lucky to have read other kinds of books," she said. "I've only read lesson books and the like, and then when my father was away I might steal into his study and try to read poetry and historical texts. He didn't have any Western novels among his books, which I would have loved. He would never have them in his library. He always told my brother that we should revere our Asian heritage and protect it from foreign influences, that whether Chinese or Japanese or Korean we were rooted of a common culture and mind and that we should put aside our differences and work together."

"This is exactly our Emperor's mandate," I told her, "to develop an Asian prosperity, and an Asian way of life."

"Though it seems it is to be a Japanese life," K said, her tone somewhat ironical. But after a few moments she sensed my quiet and said to me, "I wish that we could read one of those novels you mentioned, and then talk about it. A story set in another land and time in history, with completely different sorts of people. Since I was a little girl, I always wanted to live a completely different life, even if it might be a hard one. I was sure I wasn't meant to belong to mine. Maybe you can describe the stories to me, and we could pretend we were in their lives, those European people in the novels, involved with their own particular problems, which I am sure must be very compelling."

"They are interesting," I said, recalling the figure of a woman in a small French provincial town that was her world, and prison. "And sometimes even tragic."

"I suppose it ought to be so," K replied. "Or it wouldn't be much of a tale, would it, Lieutenant?"

"No," I said to her, gazing at her face and wondering if she knew how difficult the present life would soon be for her, and for me as well.

Near midnight, I acceded to her request and walked with her to the place where her sister was buried. There was no marker, no sign, just a slight mound of dug-up earth barely noticeable in the moonlight. I waited for her at a respectful distance. As we returned she told me of her two other sisters, who were already engaged to be married and so could not be sent away from home. A recruiter had come to the door with some military police, carrying a list of single young men in the town. They were going to conscript her brother, and as her father had lost his influence and standing and had no money left to bribe them, he could do nothing about it; but he pleaded with them in his study and soon thereafter they left. The next day the recruiter returned by himself, but for K and her sister. Their mother had already prepared each of their bags, their father having spirited his son off somewhere before dawn. She gave them each a fancy silken doll, stuffed inside with a little traveling money. They would help the family, she told them while crying, by going to work in a boot factory outside of Shimonoseki. But when they arrived at the harbor they were immediately transferred onto a cargo ship bound for the Philippines and Singapore, and then boated to Rangoon, before finally being trucked through the forested hills here to the camp. They had not known at all what awaited them, no idea what their true service would be.

I was somewhat taken aback by her account. I could not quite accept the whole truth of it. But it was more perhaps that I had reached the limits of my conception, than thinking there was something in her story to doubt. Although it was the most naive and vacant of notions to think that anyone would willingly give herself to such a fate, like everyone else I had assumed the girls had indeed been "volunteers," as they were always called. To the men in the queue, they were nothing, or less than nothing; several hours earlier I had overheard a soldier speak more warmly and humanly of the last full-course meal he remembered than the girl he'd been with the previous afternoon. He was a corporal attached to the motor pool, a typically decent young man. He crudely referred to the comfort girl as *chosen-pi,* a base anatomical slur which also denoted her Koreanness. Though I knew it was part of the bluster and bravado he displayed for his fellows, there was a casualness to his usage, as if he were speaking of any animal in a pen, which stopped me cold for a moment. I certainly did not think of the other girls as animals, and yet I cannot say they held any sort of position in my regard; perhaps my thinking was as a rich man's, who might hardly acknowledge the many servants working about his house or on the property, their efforts and struggles, and see them only as parts of the larger mechanism of his living, the steady machine that grinds along each night and day.

In fact a few minutes later I found the soldier and asked him to explain himself and his usage, but he was so bewildered by my question he could hardly speak. "I don't know what to say, Lieutenant," he said sheepishly after a pause, "but isn't that what they are?"

From his perspective, I suppose, he was telling only what he knew. And had I been of the slightest different opinion, I too would probably have thought of them that way, as soft slips of flesh, a brief warm pleasure to be taken before it was gone, which is the basic mode of wartime. But with K, I was beginning to think otherwise, of how to preserve her, how I might keep her apart from all uses in any way I could.

After returning from the gravesite, we sat under the cool cast of the moonlight in the small yard behind the infirmary. There was a dense ring of wide-leafed vegetation enclosing the space, and no one could see us. She was not so obviously upset at having seen her sister's grave; she had not cried out or made any sound of mourning. Now in fact there was a lightness to her voice, as if she were almost being playful with me, though I knew it wasn't that either. It was something different, a strange kind of release or relief. For the first time she seemed truly vulnerable to me, not just her physical body, which was always endangered, but her spirit. She would not come closer to me, as much as I thought she wished to, hungering not for anything like love but for plain, humble succor. And though I wanted to, I did not attempt to embrace or touch her or reach out. I did not shift or move at all. What prevented me I can't know, whether it was deference or detachment or a keening heart of fear.

Earlier she had wanted to speak in the darkness, and now, too, she asked if we could sit close to the building, beneath the low eave, every part of us in the shadows. I could finally understand what she was wishing for. I believe it was so she couldn't see my uniform or the shine of my boots or even my face; I realized that she was trying to pretend we were other people, somewhere else, with the most ordinary reasons for keeping such furtive company, just our whispering voices apparent to the night air.

We stayed there until just before the light began to rise again. Then I led her back inside and to the closet-room where she slept. I undid the brass spike lock and opened the door and she quickly stepped inside the cordoned blackness. Again I could hardly see her. I bid her good night and told her I would be shutting the door and locking it again. She didn't answer, and as I was closing the door she pressed her weight against it, and I thought for an instant that she was trying to force it back open. But the pushing stopped and it was her pale fingers curled around the door edge, and then the fall of her long straight hair loosely covering the side of her face. Her eyes were cast downward, and as the door swung open a little, I took her hands cupped weakly into fists and she let me open them and hold them, her hands in my own tremulous hands. I was breathless. I had closed my eyes. And I remained there for what seemed a very long time, drawing no closer to her as we stood in the threshold of her cell, unmoving, unspeaking, barely resisting all.

TWO MORE WHOLE DAYS I had, before I saw the black flag raised upon the tilted pole of the infirmary. I was heading there in the early morning, in my hand the long, flat, two-pronged key for the lock to the supply closet, when I saw that piece of cloth. At first I thought it was a blank spot in my vision, a colorless void. Then a patch of sky opened low in the east and the light hit the door, and the flag next to it became unusually lustrous, reflective and yet flat-seeming with its absolute stillness. It was larger than I had first thought, a perfect square of black silk. I thought it was of the Chinese kind, its texture subtly striated and banded; and the way it fell stiffly from the two holes cut out along one edge, through which a rough twine was looped and then lashed to the short pole, it was like a piece of shiny, burnt parchment.

I did not touch it. Instead I let myself inside and went directly to the back of the building, to the closet where I had left her. I took my key and pushed it up through the brass slots of the lock. When I opened the door she was already standing up, waiting for me. I gave her the rice balls hidden in my pockets; I had saved them from the officers' mess the night before, not eating two of my own and taking two others when I saw that the cook had stepped outside for a smoke. We sat on the blankets she had laid out over the floor. I let her eat a little while before speaking.

Then I said to her, "He did not come here last night?"

She shook her head, swallowing the last of the rice balls. "I woke up when I heard someone walking around this morning. I listened but he seemed to go away. It was the captain, wasn't it? Wasn't it?"

"Yes," I said to her, not meeting her eyes. She was staring at me, I could feel it. I told her, "I think it is this evening, K, that he will come to the infirmary."

She nodded to herself. We were quiet for some time, and I felt I ought to do something for her, or at least say a few words. I had nothing ready to offer, however, though not because there wasn't any feeling inside me. I had too much feeling, perhaps. I felt a stone in my chest, which seemed almost to pin me down.

She spoke softly now: "I must ask you again if you will help me."

"I am sorry, K, but I have told you there is nothing I can do."

"Yes, I know, but we are friends now," she said, "and I only ask that you give me something now. I don't expect you to help me in any other way. You're a medical officer, and you must know what to give me, so I won't wake up again."

I could hardly bear to picture her that way.

"Please, Jiro," she said, using my name for the first time. She had asked what it was the night before, and I had felt strange telling her, though now the sound of her speaking it was like a balm. "Please. You can help as no one else."

"I won't."

"How can you not wish to, knowing the captain will come here tonight?"

"I do wish to help you."

"Then you ought to do so," she said, somewhat harshly, her voice ringing in the ensuing silence. But then she gathered herself, her hands clutching her elbows. She tried to smile. "You have been too kind, spending time with me and bringing me extra food. I have told you how you're so much like my brother, generous and innocent like him. Blessed that way. But I've thought you've been a little brave, too."

"I don't think I am brave."

"You are." She sat up on her knees. "I don't know what risks you're taking by being kind to me. But I know you are taking risks. What would the captain have done if he had found us in the other room yesterday or the day before that, sitting and talking as we were? What would he have done then?"

I couldn't say what would have occurred. I still couldn't imagine myself challenging him, or being insubordinate in any way, and yet the thought of accepting whatever punishment he deemed deserving for me, and especially for her, seemed equally impossible. In the last few days I had begun to find myself defending her, at least in my mind, stepping between her and others, or pulling her from some faceless danger. But in truth it was solely the doctor and surgeon, Captain Ono, who ever had any purpose and intention for her, who even knew, besides myself, where K was, and it was his narrowed, severe visage that I could not yet conceive of repelling.

"I want to help you," I said to her. "But I can only do for you what I have done already, and nothing more. I have tried to keep you in a state of healthfulness, which is my responsibility, and the captain would ultimately understand that, I believe."

She shook her head. "You don't have to speak like that, Jiro. I know you don't believe only what you say. You're not just being a dutiful medical officer. I thought we had talked yesterday about what might happen after the war. What your hopes and plans were, to go to medical school and become a respected physician in Kobe.

And then meeting a nice girl from a good family and having many children, all of you in a fine house with beautiful grounds. I enjoyed talking like that, about what the future would hold. Didn't you?"

"Yes," I answered.

"And remember what you said? How we could perhaps meet again, in an interesting place like Hong Kong, or Kyoto. What fun times we might have, seeing the sights together. We were just talking, I know, but sometimes that's enough to make everything seem real."

"I would like it to be real," I said, recalling the serene temples I had described to her, the ones in Kyoto I had visited on school trips, the plum trees blooming about their hilltop perches in fantastical color. "I stayed awake until almost morning, thinking of other places you might like to see."

"What were they?"

"I thought of the rocky seasides on Shikoku, the steep cliffs above the water, the humble fishing villages there. Because you said you liked the water, and swimming. And then of course there is Tokyo, which I have not yet been to, but which must be wondrous in all its activity. They say it is a hundred Kobes, put all together."

"My father was there once," she said, surprising me. "When I was eight or nine. He brought back a fancy set of brushes for us girls to share, and brand-new English lesson books for our brother. For my mother he brought a tiny chest filled with European face powder and perfume and lip pencils."

"Why was he there?" I asked.

"He was a kind of ambassador, I think. My mother told us that a number of noblemen and civic leaders were going to Japan, to have discussions on the issue of the Japanese colonists coming to Korea. They were trying to come to an agreement, of sorts, to make it better for everyone, and fairer for those who were being displaced from their homes and shops. I remember how pleased my father was when he returned, as pleased as I have ever seen him, even taking us girls to be photographed the next day, with our mother. But by the end of the year he was most disillusioned. Nothing had changed. In fact there were more settlers than ever. And in town people began to blame my father, as he was the local official who had gone on the mission. One night we came home from a farmers' festival to find our house burning down. We had to leave our land and move into a house-for-let, and soon after that he hardly spoke to anyone. Even our brother. He just stayed in his room of books, reading Chinese poetry and practicing his calligraphy."

"You never mentioned what kind of family you were from."

"Would it have made a difference in anything?"

I shook my head, knowing that it would not have. But nonetheless it explained her speech, her education, what I was finally understanding to be her *class,* which I hadn't quite fathomed until then, having had no contact with such Koreans. In fact she had poked fun at my own talk, which was to her rough and slangy and of the streets, the twisty, cramped ghetto alleys of Kobe. And it seemed incongruous, as well, how it was that I, the only child of a hide tanner and a rag maid, should come to wear a second lieutenant's uniform of the Ocean Sky Battalion of the Imperial Forces, and that she, born into a noble, scholarly house (if perhaps one fallen), would have to sleep in a surplus closet of a far-flung military outpost, her sister already dead and buried, wishing upon herself the same horrid end.

"I want to believe that you and I will do all the things we spoke of," I told her. "I am hoping the war will end soon, as has been rumored, and perhaps much sooner than anyone knows. It is said the war in fact has been going very badly. There is even talk the Americans will soon attempt to invade Japan itself. No one will say it, but the end is likely coming, and an accommodation will be made. It must. Perhaps it will be next month, or next week even. Then we can go out of this place, we can go out of this place together, and I will take care of you and protect you no matter where we go."

"But you say he is coming tonight," she said sharply. "The doctor will come here tonight. Tonight! Will the war end before then? This afternoon? Will you spirit us away before the dusk falls, Jiro? Because if not there is nothing more to talk about in a real way. There is dreaming and dreaming talk and little else, which is happy enough, and maybe all that remains to us. But please don't try to make things sound real anymore. It makes me feel desperate and mad. You're a decent man, Jiro, more decent than you even know, so please. You can pretend, if you wish, and I'll pretend with you, as much as I am able. But I ask you please no more than that."

She became weary all of a sudden, and let her arms fold beneath her as she lay on her side on the meager blanket. The crown of her head was almost touching my knee where I sat beside her, and after a moment I reached out and began stroking her hair. She had let me do this before and she did not mind now. Her hair was unwashed and heavy and unsweetly redolent but to me it was a perfect mane. Two nights before I had done the same when she grew tired and lay down, stroking her gently at first but then more vigorously and deeply, running my fingers down to her soft scalp, until my hands were warmed and smooth with her oil. She fell asleep and I went to my tent and could not sleep myself, the rich, bodily smell wafting over me. I held up my hands as I lay on my bedroll, and before I knew it I had tasted and kissed them and rubbed them on my face and neck and elsewhere, and in the morning I wanted to be with her like nothing I had ever known. But on sight of the closet door I had to retreat and scrub my hands in the exam room, ashamed by the feeling that I had secretly profaned her.

But now she closed her eyes as I stroked. She had told me she was no longer sleeping much at night or any other time, hardly shutting her eyes even a few minutes a day. She wanted to fall asleep but could not. But I thought now she was very near it, her breathing steady and rhythmical, and it seemed with each pass of my hand through her hair her exhalations grew longer and lighter. It had been many years since I had watched a woman sleep; the last time was when I lived with my first parents in Kobe, where we slept all together in a one-room house. My mother and father would be heaped in the corner like a mound of sackcloths, the noise of their exhausted slumber keeping me awake, my mother tittering in her dreams. Some mornings her pants bottom was pulled half-down, her long straight hair fallen down into the corners of her gaping mouth, my father's hand clutching her breast. I remembered wanting to brush the loose strands away from her mouth, to cover her nakedness with the blanket.

But here beneath me, K was falling away, the line of her mouth softening, and though someone (even the doctor) could come by at any moment, I crawled around and lay down behind her, so that our bodies were aligned, nestled like spoons. She was warm and still and I gently pressed my face into the back of her neck and breathed in the oily musk of her hair. And it was so that I finally began to touch her. I put my hand on the point of her hip and could feel all at once the pliancy of it and the meagerness and the newness, too. I felt bewildered and innocent and strangely renewed, as though a surge of some great living being were coursing up my arm and spreading through my unknowing body. She was sleeping, or pretending to sleep, or somehow forcing herself to, and she did not move or speak or make anything but the shallowest of breaths, even as I was casting myself upon her. I kissed as much of her body as was bared. I kissed her small breasts, which seemed to spill a sweet, watery liquid. I gagged but did not care. Then it was all quite swift and natural, as chaste as it could ever be. And when I was done I felt the enveloping warmth of a fever, its languorous cocoon, though when I gazed at her shoulder and back there was nothing but stillness, her posture unchanged, her skin cool and colorless, and she lay as if she were the sculpture of a recumbent girl and not a real girl at all.

I said then, *I love you,* and she didn't answer. *I love you,* I said again, in Korean, not whispering it this time but speaking it as clearly as I could, and when she didn't reply I assumed she was completely asleep. I rose carefully and stepped back and buckled my trousers, wanting desperately to wake her and kiss her on the mouth but instead letting her remain, recalling how restive and sleepless she said she'd been. I would have done anything then to lend her some peace. I would have executed whatever she asked of me, helped her even to escape. I would have willingly injured another human being had she asked, or needed me to. And it unnerves me even now how particular and exacting that sensation was, how terribly pure. That a man pleasured could so easily resolve himself to the whole spectrum of acts, indifferent and murderous and humane, and choose with such arbitrary will what he shall have to remember forever and forever.

I went out of her closet-room, whispering to her that I would return in several hours, with food for her and maybe something to drink, and thinking ahead to an entire evening in her company; but as I gently shut the door I thought I heard a murmur. I couldn't lock it; to do so seemed at that moment too cruel. Instead I stood quietly for a moment and waited and indeed it was K, saying over and over very quietly what sounded most peculiarly like *hata-hata, hata-hata.* But as I listened more closely I realized that she was fitfully crying, though in quelled gasps, as if she were trying to hush herself. I was afraid to move, lest she hear me, and so I remained, my ear lightly pressed to the worn wood of the door, until she quieted and was silent again and in fact fell asleep, her breathing deep and certain.

After I left her I found myself in a state of unease and exhilaration. I could understand why she should become upset, that she was perhaps sad for the end of her maidenhood (which I thought then was the most precious ore of any woman), but hadn't I professed my devotion to her, hadn't I in mitigation said the words that should let her know what I was intending for us, after the war? I thought I should have also told her that I was now resolved to speak candidly with Captain Ono, that I was prepared to suggest to him my keeping a log of my duties around the camp and infirmary—which I had indeed begun compiling. At least I would not wilt and fade and disappear before him, as I had score upon score of times.

And yet I had no other, further plan; there was no good recourse from her required duties to the camp, there was no actual reprieve I was offering her. I loved her, though I cannot say how that love was or if it was true or worthy in any sense, having never in my life been sure how such a thing should be. I can say I wanted her and could not bear her being with another, and if those are veritable signs, then I should rightly hold her in memory in every way that I am able, and to the last of my days.

Captain Ono, however, was seemingly nowhere to be found; I even sought him out at the commander's hut, rapping on the door sharply until the new sentry ran up around the side and requested that I stop, saying the colonel was "resting" for the afternoon. The captain had indeed been around, he said, with his medical kit, as he had each morning for some days, and in the afternoons the colonel required strictly undisturbed quiet, as ordered by Captain Ono.

I recalled then the multiple requisitions I had just sent by courier to Rangoon for morphine and ether, as our supply for surgery was curiously dwindling, despite our not having conducted any recent procedures. I had long suspected he was medicating the commander, though certainly not against the man's will, as one sometimes saw them talking in the evenings on the veranda of the hut, the colonel's demeanor familiar and jovial, if a bit too loose. The probable fact of this further emboldened me, and as I went around the camp in search of the doctor I felt more determined than ever to withstand whatever insult he might level at me, and somehow influence him to agree to my sole stewardship of "the girl" under some obscure technical or medical rationale.

So sure of myself was I, so certain of my imminent resolve, that the thought of committing an aggression seemed again suddenly quite natural to me, as if I were a man long accustomed to the necessity of such things. I remember suddenly feeling suited to the notion, perhaps even bristling with it as I strode purposefully about the camp, the image of Ono desperate and pained beneath the weight of my will. For I had been quietly considering various revenges upon him, drawing up the ways I would pay him back for his diatribes and affronts, my plans including, too, the most extreme of acts. Had someone asked, I would have denied any such thoughts, but in the core of my heart I was tending the darkest fires. I had certainly despised others before, particularly the boys in the school I attended after being adopted by the Kurohatas, boys who treated me with disdain most of the time and at worst like a stray dog. Each day I vowed to wreak vengeance upon them, see them through some terrible circumstance I'd contrived, or else await the hand of fate. But nothing ever transpired. I never attempted to mark them, and soon enough we passed on to the upper school and there were plenty of others to befriend, both cause and enmity mercifully fading from my mind. I say mercifully because it was never my nature to harbor such thoughts, which have always been near-caustic to me, but in respect to the doctor a vital, searing charge was propelling me, an ashen, bitter hate whose taste I no longer abhorred.

And though exactly how I cannot describe, mixed up with this was my feeling for K, and my sudden sense of her nearness to me. It was a connection aside from what we had just done, what I should say I believed already to be a special correspondence between us, an affinity of being. This may sound specious—one may rightly think here was a young man in the blush of his first sexual love, typically conflating sensation and devotion—but I was not thinking so much of her body or even the desirous tentacled feeling of mine. I was considering what she had suggested about our pretending to be other people, like figures in a Western novel, imagining how we could somehow exist outside of this place and time and circumstance, share instead the minute and sordid problems of such folks, the vagaries and ornate dramas of imperfect love.

So when I finally came upon the doctor, when I finally saw the angular shape of his back and his wiry neck as he berated several soldiers for the dilapidated state of their quarters, it seemed I was summoning the picture of my plunging a long blade into his throat, terrorizing him not with pain so much as the fright of an instant, wholly unanticipated death. In reality I was carrying a scalpel in my holster (pinned against the pistol), and I actually reached into the leather pouch as I approached him and felt the metal handle. I could simply pull out the razor-sharp instrument and insert it a few centimeters into his skin and run it down the length of the carotid. None of the men would protest, and if one did, it would be too late. The doctor would clutch at his throat, the blood would flow forth freely, and in less than a minute he would quietly expire.

Captain Ono turned to me just as I was a few steps away. But my hand was at my head in salute and he said, with no little irritation, "What must it be now, Lieutenant?"

"I would request to speak with you, sir. It's an important matter."

"Is that what you believe?"

"Yes, sir," I answered. The enlisted men were holding themselves in, pleased as they were to witness an officer receiving the captain's harsh treatment.

"And what would this concern, Lieutenant?"

"I was hoping to speak in private, sir. It concerns one of the volunteers."

"You surely are being scrupulous, Lieutenant Kurohata. And is right now the most necessary time for you to tell me what's on your mind?"

"Yes, sir," I said sharply, nearly barking. One of the enlisted men couldn't help himself and let out a snort at my pained rigor. The captain at once wheeled and struck him across the face with his open hand, and the man fell down, more, it seemed, from sheer surprise than the force of the blow. He quickly stood up without any help and stood at attention, as were his fellows. A wide red welt rose up over his eye and the side of his face. The doctor waited and then hit him again, and again the man fell down and then got back up to his feet, this time more tentatively. The whole action seemed somehow self-evident, being strangely mechanical. He then turned to me and in no different a voice said, "Then perhaps you and I should talk elsewhere, Lieutenant Kurohata. I require a few more moments with these men. You'll meet me at the infirmary shortly."

I did not of course want to go back there with him, but he had already dismissed me and immediately resumed addressing the men, criticizing them for their indolence and disorganization. Such a sight was becoming more and more common. Like most others in the camp, the doctor himself seemed caught in a state of increasing agitation, the protracted stretch of waiting and inaction and ennui causing flares of anxiety and disruption. A rash of fights had recently broken out among the men, and the feeling within the officer corps had, in fact, become distinctly chilly and distant, what with the system of command ever loosening and the threat of fighting having clearly passed us over.

I was walking quite slowly, as I was loathing the thought of the three of us together, her so near to him in my presence, and the doctor actually caught up with me before I reached the infirmary. He took me by the shoulder to stop me, the windowless back wall where K was locked in the closet just in our sight.

"Perhaps you'll realize someday, Lieutenant, why I've been so hard on you," he said flatly, no more avuncular than he ever was, or could be. "I say this not because I care what you think of me, or even for your sake. I cannot be concerned with you, as an individual. I think you well know this."

I assented openly, for the first time feeling somehow equal to him, imminently free.

"Good," he said, taking out a small case of etched silver. He offered a brown-wrapped cigarette to me, but I declined. He took it for himself and lighted it, smoking quickly and deeply. "You are not an incapable young officer, Lieutenant Kurohata," he said, exhaling the spice-edged smoke. "But you are gravely misguided, most all of the time. I fear I shall believe this about you to my death. You probably don't care. But I know you believe I take you to task because of your parentage. I've always known of this, yes. But that never mattered to me. It's for the weak and lame-minded to focus on such things. Blood is only so useful, or hindering. The rest is strong thought and strong action. This is why, Lieutenant, I find myself unable to cease critiquing you. There is the germ of infirmity in you, which infects everything you touch or attempt. Besides all else, how do you think you will ever become a surgeon? A surgeon determines his course and acts. He goes to the point he has determined without any other faith, and commits to an execution. You, Lieutenant, too much depend upon generous fate and gesture. There is no internal possession, no embodiment. Thus you fail in some measure always. You perennially disappoint someone like me.

"Right now, you want to speak to me about the girl in there," he went on, pointing up the path to the homely building. "You wish to be resolute about something about her and yet I see nothing in your face or posture that will convince me of your desires. You sound as if you would trounce me, but I look at you directly and what is solid in you but your sentimental feeling and hope? Tell me, tell me freely, in any way you wish."

"I think you have taken questionable liberties about the camp. With the girl, and then also with Colonel Ishii."

"What exactly?"

"You have steadily usurped command, sir. Everyone knows how the colonel remains inside all day and night, how he is hardly awake anymore."

"And what do *you* know?"

"That we are again out of certain anesthetics and painkillers, which I believe you are offering to the colonel too frequently, perhaps even with the intent to incapacitate him."

"Why should I wish to do such a thing, Lieutenant, when I have always had the commander's ear, on all matters? What pleasure or advantage would it give me?"

"I don't know, sir. Perhaps you want complete control," I said, amazed at my own directness.

"Over what?" he rasped at me. "Over this meaningless outpost? These stupid, backward herds of men? You are less observant than I gave you credit for. I accepted this posting because I was assured there would be steady fighting in the region, and that I could institute a first-rate field hospital and surgery ward. I expected there would be plenty of casualties, with constant opportunities for employing new techniques and procedures. At minimum there would be the regular exercise of autopsies. Of course there's nothing now of any interest. It's a cesspool of nursery maladies, insect bites and rashes. This is a situation that you might appropriately command, but not I. Colonel Ishii naturally understood my frustration and formally requested long ago that I be transferred, but his request has yet to be acknowledged. Meanwhile, I cannot optimally serve our cause, and my skills are no doubt eroding. The colonel, if you are curious, has chronic, severe pain from a shrapnel wound suffered in the early years of the war, in Manchuria, and he chooses to relieve himself of it. It is never my place to regulate him, unless his doing so affects the battalion, which it has not.

"About the girl, Lieutenant, I will say this. You have obviously taken an interest in her, which is of course unavoidable. She is most comely, though I say that not to describe her sexual attraction, which in this forsaken place and to these men any girl or woman would possess, even that annoying shrew Matsui-san. But as for this girl, she has a definite presence and will and lively spirit. There's clear breeding there, if you didn't quite know. Unlike what you were probably taught in your special indoctrinational schooling, Lieutenant, there are indeed Chinese and Koreans of special and high character, in fact, of the same bloodlines as the most pure Japanese. There is a commonality between someone like her and me, a distinct correspondence, if one very distant. This is one of the reasons I've separated her—you could say as a means of acknowledging that relation, particularly with her sister having been killed. But you, Lieutenant, you can of course look narrowly upon someone like her, for private uses and pleasures, rather than the larger concerns."

"What are those, Captain Ono?" I said sharply. "Will you inform me, sir, as I have little idea."

The doctor grinned, the corners of his mouth tight, half-appreciative of the acuteness in my voice. "What are they indeed, Lieutenant! What do you think the Home Ministry has been promoting all these years, but a Pan-Asian prosperity as captained by our people? Do you understand what that really means? I can see you don't. We must value ourselves however and wherever we appear, even in the scantest proportion. There can be no ignoring the divine spread of our strain. You, it is obvious, are helplessly concerned about the girl—that one female body, there in the infirmary. There is something to this, no doubt. But I am not confined to such thinking. I don't care about *her*. She is not of any consequence, except as a kind of rare vessel of us, to be observed and stewarded. For the present time she is important to me, and when she is no longer I shall give her over to you, to do with her what you wish, whether you would bed her or journey the world with her or drown her at the shore. But as long as you see the banner there, Lieutenant, you shall keep to the duties I've set out for you and retain her in the manner I command. I raise it for you and you alone, and you will heed it without hesitance or prejudice."

"I cannot promise such a thing, sir," I said stiffly, stepping forward slightly. "And I cannot let you visit her tonight, or on any future day."

He stared at me incredulously, searching my face, and then laughed, surprising me, as I thought he would rage and explode at my insubordination.

"You are an immense fool," he said. "I almost feel sorry for you. What do you think you are doing, protecting her honor? I suppose you imagine she's your maiden, and you her swordsman. You do, indeed. And you also think that I've been saving her these last few days in anticipation of some memorable evening?"

"She said you had not visited. . . ."

The captain shook his head, grinning again, though he was not amused. "The girl is telling stories, and you are believing them. Did she tell you how much she thought of you, too, how much she loved you?"

"She never professed such things."

"Perhaps she suggested how she would like to meet you again, after the war?"

When I didn't answer, the captain scoffed and said grimly, "Shut up now. Or better yet, go away. I can't stand to look at you. Your presence is demoralizing me."

"I will not let anyone else go to her, sir."

"No more of you, Lieutenant!" he shouted, waving his hand. "You had permission to address me freely but now you will silence yourself and leave me."

"I wish her to be my wife. I will marry her when the war ends. I have already decided this."

The captain stared at me with an expression of pure disgust, as if I had violated every law and code of his living. "You have 'decided' this, Lieutenant? So you have already had your sweet trifle with her, I suppose; you have taken her there on her dirt bed?"

"I will love her," I said as fiercely as I could, though the words immediately rang shallow and distant. "No matter what you say."

He laughed terribly. "Even if I tell you she is pregnant? Oh indeed, yes. I suppose she must have tricked the commander about her menses. It doesn't matter now. I'm letting the pregnancy go, in fact, to see how long she'll stay that way, once she begins servicing the whole of the camp. She was pregnant before even I was able to take my pleasure. Before anyone here had her. Who knows who her real master is? The commander and I certainly aren't. So now you can fancy yourself to be her foster lover, her foster groom, as it were. And then stepfather to her child, if it ever comes to be. . . ."

But before he could finish speaking I tackled him square in the gut and the force of the blow knocked the wind out of him. He lay for a moment beside me trying to get back his breath, then rose slowly to his knees. I wanted to get up to strike him but my right shoulder seemed to shear like wet paper when I put weight on my hand, and I knew it had completely separated. The pain was severe enough that it didn't feel like much of anything when the captain punched me in the belly. I watched, numbly estranged from myself, as he unholstered his service revolver and struck me again, once or twice or several times. He then pulled back the hammer and placed the cold ring of the barrel end to my forehead. He seemed very close, as if he were peering into me. He had no malice or rage in his face, simply a plain expression of purpose. I passed through then to another reach of bodily suffering, the pain already become a thing memorial, an insolvent fever in the tissue and bones.

13

AROUND THE TIME that Tommy was likely born, I began to entertain a certain waking nightmare. Sunny was of course long gone, having departed many months earlier without leaving a forwarding address or phone number. I knew she had taken up with Lincoln Evans, living with him (and probably others) in a squalid flat down in the city, though I no longer had either cause or interest in finding her. I didn't care to see what was becoming of her. I was saddened, of course, but also in good measure angry, hurt by the completeness of her departure, as if she were a night's guest at any roadside inn, the room hastily checked out of with that rumple of early morning disorder and abandon. I had offered her all that I possessed or could muster, the run of my house and my business and the willing graces of my town, which I must say is what it felt like in those last days just before I sold to the Hickeys. The streets and sidewalks of Bedley Run truly seemed as much mine as any person's, their almost affirming solidity underfoot, bouncing me along on my diurnal way.

The dream, if I can call it that, would come to me at the end of the working day, in the last hour between six and seven when there were never any more customers or calls from salesmen and I was hungry and enervated and in a state that must be a kind of retail beatitude, a mind of placid emptiness and vulnerability. Somewhere in my thoughts I knew that Sunny was close to term, sustaining herself in whatever unhealthful and meager manner, and I summoned an image of myself as a physician, old and wise and sure, who ran a tiny free clinic on the ground floor of a tenement building in the city. Each day until dusk I would treat the ills, both trivial and grave, of the modest neighborhood folks, attending with patience and close application every complaint of cough and rash and ache, gently and somberly addressing the more serious indications, my corner windowed office known all over as a kindly haven, the seat of good Doc Hata of Whatever Street.

And so on a typical day of full appointments with the sick and injured and scared, who should walk in but an adolescent girl, unescorted, safeguarding with one hand an immense belly in that tender, cupping way, asking if she might see me immediately. My beleaguered but generous-spirited receptionist would try to explain the tight schedule, indicating the overflowing waiting room, but I'd come out in my white coat and her sallow face would brighten, the simple sight of me enough to lend some calm and relief. But just then the girl would shudder, momentarily swoon, and tip like a felled tree into the arms of the nurse, saying weakly that her water had long ago broken. We rushed her into the back room and laid her down, and when I lifted her long skirt the baby was already showing itself, not by its crown but with a tiny, perfect foot, unwrinkled and pink. I was alarmed but not nervous, as I was a doctor of long experience, having turned many a breech fetus and safely delivered a near-equal number. And yet this time I felt myself faltering, the little body inside somehow unfathomable to me, unreadable, my hands stricken with a sudden numbing weakness. I thought then to attempt a breech delivery, but here, too, I seemed to forget the delicate procedures. I still couldn't sense the baby's contours, the hip, the shoulder, the orientation of the head, and when my nurse warned that the foot was turning color, grayish blue, a hard tick of panic set off in my chest. The girl was writhing in pain, unable to listen to me and pushing too much, pushing when she shouldn't have been, and as the precious minutes passed, the foot grew grayer and bluer and I knew I would have to open her up and lift the baby out. The girl was now delirious with pain. The nurse placed in my hand a shiny blade, and I realized then that it was a travesty and I was not a surgeon, that I had never cut into living flesh. That I was a fraud and a coward and should not have coveted and accepted as I had done the confidence of people, their singular regard and trust.

At that point my conjuring would cease, and I would close up the store, go home as I did every evening, to a long swim and dinner in a bowl and a pot or two of tea. Of course it doesn't require a psychologist or guru to figure the significance of my fantasy, and I don't recount it here to suggest anything but the most simple truth. I felt guilt about Sunny, no doubt. But I know I was also truly concerned for her, and taken hold of by the worry a real parent must have, the kind that reaches far down into the gut, that wakes you from sleep and constantly breaks your thoughts and keeps you from sitting still. As much as I had hoped to, I never quite felt that way when Sunny was living with me, not when she fell down once and chipped several permanent teeth, not when she went off to sleep-away camp for the first time, not even when I let her drive alone to the city in my newly delivered Mercedes-Benz coupe. I was uneasy at those times, quite thoroughly concerned, but never gravely ill-feeling, never infected to the marrow as I assumed a real father would or should be, lying there in bed inconsolably perturbed, unable to think, to read, even to drink calmly from a glass. And though I never thought I would desire such a set of sensations for myself, in the days and weeks after she was gone from my house, in those cycles that seemed to pass like fast-turning epochs, as if I were some inconsequential rock hurtling past the warm blue sphere of human time and history, yet unseen and unknown, I finally wished I might remain in the sickness I was developing when I was sure Sunny was about to be a mother. It was not pleasant at all but somehow distinctly worthy and inhabitable, a nightly pool of deep worry and remorse and unexpected comfort that I could wade into and do my long-distance crawl, for once not forgetting who I was, for once not blacking myself out.

And yet, eventually, this feeling passed as well. Routine triumphs over everything, as it always does with men like me, and I returned to the living of Bedley Run and its vested, untouchable ways. In truth I was beginning to understand my position after so many years, my popularity and high reputation, one that someone like Liv Crawford would say was "triple mint," or "among the finest in town." Because that in fact is what it was, and has been, and no doubt will be until I die. It was during Sunny's absence that I finally awoke to this notion, that I was perfectly suited to my town, that I had steadily become, oddly and unofficially, its primary citizen, the living, breathing expression of what people here wanted—privacy and decorum and the quietude of hard-earned privilege. And so much so that my well-known troubles with Sunny were not a strike against me or a sign of personal failure but a kind of rallying point, silently demonstrated by somebody's solemn, shut-eye nod at the lakeside gazebo on the Fourth of July, or a lingering handshake out front on Church Street, or a light, friendly honk from a passing car I knew.

So why am I not fine now? I ought to be, for I'm unexpectedly driving over to pick up Thomas and bring him to the Bedley Run pool club, as the one in Ebbington has been derelict for several summers now, fenced shut and emptied of water. Sunny has relented on never letting him step back into my town, his eyes begging for a day in the water. The Bedley pool is actually a small man-made lake, chlorinated and filtered, and I've told Thomas I'll teach him how to swim, a lesson a week until the season ends, and then indoors at the racquet club if he wishes to continue. I believe he likes me. He calls me Franklin now, and not Mr. Hata, after he asked what my full name was. I don't mind at all. "Franklin," he says, as though we have been associates for many years, "I think we ought to stop for a snack now." He seems satisfied that I am a "family friend," not questioning me any further.

One day after that first shopping trip, I took him down to the city, to the natural history museum, where we toured the longtime exhibits, and then a new one on the development of mammalian sea life, in particular the evolution of dolphins and whales. All he could talk about after I read the accompanying plaques to him was how he would like to be a fish but breathe air, so that he would be jumping out of the water all day and all night. He was focused on the joys of leaping, of course, but I was thinking of the endless necessity of having to leave one's element for another and so depend on the resource of another realm, that no matter how automatic and natural it was or became there should always be the pressure of survival, this pointed, mortal condition of being.

I didn't speak of this to Thomas, for obvious reasons. I didn't tell him, either, of my other notions of the pastime, that in fact some of us longtime swimmers often wish for ourselves that submerged, majestic flight, feel the near-desire to open one's mouth and relax and let the waters rush in deep, hoping that something magical might happen. Once, I will admit, during the very time I was thinking often of Sunny and her pregnancy, I attempted this, or let it occur, just a tiny inhalation, just a little taking in, and though my mind was clear and placid, every cell in my body at once objected, my limbs practically jetting me out of the water and onto the slate surround of the pool, where I lay on my side coughing violently. Did I wish to do away with myself? Did I truly wish to die? Or was I hoping for a transmogrification, complete and however strange, a wholly different heart and shell and mien that would deliver me over to a brand-new life, fresh and hopeful and unfettered?

And here, perhaps, it is. I turn up the steep drive to The Conifers, a rental condominium in what might be described as the "better" section of Ebbington, a string of modern attached units set in a sparse stand of evergreens, each with a carport in front and a private balcony in back, overlooking the humble town below. There is a guardhouse halfway up, though it's locked shut and unmanned, and the only thing preventing me from going through unchecked is an old speed bump worn down to a nub. This is the sort of place that in Bedley Run would have a clubhouse for the tenants with a large-screen television, a wet bar, an exercise room and sauna, perhaps even a pool and hot tub and tennis courts, where Liv Crawford or Renny Banerjee might privately and conveniently reside until they settled down and began a family. But here at The Conifers you see tricycles and candy wrappers strewn outside; you see perennials and shrubs aplenty but all badly in need of sprucing and

pruning; you see the domestic cars and economy imports; you see
the subtle and varied indications of both decency and decline. By
living here it's clear these folk are aspiring to a more privileged life,
though perhaps it's true that most will never see better than the
West Hill of Ebbington, which by all rights should be as good as any
place in what really matters, just as righteous, just as valued, but
isn't all the same.

When the door opens it's Sunny, dressed in a smart-looking
dark business suit and white blouse, fastening a string of pearls
about her throat. The reason I have the chance to take Thomas
swimming is that she has an interview in Stamford and two hours
earlier was called by her sitter, who canceled for the afternoon. But
I'm late when I needn't have been, and I apologize.

"I do appreciate this," she says tightly to me, not having to add
that I am indeed her last resort. "I had to send him to the neighbors
so I could get dressed in peace. He's absolutely crazy that he's going
swimming. I'll call over there now."

While she rings for him I sit on the sofa in the living room,
where she also has a comfortable armchair, and cocktail table, and
mini-stereo on the mantel of the gas fireplace. There's a small dining area next to the open kitchen with a pine table and four chairs,
and then two bedrooms down the short hall in the back, the whole
place perhaps just a bit larger than the family room of my house.
But she's painted the walls a creamy, warm peach and the trim a
glossy white. There's a nice rug here and under the dining table, and
the kitchen is papered with Thomas's handiwork, the career of his
finger paintings and scrawls. A soft, sweet smell of lavender lingers
from the bowls of dried flowers, and all throughout there is a
sparkle to the surfaces, a steady gleam that goes straight to this old
man's heart, even as he knows it's not in the least for him.

"He's having lunch over there, so he'll be a few minutes. Do you want something to drink?" Sunny says to me, poking her head around the kitchen opening. "I have soda and tea. You probably would like tea."

"If there is time."

"There really isn't," she answers, but I hear her running the water in the kettle anyway. She calls, "I don't have green tea. Just black, and herbal."

"I will have the herbal, thank you."

"I thought you never had anything but green," she says, bringing out a saucer with three butter cookies. I want to say thank you but don't because I'm afraid of being ardent and scaring her off. But this is her place and she seems only slightly disturbed by my presence, the way she might be if a small, tame bird had somehow flown in.

"May I ask what you're interviewing for?" I say, taking a cookie. "Is it in retail again?"

"It is," she answers, sitting forward on the armchair. "It's to be a manager. It's a chain store for younger girls, teens and preteens. It's not exactly what I know, but I guess selling clothes is selling clothes."

"You'll have to move out to Connecticut?"

"No, they're just interviewing there. The chain is actually out in the west, in California and Arizona and Texas. They're expanding, and they need experienced managers, which I guess they don't have enough of out there. I haven't said anything to Thomas, nothing at all, so I'll ask you not to mention it."

"I promise to be quiet about it."

"I'm sure you will," she says, her old Sunny-soundingness almost sneaking back into her voice. But she catches herself, or I think she does, and she reaches over and takes a cookie, biting just the edge of it, a tiny nibble. It's a nothing act but I'm taken back instantly, many years, when I would offer her those popular vanilla wafers and she would refuse, not because she didn't want them but for fear I would think her greedy and selfish for taking more than one, this orphan girl. I would almost have to scold her to make her understand it was all right.

"I know Thomas is going to want to see you more after today. He asked about you a couple days ago. Out of the blue he said he wanted to go to 'Franklin's house.' Did you tell him you had a pool?"

"I may have accidentally mentioned it. I'm sorry."

"I don't want him to go over there. I'm firm on this. He'll see the house and the yard and pool and he'll go crazy. He's difficult enough, and if he thinks he can go over there anytime he wants to play and swim, I don't know what I'm going to do. He needs to work on his reading this year. He's going to be left back this fall, you know. The school said he has to repeat the first grade, unless he passes a test next month."

"Is that right?"

"I don't know. I think so. I've been trying to read with him, but he's not really picking it up very well, and I've had to leave him with the sitter while I'm finishing up at Lerner's and interviewing, and we haven't had much time for it. The sitter says she reads with him, but I'm pretty sure she does nothing but watch TV and call her boyfriend."

"Why don't I help?" I say to her. "It's a good situation for everyone. I'm home all day, or just doing errands, and though I can't promise what kind of reading teacher I'll be, I'd be happy to try my best with him. I certainly would be attentive, and I'll only allow him to play and swim as much as you say. I'm free of charge, too, if that's all right with you. It's perfect, as far as I can see."

"It's not exactly perfect, you know. . . ."

"But why? You can focus completely on your job search, and Thomas will have constant attention. I'll come over here, if you don't want him to come to the house. Or if you're uncomfortable with that, we'll go somewhere different each day. The zoo or museum, or the water park. I'll take him to Jones Beach. You can think of me as his personal day-camp counselor. I'll make sure he eats well, too, and healthfully."

"I doubt you'll be able to do that."

"But I promise I'll try. Please don't invite more difficulty on yourself. I can help, and I ought to help, and I very much wish to. And there would be nothing in this that would be detrimental to Thomas, except that I might spoil him a little. But who shouldn't do with a little spoiling, especially a good boy like him? I wish I could have done better by you when you were young, but I was just opening the store then and circumstances were spare—"

"Please—"

"I'm not trying to excuse myself," I tell her firmly, enough that it's a surprise to me. "I'm not so naive as to be ignorant of how you must feel about things. You have not been anything but generous. But I know I'm on tenuous ground, and I accept it."

"Do you?" she says, though not unkindly. And I note, too, that there is a certain give in her voice, a new gentility, and whether it's from the passage of time or a heart of pity or just the automatic lilt of our line of work, I don't care, I don't give "two darns," as Mary Burns sometimes allowed herself to say, I don't want to understand anything but that I am here and she is here, and that there is a glimmer of gentle days ahead.

She goes on, "I'm sorry, but I don't think that you do. I don't want to fight today. Or really anymore. There's just too much to do. I'm grateful for whatever you want to give to Thomas or do with him. I'm not going to be stupid about it. Not about him. But I won't have you forget or conveniently put away how you felt back then."

"I simply didn't want you to go off with that man and bring ruin on your life. You were too young."

"Of course I shouldn't have gone with him," she says with finality. "But I really don't want to talk about him now."

"No, Sunny, we shouldn't. Why don't we speak about Thomas. It's Thomas we are concerned with, yes?"

"That's right."

"Well, what shall we do for him?" I say, thinking and meaning for the far future, his schooling and training and vocation, what shall remain after I am gone.

But Sunny doesn't answer, and I realize how much she is restraining herself, though for what reason I do not know. It is as if she has "gotten religion," as they say, found some secret store of forgiveness in herself, even as I have long been depleting it. Or perhaps it is truer that forgiveness is inexhaustible, that it is miraculously depthless and renewing as long as you so wish it, no matter what has become of it, no matter how residual and meager.

"It's funny to think now," she finally says, "that if I had had that first baby, I probably wouldn't have had Thomas. Or not exactly Thomas. Which is terrible to imagine."

"Yes, of course."

"But I didn't wish for it. Tell me now. You had already paid him, hadn't you? Doctor Anastasia. Before I even agreed."

"I did nothing of the kind," I answer, sitting back a bit into the soft sofa. "I merely discussed possibilities with him, about options for you."

"It was only just one option."

I don't answer, because again for me there is nothing to say.

"I didn't really blame you, actually," Sunny tells me. "I certainly don't now. It was my decision to do and live with. Most any parent would have wanted the same. I was afraid, and you were so certain as usual how my life should be."

"You seemed to be sure yourself."

"For you I was," she answers, gazing right at me. "I wanted that baby more just to be against you. And I'm not happy that in some way, maybe, even though it was years later, that Thomas came from my spiting you. But often I think, where would I be now if I didn't have Thomas? He's always been a difficult kid but every day I think he's saving me, too. I had him maybe for the wrong reasons and now he saves me. Over and over, a thousand times."

"Yes," I utter, for in listening to her a bloom of well-being is opening immediately and fully in my heart, the kind of pleasure I have hitherto only read about or imagined, what must be the secret opiate of all fathers and mothers.

Sunny says softly, "You know, I often think it was a girl. Sometimes I miss her. I didn't know her at all of course but I miss her. But you always knew I felt this way, didn't you?"

I nod, even though I'm unsure whether I did or not, whether I ever understood at all how deeply that time might have affected her. I was so thoroughly organized in my convincing her (though none of it would have worked had she not been plain scared inside, a frightened girl of seventeen, no matter how sure of herself she was, or believed she was), that I couldn't stop until it was complete. I forced her to do it. Had she decided not to, I don't know what I would have done. In a way, it was a kind of ignoring that I did, an avoidance of her as Sunny—difficult, rash, angry Sunny—which I masked with a typical performance of consensus building and subtle pressure, which always is the difficult work of attempting to harmonize one's life and the lives of those whom one cherishes. It is the systematic operation, which always and obtusely succeeds, the well-planned response to life's uncertainties and complications. And then, too, it is a profoundly arresting thing to realize the exact mode and matter of one's own life at the very moment it is becoming incarnate and true, namely, how after you have pushed aside and pushed aside and pushed aside again, the old beacons will bob up once more, dotting the waters before you like a glowing ring of fire.

14

NOW AND THEN, I sometimes forget who I really am. I will be
sitting downstairs in the kitchen, or on the edge of the lounger by
the pool, or here under the covers in my bed, and I lose all sense
of myself. I forget what it is I do, the regular activity of my walk and
my swim and my taking of tea, the minor trappings and doings of
my days, what I've made up to be the token flags of my life. I forget why it is I do such things, why they give me interest or solace
or pleasure. Then I might get up in the middle of the night and dress
and walk all the way to town, to try to figure once again the notices,
the character, the sorts of actions of a man like me, what things or
set of things define him in the most simple and ordinary way. But I
forget the usuals, who his friends might be, his associates; I forget
even that he has a tenuous and fragile hold of family, this the only
idea that dully rings of remembrance in his heart. He walks at night
in the center of town and it is too dark to see even a reflection in
the glass of his old store. He's stopped by a patrol car and asked
what he's doing and he says nothing, I'm not really walking, I'm not

really here, and he turns for home with the cruiser slowly trailing him, unintentionally lighting his way.

When I reach the house and close the front door it's then I think K has finally come back for me. It is the moment I think I feel at home. I am sure I was regarding her last night, her figure naked and pale, loosely enrobed in a black silken flag. The sight of her shook me. I saw her more clearly than I ever had before, as I was not dreaming or conjuring but simply reacquainting myself with her, as I might any friend of my youth. And so she visited me. Last night she lightly pattered up and down the hallway in her bare feet, pausing outside my bedroom door. I knew it was she. I sat up and told her to come in and she stepped to the foot of my lone twin bed. Though she sat down I couldn't feel any press of her weight, and once again, for a moment, I was almost sure she was a spectral body or ghost. But I am not a magical man, and never have been. I am unversed in the metaphysical, have long become estranged from it, and if this can be so, I believe the metaphysical is as much unversed in me. We have a historical pact. And as deeply as I wished she were some wondrous, ethereal presence, that I was being duly haunted, I knew that she was absolute, unquestionably real, a once-personhood come wholly into being.

"Lieutenant," she asked demurely, her voice full of penitence. "Did you sleep peacefully last night? I hope you'll forgive me if I say you look somewhat weary this morning."

"I do feel weary," I answered. "Thank you for your concern. But what is it, K? It seems something is on your mind."

"I'm sorry to ask this once again."

"Please, K. You may ask me anything."

"I like to think so, Lieutenant."

"Well, then?"

"Will we be going away soon, Lieutenant?"

Her question was brand-new to me, but somehow I felt vaguely annoyed by it anyway. Even angry. I said to her, the hairs tingling on the back of my neck, "Where would we be going to, K?"

"I had hoped we would finally travel to all the places we have spoken of. To Shanghai, and Kyoto, and perhaps even Seoul. Or some other place."

I didn't answer, and she noticed this and asked if I was upset.

"I'm not upset," I said, quite tersely, causing her to inch back on the bed. "But I have to wonder, why being here is so abhorrent to everyone but me? We have everything that we require. And much more. We have an impressive house and property in the best town in the area, where we are happily known and respected. We have ample time and quiet and means. I have tried as hard as I can to provide these things, and we have been welcomed as warmly as anyone can expect. Everything is in delicate harmony. And yet still you seem dissatisfied."

"I am not dissatisfied," she said, her eyes glassy and full-looking. "But I am anxious, Lieutenant. I do hope we might move on from this place. Nothing is wrong with it, nothing at all. But I know I will not die here. I cannot die here. And sometimes, sir, I so wish to."

Her words at first confused me, as I thought she was saying this wouldn't be a suitable place for her to pass over to the next life. But then I realized she meant that it wouldn't be possible, as if this house were some penultimate trap of living, sustaining her beyond the pale.

"I don't want you to die," I said to her, feeling just as suddenly that this is a daily conversation we have, that we have gone over this ground before, and before. So I told her, as I always do, "I want you to live with me forever."

A faint, sad smile softened her face, and she let slip the black cloth from her shoulders and lay down with me beneath the covers. Her skin was cool and chaste to me, almost sisterly, alabastrine, and I thought I had convinced her to remain yet again, remembering now how many times I had done so, today and yesterday and all the days before that, in a strange and backward perpetuity. I keep winning her over with hardly an argument, though each time an ill feeling comes over me, the soiling, resident sickness you develop when you have never in your life been caught at something wrong, when you have never once been discovered.

I lay back down and closed my eyes to sleep, sure that K would stay with me through the night. But when I woke up in the dim of predawn she was gone, and I put on my slippers and robe and went about the house, upstairs and down and even in the basement, in steady search of her. There were the remnants of a fire in the family room hearth, and I could not remember if I had lit one the evening before (I had been doing so periodically, if carefully, since that sudden conflagration). The scent of moist ash lingered in the air. For a moment I thought it smelled naturally of freshly tilled ground, of just-disturbed earth, but then I realized it was in fact not earth at all I was sensing but water. The scent was of the sea, a warm and gentle southern sea. Then I thought I saw a shadow pass outside the French doors of the kitchen, and being certain it was K, I quickly stepped outside. I called out and waited but there was no answer, no sound at all, not even the movement of wind through the tree branches. From the far end of the property the light of a reflection caught my eye, and with sharp anticipation I went to it, going around the pool and past the small cabana to the part of my property where the lawn ends and the wooded area between my land and the neighbor's begins. I was quite sure I would find her, or come across the black silken cloth, left in a hurry by her on the ground. But there was nothing but brush and fallen leaves and the silent trunks of the trees. When I looked back across the precious, stately landscape of my property, it seemed I had traveled far miles to the place I was standing, as if I had gone round and round the earth in an endless junket, the broad lawn a continent, the pool a whole ocean, the house the darkened museum of a one-man civilization, whose latent history, if I could so will it, would be left always unspoken, unsung.

When I was once again inside I thought to run the water in the upstairs hall bath, the one Sunny used when she was still living in the house. The faint smell was of a shut-off dampness and mold. As with her bedroom, I had completely gone over the surfaces with spackle and paint, and then had the tiles on the wall and floor regrouted, but the work was still old enough even with the room left unused that it looked quite grim and shabby. A hard crust of greenish scale covered the spigot, which ran very slowly, and over the years the drip had discolored the area around the drain with a watery-edged patch of rust. When I turned on the hot water the tap shook and coughed, and then with a violent spew a stream of reddish-brown liquid began to flow. When it finally cleared I shut it off and flipped down the lever for the drain, but it was slow and I had to wait for some time for the dirty water to swirl down and away before filling up the tub again, nearly right to the top. I stepped out of my clothes and sat in the minerally, prickling water. It was hot enough that I thought my flesh was dissolving, as if I were being rendered away to leave only the hollow drift of my old bones.

I must say I appreciated the feeling. There is something exemplary to the sensation of near-perfect lightness, of being in a place and not being there, which seems of course a chronic condition of my life but then, too, its everyday unction, the trouble finding a remedy but not quite a cure, so that the problem naturally proliferates until it has become you through and through. Such is the cast of my belonging, molding to whatever is at hand. So I dipped my head beneath the surface and could feel the water swell over the edge of the tub and onto the tiled floor but I didn't care. The intense heat felt so pure and truthful to me, so all-enveloping, that I wished there was a way I could remain within it, silently curled up as if I were quite unborn, as yet not of this life, or of the world, of anything moored to the doings and traces of humankind. I did not want innocence so much as I did an erasure reaching back, a pre-beginning, and if I could trade all my years to be at some early moment and never go forward again, I would do so without question or any dread.

But perhaps the thought itself smacks of innocence, wanting not to know what I know, which is a fraudulent and dangerous wish for most anyone but the youngest child, but particularly for a man who is approaching the farthest region of his life. In fact a man like me should be craving every last bit and tatter of his memory. He should consider the character of all his times whether pleasurable or tragic or sad. He should at last appreciate the serendipity and circumstance and ironical mien of events, and their often necessary befalling. He should, some god willing, take firm hold of all these and call himself among the fortunate, that he should have survived such riches of experience, and consider himself made over again for it, gently refitted for his slow stroll to the edge. But all I seem to think of doing is to stop, or turn around, or else dig in for a sprint, a stiffened, perambling, old-man leap off the precipice. And if I could just clear the first jutting ledges and simply free-fall, enjoy the briefest flying, I should be very thankful indeed.

BUT PERHAPS RIGHTLY, there is none of that for me. And I recall now that it was K I saw when I finally regained consciousness after suffering the captain's pistol blows. I was lying on a cot in the empty infirmary, where she was watching over me. I asked her but there was no guard or sentry inside, only she, though two men were stationed outside. Captain Ono had simply ordered her to sit with me, telling her that we should not attempt to leave, and so for several hours she had been changing the bloody dressings on my head.

"The worst is a gash at your scalp, Lieutenant," she said, touching her own head just above the temple to indicate where. "It's not too deep, I think. But it is still bleeding. I don't think you should try to touch it, or even move."

I wanted to speak but my jaw felt as though it were wired shut, not from injury but from a terrible swelling in my face. The bones around my eyes ached with sharp pain, and I could hardly see her for the poor light and the rheumy tears clouding my vision. They had already put my arm back in its joint. With a firm hand she lifted my head to give me a drink of lukewarm tea.

"You are fortunate to be alive."

I nodded.

"The captain could have killed you right there and then," she said. She brushed my short hair with her hand, trying to unmat the dried blood. "I watched through the cracks in the wall. He could have shot you where you lay. He put his pistol at your head and he stood there but he didn't shoot. Then he looked over at the infirmary, right at the spot on the wall where I was crouched, and he called to me and asked me what he should do."

"You?"

"Yes. He was staring at me, at the wall right where I was peering out. He said I should tell him what to do. I couldn't answer him because I was frightened and I thought he was taunting me, that whatever I said he was going to shoot you anyway. I was sure he was going to shoot you. But he waited and then asked me again, and finally I said he should spare you. He backed away, and I thought it was finished. But then he walked over and leaned down on the outside of the wall. He said he wouldn't kill you, but only if I agreed to his bidding."

"Which was what?"

She gave him another drink.

"What was it, K?" I said, the tea running down my cheek.

"It doesn't matter."

"Then you must say."

"No."

"Tell me. Please."

She said quite plainly, "That I would give my life for yours."

"Your life?"

"Yes, Lieutenant." She gazed at me coldly, then looked away. "But then the doctor already has that, doesn't he, no matter what?"

She then let out almost a laugh about it, as if the notion of her life being worth something was ridiculous, which of course it was, absolutely ridiculous. But I was as yet incapable of acknowledging that before her or myself or anyone else. Instead I wanted to tell her that everything about us wasn't really as it seemed, that nothing was, not even the war, which had never quite arrived and probably now never would, that we—the soldiers, officers, the girls—all had somehow entered an untoward region of stasis from which we would soon find deliverance, that we needed only to persist for a short time longer, that we must hold fast to the general order of things.

I said, "I will protect you."

K made a noise in her throat, as if to affirm me and rescue me at once. She said, "Please don't try to be brave for me, Lieutenant. I have not given up anything. Do you think if any of us girls is still living they'll let us walk out of here when the war ends? That we will go unharmed if they do? In my mind I didn't give the doctor my life. All he really wanted was a last small concession from me. What was left of my will. So he has that. But the doctor has always had my life and my death. Perhaps now, Lieutenant, he has yours, too."

I shut my eyes for a moment and tried not to listen. Though she was right, I suddenly didn't wish to hear such words from her. There was also a seam of anger in her voice but it was the anger that arises from fear as well as mistreatment or injury, and I could tell the doctor was haunting her, his specter making her see him even as she was looking at me. Of course I feared him, too, and the pained creature in me wanted to crawl deep inside a hole at the flash of his memory. But another part of me was drawn to that same receding, that awful, singular stillness of flesh one notices before the first stroke of the knife.

And I said to her, strangely thinking of that, "I remember now, how he said you were with child."

"I heard him tell you."

"Is it true?"

"No."

"He said you were pregnant not by him but by another, even before you came here."

"It's not true."

"Are you lying to me, K? You don't have to lie to me."

"I'm not lying," she said. But she rose, turning away, her arms tight about her.

"Let me see your body, then," I asked, trying to figure if she were, and trying to believe how it could be mine.

"There's nothing in me. There can't be. If there is, then God forgive me for what I'll do."

"Let me see you."

K stood still for a moment, then went over to the lone slatted window. The light from outside was gray and soft; an afternoon rain was falling gently, and in its cast she looked even younger than she was. Like a girl waiting to go play outside. And I thought she was about to leave through it, that she might really try to climb out, though of course there was nowhere to go. But instead she turned and gazed at me for what seemed a very long time. Her expression was not sad or fearful or confused. She untied the string of her baggy trousers and let them fall down at her feet. Her rough cotton blouse hung loosely over her belly, the patch below that showing darkly through the gauzy material. Her calves and ankles were thin, but her feet especially so, the tops of them shockingly bony, reedy and translucent. Though I was weak I sat up, not from desire but because I wanted her to stop. Though I could not say so. She loosened the waist knot of the blouse so that it came open and fell, and then she was wholly naked before the window, coolly burnished, smooth. Her middle seemed no fuller than the rest, which was underfed and thin but still of amazing riches to me. I thought she was the most beautiful statue of herself. I put out my hand and she came to me, not looking at me anymore, and I kissed the tepid skin of her, at her belly and below, and I could taste her, her sharp-sweetness and unwashedness and her living body underneath. My eyes and cheeks felt shattered but I pressed against her anyway, more than I could bear. I was nearly crying from the pain. She did not hold me but she did not push me away. I never meant for this but I could no longer balk, or control myself, and then something inside her collapsed, snapped clean, giving way like some storm-sieged roof, and then I descended upon her, and I searched her, every lighted and darkened corner, and every room.

And yet afterward—I don't know how long, for time seemed to bend upon itself inside the small ward—we were simply sitting on either end of the cot, not speaking, not meeting each other's eyes. I could only glance over at her and see how she was bent over her knees and cradling her face in the crook of her arm. Not weeping or moaning, but figured in certain quiet. Almost hiding there, though I was sure—even as young and earnest and fearful as I was—it was not just from me; it was from that place and time, the whole picture and small detail, from the homely, dim structure about us, the squalor of the heavy air, from the ennui and restiveness of the entire encampment, the surreally distant war, and then of course from who I was as well. For in my own way I comprised it, my yearning and wishing and my wanton hope, the sum of which, at end, amounted to a complete and utter fraudulence. For that is, finally, what she would escape if she could, not the ever-imminent misery and horror but the gentle boy-face of it, the smoothness and equability, the picture of someone heroic enough to act only upon his own trembling desire.

One could say, I suppose, that I was a very young man. Which

of course I was. But I bring this up not to excuse myself or to try
to mitigate my actions or to confess. Rather, I mean it to stand
simply as a fact. I was young and callow, but that youthfulness was
also inescapably pure. It was wholehearted, and so native to me.
Completely mine. And that was the terribleness of it. For I must
have wanted her unto death, and I could not bear anyone else having her, and I allowed events to occur because of that feeling, even
if it meant I would lose her forever.

I must have fallen asleep, for I awoke to the sound of footfalls
outside on the landing. It was Captain Ono, I knew, by the dull
ring of his keys. K was no longer with me in the ward room. The
captain told the sentries they were relieved of their posts for one
hour. One of them barked a response and then they marched away.
The captain unlocked the infirmary door and stepped inside. I could
hear him going to the examination room, where his desk was, and
I tried to get up quickly but I lost balance and had to pause a moment. Then I heard him say, "You are looking quite wonderful this
afternoon."

There was no answer, but he said anyway, "See now, how I've
brought you something. Some mochi, the last of a box I received
last month. They're hardly perfect, but one can still eat them. Go
ahead, they're for no one else."

I would have gone right over to them and confronted him but
the sound of his voice, the way he was speaking to her almost deco-
rously, froze me. To hear him was to realize how I must have
sounded when I was with her, though his tone was elegant, still circumspect, only the least bit attenuated. He knew I was there in the
ward, of course, but there was no care of that, as though he truly
did own my life, or more, that I wasn't really living anymore, that
I'd never set foot again outside the sick house. I went to the door,

which led to a tiny hall, and I could see them there, her sitting on the exam table and him before her on the chair, his back to me.

"I wish for you to eat them," he said, holding them out. "They come from a venerable sweet shop in my hometown, which is famous throughout the province. My mother sent them to me, and it is amazing that they actually arrived. These last two are quite delicious. You can see one is rolled in green tea, the other in black sesame seeds. If you are bashful we can share. Take one, and I'll have the other. Come now, or you'll force me to choose for you."

The captain tried to make a show of picking one, but she didn't move or say anything. He held up the box to her again and she could hardly shake her head. He rose then with gravity and I was sure he was going to strike her, but he suddenly embraced her instead, roundly and warmly, clutching her as if he feared he might never see her again. And without realizing it, I found myself in the center of the exam room, mere steps from them. I could have reached and touched his shoulder, the blunt back of his head. I was unarmed and weakened but I could have struck him. And yet on sighting him, on seeing him holding her so, I felt a certain sadness for him, the humane sorrow one has when one witnesses the briefest moment of another's abandon and self-loss, which is a levity, and a phantom death, and enviable enough.

K was now staring hard at me, her arms stiffly around his back. She was quiet, not trying to hide my presence from him—for he well knew I was there in the room with them and was completely unconcerned, as if I were still his loyal assistant—but directing me, motioning with her eyes that I go to the cabinet of surgical tools and instruments. The wide, rotting planks of the floorboards groaned under my movement, and the captain only said, stepping back from K and hardly glancing at me, "There you are, Lieutenant.

I expect when you're recovered you'll resume your duties. You'll remain here a few days. Now leave."

I didn't answer him. I was seeing only that one of the cabinet handles had been turned, its steel door unlocked. And then I knew what she was telling me. Here is your moment, Lieutenant Kurohata. Take up the scalpel. Deliver him swiftly from us. Stand in your place and strike him down. And as I was listening to this, finally hearing the silent running of my own heart, the dull submarine click, I found on the leather-lined shelf the honed steel instrument with its crosshatched handle, the pen-like blade lithe and insignificant in my hand. It would be simply like writing his death. And as I faced them the captain was already turned, ready for me, knowing as he always did what I would do next, as if he were my partner and my twin, my longtime synchronist. He had unholstered his pistol and was aiming it at my chest. If he would fire I would fall murderously upon him, to rid her of both of us. But he winced and a quizzical expression rose up in his face, and with his free hand he touched the side of his neck, as if he had just been stung by a wasp or spider. K stepped away from him, in her hand a red-tipped scalpel, one just like mine. He said her name and then it poured from his neck, the wine-dark spew, a bloody epaulet alighting on his shoulder. Falling to his knees, he dropped the pistol. It lay there, darkly lustrous. He sat heavily on his haunches and motioned to me, with genuine wonder, as if I should take his hand.

He fell over then. We could only watch until he stopped moving, the life running out of him and down through the cracks of the floorboards. I wiped and examined the wound after he was dead. It was amazingly precise. K was still holding the blade, standing stiffly above us. She was not exultant; the color had left her face. She had stabbed him with a deep, short incision through the major artery, which had been rent open like an undammed stream. He looked quite peaceful to me then, slighter as he lay, as if the dying had made him youthful.

And for a brief moment, too, I almost felt her hand hovering over me, angled high, and I closed my eyes in anticipation of the sundering edge. She could have stabbed me just as swiftly. For as with any man in the camp, she should have tried to kill me. And if I believed then that she did not do so because she valued me or hoped to be saved by me, I realize now that it was neither of those things. Not at all. She had not hurt me for the same reason that she had given over her body some hours before, not for passion or love, or mercy or humanity, but their complete absence and abasement, such that there were no wrongs remaining, no more crimes, nothing to save herself from.

In an odd way, I think now that K wanted the same thing that I would yearn for all my days, which was her own place in the accepted order of things. She would be a young woman of character, as significant to her father as was his son. She would have the independence that comes from learning and grace. She would choose her kind of devotion; she would bear children and do her necessary work, a true vocation, and she would grow old as I have grown old, though she would look backward with a different cast than mine, a different afterlight. All I wished for was to be part (if but a millionth) of the massing, and that I pass through with something more than a life of gestures. And yet, I see now, I was in fact a critical part of events, as were K and the other girls, and the soldiers and the rest. Indeed the horror of it was how central we were, how ingenuously and not we comprised the larger processes, feeding ourselves and one another to the all-consuming engine of the war.

K leaned on the examination table and doubled over, gagging, still gripping the surgical knife. Nothing came out but some watery spittle. I tried to help her but she pushed away my hands.

"Please," she said, wiping her mouth with her forearm. "Please, Lieutenant. Don't touch me."

"I'll only ever do so when you wish."

"Then please . . ." she said, her eyes sickly, desperate. "I won't be touched anymore."

"You will come with me when the war is over."

"Don't speak of that," she said wearily. "I don't wish to think of it."

"You will, I promise . . . there's nothing that can prevent it. Not even this."

"I am not going anywhere with you!" She was crying now, suddenly mad. "I am not going with you! Do you hear me?"

"I'll help you."

"I don't want your help!" she shouted. "I never wanted your help. Can't you heed me? Can't you leave me be? You think you love me but what you really want you don't yet know because you are young and decent. But I will tell you now, it is my sex. The thing of my sex. If you could cut it from me and keep it with you like a pelt or favorite stone, that would be all. You are a decent man, Lieutenant, but really you are not any different from the rest. I'm sorry I gave myself to you, not for me but for you. Perhaps it was a second's hope. For that I'll be sorry to my death. But if you loved me, Lieutenant, if you truly loved me, you could not bear to be with me. You could not see me like this, you could not stand for one moment longer the thought of my even living."

"I love you," I said, in hardly a voice.

"Then show me, Jiro," she answered. "I'm too cowardly to do it myself. I want to but I can't. There is his pistol. The guards are going to return at any moment and they will announce themselves. When he doesn't answer they'll come in. You must say I killed him just as I did, and that you took his pistol and you shot me. If you cannot do it yourself, then say so now. I'm afraid, but I have nothing left to do. There's no escape. I know you dream of one but it doesn't exist. This time won't end. It will end for you, but not for me."

K bent and loosed the weapon from him and put it in my hand. She moved back a little, stepping away from the body of the captain. She wasn't crying anymore. "Jiro. Please. You are a good man. Yes, you are. A good man now."

The pistol weighed heavily in my hand, as though I'd never held one before. I had shot in training and for practice but never once fired at something living, much less her. But she was right, I knew. It was incredible to think there was a way for us, the hope akin to how a boy might fancy that he could truly fly, perched up high in the limbs of a tree. And he might even fashion paper wings and lash them to his arms, he might feel the airy hollowness of his bones, he might know like the sun the perfect certainty of his flight, and yet his first step tells, it tells with prejudice the rules of the world.

Yet I could not shoot. I could not. Whether for love or pity or cowardice. Then we heard the men returning, and I looked out and saw they were accompanied by a first lieutenant, a hulking, boorish man named Shiboru, who was in charge of the guards. They were but steps away from the stair and landing. I pulled Captain Ono by the neck and sat him up and stuck the muzzle to his wound. Then I fired. K shouted out, in surprise and dread. I dropped the pistol and let him fall dully. Shiboru came running in with his sidearm drawn as I was kneeling beside the captain.

"He's shot himself," I said. "Get the large bandages in the cabinet."

Shiboru looked confused, but I pointed at the cabinet and he complied. I realized it was he who had executed Endo that day. He hurriedly brought the gauzes but when he gave them to me I told him it was already too late.

"How did this happen?" he said, not yet holstering his revolver.

"It was an accident," I replied, picking up Ono's gun. "He was playing with the girl. Doing tricks for her. He was switching hands when it went off."

"What happened to you?"

I told him the captain had beaten me the day before, not explaining any further, and Shiboru naturally didn't question it. He looked down at the captain's body and said haughtily, "Only real soldiers should toy with such things. And even then. So I suppose you're the base doctor now, eh, Kurohata?"

"If the colonel wishes it."

"Oh, that he will," Shiboru answered, nodding to the hall. "It seems the old man needs his medicine. He insisted on me coming here and getting the captain. Right off, too, with the needles and all. I suppose you'll be by daily as Ono here was. I'll let my men know."

He snorted when I didn't answer, and he said gruffly, "He's in his house. You better go there now. The sentries will take care of this mess. She'll come with me."

"What do you mean?" I said.

"She's got no reason to be here. I know what was going on, Kurohata, like everybody else. The doctor, having it special. In fact, maybe you, too? But no more, eh? Everybody's bored with just the three others. They're nearly useless now besides. Fucking skeletons. Can't you fix them up or something? It's almost better with your own hand. At least you don't want to throw up when you're doing it. But this one, she's a doll. Skinny, but she's a real beauty. Come here, doll. Come here to your big brother."

I went to the storeroom to get the vials of the tincture, trying desperately to think of what to do. When I came back the guards were waiting to escort me to the commander's house, but I stopped at the exam room to try to stall or convince him to leave her to me. It was strange, then, when I looked inside; I thought I saw her gazing at him almost tenderly, with a last human glimmer, and then I knew in an instant how terrible all the rest of it would be. She reached out with one hand and seemed to caress him, but he groaned instead, clutching one side of his face. When he let go there was a fine red line, from the corner of his eye down to his mouth. He started bleeding profusely. She had cut him, but not too deeply, as though she were trying only to mark him. She didn't move away. Then he punched her hard enough on the mouth that some of her teeth flew out, like tiny white birds.

One of the sentries pulled me along, saying, "Don't worry, the lieutenant has his certain way." Outside, through the window, I could see that K had risen up again, bloody-mouthed, and he struck her again.

When I finally finished administering to the commander and returned to the infirmary there was no one there. I had injected him and sat with him as he requested but it still took nearly an hour until he fell asleep. Just before he did he suddenly realized that it was the first time I had administered his medicine, in place of Captain Ono. He wasn't disturbed or even suspicious; he was already too deep in the thrall of the injection. All he wanted was that I sit beside him as he lay prostrate on his bedpad and gently pat him on the back with a slow, steady rhythm. After a few minutes he began half-humming a sentimental folk song, his faint voice breaking in beats as I patted, so that he sounded almost like an old woman consoling herself at day's end.

As soon as he was asleep I went directly to the comfort house, but there, too, it was quiet, being late in the afternoon, when the girls were allowed to sleep before the evening and late night. Behind their communal tent I found Mrs. Matsui, crouched over a dented washing pail of gray water, wringing undershirts. I asked if she had seen Lieutenant Shiboru, and of course, K.

She nodded.

I asked where.

"Aren't you going there, too?" she said, wringing out an undershirt.

"No, where?"

"They're at the clearing." She picked at her teeth with her fingernail. She was angry and even a little upset. "A whole bunch of them. I told that bitch this would happen to her. Stupid little bitch. 'You're going to get yourself killed,' I told her, if she goes on like that. Or worse. But now see how it is? It has to be worse. Something worse."

I ran up the north path by the latrines, toward the clearing, as it was known, which was where Corporal Endo had taken K's sister. But I wasn't halfway there when I met them coming back, singly and together and in small groups. The men. It was the men. Twenty-five of them, thirty of them. I had to slow as they went past. Some were half-dressed, shirtless, trouserless, half-hopping to pull on boots. They were generally quiet. The quiet after great celebration. They were flecked with blood, and muddy dirt, some more than others. One with his hands and forearms as if dipped in crimson. Another's face smudged with it, the color strange in his hair. One of them was completely clean, only his boots soiled; he was vomiting as he walked. Shiboru carried his saber, wiping it lazily in the tall grass. His face was bleeding but he was unconcerned. He did not see me; none of them did. They could have been returning from a volleyball match, thoroughly enervated, sobered by near glory.

Then they were all gone. I walked the rest of the way to the clearing. The air was cooler there, the treetops shading the falling sun. Mostly it was like any other place I had ever been. Yet I could not smell or hear or see as I did my medic's work. I could not feel my hands as they gathered, nor could I feel the weight of such remains. And I could not sense that other, tiny, elfin form I eventually discovered, miraculously whole, I could not see the figured legs and feet, the utter, blessed digitation of the hands. Nor could I see the face, the perfected cheek and brow. Its pristine sleep still unbroken, undisturbed. And I could not know what I was doing, or remember any part.

15

HOW SHIMMERS the Bedley Run pool in this flood of last August light, the groups of mostly mothers and children on this weekday crowded about the man-made shoreline where it curves in full beam of the sun. The whole town seems to be here. Thomas and I have set up our chairs on the sand down-shore, under the breezy shade of large maples, the part of the beach preferred by older folks and those concerned with overexposure to the rays, or others, like the handful of our town's black families, who are enjoying their own lively, picnicking circle a few steps from us. Thomas has found them, or they have found him, and he plays with their children with a quiet, unflinching ease, something I have not seen in him until now, overexcitable as he often is. I have already given him the first lessons of flotation and breathing and treading, and as much as he was eager to try out the deeper water (with me at his side), he's caught up now with his new friends, filling buckets of sand as they build a wall around their talkative mothers. I am happy for him, happy that I can sit close by and hover and let him do his child's good business. I am pleased enough, too, that Sunny and I have so far remained on decent and civil terms, no matter if they are ones eternally provisional. They shouldn't be, certainly not if we were real father and daughter, but maybe even those who share blood and love believe only their devotions are unconditional, to be sustained through every crucible.

I'm on the lookout for Renny Banerjee, actually, who called me earlier this morning to chat. He sensed my less-than-ebullient mood, and thus determined to take the afternoon off to visit me. I told him that I would be at the town pool, which he gleefully misread as a romantic meeting (for I had gone there only once, for a town event with Mary Burns), but when I told him I was watching a friend's boy, he was curiously unprobing, as if he knew the legacies of my complications. But he also mentioned something he was supposed to tell me concerning a woman named Hickey.

"Mrs. Hickey?" I said to Renny, hardly able to speak aloud the words. "Is it that her boy . . . is it something about him?"

"The boy? Oh, no, Doc. It's not the boy."

"Thank goodness. He has a serious heart condition, you know, Renny. He's in the PICU."

"I recall that now. No, Doc, it's about his mother. Apparently she was brought in last night to the emergency room. I'm sorry to have to tell you this. A nurse there told me you sort of knew her, and that I should probably tell you."

"Yes."

"She was in a car accident last night driving home from the hospital. I guess the other driver was drunk. She didn't really have a chance, that's how fast he was likely going."

"I don't understand."

"She died soon after the paramedics brought her in. I'm awfully sorry, Doc. I don't really know much more than that. Gee, Doc, was she a good friend?"

"No, not really. She was an associate," I think I said.

"I'm very sorry."

"That's quite all right, Renny."

"Listen, Doc, I'll try to see you this afternoon. I have to go now. Will you be okay?"

"I'm fine," I told him, and after some more chat we agreed to try to meet here at the pool. There was another thing he wanted to mention, but it wasn't so important and could wait.

But later, as I drove on an errand before going to Sunny's apartment in Ebbington to pick up Thomas, I began to find the information about Mrs. Hickey so profoundly untenable that for a few minutes I had to park along the side of the road with the engine shut off and the windows rolled up. The cars were steadily whizzing by me on the narrow two-way of Route 9, the muffled slingshot of their passing buffeted by the safety glass. I wondered which tight suburban road it was, if not this very one, that Anne Hickey should not have driven on late at night when everyone knows the saloon revelers would be speeding to the next place. I wondered why she hadn't known to stay at home with her husband or in the intensive-care ward with her son, that good people like her should take the most extreme caution with themselves and practice wariness and avoidance for the sake of their beloved, and then, too, for the rest of us. And sitting at the wheel I became angry all at once, angry at her lack of care and circumspection, and if she had been in the passenger seat looking at me with her comely palish-pink face and sea-blue eyes, I would have scolded her as hotly as I wished to scold Sunny when she was a teen. But I found myself instead struggling for breath, the simple draw of it, my still weakened lungs smarting with each gasp, and whatever life-spirit I possessed at that moment I felt desperate to abdicate, if but for empathy and the wish for a penance that would likely never come.

There was still some time before I had to get to Sunny's, and so I made a U-turn in the road and drove to Bedley Run, through town and then up the road past my house, and I kept going up the hill until the very end of the street, where there is a small Catholic cemetery, the pedestrian entrance to which is bowered by a delicate wrought-iron arch. It is pretty, and modest, like the well-tended plots inside the grounds. The elevation is high enough that from most every spot—at least on a clear day—you can almost make out the city skyline to the south, the high spires looming like the far parapets of a strange, empyreal country. And then, in the middle distance, when you view the dense overlay of towns and villages laid out in contiguous patches, the multiple strands of the interstates and the parkways running straight through the heart of some and bending deferentially around others, bounded and marked by the shimmering waterways and reservoirs and the gently sloped hills, you feel as though this place in which you stand is a most decent and comely kingdom, even as it is a solemn province of the dead.

The monuments are mostly severe and plain, and even the few miniature mausoleums are unadorned, dignified structures, squarish blocks of polished black granite fitted with engine-turned doors of patinated brass. As I gloomily thought of Anne Hickey and her unsettling, instantaneous end, I remembered, too, with a start, that it was in one of these tombs that the Dr. Bradley Burnses resided.

Mary Burns didn't altogether favor the tomb her husband had pre-built for them. She would have preferred a simple set of headstones over any free-standing structure, but of course she was always typically dutiful and made sure to keep up its appearance. One spring day I accompanied her to help her plant several evergreen shrubs on either side of the tomb's door. I called the owner of the local nursery to deliver the plants to the cemetery entrance, and Mary Burns and I each rolled a wheelbarrow up Mountview Street to pick them up. We must have appeared quite a pair, dressed in our heavy canvas gardening trousers and work shirts beneath our wide-brimmed sun hats, clodding along in black rubber boots like an odd pair of itinerant landscapers. Though part of me was distracted by the idea that our neighbors might be peering out their windows at us, wondering what the exact nature of our relationship was, I was also, to be honest, almost discomfitingly flushed with a sensation I had not believed I would ever experience again. For even as we set about the work of sprucing up her late husband's gravesite, with all the typically complicated specters and notions attending such a task, I was in fact nearly giddy, and I believe she was as well. We were happily basking, as one might say, in the warm glow of our passion, our union still in the early, intimate weeks when there is not yet talk of past or future days but only the too-swift dwindle of the hours.

That day we walked up to the cemetery we didn't go directly in, as the nursery truck hadn't yet arrived with the delivery of shrubs. I sat on a bench to wait, but Mary Burns suggested we leave the wheelbarrows inside the wrought-iron gates of the entrance and take a brief hike on an old bridle path, whose almost completely hidden trailhead was a block or so back down the hill. I thought we should wait for the delivery, in case the driver was unsure of what to do, but she tugged at my hand and cajoled and even pecked me on the cheek, and soon enough I agreed.

It was clear that the trail was hardly used anymore, if at all. Mary Burns said that many years ago there were a number of people in the neighborhood who kept horses, and that you could see them on the weekends strutting up Mountview, fathers and daughters in rustic dress setting out for a day-long ride. Over time the riders had fashioned a clear path, which went up over Bedley Hill and down the far side, where it meandered through several square miles of undeveloped county land. I was surprised to learn that Mary Burns often took solitary walks here for hours at a time, and that she hadn't until now invited me along. I was also a bit concerned for her as it grew quite isolated the farther we went, the path narrowing steadily until it was no wider than a deer trail, with the ever-thickening underbrush tugging at our trouser cuffs. For even here in Bedley Run, something terrible could occur, in a place like this all cloistered and shady. A certain kind of man could happen upon her in her light cotton sweater and willowy walking shorts and think he was exempt from the prevailing laws, that everything in the domain was his to master.

After we'd hiked a quarter mile or so, I said, "You don't find it a little dark back here?"

"Are you trying to scare me, Franklin?" she said lightly, her eyes archly narrowed. "Because you should know I don't frighten easily."

"I'm not trying anything of the kind," I answered. "It just is very much removed here. Our street seems already to be miles away. There aren't any sounds but ours."

"That's why I like it."

"How far do you usually go?"

"I don't know," she said, continuing to lead us. I was following closely behind her, the faint scent of perfume trailing her in the damp, spring air. "I don't keep track, I guess. But don't worry, I know where we're headed to."

"I don't mind, Mary. Wherever you take us . . ."

"I'm glad," she said, suddenly turning about. She put her hands up to brace herself but I ran straight into her. She went down with a crash, instinctively grabbing a branch of a sapling that snapped and tore along the trunk as she fell. I felt awful, even as she was fitfully laughing, and I knelt to examine her. She had a trickling nosebleed, and her eyes were teary, and I had her lean against my shoulder, her head tipped back.

"My goodness, that was a surprise."

"I'm so sorry, Mary. It's my fault."

"Don't be silly," she said, her hand around my knee. I could feel her letting all of her weight ease back into my chest. "Brainy me did the about-face. Will I be getting two black eyes now?"

"I'm sure you won't. Does this hurt?" I gently pressed my fingers against the bridge of her nose. She didn't flinch. The blood was still coming, though in tiny rivulets, and as I had nothing to stanch it with I unbuttoned the cuff of my work shirt and she nodded that I go ahead. We stayed a minute or so that way, her face nestled into my forearm, and had someone come upon us in the narrow path, with the bright blood soaked into my sleeve, they might have thought I was attempting to snuff the life out of her. And the strange thing is that I kept having the thought that I was, or at least imagining the horror of it, for even as every cell of me was reaching toward her with utter tenderness and warmth and the drug of an amorous bloom, it seemed I could just as easily summon the harshest want in my hands, the tightness and pressure that might have no bound. And if some keenly sick man could have committed the act in a flash, for reason of mere possibility or nihilistic whim or curiosity, a man like me would have done so for the avoidance of a future day, whose complications—whether happy or not—might simply overwhelm.

But she tightly embraced me then, turning her face into my neck. She cupped my cheek and she kissed me, deeply, with an instant fervor. Her fingers ran through my hair, along the back of my head. Before this we had held hands and hugged each other after a dinner out or a movie at the village theater, and I'd only politely kissed her good night, despite her clear willingness to linger in the car or before her front door. She would invite me in but I always made the excuse of having to go home to Sunny, which was true enough, though not because I was needed there. In those first weeks with Mary Burns I was still hoping to provide my daughter with a complete family life, and while it was obvious how nearly perfect Mary would be as a mother, how well she could run a house (even mine), I began to wonder if I were up to the tasks of being a worthy partner and husband. I worried whether I knew what to do, like any pubescent boy might be concerned, for honestly it had been quite a long time, long enough that I was as fearful as I was anxious and expectant. But that afternoon, on the impromptu hike, she held me tight and wouldn't let me go and at some point I began not just to relent but to kiss her back, and with a sudden, spurring ebullience that caught us both off guard.

"You're such a surprise," she said, when we finally ceased for a moment. "Come with me."

She got up and started walking the path again, in the direction we had been hiking.

"Where are you going?"

"Where we were headed."

"But what's there?"

"You'll see. Just come on."

She was going more quickly than before, almost running, and soon enough we found ourselves in a silly bit of a chase, her slowing down until I could reach and touch her and then rushing forward again, the two of us acting a third or perhaps a tenth of our years. She disappeared around a turn and when I reached the spot, she was no longer ahead of me. I called out and she answered, and when I looked down I saw a small opening within a thicket.

"Come inside," she said.

"Shouldn't we go back? The nursery man must be there by now."

"Please, Franklin. Don't be a spoilsport."

I got on my hands and knees and crawled in. It was a small place, open to the sky, a lair that must have been used by deer. Mary Burns sat on the tall, matted grass.

"I think high-school kids sometimes come here at night," she said. "But don't worry. I sit here all the time, and no one has ever come by during the afternoon. Today's a school day, you know."

Of course I did know. I'd decided, for the first time ever, to close the shop after a half day in order to be with her.

I said, "I'm not worried at all, Mary."

"Then let's sit next to each other again, just like before."

And so we did. And we began to kiss, and eventually our hands were purposefully exploring each other, lingering and caressing and soon enough undoing buttons, clasps. It would have been scandalous in town had someone caught us. But it didn't seem that we cared. We were only half-clothed in the open-air cloister, and if it hadn't been so patently unshaded and bright we might have done something right there and then that was quite extreme, and perhaps even wonderful. For I am almost sure she wanted me to make love to her, this by the open, willing character of her body, and then by the strength of her limbs, the way she so tightly wound my legs with hers. It was as if a vast store of energy had been held inside her, bounding about in a terribly long, great waiting, such an abeyance really being the most lovely thing to me, and harrowing as well. For I did desperately want to make love to her; she was so wonderfully pretty lying there beneath me looking up, her silvery-streaked flaxen hair loosened from the headband and splayed against the grass like a fan of shimmering, threaded light. Beautiful, too, I thought, were the many fine creases and lines in her rosy face, the supreme paleness of her lips, and then the fresh smell of her, faintly sour-sweet like unripe plums. I felt awfully young, touching her, and the wanting I had wished never again to know was rushing back to me, a disturbing shiver in my fingers and in my mouth and in my eyes.

I stopped everything then, perhaps too abruptly, for Mary Burns had the impression that she had done something terribly offending or wrong, and I knew I could not convince her otherwise, at least for the moment. We quickly dressed and without speaking hiked back to the cemetery entrance, where the delivery man was waiting with two pairs of evergreen shrubs. He insisted on helping us wheelbarrow them inside, and doing some digging as well, and I was glad that he was there, and even Mary Burns seemed relieved. In fact we never spoke again of what had happened. And though in near time we did sleep together (with a genuinely pleasing, if sober, conviviality), I came to think of that first interlude with a somewhat sorrowful fondness, for I saw that our days together were perhaps sullied from the very beginning and all the way through, right up to the last.

NOW, MY GRANDSON THOMAS, overfilled with energy and pluck, runs up the short beach holding out his inflatable water wings and dumps them in my lap. He doesn't need them anymore, he insists, this after a mere week of pool-going. Soon enough he's practically performing for his newfound friends, as he holds high aloft a bucket of sand and with some ceremony dumps it on his face and neck and chest. I'm a bit alarmed, but the other children laugh at this, and Thomas repeats the action and I realize I've seen this from him before, how he often makes a buffoon of himself for others. At the roller rink last week, he spilled wickedly several times, falling flush on his back as he tried to whip around a group of children his age, each wipeout a bit more thunderous than the one before. They snickered, but then seemed more frightened by him than amused; soon after they were ushered off by their mothers. As I was watching from the stands I could only shout my warnings to him, but once they were gone he was perfectly fine as he skated, whipping past my spot with aplomb and cool abandon, his stout little figure apparently unaching, unhurt. Another time, in the toy store, a floor display of boxed firetrucks fell over on him, though I suspected at the time that he had meant to cause it, if not expected them to fall directly on him.

But now I'm deeply worried, having sensed the strangeness in the pattern, his obsessive, self-taunting behavior, and I get up from my folding chair and go over and hold him as I brush the sand from his hair, his thick eyebrows and lashes. He pulls hard away from me.

"What are you *doing?*" he says, jerking his arm away from me. There's a flash in his eyes that perhaps only I as his mother's father can recognize, a cold light of refusal.

"That's not good for you," I say, lamely. "The sand will get in your eyes. It could injure them."

"I'm having fun," he answers resolutely, filling up another bucket. For the first time in our two weeks of knowing each other I am not having so much fun, though still a great part of me wishes him to go on, to do whatever he wants no matter what I might say.

"Perhaps we should get back to the water. Why don't we all go in? You and your friends can have a splashing contest."

"Hey! We don't just splash, mister, we swim just fine!" one of them shouts, a girl with hundreds of white plastic beads woven into her hair.

"That's right, mister," Thomas pipes in, though now sweetly again. "We're all going in the water, aren't we? We're going to have a swimming contest."

"You got that right!" the girl replies.

I begin to peel off my shirt but the girl in braids shoots me a stare and Thomas immediately cues on this, holding up his solid little hand. "Sorry, Franklin, but it's just kids only."

"Yes, Thomas, I understand. But I promise I will remain off to the side. Or I'll swim in the deeper water, if you don't mind, and watch from there."

"Adults have to stay on the beach, Franklin," he tells me, as though it's out of his hands. And he points to my folding chair with a silencing finger and an almost wry smile, and it's all I can do but sit down again as they stomp and leap their way into the water.

One of the mothers declares to me, "You don't have to worry, Gramps, they're all like little seals," though this only serves to alarm me more, as I know exactly what Thomas can and cannot do. I tell him to go no farther out, and he nods. But he's already chest deep, and one of the boys is behind him, pushing down on his shoulders in order to dunk him. I call out for them to stop, but against the din of play and constant reverberation along the shore my weak voice thins, and I lose sight of who's who among this brace of kids roughhousing in the water.

"Hey, there!" I hear, and I turn to see Liv Crawford, wearing oversized cat-eye sunglasses, stunningly trim in a cream-white one-piece, a batik wrap smartly knotted about her waist. "You look really good, Doc. This convalescence is doing the job." She quickly scans about. "Are we really sitting here?"

Renny comes up, carrying chairs and towels, and says, "Yes, darling, we are."

"I prefer the sun," she answers, casually looking over at the mothers of Thomas's friends, who are passing around a plastic container of BLT sandwiches. "But if you two insist."

"We do," Renny says brightly, unfolding a chair on either side of me. He doesn't wear a hat or sunglasses. He flicks at one of the seats with the towel and then spreads it out for her, holding her hand as she sits.

"So who is this young person you're looking after today?" Liv asks me, taking my hand, too. "Renny wouldn't say anything more."

"He's in the water," I say, pointing to the group of them some fifteen yards from shore. Having already tested it, I know the water deepens very gradually, though past the line of buoys it drops off quickly, as if off a shelf. "Perhaps you can tell which one he is."

"I'm not sure how."

"Isn't he your daughter's son," Renny says, "the one right there?"

"What? Where?" Liv says with a sort of pleased alarm, craning forward, her hand over her eyes. "Your daughter is back in town, Doc? You didn't mention it to me. She must be staying with you at the house."

"She lives over in Ebbington."

"Ebbington? Oh goodness, but why?"

"She's probably making a living and supporting herself, that's why," Renny scolds her. "Not everybody in the world, Liv, has to live in this over-blessed, over-prosperous duchy of a town."

"I one hundred percent agree with you, dear, but for Doc Hata's girl, who I must say I didn't even know existed until last week? I won't say for her to go live in your house because it's against all my interests, but really, Doc, you ought to set her up in an apartment in the village. My office holds the few good listings, you know. Especially if she has a boy who goes to school. There's nothing much going on in the Ebbington school system except gym and metal shop and prenatal classes."

Renny groans and says, "You can be the most terrible snob."

"I'm thinking of the welfare of the boy, Renny. Anyway, you're the one insisting on my marrying you."

I turn to Renny and he nods, half-grinning, half-grimacing, a difficult state of being which I know more and more finds its own measure of dignity, and joy. "I wanted to mention it on the phone, but then Liv wanted to see you in person to tell you, and I guess so did I."

Liv says, "Renny and I realized that you were really the only person in town, Doc, who could extend his mature and wise blessing over us. You're our private elder, you know, neither of us having parents still alive. Really, that's only if you think it's a good idea, for us two to get married."

"Yes, yes, yes," I say, dumb and glad that I am affirming both notions of Liv's, especially because they immediately occur to me as somehow off, not at all wrong or terrible but perhaps improbable; and I feel, too, suddenly overwhelmed with the wide flows of information that have come to me today, the flash flood after the rains, and perhaps naturally I imagine good Anne Hickey again, though more clearly now, in her white turtleneck and leaf-colored sweater, greeting me on a wondrous autumn afternoon in front of the beveled glass door of my shop, her hair and eyes aglow in the lovely, burnishing light. The sight isn't so romantic or sentimental, it's merely a picture, caught in my memory, the nearest thing I have to something remotely real.

"You don't seem convinced, my friend," Renny murmurs sheepishly to me, his fingers raking the soft sand.

"No, Renny, I'm very happy for you both. I'm very happy and I think you ought to get married as soon as possible."

"I'm not *pregnant,* Doc," Liv croons.

"I know that but I would hope you two don't let pass any more time. Why I should be the one to heed I don't know. But it seems you two have a special love for each other, and despite some of your difficulties in the past and whatever ones that may arise again, I believe you ought to use this time for best advantage."

"Who knew you were such a carpe diem sort of guy, Doc?" Liv asks.

"But I am not," I tell her, practically arguing with her. "I am not at all. I'm simply excited for you both." And though the implication is that I am the sort who is always careful and preparing, I think that's not right, either; in fact I feel I have not really been living anywhere or anytime, not for the future and not in the past and not at all of-the-moment, but rather in the lonely dream of an oblivion, the nothing-of-nothing drift from one pulse beat to the next, which is really the most bloodless marking-out, automatic and involuntary.

Renny says, "I suppose Liv and I are relenting, which I hope is as good a reason as any."

"It is, Renny, it perfectly is," I listen to myself say. "Please understand me. There are those who would gladly give up all they have gained in the world to have relented just once when it mattered."

He gazes at me curiously, and though he hasn't a clue what I'm talking about (nor, in truth, do I, at least in a pointed way), he knows enough of me to note the brief fervor in my voice, and this quiets him for a moment. Liv is stretching out her long, thin legs and rubbing lotion on them from the ankles up, and if she doesn't seem to be listening there's no mistake she hasn't missed a word. But she's atypically reserving comment as well, and I think I must be sounding something unusual indeed, to quell Ms. Crawford and Mr. Banerjee, affable gabbers both. I want to engage them further, I want to tell them the first thing that comes to mind, whatever history of my days, when a commotion erupts next to us.

"Tess!" one of the mothers cries sharply. "Where's your little brother? Where is he!"

"I don't know! I've been looking for him. . . ."

"What do you mean! I asked you to stick by him every second! I told you to keep a hold on him."

"I know! I know!"

Her mother frantically scans the water but the kids are splashing wildly, so much so that it's impossible to tell who or how many there are. Then she see a lone yellow float that attaches to the arms.

"Bobby! Oh my God, Bobby!"

Renny immediately leaps up from his beach chair and goes to

the woman, asking what has happened, and then he runs into the water, his knees high and dragging, shouting out the boy's name. The woman starts yelling for the lifeguards, most of whom are stationed where the people are crowded in the sun. The playing in front of us has stopped for the moment, the kids frozen as though there were something lethal in the water. I see right away that Thomas is nowhere apparent, being neither among the group of them nor farther out near the buoys nor anywhere along the shore. I check again and again. Renny is searching in the water, ducking his head under and then coming up. I take off my hat, my sandals, my eyes offering only slow-motion vision, and I take the deepest breath I can and dive in among the bodies standing about.

The water is clear and silent and surprisingly refreshing. I see the green-tinted legs and feet and resting hands up at the surface, the child limbs rooted on the bottom like an otherworldly forest. I go past them and deeper and I'm terrified of what I might see, a limp figure floating in the mid-level, the mouth agape, eyes unfixed and cold. But my chest is burning and though I want to stay under I have to rise. And it's now that confusion and unrest ripple over the water. Young lifeguards are swarming about, and I cry to them that there's another child in trouble—another who is mine—and they order me to go ashore and leave the water clear. But who can? The mother and her friends are knee-deep in the water, Renny is somewhere I can't see, and even Liv has waded in to her waist, her silken wrap ruined, her hands waving spastically in a way that frightens me; I think I have never seen her like this, anything but perfectly poised and comported. And I hear what must be Renny, the tenor bell of his voice, letting out a small cry of pain. I'm the closest to him, and I watch as he begins to slip beneath the surface, where the water is not even over his head: He is having, I murmur to myself, a heart attack. But at the same time the lifeguards are diving and rising near the line of buoys, searching for Thomas and the other boy, not aware of Renny's distress. I can't tell if he sees me. He's grimacing, and his hand comes up weakly as if to say, *I'm here, I'm here.*

Everything is happening instantly and simultaneously; his hand seems to be a sign not only from Renny but Thomas, too, and the long knives of panic pierce my chest and belly. I want to have faith in the lifeguards but they're so young, and not turning back to check Renny, I swim as fast as I can out to the line of red-and-white floats. It's deep out here and I realize that this is where Thomas would be, this is where he would put himself, and when I dive I am absolutely sure I'll see him. And I do: a stocky little figure, crouched as if sitting, his shape hardly discernible. I kick and swoop under him and then lift us upward. When we surface, two lifeguards take him and swim him quickly to shore. I let them because I think I wish to have faith, because there is really nothing but that for someone like me, and because of Renny, because I can't stand yet another abandonment in my life, even if it's for a brief moment.

Just as I reach him, Renny's mouth dips beneath the water. I brace him and he coughs weakly. His rich brown skin is muddy, grayish about the neck and face and hands; his breathing is labored. His eyes are glassy. On the beach Liv is bleating something in a tiny voice, shuffling back in half-steps. It is in fact a natural reaction, one of the many that people can have. Against my back I can almost feel the thrum of Renny's heart racing, then arresting, then racing again. I shout ahead to an onlooker to call for an ambulance. Some steps away the lifeguards are working on Thomas, and I hear his gasp and hack and he instinctively sits up and looks about. I nod, and he begins to cry. The presumed missing boy is walking up the shoreline with a hot dog in his hand; he's not been in the water for some time. But Renny spasms then, as if he's hugged me, a broad, low electric shudder, and somehow I carry his big frame right up onto the shore.

"Oh my God, he's dying," Liv says, collapsing to her knees. "He's dying."

I do not answer, not from fear that she is right but that I am so certain she is wrong, for there will be no dying for him today, I think, I cannot allow it—in the way a doctor, perhaps once or twice in his career, might not simply abide—and if I have to reach inside his chest I shall, reach inside and roughly clasp his heart and will it back alive.

16

WHY MUST ALL MY PATHS lead to the forlorn, unpolished wards of some hospital? Sitting here in Renny's cramped but tidy office, I fear I am afflicted. Or even worse. For how can one slight, shrinking-in-the-bones fellow be such a lingering pall of sickness and mortality, casting darkly upon his associates and friends and recently discovered loved ones, who (almost) to the last profess their happiness for having known him, and for knowing him still? They phone him and say grace for him and invite him to their rooms, and then they even send flowers to his house when he should be bearing flowers tenfold back to them, a veritable nursery of grateful tidings.

Renny, thank goodness, will survive. Indeed, as I suspected, it was a first heart attack, and had not the paramedic unit arrived so quickly (having stopped for lunch, by chance, a few streets away at the time of the call), the damage to his heart muscle would have been dangerously severe, perhaps forever debilitating. He was napping this morning when I visited him, still propped up in the tilted bed, the lines to the various monitors and saline drip and his oxygen crisscrossing his wide, bared chest. The fluorescent light fixture above his bed had been left on, and beneath its cool, icy cast, he appeared as if he were alive but being preserved in a kind of science-fictional stasis, his hair unevenly matted from sleep, his skin dull of sheen, the beeps and hums of the machines standing in for the sounds of his living.

Thomas, whom I brought along with me, was initially frightened by the congealed, webbish sight of him, as was I. The boy wouldn't step immediately into the room; he needed a moment or two to gather his courage. When I finally led him in he wouldn't go past the foot of the bed, standing there as quiet and unmoving as a stone, as quiet as I have ever seen him until last week, when he was curled up in his own hospital bed after the jarring, frightening events at the pool. His mother, to my surprise, had been the picture of calm when she arrived in the ward. Thomas was by all accounts fine, solely in for a night's observation and monitoring, and she had listened studiously to young Dr. Weil, nodding and even taking notes in a black leather organizer. She asked him questions about what to expect, what signs of complication might appear, infections and fevers and whatnot. She inquired earnestly after Renny, whom she didn't know. I stood by and listened, not saying a word, though not avoiding her eyes, either, which weren't accusatory or angry but rather relieved and a little frazzled, with the depth of that life-worn knowing, that hushing stare of all loving mothers and fathers. I would have gladly endured a fit of rage, or a frosty harangue of disappointment, and yet it seemed she was making efforts to assure the clearness of my conscience, despite the unavoidable fact of my momentary carelessness and lack of vigilance, which I didn't attempt to diminish when I first phoned with the news. Why she should be so gentle with me I couldn't figure, except for my obvious tender feeling for the boy, which I suppose anyone would see. But I heard something else, too, or so I wished I'd heard it, the willing sufferance of me in her tone, the first hint of a generous, filial allowing that I probably ought never to deserve.

In Renny's case, I have deep regrets. He believes I saved his life, when in fact I likely endangered it by not going to him right away. But nothing I say will convince him; I'm his hero, his savior, his lifelong guardian angel. He sleeps much now, so I can't educate him with what really happened. And then Liv, too, must be misremembering the scene, for she's been equally grateful and then nervous, no doubt abraded by this rough brush with mortality.

"I still feel jittery, Doc," she said to me this afternoon, in the corridor outside his room. I had taken Thomas back to Sunny and had returned to resume my vigil. Liv had arrived from her office in the interval, and she was not looking like herself; she was disheveled and not wearing makeup and drinking a non-diet Coke.

"I'm weak," she moaned. "Terribly weak. I can hardly drive. God, I can hardly dial a number on my car phone. It's all hitting me. Tell me it'll soon go away."

"I can't truly say, Liv. But I wish I could."

"Well, please just say something helpful."

I asked what that might be.

"Something reassuring and wise."

I didn't know what else to say, so I told her, "Then I am certain your strength will return. So will Renny's. Completely for you both. And you will live together in contentment and happiness. You will grow very old together."

"Please don't say *that*, Doc!"

"Your strength is increasing already."

"Ha!" she cried, squeezing my hand. "You're a good doctor, Franklin Hata."

"You know as well as anyone, Liv, that I'm not."

"I know, I know," she said, brushing lint from my shoulder. She sounded a bit arch again, though still tensed up, wound tightly with everything. "But you are, aren't you? I mean inside, you *are* a doctor, whatever you actually know. I can tell. It doesn't matter if you have a degree or not. You have the spirit of one in you. The essence."

"I don't know, Liv. I don't know what that is."

"Well, I do," she said firmly. "And you have it. It's not empathy, exactly. It's just that you know what people are feeling, and what they want. You sense their pulses, I guess."

"Perhaps," I said.

"You bet, Doc." She hugged me and, to my surprise, kissed me on the cheek. I told her I would stay at the hospital and keep Renny company, so that she might go home and shower and change her clothes. She hugged me again, and on leaving she cried out, as if for the whole ward to hear, "I know the truth, Doc, and so does everybody else."

But the truth, I am beginning to think, is not something that can be so clear. Not in even the best circumstances. My friend, Mrs. Anne Hickey, wherever her good spirit may be, would have been among the first in line to testify to the "truth" about me. And yet what have I ever done for her, then or now? For another passing hour her boy, Patrick, lies in his solitary ship of a bed with the clear vinyl curtains drawn down around him, unvisited by me since that first night I stole into his room. It's not the chance of seeing his father I dread, but the hard posture of Patrick's stillness, the limpid quality of his skin, the clocklike winding-down. His is an old man's demise, a chilly lessening, which is not right for a child (if any end is), who in the terrible waiting matures with a bittersweet swiftness, a quickened growing up in order to die.

And how further depleted might he appear with his mother now gone? I wonder if he even knows. If I were Mr. Hickey, I wouldn't tell him, I couldn't tell him, I'd say his mother had to take a trip, that her old friend across the ocean had died. I'd keep up a lie for as long as he could bear. I'd tell him whatever story he would hope for and believe. I would pool about him a whole history of her absence, too wide to cross and too deep to plumb: a dusky, flooding water in which he might forever gently tread.

I watched yesterday, as she was interred in one of the two small cemeteries in town. I waited outside the chapel in my car and then followed the procession along Church Street and then up past Boling Street and McKinley, to the large memorial grounds where many years ago I purchased my own plot, and one for Sunny as well. It was a day when one suddenly thinks one should prepare for such a thing, automatically and immediately. And it was an unusual decision as well, I realize, to buy one for such a little girl, but I wasn't married or expecting to be—the other plot one buys being normally for a spouse—and I thought that it would be something like insurance, that we would always have a place for ourselves in the end, which no one could encroach or buy back or take away. But I never told her about it, feeling it was morbid; and then later, when we were having so many difficulties in our relationship, it seemed inappropriate to mention, too easy for her to misinterpret or misunderstand.

Once there I parked just inside the entrance and let the hearse and the long line of cars wend their way to the burial plot; I didn't want Mr. Hickey to have to see me or acknowledge me or have to consider my presence in any way, and so I walked slowly toward the site, keeping an eye on him so that I might turn or step away whenever he looked up from the ground. Of course he would have noticed me immediately, had he gazed about. But he didn't. In the warm, slanting light of the autumn morning he appeared still quite pale, moon-faced, his dark suit rumpled at the armpits and shoulders, one collar point lifting. His son was not there, of course, and so Mr. Hickey appeared that much more alone, standing as he was some steps away from the other family mourners, upright in an almost military style, his feet set apart, his hands clasped behind him. He wasn't angry-looking, as I selfishly expected; he was bewildered, as everyone there was, though his body seemed not to wish to know it, not bent over and miserable but unmoving, completely still.

The minister was speaking in a broad, calling tone, and though I couldn't hear what he was saying, I felt sure from the waves of sound that his sermon was deeply and earnestly uttered and thus worthy of Anne Hickey, who was nothing but kind and straightforward and estimably ardent, the sort of woman I might wish for if ever I would enjoy the company of someone again, the sort of woman Mary Burns was to the core and that I'd always hoped Sunny would someday become, and perhaps is now.

The minister ended with a long prayer, and then he motioned to the undertaker and his assistants (they were no doubt his sons, from the facial resemblance) to lower the casket into the ground. He began speaking again, perhaps a final consecration, when Mr. Hickey broke from the rank and began walking away, down the hill, in my general direction. *This is not acceptable,* his body was saying, *This is not something for me.* Everyone turned to watch him, the minister and others feebly waving for him to come back. Then Mr.

Hickey began to jog, then run, almost coming in a sprint down the grassy incline, his suit jacket still buttoned. He passed by quickly, and he must have noticed me, for he glanced back over his shoulder, and it was then his footing slipped on the dry sod, causing him to fall in an awkward, tumbling heap. Several mourners had rushed down to him, and when I reached him I could see that his leg was traumatically fractured at mid-calf, the splintered tip of the bone poking out through the bloody material. He was sitting up and gripping his thigh, puffing furiously through his teeth, and I thought he would soon pass out. An older man, whom I recognized as a retired physician from the county hospital, was urging him to lie back, to hold still so he could make certain the main artery hadn't been severed, but Mr. Hickey saw me then and tried to rise, reaching out toward me, moaning, "Don't anyone touch me! Don't touch me. I want him to help me. . . ."

Then he lost consciousness, and everyone was staring, wondering if I had even been part of the gathering, or if Mr. Hickey had momentarily lost his mind. They seemed to pause, so that I might actually do something, but the retired doctor had been regarding me most skeptically and then purposefully set about his business, asking someone else to run and call for an ambulance.

Under sedation, Mr. Hickey was transported to this very hospital, and one of the best orthopedic surgeons in the area, a Dr. Peter Milhoos, set the leg. I had followed in my car and informed the nurse at the admitting desk that I would cover all the expenses of his stay, writing a large check as a deposit. She thought it suspicious, but on calling the billing office she mentioned my name and Ryka Murnow remembered me and it was approved. I waited until the procedure was finished, and instead of going home I felt I should stay close by. Sometime late in the night, with a key Liv had given me, I came here to rest a moment and somehow fell asleep until morning in Renny's wide, soft-seated leather chair.

I had dreams, many of them, all pressed upon one another like bits of photographs in a child's scrapbook. And they were vivid to the extent that although I don't remember their particular images or events—for I very rarely do—I still even now have the pulsing feeling in my head of near-exhaustion from the force of what must have been their great number and intensity. What is unsettling is that for so long a time my days and years flowed by with an estimable grace, the most apparent processionals of conduct and commerce, and yet in the last weeks the gradual downflow has loosed into a sheer cascade, an avalanching force that has caught me deep and sure.

And I think that like Mr. Hickey, I can hardly bear to be a witness anymore. I couldn't watch for long as his wife's casket was slowly cranked down into the earth, the ending-ness and rank finality brutally apparent, the nothing-more of that lowering. It wasn't only poor Anne Hickey I felt going down into the ground, but her husband, and Patrick, and the mourners who stood there decently and stiffly over the fresh hole (if preternaturally leaning back), and then myself as well, who is afraid not of death but of the death of yet another living chance through whom I might reconsider, and duly reckon.

It seems in kind then that I am developing a quick nerve for whatever I happen to see, like the girl and her brother at the Ebbington Mall. It strikes me as almost pathological that I should be this low about Anne Hickey, whom in most every way I hardly knew, when in the past I could shed loss and leaving like any passing cloud of rain. I'm nearly afraid to leave this tiny office, for fear of what else I might see, what else might ensue, like any boy who is sure his very observation and presence makes the world hitch and turn; but in my case those turns are real and have come too ponderously, bearing ever heavily on my minor realm. Too much now I'm at the vortex of bad happenings, and I am almost sure I ought to festoon the facade of my house and the bumpers of my car and then garland my shoulders with immense black flags of warning, to let every soul know they must steer clear of this man, not to wave greetings or small-talk with him or do anything to provoke the hand of his agreeable, gentle-faced hubris. Now I finally think how much sense it made years ago, when perhaps without exactly knowing it herself, Sunny was doing all she could do to escape my too-grateful, too-satisfied umbra, to get out from its steadily infecting shade and accept any difficult and even detrimental path so long as it led far from me.

Now of course I fear darker chance lies ahead for her and Thomas if I don't soon retract myself from their lives, that something terrible and final will befall them as did Anne Hickey, smash them without any sign of admonition. Even the thought of this makes my heart leap and hurdle, and I can say once and for all that if a guarantor came forward and promised their lives would be good and full and only sporadically miserable in exchange for mine, I'd tie a twenty-five-pound bag of driveway salt onto each of my wrists and ankles and fall one last time into the pool. One might argue that this would be no sacrifice to me at all, and yet I must confess as well to a strangely timed current of happiness, despite what traumas have just occurred and are occurring, and say that I have never before quite felt the kind of modest, pure joy that comes from something like simply holding Thomas's hand as he

leads us through some mall, or watching as he and Sunny orches-
trate the pulling of a T-shirt over his head, his sturdy little arms
stuck for a moment, wiggling with half-panic and half-delight.
And it's not just these sightings, of course, that elevate me, but the
naturally attendant hope of a familial continuation, an unpre-
dictable, richly evolving *to be*. For what else but this sort of complication will prove my actually having been here, or there? What
else will mark me, besides the never-to-be-known annals of the
rest?

There's a knock at the door and to my great surprise it's Sunny,
holding a white paper bag of deli sandwiches and a cardboard tray
with two cups of tea. It's a little lunch for us, she says, stepping inside the cramped space. There's only one other chair for her to sit
in, and she sits in it, across Renny's desk from me. She's neatly
dressed again, in business clothes, though I know she's already
stopped going to work at the mall.

"The nurse said I could find you here. I kept calling the house
but no one ever picked up. I was starting to get worried. You ought
to get an answering machine, you know."

"I often mean to, but I never do," I say. "I like to answer the
phone in person, as I always did at the shop. Where is Thomas?"

"I left him with the neighbor."

"He didn't want to come along?"

"Of course he did," she says. "But I think he's a little frightened
of hospitals. Like his mother, I guess."

"You?" I say, accepting one of the turkey sandwiches from the
deli I used to frequent. "You never told me this. All the times I
brought us here when you were younger, while I was doing business, and you never let on."

"That's why I didn't like being around the store, either," she answers, almost smiling. "All those depressing devices. Before I came to you they had me in a place like this, but much worse, of course. I know they told you I was at a Christian orphanage, but really it was like a halfway house, I guess. I wasn't put up for adoption. I was abandoned. I can't believe you're surprised. Did you really believe they would give you a wanted child?"

I answer, "They said I would be an ideal candidate, if it weren't for the fact I wasn't married. But they were convinced of my intentions, and so sent you to me anyway."

But I feel myself addressing her in the lawyerly and justifying way I always employed when she was growing up, and I am quite sure I should stop speaking now, or at least speaking like this, and I suddenly say, "You probably wish you had never had to come live with me."

Sunny looks down, slowly unwrapping the white butcher paper from her sandwich. Her short dark hair is combed back neatly, away from her temples and eyes, the soft, maturing shape of her ever-beautiful face.

She says, "I don't wish that anymore. I used to. And I used to wish I had never been born. But all that's natural, isn't it?"

"Yes."

"Right. But with you, I just didn't understand. I thought this even when I was very young, why you would ever want a child, me or anyone else. You seemed to prefer being alone, in the house you so carefully set up, your yard and your pool. You could have married someone nice, like Mary Burns. You could have had an instant, solid family, in your fine neighborhood, in your fine town. But you didn't. You just had me. And I always wondered why. I always thought it was *you* who wished I had never come, that you had never chosen to send for me."

"I never once thought that," I tell her, "not for one moment."

"It doesn't matter if you did," she says, with a gentle equanimity. "We're here, aren't we? Whatever has happened."

I let the notion suspend, and even happily, for I've long wished to taste the plain and decent flavor of being with someone who is likewise content to be with me. It's a feeling not necessarily happy or thrilling or joyful but roundly pleasing, one that I am sure most people in the world know well, and others, like Sunny and me, both orphans of a sort, must slowly discover, come to learn for ourselves.

"How is Renny, by the way? Was he awake?"

"He was," Sunny replies. "We talked for a little while. He was very tired, and I wanted to leave him alone, but he kept asking me questions."

"About what?"

"Guess."

"Oh. Well, I suppose Renny was curious about you being my daughter."

She carefully peels the tops from the cups of tea. She hands me one. "I think he knows you adopted me. But he wasn't so interested in that. He wanted to know what it was like, having you as a father. Growing up together in the house."

I tell her, "You don't have to tell me what you said to him. I don't mind."

"How are you so sure you don't want to hear it?" she answers. "You think I would say something bad?"

"No, I don't," I say, trying not to sound pleading. "It's just that I see no reason to put you in a funny position now, when it was probably awkward enough with Renny. I know this will sound terrible, given what's happened in the last few days, but I'm almost grateful for the way things have gone of late, by which I mean between you and Thomas and me. It's certainly strange and unexplainable, but I can't think of another time in my life that I have been as hopeful as I am now, and I am sure it is because you have come back here with your son. I will take that over everything else. So you see how you could have told Renny whatever you wished or felt compelled to, and it would be all right with me. With the misery that has come, there is some fortune. Perhaps even for me."

Sunny says, "You're not someone I ever think has had too little fortune in his life."

I don't answer, though I glance at her somberly, to try to tell her somehow that she's both absolutely wrong, and right.

"I think that's why Renny likes you so much," she speaks up. "You're a charm to him. He looks up to you. He's obviously a nice man, too, and I could never tell him anything bad about you."

"But you very well could."

"I could," she tells me straight, but without any malice in her eyes. "I could. I guess I could have told him a thousand things about you and about me, none of them alone so terrible and damning but taken altogether."

"But there is that one thing. . . ."

She lowers her eyes.

"I've been wishing it never happened."

"Yes," she very firmly and quietly says. "But we've talked about that already, haven't we? I don't want to bring it up again. Please."

"Okay," I say to her, though somehow I feel an impulse to lead us to some brink. So I say, "But in fact everything with Dr. Anastasia was all my fault. It was."

Sunny doesn't answer. There's a cross wrinkle in her brow, but she somehow sloughs off my likely ruinous charge and asks instead if the turkey sandwich is all right for me. I can only answer that it is. Before I know it we're on to something else entirely, namely, her round of interviews in Connecticut, and while she's telling me how it doesn't look promising that she'll get the job or really want it if she does (the store being somewhere in northern Arizona), I see how far past those events and times my daughter is, how (whether psychologically healthful or not) she's for the present moment put it well away, just a box in a trunk in an upstairs garret closet, this for her sake and Thomas's and maybe even for mine.

We finish up with lunch and drink our tepid tea. We don't say much of anything more, except to laugh about Thomas a little bit, as she tells me of his renewed love for all things on dry land. When she leaves I decide to go out of the hospital with her and escort her to her car, which she lets me do without a word. And I think a simple thought, that we can walk like this across wide parking lots, we can have a lunch together in a tiny basement room, and leave off mostly decent and all right.

I'm heartened on my own drive home, and yet I can't seem to shake what I thought I had put well past me. For it was not in the hospital but in an affiliated clinic that I had arranged for Sunny to take care of her difficulty. She had returned once more to the house, after having been away for nearly a year. She was barely eighteen years old. She had been living with her friend Lincoln in a tenement apartment somewhere in Upper Manhattan. One evening as I was reading in bed the telephone rang and it was Sunny on the line. Her voice was very quiet and shallow, and for a few seconds I thought it was someone else, a prank caller of some kind. But then it was unmistakably Sunny, the reserve of her coming through even the anxiousness in her voice. Of course she would not say a word of how scared she was. But I listened and did not try to interrupt, and by the end of the conversation I told her I was glad that she decided not to go to one of the crowded, dirty clinics where she was living, and that she had nothing to be concerned with anymore. When I awoke I made several discreet contacts and by the afternoon the procedure was arranged and scheduled for the following Monday. Sunny would take the train up to Bedley Run on Sunday and I would meet her at the station and take us to the private clinic for an examination, which the doctor insisted upon before any procedure the next morning.

When I saw her step out onto the platform I was taken aback by the broad, curving shape of her. Her face was full. She hadn't said how far the pregnancy had gone, and I had assumed it was but a few weeks past her date, perhaps a month or two, no more. Anyone else would have thought that she was too long with the child, that it was much too late, that there was nothing left to do. She was indeed quite near full-term. But when she came out of the train the first thought that came to me was that it was a Sunday and quiet, when there was hardly anyone about, and that I ought to spirit her to the private clinic and to Dr. Anastasia as quickly as possible.

In the car I didn't speak. What was there to say? If anything, I had only criticisms, and though I chose not to air them I was feeling edgy all the same, driving brusquely, speeding and changing lanes without signaling. Sunny didn't seem to notice, swaying on each turn, unseatbelted as always, and suddenly I was furious with her. How could she get herself into such a predicament? How long did she believe she could delay? Where now was her "lover," whom she always talked of being so genuine and serious and gentle? Perhaps he had made a few recordings some time ago, but did he even own his trumpet anymore, or was it pawned for a few weeks' phantom plea-sure and delirium? And glancing over at her I felt my fury redouble, seeing that she had little need to apologize or excuse or otherwise explain, and I thought—darkly, for a bare millisecond—that I could unbuckle myself now, too, and let the car's momentum carry us straight through the approaching sharp turn, into the stone farmer's wall that bounded the old suburban roadway. I wanted an end to us, inglorious and swift, just another unfortunate accident on Route 9, to leave a few lines hardly noticed in the local paper concerning a longtime Bedley Run resident and his daughter, with no survivors.

And yet what did I do but nothing unusual, save elicit a sighing murmur from the tires as I wheeled us wickedly around that bend, the same one that I would grimly consider on countless future oc-casions, and that one rainy night years later my friend Anne Hickey would not survive. If only once I could cease imagining the various motions, and instead of conjurings and dummy musings that leave one subtly affected, take hold of some moment and fully acquit myself to it, whether decently or ignobly. This is not to say I wish I had smashed us into the wall, but that I might have at least stopped the car along the road and turned squarely and given her every last angry bit and piece of my mind. But what happened of course was that I drove home and let her inside the house where we separated until the appointed exam, Sunny upstairs in her old room stripped of everything but the bed, and I down in the family room, listen-ing to the records of Chopin and Mozart I had bought for her to use as models and inspiration. And while I listened to those stirring, ambling notes I might have realized how frightening all this was to her, how overwhelming and awful, but I sensed instead only the im-minent disgrace and embarrassment that would hang about the house like banners of our mutual failure.

At six o'clock I went up and had to rouse her. Her eyes were puffed and red; perhaps she had fallen asleep crying. I told her to come down to the car, and she said weakly she didn't want to go to the doctor that night, asking if I could take her the next day. I reminded her that it was the waiting that had placed her in such trouble, that it was only an examination and she could talk to Dr. Anastasia about whatever she wished. Then she said she wasn't sure anymore about going ahead. I didn't protest; I only repeated that it was an examination and that nothing was yet determined. She finally nodded, still groggy, and excused herself to go to the bathroom. I fully noticed then the change in her as she walked down the upstairs hall, the outwardness of her feet, the slightest waddle to her gait. To remember that now makes me feel the way I should have felt, to brim at such a sight with sober pride and happiness, a grandparental glow, though then it was, I must recall, a most sickening vision to me, being the clearest picture of my defeats, familial and otherwise.

We arrived at the clinic well after dark, a few minutes before Dr. Anastasia. We waited in silence. When he drove up he got out of his car quickly and went straight to the doors, his keys out. He nodded at us and let us in and locked the doors behind us. I'd known him only casually; he was one of many obstetricians with privileges at the county hospital, but the only one I knew of who also worked at such a clinic. He was older than I, and not originally from this country, and he always seemed utterly purposeful and competent if not always warm, the sort of professional one could admire for his straightforward nature and his efficiency. I believe he sensed my appreciation and so obliged my request for an afterhours appointment. But when we were gathered in the brightly lighted waiting room, he looked somewhat put out, disturbed. I didn't offer anything and then he asked Sunny if she was ready to be examined. They went into the next room. After a mere five minutes Sunny came out, and Dr. Anastasia called me in. Sunny walked past me and sat on the waiting room sofa.

When he closed the door the doctor said, "What are we doing here, Mr. Hata?"

"Excuse me, Doctor?"

"You told me she was around twenty-eight weeks. Are you mad? But then you, especially, should know better, being in your profession."

"She was unsure of her dates."

"Notwithstanding," he said, thoroughly annoyed. "It's not possible now. She's no doubt past an acceptable point."

"But you hardly examined her."

"I didn't have to," he said. "Anyone with eyes can tell what's the case. She has no option left but to carry to term."

"I tell you she does not want it."

"It doesn't matter, Mr. Hata. . . ."

"Let me speak, please, Doctor. I tell you she cannot have it. There are many unhappy reasons. She barely finished high school last spring and doesn't have a job. The father is somewhere in Washington Heights, and he has practically abandoned her. He is a long-time drug addict besides. I'm afraid she has also begun taking the drugs with him. You well know there's a chance the fetus may have grave injuries as a result, if not certain mental deficiencies. I'm here now to help her but I've run out of patience and willingness. I am sorry and ashamed to say that this is the last effort I have for her. But I will do this. So I'm asking you to help because of who you are and your experience and skills, so that she won't go to someone else, which she will, and no doubt suffer terrible injuries. You will be preventing further trauma. I apologize for not being more forthright on the telephone, but you see I had to speak to you in person. I feel I must convince you."

"I do not involve myself in the lives of my patients, Mr. Hata. I attend to them after they have made decisions. But this decision comes far too late."

"It's not too late," I told him. "There can be medical necessities, as I have mentioned. I understand these operations can be very complicated, particularly at this stage, and much more costly than usual. I am willing to do everything I can to have you help my daughter. This is not to insult your professionalism but only to make clear how resolved I am. And I am resolved. We are desperate, sir, and I will do all I can to get her out of this trouble."

He was quiet for a moment, and then said, "I have done them this late but not in this country. There are different standards."

"Yes."

"She appears unsure as well."

"Perhaps she is," I answered. "She's naturally fearful, as I am. But she has confided in me, and I tell you she is ready. We are ready even tonight, if it's possible."

"My nurse won't come here now," Anastasia said. "I can anesthetize her, but I need my nurse to attend me. I believe, however, that she would likely not agree to assist such a procedure."

I told him, "I'll stand in for her."

"You?"

"I was trained, once, in surgical methods and nursing. A long time ago, during the world war. I'm sure all you in fact need is another set of hands, to give you instruments and such."

"This is mostly true. . . ."

"I can do that for you. I'm willing to do that."

"Yes, but Mr. Hata," he said, considering me grimly. He spoke slowly and resonantly. "You understand what you will have to see. What you will look at. This will be an indelicate action, which I would not wish upon anyone."

"I understand, Doctor," I said. "I've witnessed such things. Similar things."

"Perhaps you have. But she is your daughter, Mr. Hata. It will be different."

I said to him, "I understand."

"Do you really?"

"Yes, I do," I said to him, as unwaveringly as I could utter the words, enough so that I was quite convinced myself. He took me at my word, and within an hour she was in her gown and he had given something to relax her. All I had asked of him was that she be heavily sedated, even before being administered the numbing spinal, so that she wouldn't realize I was there, or much remember anything of what was done, which he did for me, and with success.

The following evening, in fact, when she was recuperating in her bedroom, she would ask if I had come into the operating room, and I told her that I had done so only briefly at the end, as she had called for me. This was true, for she did say, "Poppa," out of the blue, and I had held her hand for some moments, patting her fingers gently to try to comfort her. It was the first time since she was quite young that I had caressed her so, and the final time, too—still right up to now—for she would leave again just as quickly as she arrived, having a taxi come to the house and take her to the train station for the first express of the morning. She didn't know that I had been awake all night, or that I'd heard her walk down the hall and slip a note under my door, which read, "Sorry for all my trouble to you. Goodbye." I almost went to her then, to plead that she remain, but I saw a beam of headlights sweeping up the drive, and before I could even pull slippers on my feet she was quickly down the stairs and outside, closing the cab door behind her.

If Sunny were to ask me now, I would not tell her I was in the operating room throughout the procedure. I would have to lie. For it was much more difficult than even Dr. Anastasia expected, and owing to his skill and great care he didn't injure her at all, Thomas being proof enough of that. And so I remain grateful to the doctor, for the force of his patience and focus, as it was obvious how much heed he gave to each operation and step. I watched his face and the movements of his hands, his concentration and purpose astounding to me. Once he began he never showed even a shade of consternation, comporting himself with utter professionalism, as though it no longer mattered how much I would pay him (which I did, over-generously), nor that she was much too far into her term. Sunny was eerily quiet while he worked, her eyes glassy and unfixed, though every so often she would gaze up at me almost searchingly, as though I were some faraway figure in her dreaming, this dimmed man in the distance, made of twilight and fog.

The doctor was right about my presence and participation. For what I saw that evening at the clinic endures, remaining unaltered, preserved. And if in my life I've witnessed the most terrible of things, if I've seen what no decent being should ever look upon and have to hold in close remembrance, perhaps it means I should be left to the cold device of history, my likeness festooning the ramparts of every house and town and district of man.

But it is not. And I do not live in broad infamy, nor hide from righteous pursuers or seekers of the truth. I do not mask my face or screen my doings of each day. I have not yet been banished from this earth. And though nearly every soul I've closely known has come to some dread or grave misfortune, I instead persist, with warmth and privilege accruing to me unabated, ever securing my good station here, the last place I will belong.

17

MARY BURNS once said to me, "You're truly an unexpected sort, Franklin Hata. Like no one I've ever known."

I've been reflecting on those words in recent days, as I've not felt like swimming much, opting instead to walk longer than usual, my new route taking me past her old house twice, coming and going. It was her compliment to me, spoken early in our friendship, in those heady though still reposeful weeks after we had become physically intimate with each other, if not yet as lovers. Later on she said something quite similar to me by the poolside, but of course it was meant then as a sober appraisal of our all-but-dissipated relationship, which was as critical as Mary Burns could ever be of me. I remember that day as being just as it is now, late one afternoon near the end of the season. She sat in the teak deck chair with a towel tied around her waist, her navy blue one-piece still wet from her twenty laps. When a chilly wind swept through she pulled on the rumpled white men's dress shirt she often used as a wrap, her silver-golden hair swept back neatly with a velvety black band, the cast of her eyes opaquely shaded behind the large ovals of her sun-glasses.

She was particularly laconic that weekend, for she'd had a most unpleasant phone conversation with her eldest daughter some days before. The young woman had been asking about her mother's will for some time; she and her husband were apparently a high-earning couple who somehow still lived beyond their means and were constantly in debt. For several months once, Mary Burns had to make the mortgage payments on their Manhattan apartment, lest they lose it to the bank. Her daughter had called that week not because they were in trouble again, but rather because they were "looking ahead," and wanted to know exactly how much Mary Burns would be leaving to them in stocks and bonds and cash, as well as whatever interest she could expect in the Mountview house and a large bungalow with acreage on Fisher Island. They wanted a financial picture for themselves, she told her mother, in order to plan their lives accordingly.

I was visiting at her house that day when she received the call. When she hung up she returned to the living room where we'd been reading together after lunch, and though I hadn't heard her speak any way but placably to her daughter, I could clearly see that she was distracted. She sat down at the other end of the long sofa, and when I asked she briefly recounted to me what her daughter had wanted.

After a while I said, "I hope she was satisfied with what you're leaving her."

"What?"

"Her inheritance."

"I don't know," she said, suddenly looking at me, stunned. "I don't know how much it is."

"Oh, you couldn't tell her anything?"

"No," she answered, with great somberness. "I never knew she thought about me that way."

"Well, surely she will be pleased," I said, something in me trying now to put the subject to rest, "no matter the amount."

Mary Burns was silent, and despite the fact that for the rest of the afternoon we didn't converse much at all, everything seemed mostly fine. She offered me as she always did a thick slice of her homemade marble pound cake to go with my tea, and when it was time for me to leave she let me peck her on the cheek. I felt all was well again, or at least as well as it had been during that last month, which I see now was a period of the most agreeable passivity, an inert state that neither of us—being alike in many ways—was willing to disturb. And yet the differences were crucial, too, for while Mary Burns was just the kind of woman I could have befriended and come to love, being exactly partnered for someone like me, for her I was perfectly wrong. Better for Mary Burns that I should be a man who could set her afire like a bowl in a kiln, better that I could so frustrate and anger her that I'd breach the thick jacket of her grace and unleash her woman's fury, to make her finally crack, or splinter, or explode.

The next morning she came by to swim as she did most Sundays. She would simply walk around the side of the house and begin her laps while I was still in the kitchen preparing breakfast. She liked a plain meal of oatmeal porridge with diced apples and a cup of black coffee, and I was more than happy to make it that morning, seeing her there leaning on the curved stainless steel ladder as she tucked her hair inside her swimming cap. Her body was trim and fit, her longish legs tanned, and from where I stood she could have been a woman in her late twenties or early thirties, not yet even in the prime of her life. I was amazed and humbled. She looked toward the patio and the kitchen but didn't wave back at me, and I thought the reflection of the sun against the panes of glass must be blocking her vision. The next I saw she was gone, the surface of the water gently rippling with the wake of a neat dive. I watched from the stove for her to reappear. When she didn't I thought I had miss-seen her go in and quickly surveyed the rest of the property, and when again I didn't find her I stepped out through the French doors onto the patio. The water was astonishingly calm. I kept searching the far end of the dark pool for the bob of her head, and yet nothing would rise. The seconds passed. A bubble of panic came up in my chest. I knew I should run and dive in but another feeling was holding me back, like tethered weights on my legs, this pulling-down horror of what I might see.

But with a great gasp she rose, like a shot, by the near edge of the pool. She had gone the whole length and back. She leaned over onto the slate surround, hacking and coughing terribly. I rushed to her but she said weakly, "Something's burning," and I realized the porridge was probably boiling over onto the coils.

"Are you all right?" I asked her, and she nodded. I rushed back to the kitchen and took the pot off the burner, though by the time I returned to her she was sitting in the deck chair as I've described, with nothing so unusual about her except the slightest tinge of blue in her neck and face. And we sat that way for a while, neither of us having anything to eat or drink, just sitting and listening to the westerly breezes filtering through the first dry-edged leaves of the treetops.

At some point she said, "I suppose you'll be leaving all of this to Sunny."

"Yes," I quickly replied, though of course I hadn't really considered such things yet, as she was only fifteen at the time. But almost immediately the notion seemed more complicated than I expected, as my trouble with Sunny was deepening by the day, enough so that I'd begun to wonder whether she and I would have any relationship at all in the future, or if we did, what kind of feeling she would have for me when both of us were old. It was then I understood better what had upset Mary Burns about her daughter's phone call. There is a need for the belief—even if illusory—that despite the ever-obvious evidence of familial messiness and complication, one's child will always hold the most unconditional regard for her parent, the same one no doubt that Mary Burns felt her heart spill over with when she was handed her newborn daughter, and which I am sure washes over me whenever Thomas tugs my hand. We wish it somehow pure, this thing, we wish it unmixed, unalloyed with human hope or piety or fear or maybe even love. For we wish it not to be ornate.

And yet it always is. And when I tried to have Mary meet my gaze, so that I might show at least one momentary glimpse of what I could offer, she patently refused, sitting stolidly behind her shading sunglasses, her wide, thin mouth set with weariness and rigor. Soon enough she got up and slipped the towel from her waist, then quickly stepped into her loose athletic pants. I rose, too, and she hugged me tightly, and she kissed me on the ear and cheek, and held me fast once more, such that I was almost sure our day would simply resume. But she shouldered her jute bag and, smiling weakly, said without a trace of irony, "You're a marvel, I think." Then she spoke a barely audible goodbye. And then she walked around the house and was gone.

That was the last time I saw her up close. We spoke on the phone several times, but she was too well-bred and kind to be

abrupt, despite the halting awkwardness of our conversations. She
had an amazing discipline when it came to me. All I could think to
bring up was what I was planning for my autumn garden, the certain coles and lettuces which were the same that year as every
other.

Which, I'm thinking, as I slow my pace across the street from
her old house, might in fact please her if she were still alive. Perhaps she would make fun and say it was my "habitation." And I
think I miss her, seeing the activity of the young family inside, the
movements in the kitchen and the children's rooms upstairs, the father in the paneled study watching Sunday golf on a large-screen
television. I imagine this is more or less how it was for her twenty-
five or thirty years ago, those times before her daughters grew up
and Dr. Burns passed away and before she ever came upon me
working in the front of my yard, the hours spent in those gently
lighted rooms not necessarily ideal or happy but full at least with
the thousand tiny happenings of her life.

It is those same notices, of course, that have never blessed my
house. And as I make my way up the rise of the hill, it now comes
fully into view, the staggered pointing of the chimneys, and the
double steeples and bluish leaded panes, and the crossed beaming
of the stuccoed Tudor style, my house a lovely, standing forgery,
pristine enough and old enough that it passes most every muster.
Liv Crawford could speak to these elements and others, and then
point out the work invested in the grounds, the mature and various species of tree and shrub, the well-chosen perennials and an-
nuals and judicious use of ornamental stones, the scale and shape
and proportion of the entire site a realty dream come true, so that
all one need do is simply move right in. And yet it seems nearly

wrong that the next people will never know what sort of man walked the halls within, or know the presences of his daughter and his lady friend, or wonder about the other specters of his history. Of course I don't wish them to be haunted. But if they might be somehow casually informed, whispered to that this man was nothing special or extraordinary but, as Mary Burns suggested, particular to himself, I would feel a certain sentence had been at least transferred, duly passed.

There's a familiar car parked down the driveway near the garage, and when I step around to the back I see Liv Crawford on the patio, peering into the windows. I remain still for a few moments, to watch her looking in as she sizes up the results of her many restorations. She doesn't seem the least bit covetous, only rather proud. I clear my throat and she wheels, her face beaming, and she floats forward with her arms open wide to embrace me as if I were her only child.

"Where were you, Doc?" she practically cries. "Your car was here and so I figured you went for a walk, but it's been here over an hour. I don't care because I had about a million calls to make from the car but I was getting worried. Where on earth did you go?"

"I have a new route," I tell her. "To the village and the state park but then up past here, to the cemetery. You should have let yourself in. I don't mind at all, you know. We didn't have the appointments, did we?"

"That's tomorrow," she says, though checking her calendar book anyway.

"How many?"

"Just three of them, Doc. That's all we'll need to get it done.

I've spoken to the parties again. They're primed, ready for battle, and it looks like we're going to be holding our own little auction by tomorrow night."

"I do hope so, Liv."

"Don't worry, Doc. It's already there. Truly. I'm the best."

And so you are, I think, and mostly I'm content and happy that she's back to her old self, Crawford Power and Light becoming operational again once Renny Banerjee left the hospital with an excellent prognosis for a full recovery. I haven't been to visit him at his condo in several days, but I hear from him that he and Liv have been shopping for their matrimonial bed, each of theirs a bit too historied for the spending of restful nights. Like everyone else who has learned I'm about to sell my house, Renny was concerned that it should happen so soon, or at least before I've made any decisions about where I'll go. Liv herself was dubious and hesitant to place it in her listings once she asked a few questions about my grand plans, but I insisted that she do, and when she kept balking I even threatened to call a rival agent at ERA.

"I'm kicking and screaming, Doc," she replied, and then told me she'd bring over the paperwork for me to sign right away.

That was two weeks ago. In the interim Liv has come by nearly every day, noting all the last-second fixits and sending over workmen to replace some kitchen cabinet hinges and a light fixture, and touch up the chair moldings in the dining room and polish all the brass doorknobs in the house. She's brought in a crew of professional landscapers as well, to tidy and manicure my admittedly derelict yard work of late, to clip and prune and then rake the lawns and beds of the first fallen leaves of the imminent season.

Liv steps inside to make a last inspection with her pen and pad at ready, as she wants to make sure there's nothing left to do. I tell her I'll stay out here. I'm sure there is an important detail left, though I would never see it, as I would never think to order a half-dozen bouquets for around the house, and even rent lead crystal vases to place them in, as Liv has done. Each day up to now has seemed to me a kind of ritualized processional, this step-by-step advance to some defining ceremony, like a wedding or a funeral. But whether it will be a commencement for me or else a last crucible, I do not know.

For my plans, to be true, are nonexistent yet. At least those for me. I've instructed Liv to bring all her selling acumen and brinkmanship to bear on this, as I need every last dollar to carry through my other aims. After the sale and closing I'll call Mr. Finch at the bank and instruct him to buy out Mr. Hickey's mortgage on the vacant store and building. I'll ask him to stop the foreclosure, then state any extra price the bank might want for selling the property back to me. Then I'll call my acquaintances at the hospital billing office and issue an anonymous line of funds for Patrick Hickey, so that he might remain in the PICU for however many days he can hold on and wait.

Concerning Sunny, who didn't protest that I was selling the house but did ask quite worriedly and sweetly if I were going to move very far away, I'll place her name on the legal title to the store and building along with mine, and ask if she'll accept this one thing from me, if she'll sell the remaining medical stock and inventory and open whatever shop she wants and—if she and Thomas please—come live in the apartments above, which Liv's contractors are presently reconfiguring and remodeling into one.

And with what remains, if Liv is right and all goes well, I'll have just enough to go away from here and live out modestly the rest of my unappointed days. Perhaps I'll travel to where Sunny wouldn't go, to the south and west and maybe farther still, across the oceans, to land on former shores. But I think it won't be any kind of pilgrimage. I won't be seeking out my destiny or fate. I won't attempt to find comfort in the visage of a creator or the forgiving dead.

Let me simply bear my flesh, and blood, and bones. I will fly a flag. Tomorrow, when this house is alive and full, I will be outside looking in. I will be already on a walk someplace, in this town or the next or one five thousand miles away. I will circle round and arrive again. Come almost home.

While writing this novel, I was fortunate to meet with a number of people whose help was invaluable. I would like to thank Prof. Yun Chung Ok, the Rev. Kwon Hee Soon, and Kwon Hyuk Ju of KBS-TV in Seoul. Also, for her help in contacting surviving comfort women and for her translations during our interviews in Seoul, I wish to thank Son Hi-Joo.